Armando's Havana Loves

WILLIAM M. iEZZI

HBB PRESS, LLC

Chapter 1
Glitterati, Mafiosi, Politicos

Armando "Army" Lobo knew what was happening at the Presidential Palace nearby, but he didn't let on as he greeted important guests, some of whom knew too.

On the evening of March 10, 1952, the Who's Who of Havana had joined him to celebrate the opening of Army's Fox Hole, an American bar situated halfway between the palace and the capitol building. It was the only Yankee bar in a Spanish-speaking city brimming with salsa music, spinning roulette wheels, sizzling señoritas, sexy cabaret singers, and men from the states sucking it all up ninety miles from Key West.

"Good-looking crowd, Fay," said Army, feeling fit in a black Rudofker tuxedo handmade in Philadelphia.

His inamorata waived a multicolored silk fan in front of him to create a breeze. "Some of the haute couture is spectacular," she said, spreading her arms for him to admire her own brown silk taffeta cocktail dress and beige-tip, taupe pumps.

He laughed. "*You* look spectacular."

The couple formed a two-person reception line at the Fox Hole's entrance on Calle Zulueta as ceiling fans did their best to move the heavy air. They greeted political gangsters-turned-senators and congressmen, mafia bosses, police officials, indicted bankers, big business barons, sports stars, authors, and Hollywood actors.

A tall, middle-aged gentleman winked at the host and addressed Fay. "You look as beautiful as ever," he said as he bowed and kissed her hand.

She smiled and leaned over to show cleavage. "And you are as sweet as your sugar plantation."

The man laughed and turned to the host. "Where's your dad?"

"He said he wasn't up for the trip from Philly. He's running our business in the States."

"How many states are covered by your chocolate now?"

"All of Pennsylvania, roughly the size of Cuba, and most of the others."

A cavalcade of stars followed: including actor Spencer Tracy, baseball player Mickey Mantle, and novelist Ernest Hemingway.

The glitterati and others had come to welcome Army, heir to the sugarcane, chocolate, and railroad fortune of his revered father, Lazaro Lobo.

He casually lit a cigarette and blew smoke into the humid air when he spotted the spy, incognito with bushy brown hair and black-framed eyeglasses. His blue suit didn't fit properly.

No stranger to the spy world in a city inhabited by them, Army had firsthand knowledge of American government agents all over Havana, disguised as everything from barbers to sports writers. There was a lot to watch: gangsters from New York and Europe, communist agitators, money launderers, drug lords, card sharks, and a malleable military on an island nation strategically important to the United States.

"Can you take over for a moment, honey?"

Fay looked at him quizzically. He turned and followed the suit to the men's room. They checked all six stalls for patrons. Satisfied they were alone, Army slid a bolt to lock the door to the entrance.

"It's happening tonight," the spy said, wiping perspiration from his forehead with toilet paper.

"I know." Army dabbed sweat from his face with a white linen handkerchief.

"We've alerted our embassy, the doors are open to the president and his men if they choose refuge in the US."

"What if they fight?"

"They'll die."

"Then they won't fight, but I'm still in either way."

"You're in?"

Army grinned. "Somewhere in the government."

"How do you know?"

"I have an insider among Batista's insiders."

"You gonna be able to work with that crowd?"

"You're a CIA guy. You know Cuba. Cutthroats and crooked politicians running the show here since before the Spanish-American War. I don't want to, but I'll have to. Besides, I'm no choirboy."

"You're right about that, amigo. Remember Istanbul? You jujitsued that guy over a fourteenth-floor balcony."

There was a knock on the door.

"Maybe I can do a jujitsu move on the power brokers here. Get them to help these poor Cubans to a better life."

Another knock.

"Maybe. Maybe not. But it's nice to know that we'll have you on the inside."

Army wouldn't acknowledge the comment. The knocking grew louder. So did the man rapping on the door.

"Anybody in there? I gotta go. Bad."

The informant looked him in the eyes. "You're with us, right?" Again, no response. The impatient guest knocked louder. Uneasy, Army slid open the bolt and the spy ducked into a stall. The irritated interloper raced to a urinal without acknowledging his savior, who exited quickly, thinking this was his night in more ways than one. Most of the movers and doers in the capital were shaking his hand. Good for business. Some were involved in the government. Good for politics. Others were in the mob. Good to know.

Guests sidled up to the fifty-nine-foot oak bar. They were smoking cigarettes and cigars and tipping mojitos and other rum cocktails, ignoring the sticky air.

A salsa band near the entrance played softly to avoid drowning out the conversations of the invited guests.

Four bartenders poured and stirred in sync with the music as clouds of smoke rose above the spiffy hairdos. Square oak pillars sixteen-feet around supported a forty-five-foot-high ceiling on which eight fans turned continuously to prevent tobacco smoke from choking the human chimneys below. Each of the eight beams displayed photos of American sports stars and entertainers as well as a poster of the family's trademark: a white wolf with a brown-and-white Lobo chocolate bar wrapper in his mouth.

Army smiled at smartly-dressed young women holding lit cigarettes near their cherry-colored lips. He heard them chatting about "*A Streetcar Named Desire, An American in Paris,*" and other films up for an Academy Award in ten days. Suddenly, he felt a tug of his arm from behind and turned to see his love.

"Where'd you go?"

"Men's room. Looks like we have a packed house."

Fanning herself, Fay raised her cocktail glass: "We do. Hopefully tomorrow, too."

"I'd like it to be filled every day. We're in a good location. Halfway between power and glory."

"Power? Glory?"

"The capitol and the palace."

She frowned. "We're also in the heart of the capital, where rabble-rousers cause problems. Remember those university students? The ones who overturned a blackjack table at the Plaza Hotel and yelled something about capitalists?"

"The communists. Yes, I remember. Bad news."

Chapter 2

Army and Fay

ARMY WAS ADMIRING Fay when a charming man with a hooked nose interrupted politely, shook her hand, and kissed her on the cheek.

"Belle of the ball," the man said in a Brooklyn accent, smiling at the host. "And you, the pride of Philly. Yous two make a great couple."

She curtsied. "Thank you, Mr. Massi."

"Oh, you know me better than that, doll," said Massi, business operations manager for the New York Mafia. "Call me Joe."

They did make a nice couple Army thought as the mob boss prattled on. Meeting the Boston beauty had provided a much-needed spark in his life after some dark days working for the Office of Strategic Services in Turkey.

He closed his eyes and saw an image of Serina, an underling whose death he felt responsible for in the war. His eyes remained closed until he was jolted back to reality.

"Army!" Fay shook him by the shoulders.

He opened his blue eyes. They were moist.

"Back in the war?"

He stared at her, blinking.

She hugged him for a moment. He wrapped his arms around her and whispered into her ear. "Thanks, honey."

A clumsy woman knocked into them, breaking the embrace. An apology was offered, accepted, and she moved on.

"I'm happy I'm in Havana, Fay. I've been so busy at the plantations that I've never been able to spend quality time with you here. But that's changing for the better now."

She listened and smiled.

Army liked not only her looks – slim and blond - but also her personality. She was outgoing, friendly, and knowledgeable about a variety of topics. He liked the smell of her perfume, too. She wore Youth Dew by Estee Lauder, combining spicy bitter herbs and sweet vanilla. He mused that her mood seemed to determine what the fragrance emitted. Sometimes it was sweet. Sometimes it was bitter. All of the time it had a hint of rum or whiskey.

He wrapped Fay in his arms again. She looked up at him.

"The plantations were so boring," she said. "I couldn't stand it."

He studied her for a moment. She broke away and he followed her to the loud, sweaty patrons at the bar, where she raised two fingers to the bartender-manager, a fair-skinned Cuban.

"What will you have, *señorita?*" he shouted.

"The new drink," she yelled as she pushed her way past patrons at the bar. "Cuba Libre."

The bartender poured two rum and Cokes and slid them to her. She passed one to her beau.

"So where's *El Mulato Lindo?*" she asked as they touched glasses.

"Batista? He's busy tonight.

"So you know why he can't make it, but you're not telling."

"Some things you don't want to know."

She raised her eyebrows. "And Meyer?"

He shrugged. "Lansky's not one for the limelight. He works from the shadows."

"Like your dad?" she shot back.

"No, like yours."

Just as he spoke, her father, a large red-nosed man in a three-piece suit patted him on the back. Big Bob, a chatty Irishman with bushy white hair, blotchy white skin and a bulbous, craggy nose that turned redder the more he drank, bent down so his daughter could kiss him on the cheek.

"Nice party," the big man said in a Boston-Irish accent. "How's my little girl look, heh? Ain't she pretty?"

Army nodded. "She doesn't resemble her father."

Her dad leaned over and whispered into his ear. "Ya know what's goin' on at the palace, don't ya. Good for business. Damn good for business. At a price. But who am I to complain? I've got a foothold here and I mean to expand."

Big Bob pulled back and spoke loudly, holding up his empty cocktail glass. "Look at this, time for a refill." He disappeared into the bar crowd.

"Your father could lead Santa's sleigh," Army said. "He should lay off the juice."

"How's your dad?" Fay said to change a subject that seemed to make her uncomfortable.

"Doing better with the new medication. He says the trip from Philly to Miami to Havana isn't easy anymore. But I know the real reason he isn't here."

She gave him a bored look. "Why?"

"He wants to stay out of the way. This is my night. He's the one who built the business, working in those hot 'cane fields as a boy.'"

"Don't shortchange yourself. You worked those same fields, too. You're always in denial. Face it. And you're paying off his gambling debts."

"Working during summer vacations isn't exactly the same as building a massive sugar business. As far as paying off his debts, well, I'm doing what any son would do. He's handed the whole Cuban operation to me. And tonight, he wants me to have the glory."

Fay drained her drink, turned to the bartender, and pointed to the empty glass to avoid shouting over the din of the crowd.

"That's why I want to make him proud of me. Did you know he once ran for Congress here?"

Responding with alcohol-induced sarcasm, she sneered. "No. For which office are you thinking about running?"

"The House, Senate, President. I don't know."

She shot him a look of incredulity. "Why would anyone want to hold office here, with all of the intrigue it entails? The communists, labor unions, police, radical students, assassins, political gangs with guns."

Army looked into her eyes. "It's about the people."

She guffawed. "The people? Please."

Fay's stubby fingers dove inside his white Tuxedo shirt collar and exited with a bent medal the size of a half-dollar on a twenty-two-carat gold necklace.

"It's about this thing, isn't it?" she said as she held up the medal bearing the likeness of an angel with wings, body armor and a spear. "Saint Michael the Archangel, the Great Protector. You have this need to protect everybody."

"Not everybody," he said with a shrug.

"Did your father give you this, this thing?"

Wounded by her comments, Army clenched his jaw for a second. "No, he didn't. He never told me what I needed to hear, either."

"What?"

He turned his head away to gather himself and return the medal to its resting place. Unforgiving, she pressed him.

"That he loved you? Come on. Actions speak louder than words," she said matter-of-factly as the bartender handed her another Cuba Libre. "I mean, he didn't steal your thunder tonight, did he?"

"So you agree with me. Funny thing about actions, Fay. You and I are having a blast right now, but I know what'll happen in the bedroom tonight."

Her answer was to point her index finger straight ahead.

"Look, Errol Flynn." She bolted.

"Now who's in denial?" he said to no one in particular as she ran away.

Chapter 3

Laying the Groundwork

WHILE ARMY PARTIED, others plotted at the palace. With the backing of the military, former Colonel Fulgencio Batista had just engineered a quick coup d'etat and it was time to get to the business of governing.

The self-installed leader removed his white shirt and tie and slipped on a black pullover. He didn't look presidential, but he felt cooler as he got to work at the presidential desk. He acted decisively as he spoke to aides seated in front of him.

"In the morning we will issue a statement. It will say that President Prio and his corrupt supporters were collaborating with the communists, condoning gangsterism. We will say that he was planning a *coup* before the November election, which he had no chance of winning. We will list his corrupt practices. We will say that the people and I are now the dictators, with the backing of the military."

He scanned the faces of his overheated aides for a reaction. He got none while many of them fanned themselves with their handkerchiefs.

"Also, I am issuing an executive order to suspend the constitution, call off upcoming elections, dissolve all political parties and prohibit strikes by labor unions for forty-five days. Statutes will replace the constitution. An Advisory Council will replace the legislature. I will appoint them. And oh, everyone in the army will have a pay raise."

"What about your cabinet?" asked Emilio Grau, the new Chief of the Anti-Communist and Anti-Subversion Squad. "You have nine ministers to appoint immediately."

Batista pulled a note from his pants' pocket and looked over it.

"I already have the people for Justice, State, Governing, Treasury, Defense, Education, Health and Welfare, and Public Works in this room. You know who you are. What am I missing?"

"Labor. How about Lazáro Lobo's son, Armando?" the Minister of Public Works said, dabbing his chubby cheeks with a powder-blue hanky. "He is up the street now, at Animas and Zulueta, opening his bar."

"Armando? The one they call Army? The American? American Army in my cabinet? We will be invincible," said Batista, laughing heartily.

Everyone chuckled.

"I like it. American Army, Minister of Labor. Will he accept the appointment? Anyone? Blanco?"

Blanco Rico, Chief of the Secret Police responded: "Sir, I believe he will accept, enthusiastically. The young man has expanded his father's business in Cuba over the last five years and he has political ambitions. He is more than capable. I hear that he wants to become president."

"Of Cuba?" Batista asked, with a wry face.

Everyone snickered.

"What did Joseph Stalin say? 'How many divisions does the Pope have?' Like the Pope, Armando has none. The army would not back him. Furthermore, his father was born here, not American Army. Our constitution would not permit it."

Blanco interrupted: "Sir, we just suspended the constitution. He could try to amend it, later. Anything is possible. He is ambitious, smart, and something else."

"What?"

Blanco picked up a copy of *The Havana Post* and fanned himself vigorously with it. "He was a member of the American O.S.S."

"The Office of Strategic Services? An ex-spy? So? The American spies are on our side. They are so afraid of communists that they are not afraid of me."

A burst of laughter filled the room

"Okay? We will give American Army a try. We will keep an eye on him. Any objections?"

"He could be trouble if things do not go well for us," Blanco said. "Washington would have an insider among us. Once a spy, always a spy."

Grau interjected: "He is also a do-gooder, like his father. He builds collectives for his workers. Like a communist. You know, housing, schools, stores, clinics."

"You forget one thing, my dear Grau," Batista said, addressing everyone in the room. "He loves money. He must. He is paying off his father's gambling debts. His dear father, who led the fight against the communists in the '40s. Maybe American Army fits his workers into a communist model, but he is no Marxist. He is The Sugar Man to many. And I hear he likes that name."

Batista looked directly at Grau. He received no response. He addressed everyone again.

"Regarding communists, as long as we crack down on them, disrupt their meetings, make their leaders disappear, the Americans will support us. American Army will be no problem. In fact, having him in the cabinet may appease Washington.

Batista scanned everyone in the room. "Gentlemen, political stability is of the utmost importance. The United Fruit Company, the Freeport Sulphur Company, Domino Sugar, AT&T and other American companies want to know that it is safe to continue investing in Cuba.

"Okay? Young Lobo is the new Minister of Labor. Grau, notify him. We will have another meeting soon."

Chapter 4
The Corsican Mafioso

A RMY GREETED AMLETTO Lora as the party continued. He recognized the House of Representatives member from his teenage years when he, his father, and Lora would dine together at the Sevilla-Biltmore Hotel's rooftop restaurant. The crooked congressman owned the hotel as well as Banco de Creditos e Inversiones, which laundered money for the Italian mobsters from New York. He also welcomed a new selection of girls from Colombia at the hotel each month.

CIA friends had described the Corsican Mafioso as a vascular surgeon. The joke was that Lora made sure the flow – money, not blood, although sometimes the red stuff smeared the green – continued unobstructed.

Army embraced the bald, thin and elegantly dressed man, whose respected title was "Don." They kissed each other on both cheeks.

"Armando, my friend. You do not mind if I call you Armando, do you? You are no longer a boy, and it is more Cuban."

"Not at all, Don Lora." He shrugged. "My father is Cuban and Armando is my birth name." Then, chuckling: "You can call me Sugar Man," but Lora waved him off.

"Your father told me all about you. And you are so much like him in stature and looks. But I am curious. Why do you call this place Fox Hole? You were in a fox hole? You were in the American army?"

Army smiled. "This is the only fox hole I've ever been in. Look around. See all the foxes? They help me to forget the war. That's why I opened it."

Lora grinned, then turned serious. Army felt the Don's hands on his shoulders. "Armando, it is good that you have relocated to our beloved Havana. I urge you. See her. Hear her. Smell her. Touch her. Taste her."

Army raised his eyebrows. The Don released him and continued with a smile.

"You are now in the city where one can put his ear to the ground and hear the stampede coming. At the plantation you were in danger of becoming a *guajiro*, a country boy, out of touch with those who get things done in the capital."

"I agree, Don Lora. But with a last name like Lobo, wolf in English, I have the ears to hear what's going on at the plantations. Fortunately, I have a good manager who keeps things running smoothly."

"The German."

"Yes."

"He has been with your father a long time, no?"

"Yes. He manages all three of our plantations. Very productive."

Lora straightened Army's black bow tie like a father preparing his son for a prom date. The salsa music and the guests were becoming louder and he had to raise his voice slightly.

"Speaking of productive, Armando, are you aware that the sugar crop next year is estimated to be 4.75 million tons?"

"Yes, I saw the International Economic Summit Report out of London. It said that Cuba is expected to supply more than half the world's sugar."

"You are a member of the Sugar Stabilization Institute?"

"Yes."

Lora smiled. "You are making the world a sweeter place to live in, my friend."

"In one way, I guess I am. But in another way, it's bittersweet."

"How so?"

Army shrugged. "The poor."

Lora frowned. "Come now, Armando, you are speaking like one of those communists. Give them an ounce of beef and they want the entire cow. To redistribute among the masses. For free. It does not matter to them that the owner of the cow bought the beast or raised it from a calf. Spent his hard-earned money to feed the animal and pay a veterinarian to treat it when it became sick."

Lora waved his hand in disgust. "Communists are dangerous. And they hate capitalists. We caught a couple attempting to set fire to my hotel."

Army nodded. "I'm a capitalist through and through, Don Lora. Like my dad. I love what business can bring to a community. My father's been good to his workers. He's taught them skills for which he pays well and provides benefits. You know the saying, 'Teach a man to fish and you feed him for a lifetime.'"

Lora shook his head in agreement: "Lazaro Lobo is a good man. And I see that the apple does not fall far from the tree. Maybe you should run for the House. With your name, money and good looks you can win. You can acquire the power your compassion deserves."

The Don added with a sigh and a roll of the eyes: "Then, maybe you can convince me and my colleagues to be more generous to the paupers. Meanwhile, call me if you would like to do business through my bank or come to one of my fiestas. See you at the Cinodromo."

Army's father had told him about the Corsican Mafioso's involvement in fixing races at the Cinodromo dog track and other illegal activities. Lobo the elder also said Lora had his finger on the pulse of the Havana underworld and he (Lázaro) had his finger on Lora's.

Army knew that the Corsican's resumé wasn't unusual in this city, which made the American Wild West seem like Boy Scouts at a jamboree. That would have bothered him before the war, but not now.

He drew on a cigarette and ruminated about the spy culture and World War II, which had claimed Serena as well as his older brother. His face contorted as he thought about the corrupt world in which he was living and how he accepted it, even though acting dishonestly went against his nature. He had money. Prestige. Celebrity. Status. But without political power he was incomplete. Or so he thought.

He blew a smoke ring and pictured reinventing himself in Havana, where the atmosphere was suitable to the temperament of a former spy. And how the Cuban side of him wanted to dance with the devil. But could he do it?

Chapter 5

Queen of the Tropicana

ON THIS SPECIAL evening police were keeping grifters, street walkers, pimps, pickpockets, and pirates who roamed the streets of the busy capital day and night from gathering around the Fox Hole's front door. Suddenly, a sleek, black 1952 Chrysler Imperial limousine pulled up to the entrance. A powerfully-built mulatto man in a gray chauffeur's uniform opened the rear door of the limo to reveal a pair of pink, three-inch stilettos swiveling to the pavement. They were attached to a pair of long, shapely legs.

A grizzled man in a tattered shirt and soiled pants whistled as a tall, stately lady in a black dress and diamond necklace rose from the back seat of the glistening automobile. A baby's breath tiara embraced her blond hair, pulled upward into a bun that accentuated high cheekbones, ruby-red lips and brown eyes. Suddenly, the horde that had been hurried along by the police stopped and made an about-face.

"Titi," the grizzled one yelled. "*Cuando Escucho Tu Voz,*" he cooed, melodically, singing a line from one of her songs.

With her right hand over her heart the Cuban heartthrob finished the verse with sincerity. "*Mi corazón laté mas rápido, mi amor,*" she sang.

The street people loved it and the cops, smitten by her extemporaneous performance, forgot about the mob, which rushed her.

"Titi," a woman screamed.

"Titi, Titi, Titi," the people shouted in unison.

Nefertiti, Queen of the Tropicana cabaret dance troupe, responded by blowing kisses to her admirers while exhibiting great dexterity in avoiding the dirty hands that reached out to touch her. The chauffeur shielded her all the way through the bar's front door.

Once she was safely inside, the power crowd was no less infatuated than the hoi polloi. However, the guests showed their appreciation in a much more subdued manner.

They nodded their heads approvingly as Titi sashayed along a parting path to the middle of the room, where the Sugar Man stood alone. She removed a white-silk glove from her right hand and offered it to him. He didn't know whether to kiss it or shake it. He shook it. After which she greeted him seductively in Spanish.

"Armando. I am Nefertiti Randal, here to welcome you to Havana."

The usually confident, composed, and suave Armando lost his breath for a millisecond. He'd observed her at all the hot spots in the city during his short visits from the plantations. But he'd never seen her up close until now. Furthermore, although he was six-feet tall, he had to look up at her. The only other woman in heels to whom he looked upward was his mother, and the beauty before him bore a striking resemblance, although about 20 years younger.

"Thank you for coming," he said in her native tongue. "I am surprised and honored."

Then, looking around the room, which fell almost silent so those straining to listen could hear what she said, Titi continued: "Where is Popi?"

Army raised an eyebrow. "You know my father?"

Titi studied him for a moment. "Yes. You look so much like him. Except for your blue eyes."

"And you look like my mother. When she was younger."

"She is American?"

"Irish. Irish-American."

A moment of awkward silence followed before Titi said in conclusion: "This is your special night, Armando. I do not want to tarnish your luster. I must go now. I have been summoned to the palace. They are having a small party."

Army gave a knowing look.

Titi picked up on it. She smiled, squeezed his hand, turned toward the door and surveyed the swarm that surrounded her.

"I'll tell the president you wish him well." Then, looking at her chauffeur, "Vamos."

The burly driver led Titi through the guests to the exit, where she turned and blew kisses to acknowledge polite applause and even a whistle that parted the lips of one of her male admirers.

Fay sidled up to her man while the guests were still abuzz with what had just transpired.

"Wow, I'm sweating."

"So am I," he said, still looking at the entrance.

"What did she say? What was all that Spanish about?"

"Popi."

"What?"

He turned to her.

"She called my father Popi."

"So?"

"Never mind. Where were you?"

"Talking to Tony."

"The baseball guy? You invited him?

"Yes, no big deal."

Army looked around the room.

"He left. I told you before, he's just a friend. I go to baseball games with him because you're always too busy. And you own the team."

She laughed. Then, playing the coquette, kissed him on the cheek.

"Besides, he's not my type. You are."

He looked askance at her.

Chapter 6
Pleasure and Pain

IT WAS 3 a.m. when Army shook hands with the last guest and turned to Fay at the bar. She was sipping another Cuba Libre and talking to Hiran, the bar manager.

"Can I get in on this conversation?" Army asked, slipping onto a nearby stool.

"Sure," she said. "We were just talking about Theodore Samuel Williams. Do you know to whom I'm referring?"

"To whom I'm referring?" he repeated. "Okay, Vassar girl, Ted Williams."

"Good. Did you know that he batted only .318 last year?"

"Yes."

"Do you know why?"

"Wasn't he hurt?"

"The year before. He fractured an elbow in the All-Star game."

"Well, Miss Boston, here's something even you don't know about the Splendid Splinter. He and the rest of the Boston Red Sox will be staying at the Sevilla-Biltmore Hotel. 'Don' Lora extended my invitation to the slugger to be my guest at the Fox Hole. He accepted. His photo's already on our main pillar. Now he can sign it."

Fay nearly fell off her stool in an attempt to hug the most eligible bachelor in Havana. She followed up with an Irish Jig. The bar manager shook his head disapprovingly. She was flagged.

19

Acknowledging the gesture, Army gently placed his hand around her waist and guided her to El Carcel.

Situated in the back of the room, El Carcel looked like its name, jail. Only this one was made of bulging black ornamental iron, some of which was gilded. It was suspended from the ceiling, 10-feet high and 20-feet square. Its solid steel floor was about 35-feet above the barroom floor. Guests sitting on one of four stools at the small bar in El Carcel, the sofa, or at the round table could see the action below and vice versa, unless blocked by a curtain made of Dacron, the latest creation of the DuPont company.

Imprinted on the black drapery was the Lobo mascot: a wolf indigenous to the Arctic. His white fur was accentuated by blue eyes. His short ears, shaped like furry cathedrals, pointed to the sky. His nose was black and wet. He was intelligent-looking despite a Lobo Chocolate wrapper in his mouth.

From behind, Army steered Fay by the hips to the black iron gate that led up the narrow iron steps. He pulled a key from his pocket, inserted it into a large, round brass lock and turned it until it clicked.

"Are you taking me to jail again?" she asked.

"Beyond jail. To my bed."

Next to a couch inside El Carcel an iron ladder fastened to a wall led to a ceiling door, which pushed open into Army's apartment. He gripped the ladder with his left hand, placed his right hand on her butt and pushed her up the steps until they were through the roof.

"What a fun way to my apartment," he muttered.

The trap door opened into the middle of the living room of a sprawling, well-appointed flat that had the latest in furniture and art. Fay collapsed onto the couch.

"Oh no you don't," he said, scooping her into his arms and carrying her into a hot and stuffy bedroom with a king-size mattress. He laid her atop the cotton sheets of an English-style sleigh bed with cherry-and-birch veneers, turned on the ceiling fans and pushed open the Plantation Shutters. Stripping naked, he laid next to his sleeping beauty, not wanting to disturb her. He watched her in repose until he could no longer keep his eyes open.

When Army awoke the next morning she was sleeping naked, next to him. He could still smell alcohol on her breath. He gently stroked her hair and her eyes opened.

"Morning," he whispered.

She smiled.

He kissed her lips lightly. Again and again he kissed them, each time a little longer, more passionately, until he slipped his tongue between them. Their mouths became one. Their breaths became one. Their hearts pounded in sync.

Army leaned over and licked around one nipple and then the other, back and forth, slowly. Fay began to breathe heavily. The more he licked, the shorter her breath until she squeezed his hard penis and went down on it. As she thrust deep and retreated over and over one of her incisors clipped the rim of the head. It was pleasure and pain, he thought, just like her. He concentrated on the pleasure until he whispered:

"On top."

He spread her legs and slipped inside her. And then it happened, as it had occurred so many times before. She began to cry.

Pleasure and pain once again. But this time the sobbing was so intense that Army stopped moving and stared at her closed eyes. She fell forward, whimpering with her hair covering his face. Blowing it away he spoke with resolve.

"I'm gonna ask you one more time, why are you crying'?"

"You have the power," Fay said as she buried her face into the pillow, barely audible.

Raising her head and sobbing: "You have the power."

"What power? What are you talking about? If you think I have power over you, I don't want it. I'm not looking for that kind of power."

Rolling onto her back and looking up at the spinning ceiling fan, she sobbed.

"I don't know, Army. I don't know."

"Know what? Lay down your sword and shield, Fay. Relax."

"Never tell a woman to relax," she snapped.

He looked at her.

"Damn it. What am I supposed to say every time you start crying when we make love?"

"Is that what you call it?"

"What do you call it?"

"You don't love me."

He sat up and buried his face into his hands before resuming the conversation. He propped himself on one arm and looked into her disinterested eyes.

"What's going on?"

Fay stared past him, at the ceiling fan, silently. He waited in quiet anger.

"You didn't like me talking to Hiran, did you?" she said.

"I'm used to it by now. You go up to every bartender, every guy in a bar to impress them with your knowledge of sports so they'll pay attention to you. As if you had to."

With his free hand he cupped her face. Sadly, his eyes engulfed her, head to toe. Her piercing hazel eyes commanded attention. Her breasts were perky, her stomach flat. Her legs were long and shapely. She had the whole package.

"Insecurity is your demon," he said.

"I'm not insecure."

Pulling his hand away, abruptly. "Then, what are you? What makes Fay the way she is? Why does she want to make Army jealous?"

"I do not do that."

"Oh really? How about the mechanic?"

"What mechanic?"

"Your auto mechanic. Remember what you said? 'Oh Army, my mechanic said he's in love with me.' That mechanic."

She rolled her eyes and he reclined in disgust.

He was hurt. He needed to do something about it, but what? When? Where? How?

Passive hostility was his modus operandi when it came to her these days, although he did his best to mask it. He was like a hand grenade that hadn't gone off when the pin was pulled, but still likely to explode.

After five minutes of silence she sat up, slipped off the side of the bed, and walked into the bathroom. Army heard the shower. He joined her in the cascading water flooding her hair.

"How do you feel?"

She handed him the shampoo bottle. "Clean."

He rubbed gel into his thick, black hair as Fay stepped out of the shower and dried herself with a white towel before wrapping it around her head. Ten minutes later they both were sipping small cups of black El Buchito coffee in the open kitchen. Frank Sinatra was singing *Why Try to Change Me Now?* on an RCA Victor Console in the living room. On a white wall next to them hung an abstract oil-on-canvas painting of a woman with large wild eyes.

She turned to the art.

"Who's the artist?"

"Willem De Kooning. A Dutchman. It's called *Woman*. What do you think?

"Complicated."

"Remember when you used to teach art to those Italian boys in reform school in North Boston? You said you were never happier."

Fay stared into her cup, seeming sheepish.

"Things ran their course, I guess."

"Like us?" asked Army.

She didn't answer. Except for the towel on her head, Fay was naked as she sat and sipped. He wore a red silk robe and smiled wistfully.

"Always naked. Nice."

"We grew up naked." She sipped from her cup.

"Naked? Your sisters, too?"

"Neither I nor my sisters wore clothing in the house. Right through high school. Besides, I have nothing to hide, sir."

"Sir? I'm not in the army."

"You're not in it. But you're not through with it."

"Why do you say that?"

"The guy in the cheap suit. At the party. CIA?"

Army feigned surprise. "What guy in the cheap suit?"

She made a wry face.

"Secrets," she said.

"What?"

"I know he's a spook."

"Who?"

"You know."

"Do you have secrets, Fay?"

"I have nothing to hide, sir," she said, unwrapping the towel from her head and running her fingers through damp straight hair.

"Then tell me why you're so jumpy. Every time I touch you. You don't sleep much, either. Something bad happen to you?"

"No."

"When you were a girl, something happen?"

"No." She sipped more coffee.

"How was your dad?"

"Well, like your father he wasn't around much. Like your father he was busy making money. But when he was home, it was fun. Big Bob, we called him that, also let us drink whiskey with him and mother."

Army lit a cigarette, folded his arms and studied her. "So why can't you sleep?

"I don't know."

"Ever dream?"

"No. Yes. Actually, I have a recurring one."

"What is it?" He blew a smoke ring.

"I'm on an elevator. Alone. Top floor of my father's office building in Boston."

She pulled a cigarette from a pack of Lucky Strikes on the counter. He lit it.

"And?"

"As the elevator descends the brakes fail. It's speeding downward, out of control. I'm trying to time my jump off the floor right before it hits bottom. Then I awaken in a sweat."

"Wanna talk about it?"

"No."

"Why?"

"Because I don't. What is it that you always say? 'Some things you don't want to know?'"

Chapter 7
The New Minister of Labor

THE HAVANA SUN was intense. High humidity sucked oxygen from the air when the couple slipped through French doors in the living room and stepped onto the balcony overlooking Calle Animas. Army could feel the heat penetrate his beige-cotton slacks and white, short-sleeved shirt. He unlocked the gate to the stairs that led to the street.

Fay's silk cocktail dress drew the heat even more. She held a wooden rail with one hand and waived the silk, hand-held fan in front of her face with the other.

"God, it's hot," he said, following her down the stairs.

"Leave God out of it. It's hot."

"I forgot I was talking to an atheist. But it's hot either way."

When they reached the pavement, Grau and another man wearing white Guayabera shirts, straw boater hats, and sunglasses approached. They removed their hats and nodded to the couple.

"*Señor* Lobo," Grau said, "a matter of great urgency requires your attention. This is Jomar, a detective who will be your bodyguard and driver.

Perplexed but not protesting, the Sugar Man shook hands with the slim young man with deep-set brown eyes, curly brown hair and a peach-fuzz chin.

Army turned to Fay. "Sorry about this, honey. I'll call you a cab."

"No," Grau said. "Jomar will drive Miss Flanery wherever she must go."

The couple looked at each other, then at Grau, who waved to a 1950 Chevrolet black-and-white police car parked a half-block away.

"Have I done something wrong, Grau?"

"*Si, Señor* Lobo. You have become the new Minister of Labor. The president awaits you and other members of his cabinet at the palace."

Army grinned.

"The president?" Fay said as the detective escorted her to his car. "His cabinet? What's going on?"

"Jomar will explain," Grau said.

The driver led her to a black, Hudson Hornet sedan while the new minister and the communist hunter took their seats in the back of the squad car. A uniformed policeman drove them along Animas to the Prado, where he turned right while Grau fanned himself with his straw boater. All welcomed a breeze that blew through the open windows.

"Did Prio go peacefully last night or did he resist the *golpe*, Grau?"

"One fatality. One wounded. Prio and his men fled."

"Who died? Who was wounded?"

"I do not know the name of the man who died, but he left this world after he shot the general."

"The general? How is he?"

"He will recover. And maybe lose some weight."

Who are the other members of the cabinet?"

"You will see when we arrive. Now we must take stern measures, of course, until this all goes away. It is important to put a happy face on this. A happy cabinet face."

The driver made a right onto Calle Refugio and parked next to marked police cars in front of the palace. The two men walked up the steps, past soldiers holding Thompson machine guns with 50-round drums and pistols on their hips. The duo walked through the entrance, where more soldiers with M-1 rifles stood in front of a white-marble staircase that led to the second floor. Perspiring, they saluted Grau and allowed the two men to ascend 37 winding stairs to the second floor, where plainclothes policemen saluted and permitted them to turn right along a wide hallway.

"It's good to be here," Army said, walking past the Salon de los Espejos, modeled after the Salon of Mirrors in Versailles, France. Soon they arrived at a short hallway with a large white door on the left. A brass plate on it read: Oficina del Presidente. A large, white door on the right had a brass plate marked: Consejo de Ministeros. Passing through that door they saw a long conference table made from caoba, the same dark mahogany the conquering Spaniards used to build ships in the Colonial Period. Around the table were seated the other ministers. Ceiling fans hummed above, creating a nice breeze as he sat between Blanco Rico and Grau, a cobra and a viper.

At the far end of the room, on a white wall hung a large oil-on-canvas painting of mustachioed Carlos Manuel Cespedes, the first Cuban to hold the office of president. At the opposite end was an empty brown-leather chair and a stained-glass window on a wall behind it.

Army and Grau were seated among chatty cabinet members. Smoke from their cigarettes and cigars filled the air when Batista walked in. Dressed in a dark suit, white shirt, and yellow tie, El Mulato Lindo stood in back of his chair and waved to his underlings.

"Gentlemen," Batista said. "Welcome to a new Cuba."

The ministers stood and applauded enthusiastically.

"This is a great day for us. We face many challenges. But we shall overcome them. Great social and economic changes are on the horizon. And I have good news from Washington. The American Secretary of State has assured me that President Truman and his administration have recognized us as the legitimate government of Cuba."

More applause from the ministers erupted as Batista smiled broadly and took his seat.

"Of course, with that kind of backing comes great responsibility. I have pledged our cooperation with Mr. Harry J. Anslinger's office, the Federal Bureau of Narcotics. I have also agreed to work with the Central Intelligence Agency to monitor closely the Communist Party and labor unions. He looked at Army, who nodded in the affirmative.

"We will do more than monitor them, I promise. That is where Emilio Grau comes in. Grau?"

Known as the Well-Dressed Assassin – he wore a suit while executing communists - the Lieutenant Colonel snuffed an H. Upmann Corona he'd been puffing, stood, and nodded to Batista and the others.

"Yes sir, we continue to cut off the head of the communist body, but it seems to grow back again and again. Furthermore, political gangsters, especially members of the now-dissolved Orthodoxo Party, and radical students and labor leaders continue to agitate the people. We have the University of Havana, a breeding ground of sedition, under constant surveillance."

Grau took his seat while Batista lit a Montecristo cigar and puffed.

"Thank you, Grau. I also want to point out that we will be working more closely with our Italian friends from New York. Under the direction of Meyer Lansky, our new casino advisor, legal gambling will be reformed and expanded, thereby generating more revenue, which can be used for economic development.

Most of the ministers looked at each other approvingly.

"There will be a boom in construction. A new banking system will assist in the building of new roads, tunnels, hotels, casinos and office buildings to accommodate the big upturn in tourism from the United States. Not to mention an increase in sugar production."

As soon as he mentioned sugar, Batista turned to his right and smiled at Army. "Which should please our new Minister of Labor, the Sugar Man, Armando Lobo."

He smiled and his peers applauded as he stood.

"Mr. President," he said. "I'm overjoyed and curious. Happy, because you've included me in a position that I cherish in your cabinet. I want to help the poor get on their feet.

"Perplexed because you haven't addressed the plight of the people: Unemployment, low wages, housing, illiteracy, poor medical care, etcetera. Outside my club last night there were enough pick pockets, prostitutes, panhandlers, beggars, and thieves to fill the jail in the Fifth Precinct."

Grau growled. "The Fifth Precinct jail is already filled, Señor Lobo, with those who are against progress. Maybe we should build another jail for those who disturb your business by loitering outside your bar."

The ministers chuckled. Army turned and looked down at the man who mocked him.

"They wouldn't be outside my bar, Grau, if they had a good education and a job that paid a living wage." He turned to Batista. "As you know, Mr. President, I'm all for making profits, even if the manner in which they're made is somewhat questionable. However, why can't we spread it around? The people will love you. You'll have the power *and* the glory."

Batista puffed on the cigar and smiled. "I know that you have political ambitions, Armando, so we will leave power-and-glory issues to you. My job right now, as I see it, is to expand the economy at a time when tourism is blossoming like flamboyant trees and our sugar production is making us the sweetheart of the world.

"On both counts, Armando, you are a winner. The Fox Hole bar and the sugar. My friend, you and your father are major contributors to our economy and we thank you. We respect your opinion. So, write a report on what you think needs to be done. Present it at our next meeting. But for now, let's leave the people to Grau and Blanco Rico."

Batista stood and made an announcement before leaving the room. "We will meet here again soon, gentlemen. Thank you for coming."

Everyone stood as the president walked out. Army turned to Grau. "Is that a spot of blood I see on your cuff?"

Grau looked. "Humm, so it is."

"I'm surprised that you'd walk around with a spot on your clothing. I mean, your reputation as a fastidious dresser precedes you."

"You misjudge me, *Señor* Lobo. To have the blood of subversives on my shirt is a badge of honor." Then, stepping toe-to-toe with Army he looked at him eye-to-eye. "Never misjudge me."

He didn't blink. The other ministers began walking out of the conference room and he joined them. Once outside he walked along the left side of the wide hallway and stopped in front of a bronze bust of Abraham Lincoln. A plaque below it read: *"When the people fear the government there is tyranny. When the government fears the people, there is liberty."*

Army thought for a moment and spoke to himself: "Liberty? Not here. Not now."

He was happy for the opportunity to put people to work in the city, as his father had done on his plantations. But he tempered his enthusiasm with the sobering knowledge that he was working with a treacherous crew.

He resumed walking to the staircase, skipped down to the first-floor lobby, picked up a public phone, and dialed Fay's number. No answer.

He stepped out of the palace, still swarming with soldiers, and turned left toward the sunny Prado, a concrete promenade of benches and trees separating a boulevard that ran for about a mile-and-a-half in both directions between the ocean boulevard and Central Park. He wanted to gauge the mood of the people so he walked along the paved public walkway toward the capital. And as he did he took in some of the aromas, sights, and sounds of Havana City.

At the first side street he sniffed the salt air that carried with it a hint of ocean fish. He could almost taste the seasoned pork cooking on a pavement barbecue. Continuing under the shade of the Laurel of India trees toward Calle Colon, he sniffed coffee and tobacco while passing Cuban businessmen drinking, talking, and smoking cigars at tables outside a coffee shop. Next door he spotted a bar, a restaurant, and a lingerie shop with male tourists walking in and out. He saw the same men walking up the next three streets he passed: Trocadero, Animas and Virtudes, known as Barrio Colon, where young women in sexy dresses wooed them from open windows with salsa music blaring. Assignations cost $1.

If that wasn't appealing, a man could always knock on the doors of Doña Marina, who owned a string of brothels inside and outside the barrio.

Satisfied that nothing unusual was occurring, he turned left to the slice-of-pie-shaped main entrance to Hotel Plaza. Bell boys and other personnel greeted him as he walked through the open doors and headed straight to the elevators, skirting the casino on the right. On the second floor the elevator doors opened and he veered left to the first door on the right, No. 220, the room with a peppermint-striped barber pole outside. He opened the door and saw his favorite barber inside.

Chapter 8

Time for a Trim

RMY OBSERVED THE spy from opening night in a different light. He was dusting hair from an elderly man's neck. The bushy brown hair was gone. The thick, black-framed eyeglasses were history.

The barber was himself with short, straight black hair and round, wire eyeglasses that magnified large brown eyes. The frame rested upon a beefy proboscis and large ears that bent forward as if they wanted to catch every sound.

With his olive skin and expressive gestures, he looked more like the Barber of Seville or a Mob member than "Mr. Cutter."

"You have an appointment, sir?" Cutter said to the customer while helping the old man out of the barber's chair.

"No sir. But I hear that you're a good barber. If you're not too busy I'd like a trim."

The barber graciously accepted $2.00 from the customer and led him out the door. He turned to his visitor.

"Sit down."

Cutter tied a white apron around Army's neck, spun the chair to face the mirror and began trimming the back of his full head of hair.

"I saw you and Grau pass by in a police car today. You been a bad boy?"

He smiled. "Batista appointed me Minister of Labor. Has word gotten around about the coup?"

Cutter shook his head approvingly. "Congratulations. Students are gathering for a protest at the university. But the streets are calm Mr. Minister. Still think you're gonna be able to work with Batista's cutthroats, thieves, and drug dealers?"

Cutter stopped cutting and looked into the mirror to see Army's reaction. Boredom looked back at him.

The barber responded. "I don't have to tell *you*. It's a dangerous place."

"And depressing and exhilarating," was Army's reactin. "Remind you of someplace else, paisano?"

"Yeah. And a couple of murders in Berlin."

Army's jaw tightened. Cutter held the scissors and looked at him in the mirror.

"Knock it off. You did the right thing sending Serena. She was the only one who could've gotten the job done."

"You're wrong. I should have gone instead."

"You followed her. Stop blaming yourself. Besides, you took him out."

"After he killed her. Five minutes. I was five minutes late."

"Man, you're too much."

A moment of silence followed before the barber dusted the back of his former colleague's neck with talcum powder and spun him face-to-face.

"A shipment of heroin and cocaine is coming in from Bogotá. We don't know when, but it'll be aboard an Aerovias Q flight that lands at a military base in Camaguey."

"Aerovias Q?"

"A small airline company fronted by a senator for Don Lora. Cargo planes mostly, DC 4s that fly Havana to Camaguey, Barranquilla, Bogotá and back.

"Lora has those drug parties at the hotel. He likes you. Think you can snoop around?"

Army pulled the apron from around his neck, stood, and stepped closer to the mirror. He grabbed a hand-held mirror to check the back of his head.

"Nice trim," he said, coolly, turning his eyes to the reflection of the barber in the mirror. He faced his friend with the scissors, pulled $5 out of his pocket and placed it in his hand.

"Well?"

"I retired after Berlin. Remember?"

Army walked toward the door, stopped and turned to the sad spy.

"Wear a better suit next time. For a CIA guy you were easier to spot than a hooker at a church picnic."

Chapter 9

Riot at the University

By the time Army made his way to the Hotel Plaza's lobby it was 2:00 p.m. He telephoned Fay again. No answer. Instead of eating lunch at the hotel he decided to walk to the Fox Hole, where his black 1950 Chevy coupe convertible was parked, and drive to La Colina, a small hotel with a patio restaurant that faced the University of Havana. He wanted to see Grau's hotbed of sedition for himself.

With the top down to catch a breeze under the hot Havana sun, he drove into Los Nortes, turbulent winds from the north, along the ocean boulevard called the Malecón. Waves from a frisky Atlantic Ocean slammed into the sea wall at different spots, sending a briny spray over the four-lane highway. The salt water occasionally flooded the windshield faster than the Chevy's wipers could chase it away. Some of the spew smeared his sunglasses, which he quickly removed with a smile on a day when the sun was so intense that a smack in the face by the ocean was energizing.

On Calle L he spotted a large crowd at the top of the hill, so he parked and walked. The closer he came to the hilltop the louder the noise, like a beehive with an amplifier. A plethora of students had spilled from the Grand Staircases of the University of Havana onto the street in front of the hotel.

Pressed up against the hotel's metal chairs and tables, some of the bare-chested male students, covered with sweat and blood, saw an opportunity. They picked up chairs along the periphery and passed them over their heads to compatriots who used them to throw at the police. The cops fought back with their wooden batons. More blood and screams. Army was momentarily transfixed.

Tourists who usually occupied the dozen outdoor tables stood anxiously inside the hotel's glass-enclosed lobby, fanning themselves and watching the action nearby. Still, one brave foreigner sat alone at a table close to the hotel's entrance, eating, drinking and watching. He had a racing form sticking out of his front shirt pocket. Occasionally he fanned himself with it.

Curious to see how police were handling student unrest Army sidled up to the stranger: "Mind if I join you?" he shouted to the chubby and tanned visitor, who looked up and pulled out a chair.

"Thanks." They shook hands. "Armando, they call me Army."

"Sal, they call me Sallie," the man said in a Brooklyn accent.

A waitress leaned over with a menu, but she was waived off.

"I'll have what he's having." Turning to Sal. "You're taking a chance sitting out here."

"Yeah. I'm a gambler. An' I can't get to the race track right now. What about you?"

"I'm curious. Why are they rioting?"

"Batista's back. He kinda took over. These kids are madder than a hit on a Hornet's nest. You missed the speeches 'n' stuff. But see that skinny fella over there, the bald one with the black beard, no shirt, in the middle, surrounded by cops. See him at the topa the steps?"

Army craned his neck and caught a glimpse of the young man. Meanwhile, the waitress placed a bottle of beer and a burger on the table.

"Yes. What about him?" He took a bite and a swig.

"He made the last speech. Beer bottles started flyin' at the cops. That's when they started whackin' everybody with clubs. The guys and the girls."

"Why are you still sitting out here? Isn't it a little dangerous?" Army said, wiping his full mouth with a napkin.

"Hey. I fought at Anzio. This ain't nothin'. I been comin' here a long time. The kids have a good beef, I mean, Batista didn't take carea the little guy the last time he was president, either."

They watched a canvass-covered military personnel truck force a path through the mob at the bottom of the university steps. A dozen soldiers with bludgeons hopped out and surged into a vociferous crowd that had surrounded police who held the bald, bearded one by the arms.

Suddenly, gunshots pierced the air. The crowd screamed as one and scattered in all directions. That gave officers an opportunity to handcuff the shirtless, bearded agitator and with the assistance of soldiers drag him down the steps to the truck. But before they could get a good grip on him to throw him in, he yelled: "Down with Batista, dictator, murderer, thief, traitor."

Young men and women scattered in a stampede of fear as more military transports arrived in front of the university. The scene became so wild that the two men picked up their plates and beers and headed for the hotel lobby.

Shaken by the action, Army thought about the possible repercussions that were ahead for him as a politician and businessman. He felt sympathy for the students, but were they being inspired by communist agitators? And were the police justified in their use of unrestrained force?

Chapter 10

Betrayal

IT WAS 9:00 p.m. when Army pulled in front of Gran Estadio de La Habana, the largest baseball stadium in the Caribbean. His team, the Cienfuegos Wolves, was playing. He looked at the scoreboard: Cienfuegos 1, Havana 1, bottom of the ninth inning.

Instead of walking to the dugout he took the stairs to the press box. As he entered, El Tigre, the Wolves' No. 1 pitcher, was at bat. He watched the hurler strike out to end the inning. The Havana home crowd roared. Extra innings.

Sitting in the middle of the box and above home plate, the stadium's announcer informed the packed house: "El Tigre retakes the mound with ten strikeouts."

"How many Ks does he have on the season?" Army asked as he sat next to a middle-aged *Havana Post* sports writer and CIA spy.

"One hundred and eighty," he said as he picked up a pair of binoculars and trained them on the pitcher. "First time I've seen you here in a long time, Sugar Man. How come you're not in the dugout?"

"Not while the game's in progress. Too much of a distraction. Who's pitching for Havana?"

"Number 7, Miranda," the writer said, still looking through the binoculars. Then, as though a distant memory surfaced, he put down the glasses.

"Say, wasn't that your number?"

"What? You mean in college? How would you know ..." his voice trailed off. "You guys are too much. Is there anything you don't know?"

"Actually, you played with my brother, Elliott. He was a pitcher. Too."

"Elliott Grey? Your brother? Small world. How is he?"

"He didn't make it home from France," the writer said, picking up the binoculars again.

Army winced, as though he'd been hit by a foul tip. "Sorry to hear that. He was a helluva competitor. Hated to lose, like me."

"How come you're not down there with her?" the scribe said as he focused in on the third-base side.

"Who?"

The sports writer passed the glasses to him. He scanned the third-base box seats and saw Fay sitting between her father and a good-looking man in a sports coat and tie. Next to him was Massi."

Army focused on the one in the sports jacket. "So that's him. The baseball guy. The one she's been going to games with while I was away."

"What?"

"His name is Tony, right?"

"Massi's new driver, Tony "The Blade" Stabo. I've seen him here with her before, but not with Big Bob. What's goin' on?"

Sugar Man looked around and whispered: "You see the file on him?"

A crack of a bat and roar of the crowd diverted the writer's attention to the score sheet, where he recorded a two-run homer for the home team. He turned to the owner.

"Your team just lost, 3-1."

But Army continued to watch Fay & Company through the binoculars as he repeated the question. "You see the file on him?"

"Small-time hood from Brooklyn. Got rid of a couple problems for Massi back home and got himself invited here to be his driver-bodyguard."

Army returned the binoculars to the writer, and headed for the exit.

"Where you going?"

"See my manager."

"What about her?"

"I'll deal with her later."

By the time Army made his way to the clubhouse the players were entering the dugout, followed by their manager. El Tigre and his teammates were in a somber mood after losing in extra inning to their arch rivals. The manager, Alain, shook hands with Army and invited him into his office for a private talk.

"We have a problem," he said, closing the door behind him. "It is El Tigre."

"Is he hurt?"

"No. But in this moment, he hurt the team."

"How?"

"I think he threw away the game."

"What? Are you serious?"

"Yes. His pitches had no spin. They were, how you say in English …"

"Lollypops, *piruletas.*"

"Si, yes, *piruletas,* and Havana hit one over the fence to win the game."

"Maybe his arm was tired."

"No, I know when his arm tires. His velocity begins to slow in the seventh. But he threw hard into the tenth."

"Come on, the guy just lost it in the ninth."

The manager shook his head negatively. "There is one more thing. My neighbor, Gensy, is his wife's doctor. She visits El Tigre's house to treat Flavita's pneumonia and the influenza of the children. She said a well-dressed American man came to the house yesterday while she was in the back room with Flavita. She could see him talking to El Tigre through the open door, but she could not hear what they said. Before the man left, he gave El Tigre an envelope with cash in it."

"How'd she know it was cash?"

"She said El Tigre pulled it out and pushed it back in."

"What did the guy look like?"

"Italian."

"Young or old?"

"Young."

Army sat down silently on a wooden chair in front of a small desk for a moment, then looked up at the manager. He scowled.

"Get him in here, now."

He was sitting at the skipper's desk when the manager returned with the pitcher.

"Close the door and sit here, El Tigre" Army said, pointing to a chair that faced him in front of the desk. Staring into El Tigre's eyes, he spoke like a prosecutor to a defendant.

"Has Alain treated you fairly, Tigre?"

"Yes, sir."

"Have I treated you fairly, Tigre?"

"Yes sir."

"Then why did you throw the game today?"

El Tigre said nothing. He lowered his eyes.

"Why did you hurt us, your team, yourself, Tigre?"

Again, the pitcher was silent. Army grew impatient.

"Talk to me. I want to know what makes a man betray his teammates. Tell me, Tigre. What makes a man less than a man?"

El Tigre raised his head and looked at his interrogator.

"My wife and children are sick, sir. The doctor, nurse, the medicine, the special bed."

"Why didn't you go to your manager?"

Tigre looked away.

"Who was the man who gave you the money?"

"I do not know, sir."

"What did he look like?"

The player shrugged. "Black hair, Nice lookin'."

"How old?

"About 25."

"What did he tell you to do?"

"Make sure we do not win."

Hearing this Army stood, picked up a baseball bat and walked to the closed, wooden door. A red heart drawn on a white sheet of paper was taped to the middle panel. The name Sonia was signed in large letters – those typical of a schoolgirl – under the heart. Army took a swing, not like a baseball player but like an axe murderer. The bat burst through the panel and remained imbedded there, a dagger in the heart. The manager and the player jumped at the sound of fury. The owner walked back to the desk and sat.

"Sorry," he said. "I hate cheaters."

He looked at El Tigre. "How many times have you done this?"

"First time, sir."

"Anybody else on the team do this?"

"I do not know."

"How much money did he give you?"

"Fifty dollars."

The Sugar Man reached into his right pants pocket, pulled out a 50-dollar bill and showed it to Tigre.

"This is for you and your family."

Sheepishly, the pitcher looked at the owner. "No thank you, sir. I cannot accept that."

"Then accept this, you'll sit on the bench until further notice. If we make the playoffs, maybe I'll let you play. Meanwhile, when your teammates ask you why you are not playing, you will tell them the truth, or you're off the team. Furthermore, I'll see to it that you never pitch or play for any other team in Cuba again. Do you understand me?"

The pitcher looked down. "Yes sir."

Army leaned over the desk and stuffed the $50 bill into Tigre's shirt pocket.

"Now get out."

Tigre stood and walked to the busted door. He grabbed the door handle and turned around.

"Tony. I hear a man in the car call him Tony."

Chapter 11

"You Should Have Lied"

ABOUT AN HOUR after the game ended, Army's car screeched to a halt in front of Fay's residence in suburban Miramar. Lights were on throughout the first floor of the two-story, stone house once occupied by Mob Boss Charles "Lucky" Luciano, on the corner of Fifth Avenue and 30th Street.

Army sprinted to the mahogany door and slammed the knocker five times. Esmeralda, a 20-year-old mulata maid, opened the door, but before she could greet him, he passed her into the hallway and yelled:

"Where are you?"

Fay poked her head out from the archway to the living room on the right.

"Hi, how are you?"

He stomped to the living room and looked around. On a black-lacquer Oriental cocktail table in front of a black couch with tiger-colored piping were two half-consumed cocktails and two lit cigarettes.

"Where is he?" Army fumed.

"Well, he's across the hall, in the bathroom. Why are you upset?"

He stomped to the bathroom door and yanked it open. Sitting on the toilet, black pants at his ankles, was Big Bob. Startled, the large man, cut down to size by embarrassment and circumstance, looked up and let out a burst.

"Whataya doin'? What's all the fussin' about? Shut the damn door."

Astonished, Army looked at the helpless big man for a second and slammed the door shut. Fay was on his heels. So, when he whirled around he accidentally knocked into her and she sent herself flying to the ceramic-tiled floor. He squatted in front of her instead of helping her up.

"Where's Tony?"

She looked up, helplessly. If she was hoping to evoke sympathy, none was present.

"Where's Tony?" he asked again, as she stood and wiped blood from her nose with her fingers.

"I'm bleeding," she shouted. "Good grief I'm bleeding."

From the bathroom Big Bob bellowed.

"What's all the commotion?"

Fay marched into the living room with a wolf in hot pursuit. She pulled a tissue from a black satin box atop the coffee table, dabbed her nostrils, sat on a cushioned, black-lacquer chair with a short back and threw her head backward over it.

"This is what you're supposed to do when you have a nose bleed," she said in a throaty voice, which sounded like someone else's. His legs splayed over hers, he leaned over the chair so that his face was even with hers.

"Where is that son-of-a-bitch?"

"What on Earth is wrong with you, Armando?" she said in that strange voice. "Tony? He went home I guess. He went to the baseball game with us today."

Raising her head, holding a tissue to her nose, Fay stood and tromped out of the living room with him trailing. Both nearly walked into an eavesdropping Esmeralda as they made a sharp left around the archway and then a sharp right under another archway, where Army felt a heavy hand grab him by the arm.

"We gotta talk," said the chatty Irishman.

He tried to pull away as Fay ascended a grand, spiral staircase, but her father held him, firmly.

"We gotta talk business."

"Bad timing, Big Bob."

"No, this is really important, more important than her."

Army looked at his captor with incredulity as the big man ushered him back to the living room and sat him down on his inamorata's nose-bleed chair. From the expansive and cushy couch the large man, wearing the same, three-piece suit he always wore, presented his case.

"I wanna buy ya out."

"What?"

"The sugar plantations, the rum, the railroad, the baseball team, I wanna buy ya out here in Cuba."

"You must be crazy."

"I'm not. The Dagos have their greedy hands on the gambling. The Cubans have most of the drug trade and the, ah, entertainment here. The only way for me to expand is through sugar and its transport. I want it all."

"You're a cheapskate, Bob. You wouldn't spend the money. How about I buy you out? Your plantation in Matanzas. The electric plant. The factory. Your train."

Big Bob shrugged. "I know that this is a touchy subject, but we both know that your father has a big gambling debt here that still ain't been paid off."

"I'm paying the vig every month. When the time comes, I'll pay off the debt."

"Sure, you're payin' the interest every month. But why work with a ten-thousand-pound boulder on your back? Ya have a nice business at the Fox Hole. Batista likes ya. The Dagos like ya. Why work under all that stress?"

"Those Dagos made you a lot of money during Prohibition, Big Bob, or should I say Bootlegger Bob? Luciano, Capone, Costello, Genovese. You still calling them Dagos? Whatdaya call us Cubans, Spics?"

"You ain't Cuban. You're all-American. You forget. I saw ya play football in the Ivy League. Damned good quarterback."

The big man leaned over, patted him on a knee and pulled on the lapels of his black suit, the only one he seemed to own.

"Think it over. I'm goin' for a stroll on Fifth Avenue. Ain't that funny? There's a Fifth Avenue here."

He started to walk away when Army hooked him by the arm. "Who's Tony Stabo?"

The large man whispered: "A friend of hers. A very good friend of hers."

Stunned by the comment, he stared up into the big man's black eyes and released him. Big Bob waved as he turned left for the hallway and walked out the front door.

Fuming, Army trotted up to Fay's bedroom and tried the doorknob. It was locked. He knocked three times.

"Who is it?"

"Me, I have to talk to you."

"I'm in bed. I want to go to …"

The door exploded. Army kicked it open. Splinters of wood were still bouncing around the room when he stomped to Fay's bedside. Startled, she sat up, frightened.

"Are you fucking him?"

Fay placed both hands to her face and started to cry.

"Oh no you don't. No more hiding behind tears."

He pulled apart her hands and looked into her eyes, his face inches from hers.

"Are you fucking him?" he asked.

The reply was feeble, meant to elicit pity. But there was no forgiveness in his aching heart. Only hurt and anger.

She nodded her head up and down.

With that, he released her hands and looked at her in disgust.

"I fell in love with you."

"You never told me," she said, whimpering.

"I never told you because I didn't love you in the beginning. I didn't want to lie."

Fay shifted from hurt little girl to domineering woman in a flash. "You should have lied!"

He stared at her for a moment in disbelief. Then, he moved closer until he was nose-to-nose with her.

"Like you lied to me?" he hissed. "Tell me. Do you cry when he's fucking you?"

The little girl returned. She'd never seen his rage. He looked as if he could kill her. She trembled, gripped the sheet with both hands and pulled it up to her chin. But suddenly he turned away and started walking to the door.

"I loved you right from the beginning," Fay screamed hysterically. "You should have lied."

Army didn't break stride as he grabbed the side of the broken door and slammed it on his way out, more splinters bursting into the air.

"One liar's enough in a relationship," he yelled as he flew down the stairs, past a frightened and excited Esmeralda.

Chapter 12

The Purge

I**T WAS MIDNIGHT** when Army pulled the Chevy convertible into his parking space on Animas, next to the Fox Hole. The bar was lively. The band was playing *Besa Me Mucho.* He could hear it. But he didn't enter.

He hit a button to raise the convertible top, secured it with the chrome lever inside, above the windshield, stepped out and locked the door.

He nodded hello to a couple patrons who waived to him on their way into the building. And then suddenly, as though a dagger had pierced his gut, the severity of what had happened at Fay's house fell heavily upon him. Crestfallen, he leaned against the soft roof of the car with his left forearm and pressed his forehead against it.

"Not again," he said.

He thought about how he'd allowed himself to fall in love only twice in his life – Serena and Fay – and both times his heart had been crushed. With his right hand he rubbed his stomach to make the emptiness go away when he felt something else under his shirt: the curved gold medal of St. Michael the Archangel. Reflexively, he rubbed it through the garment between his index finger and thumb.

"I know what to do, I know what to do," he repeated, his forehead still buried in his forearm.

There was only one thing to do at a time like this, when the pain was unbearable. Journey to the depths of Hell on Earth. To an inferno like Dante's, inhabited by the souls of the lustful, greedy, wrathful and violent. A place that harbored traitors, sodomites, fortune tellers, hypocrites, thieves, falsifiers, betrayers, and worse. The types who'd gathered to perform a devil's dance in front of Dante and Virgil. Only there'd be no paradise on the other side. Maybe he'd make it out alive. Maybe he wouldn't. He just couldn't be a part of the civilized world at that moment.

Army backed away from the car and continued to rub the medal. Passersby glanced at him curiously but didn't break stride as they walked to their cars.

Going to Hell on Earth was the only way to dispel the profound emptiness that gnawed a hole in his stomach. He knew that Hell wasn't far away. He turned, waived a taxi to the curb, jumped into the backseat and barked an order.

"Sailor's Bar," he said.

The taxi driver looked at him in the rear-view mirror and repeated: "Sailor's Bar?"

"*Rápido, por favor*," Army said.

Within a few minutes they were on Avenida Del Puerto, a two-lane highway of railroad tracks and Adoquine Cobbles, rectangular bluish stones cast from furnace slag and formerly used as ballast in Spanish Galleons. They drove past Havana Harbor's bars and brothels in the oldest part of the city, where some of the buildings had been constructed in the 1500s.

"Are you certain you want Sailor's Bar, Señor," the cabbie said. "There is a full moon tonight. Crazy things happen under a full moon, sir. Especially in ..."

Army cut him off. "Yes, I know. Just drive, please." The taxista shrugged and continued along the highway in search of Calle Cuba.

A fog enveloping Havana Harbor carried with it the odor of high-sulfur coal from a coal-burning plant. About a block before Calle Cuba, traffic came to a halt on the Avenida, which separated the Customs House on the left from tenement housing on the right. The delay made the passenger impatient.

"*Señor*, here," he said, handing the driver the generous sum of $5. The man offered no resistance. He looked relieved as he pulled over to discharge him.

The foreboding sound of a ship's fog horn blared continually in the distance as he walked along a dark, narrow, slippery sidewalk that smelled of fish.

When he turned right onto Calle Cuba, he saw a brawl about to erupt under a light post two short blocks away. A half-dozen American marines and sailors were pushing and shoving each other outside Sailor's Bar.

"I'll mess you up," a staggering American marine yelled at an unsteady US sailor. "Oh yeah?" the sailor replied. "Let's see what you got, punk."

Suddenly, gunfire erupted. A ship's horn wailed. Two more shots rang out. Would-be combatants and onlookers scattered in all directions like scared rats in a ship's galley. Unfazed by the urgency of the moment, Army moved forward with the detached resolve of a battle-weary soldier. It was as if Novocain had replaced blood in his veins, numbing him to danger or delight. He seemed dazed as he marched closer to the place from which shadowy figures were fleeing, bumping into him, nearly knocking him over as they ran for their lives.

"Get outta the way man," a fleeing sailor shouted.

When Army arrived at the front door of the wedge-shaped building that housed Sailor's Bar, he saw no gunshot victims or shooters. He heard male voices yelling over loud juke box music inside the bar, looked inside and saw four wobbly marines huddled together near the entrance singing the *Marine's Hymn*.

Army stepped around a puddle of dirty water that stood in front of the entrance, where the edifice came to a point. Suddenly, a huge bald bouncer holding up two young men by their collars walked straight at him. One was an American sailor in scuffed whites; the other was an US marine in stained khakis. Both had swollen eyes and looked bewildered. The bouncer heaved both into a polluted puddle near the front steps.

Dirty water splashed his pants. He didn't react.

The bouncer slapped his hands in disgust and complained in English: "God damned Americans."

Army looked up at him. "Hey. I'm American."

The behemoth one looked down at the Yankee, whose shirt, slacks and tan shoes betrayed his status. A smile slowly creased the big man's lips. He stepped out and gave Army a hearty pat on the back.

"Amigo, vamos," the bouncer said while grabbing him around the right shoulder.

Like a wild bull, the mammoth man charged through a raucous crowd in the smoke-choked room with blaring music. He bowled over two of the American marines, one merchant marine and two sexy chicas. He bumped into Cuban ship captains and crew members until he deposited Army at the crowded bar.

"You are American?" the bouncer said.

"Yes," he replied, reaching into his pants pocket and pulling out a wad of cash. "Cuban, too. How about a drink?"

The bouncer ignored the offer. Sensing trouble he turned, muscular arms folded, to face the crowd and guard Army's flank in case any disgruntled patrons were to take out their anger on an interloper. If there were any, they didn't show it. Unsteady American sailors and marines danced with house girls. A craps game among six sailors played in one corner of the room. In the other, two bleary-eyed soldiers and a couple of chicas sucked on tubes sprouting from a bong. Next to them, standing, were a US sailor screwing a chica from behind and another girl, seated, sucking a Cuban sailor's penis. Two girls watching the action turned to each other and started kissing.

Frankie Laine's *Jezebel* was playing so loudly on the juke box that Army had to scream to gain the attention of a bartender.

"Double shot of Fox Hole rum," he yelled.

"Fox Hole?" the barman laughed. "Go to the Fox Hole." Then something clicked. The bartender extended his hand to shake.

"I know you. Armando. The Sugar Man. From the Fox Hole."

Army shook hands with him. "Sorry. I'll have a double Bacardi instead."

The barkeep placed a double shot on the bar, but before he could take any money from the pile of cash, the man on a binge grabbed his arm and flashed a two-finger sign.

The bartender poured another double shot in front of him. He drained it.

"Another," he hollered. The bartender did so.

Meanwhile, a bearded Cuban merchant marine wearing a Greek sailor's hat and a black patch slung over his right eye stood to the left of the city slicker, sizing him up. The man was muscular, hairy and bare-chested under a black vest. He looked like Blackbeard the Pirate and wore ballooned, black sailor's pants secured around the waist by a black, studded belt with a large, square shiny silver buckle. Another Cuban merchant marine stood to Army's right at the bar, near the money.

"Amigo," Blackbeard yelled, thumping him on the left shoulder.

Swilling his fifth double, Army turned to face the man, who was his size.

"Amigo, see this hat?" he said, pointing to his head. "I take it from a Greek lady boy on the Gulf of Siam. You a lady boy?"

Without hesitation: "No, are you?"

Blackbeard responded by pulling a knife from his right boot and raising it menacingly near Army's face. Meanwhile, the second man swiped the cash and hit him over the head with an empty Hatuey beer bottle. Big mistake. The bottle should have been full because instead of going down, Army pivoted like a shot putter, spinning and striking the thief on the chin with his right elbow and catching the pirate with a roundhouse left hook to the right cheekbone – the eye patch may have concealed the coming blow – with such force that the buccaneer's head hit the top of the bar, the knife flew and its bearer slid to the floor like a sack of sour lemons.

Army stood over his attackers, waiting for them to get up, but the bartender leaped over the bar, reached down and grabbed the thief by the collar. The bouncer already had his huge hand around the pirate's throat. Once again he cleared a path and heaved the unconscious attacker into the puddle of dirty water in the street. The bartender rifled the robber's pockets and pulled out Army's cash before tossing him out by the collar and belt on top of his accomplice in the street.

When the barman returned, he slapped the stolen money back on the bar and hopped over it. Sugar Man slowly pushed a five-dollar note to him.

"Thanks." Unsteady, he ordered another double.

The bartender looked into his bloodshot eyes. "You sure you want more, Armando?"

Army waived him off, the binge resumed and the patrons continued their debauchery, oblivious to another fight and ejection.

Someone played *Jezebel* for a second time. He listened and bowed his head, with eyelids feeling like 10-pound weights as Frankie Laine sang a sad song about a deceitful woman.

The tune ended and when he raised his lids a slim, fair-skinned, pretty flirtera with dyed blond hair stood face-to-face with him. A tight-fitting red dress clung to her shapely body, delineating her assets. She looked at him curiously. In broken English she made her observations and inquiries as the cacophony of the crowd was the only background noise between records.

"You do not belong here," she said. "Your head, in back. You have blood."

He rubbed his head with his left hand, felt wetness, and looked at his fingers. They were red. The pretty stranger disappeared and returned quickly, jostling her way back to the bar with a wet, white towel. She dabbed it on the back of his scalp.

"Do not move," she commanded. "I pick glass from your head. You are okay?"

"Wanna drink?" he said as he tapped the empty shot glass twice on the top of the bar. The bartender shook his head in disbelief and poured another double. With a full shot glass, Army saluted his new acquaintance and asked again.

"Wanna drink?"

"I do not drink. You have a Jezebel in your life, no? You try to wash her out?"

Swaying involuntarily, he looked into her brown eyes for a long moment. His eyes welled.

"My name is Celia," she said as she dabbed his eyes with the bloody towel. "I have sorrow for you."

"And I have sorrow for you."

He turned to the bartender and tapped his empty glass once more. This time the barman refused to fill it. Suddenly a whistle filled the air and a stampede of khakis and navy whites surged to the exits. Shore patrol had arrived. Within 10 minutes most of the bar cleared and Army found himself standing there with Celia as a Johnnie Ray recording blared: *Walking My Baby Back Home.*

"Come. We go," Celia said as she took him by the arm and steadied him to the door where the big bouncer saw them and laughed.

"Aye, Celia. You catch a fish from another world. Now you will fillet him."

"I will not fillet him, Bravo. I will fillet you and feed the waterfront for a month."

With this, Bravo and Celia shared a laugh while the tippler toppled to his hands and knees and vomited on the front steps. He couldn't rise. He rolled onto the grimy pavement.

"You want to take him home?" Bravo asked. "I will put him in that empty fruit cart over there. But you must push it because I cannot leave here. And you must have it back before noon because Pedro will look for it.

Chapter 13
A Bumpy Ride

CELIA WATCHED BRAVO pick up Army like a helpless baby and lay him in the wooden cart that smelled of overripe fruit. Mashed mangoes, pineapples and red grapes covered the floorboards, which became Army's bed and embedded themselves into the back of his white shirt and slacks.

Celia weighed about 115 pounds, but she summoned the strength to lift the handles of a wooden cart containing a 190-pound man and push it forward. Iron wheels skipped over cobblestones on Calle Cuba. The occupant's head knocked against one of the sideboards. The ride was a rough one for Celia and her passenger until she turned the pushcart right onto a dirt road called Calle San Isidro.

At the corner other flirteras and pimps started hooting and whistling at her in the light of the moon.

"Mami, who is that big mango you have in that cart?" a scantily-clad chica in pink yelled. "Tell me where I can get one like that." The other chicas roared with laughter.

Celia stopped the cart in front of her tenement building in the middle of the street and ran inside. She returned with a bucket of water and tossed it into Army's face. He sat up, startled and saturated.

"Come," Celia said. "You must walk with me."

Still wobbly and weak, he leaned on the pretty stranger and they ascended narrow, creaky wooden steps slowly in an old building that looked as if it had housed Christopher Columbus. Gradually they made it up five flights of darkness that became hotter and hotter until Celia opened the door to a room with an open window. A streetlight illuminated the contents: a double bed neatly covered with blue sheets against a green wall, a crucifix above the headboard and a broken dresser and mirror next to the door.

A sea breeze saturated with sulfur left a foul odor in the room, but it also chased away the heat.

"You okay?" Celia asked. Her inebriated guest mumbled something in response.

Celia sat him on the bed. He fell backward as she removed his wet shoes, socks, pants, shorts and shirt. The only thing he was wearing was the gold necklace with the misshapen medal when she turned him face down. With her fingernails she picked more fragments of glass from his scalp, which had stopped bleeding, but was caked with blood. When she finished, she turned him on his side, facing her. She slipped out of her red dress, bra, and panties, and laid beside him, waiting. But he was out, cold. And as he slept, his eyelids twitched a badly-spliced movie reel of nightmares.

Army saw himself with Fay in an elevator speeding downward, faster and faster until it crashed and exploded on the bottom floor of an office building … He watched helplessly through a skylight as a man in a Nazi officer's uniform raped a young blond woman, slit her throat, looked up and smiled at Army screaming in rage with his jammed pistol…He saw his mother holding his father's hand outside the Tropicana, even though she'd never been there… He felt his hands twist a garrote around the Nazi's neck until he choked to death on the floor, next to Serena's body … and then there was the mysterious girl with beautiful, dark eyes and full lips. He tried to hear her sweet offerings but he couldn't. She shed a tear, he wiped it away with his thumb and she vanished.

———— ◆ ————

Morning arrived and the sound of a bird cooing called Army back to consciousness. He opened his eyes and saw a white dove on the open windowsill. The bird spread its wings. In the shadow created by the intense backlight, the vision frightened him.

"Holy Ghost!" he mumbled. "I died!"

Army started pinching himself to see if he was really dead. Satisfied that he was alive, he sat up and scanned the room. He glanced at the window sill again but the dove was gone. Turning his head proved to be problematic.

"Ouuuu," he said, placing his right hand on the back of his head. He felt a scab over a swollen scalp. He patted it and looked around the room. His clothes were folded neatly next to a Bible atop the bureau near the door. Under the dresser were his shoes and socks. He stood and slipped on his undershorts and fruit-stained pants. He felt for the wallet. It was gone. His heart pounded as he felt for the gold chain and medal. They were there. He sat down heavily on the bed and held his head with both hands. He tried to remember the previous evening's activities when suddenly the door swung open.

Celia barged in with a small, brown paper bag overflowing with mangos.

"Ah ha, Mister Sleepy. You wake up. Do you remember me? I am Celia. How your head is?"

"It hurts a little."

"Let me see."

She touched the scab and felt the swelling.

"Ice. You must have ice. You are so drunk last night. But first you take a shower. You stink. I have mangoes for you and me."

He looked up at her. "Okay Celia. Where is it?"

"What?"

"My wallet."

"Oh Armando. I know your name because I look inside your billfold. You never tell me your name before you go to sleep."

"Where is it?"

"You sit on it." She pointed to the mattress. "Under. I hide it there because if someone come in when I push cart back to Sailor's, they cannot find it."

"You live in this place with a door that doesn't lock?"

He stood and slipped a hand under the mattress. He pulled out the wallet, opened it and saw that the contents were undisturbed.

"Do not worry, Armando. I buy fruit with my own pesos. Now shower, please. Here is the towel, soap. Shower in the hall."

Army accepted the items with no resistance, looked down at his stained, stiff pants and disappeared into the hallway. About 15 minutes later he returned wrapped in a white towel, clean and hungover, holding his garments. The hair on the back of his head was no longer stiff. But his clothes were. His white shirt, handed to him by Celia, had become a cardboard Rorschach test of swirls and colors from the fruit absorbed in the cart. Smashed grapes were inside his loafers and on his argyle socks.

"Wait," Celia said. "I pick grapes."

In a flash, she cleared the fruit from his shoes and rubbed the socks together to pulverize the dry, stale grapes and handed them back to Army. She did the same with his shirt and pants. On top of the chest of drawers, Celia had sliced two mangoes and placed them on a plate.

"I'm sorry," he said while dressing. "I can't eat mango right now. My stomach needs toast and coffee. Please, come with me."

"Where?"

"To my bar and restaurant. We can eat there."

Celia led him down the narrow, creaky wooden stairs. A few doors opened and desperate-looking men and women stared at them. He nodded, pleasantly.

"*Todo esta bien,*" he said. "Everything is all right."

Once they were outside the ancient tenement building, the Sugar Man turned, looked at it and shook his head. He'd never stayed in a place like that. The facade was faded white plaster covering old bricks, exposed in spots by large cracks. Sagging, wooden balconies drooped over each pair of dirty windows like sad eyebrows over bleary eyes. The entrance to the building had no door, inviting those who lived there and those who did not, to enter.

Army took Celia by the hand, walked a block to Calle Cuba and looked to the left. She pointed up the street, where a middle-aged man wearing a farmer's wide-brimmed, straw hat loaded the fruit cart.

"There, Armando. The cart. This is how I bring you to my room last night. I push it all the way to my place. You are so drunk." She laughed.

"Why didn't you just call a taxi?"

"Taxi? Here?" She laughed again.

They turned right onto Calle Cuba and walked two blocks to Avenida Del Puerto, where he hailed a cab.

"Zulueta and Animas," he said.

———— ◆ ————

When the duo entered the Fox Hole, the place was filled with a lunchtime crowd of tourists, gamblers, uniformed American sailors and Hollywood actors. The odd couple drew curious looks from the patrons. His multi-stained shirt and pants looked like a clown costume. She wore the same red dress from the previous night and as they moved through the horde, a jokester plopped a black top hat on her head momentarily. She looked like an attractive carnival barker with her mutant. The circus had come to the Fox Hole.

Hiran did a double take before waiving hello from behind the busy bar. Army waived back and directed Celia to El Carcel. Once inside, they sat down at the round table near the small bar and surveyed the crowd below. Celia was beaming like a little girl in a candy store as she looked at the fancy dresses worn by the women. He spoke into her ear over the din of the crowd below.

"Most of these people are American. They like to dress up. This is an American bar."

She couldn't take her eyes off the crowd. About seventy-five patrons, thirty of whom were women, chatted, smoked and drank. Some of the ladies sat on stools at small round tables and nibbled cheese on ceramic plates while the men bit into sandwiches requiring two hands to hold.

Army picked up a telephone on the bar. He dialed.

"Hiran, I'm still in breakfast mode. Coffee and burned toast with butter for me. And for the lady …

"Mango juice, please."

"Mango juice with scrambled eggs and toast. And throw some ice into a plastic bag."

Army observed Celia looking excitedly at the scene below. "One, two, three, oh, there are so many pretty American women, and men in fine suits, Armando. And so many bartenders."

He looked at her for a moment, lit a Lucky Strike and offered her one.

"I do not smoke cigarettes."

"Marijuana, cocaine?"

"No druga. I see too much the chicas take druga and do bad things."

He took a drag from his cigarette and studied her. "A lot of bad things could have happened to me last night. But you took care of me. Why?"

She turned to him. Her manner suddenly turned serious. "Armando. I am a good Christian, except that I am a flirtera, you know, I walk the streets. I must support myself and my family. But yes. Bad things can happen to you in a bad place where you do not belong. I know you have a big hurt and do not care what happen to you. Who is Serena?"

"Serena?" he said, startled. "Where did you get that name?"

"You scream her name. You yell: 'Nazi son-of-a-bitch.' You have nightmare all night. Serena is your Jezebel? The one who make you go to Sailor's Bar and drink too much?"

Army lowered his head and stared at the floor. He closed his eyes and saw an image of Serena, the agent who'd begged him to send her on a covert operation to Berlin, where the Nazis had imprisoned her sister. He'd resisted because of the risks as well as his strong, though unspoken, feelings for her. He sensed her powerful attraction to him, too. But in an office of spies working 'round the clock to defeat the Germans, their mission was on high alert and their unexpressed feelings for each other had never blossomed into passion.

Because she was unrelenting in her desire to find her sister, Army had sent Serena on the journey. Reconsidering his decision almost immediately, he followed her. But not close enough to protect her. He'd watched helplessly as she was murdered.

"She is Jezebel?" Celia repeated

"No."

"Who?"

"Never mind."

The street walker observed him for a moment. "Armando, promise me you do not go to Sailor's Bar no more."

He looked into her brown eyes. "Okay. But you have to promise me the same. You have no lock on your door. How many times have you had unwanted guests?"

Her expression turned teary. She bowed her head. "Many times. Many times. I am too small to stop them."

"Don't go back there, or Sailor's Bar."

"Armando, you do not understand. I have to work. Outside the bar. Bravo let me in to use the toilet. That is when I see you. I have little education because I grow up on a farm in Camagüey. I leave my parents and sisters and brothers to come to Havana to make money to send to them. I am here three years. Three years I am a flirtera. Never a House Girl, a prostitute owned by the Mafia. But please do not judge me on this."

"Is there any type of work you can do?"

"No," she said, delicately wiping away tears with her fingers. "I want to learn something. But no one will teach me."

"Look down there. See all those bartenders? None is as pretty as you."

"Of course, they are men."

They both laughed.

"Seriously, you speak English, you're attractive and I trust you."

"Thank you."

"What I'm saying is that we'll teach you to be a bartender if you want. You will be one of very few female bartenders in Havana. Want to try it?"

She froze. Her shocked expression told the story. It was the chance of a lifetime. Like winning the bolito in Havana. Tears rolled down both her cheeks.

"Yes Armando. Yes, I want to try." She hugged him with all of her strength.

Hiran arrived with a tray and set down the breakfasts on the table. He handed a bag of ice to Army and nodded to Celia, who was wiping away more tears. She took the ice from him and held it on the back of Army's head.

"Armando. What happened to you?"

"I'll tell you later." Turning to his guest, he made the introductions. "Celia, this is my manager, Hiran. I trust him, too. Hiran, meet Celia."

The bar manager smiled and nodded at her.

"I want you to train her to be a bartender."

The bartender's eyes widened. "A chica? Behind the bar?"

"Yes. Can you handle it?"

"Yes, if you want. But it can be a distraction to the customers."

"Ah, you're thinking like a Cuban. This is an American bar. You have to think like an American. We want them to feel at home. Celia with her blond hair, good looks and positive attitude will make them feel comfortable. She'll be a distraction to the Cubans who come in here, a pleasant distraction."

Hiran cocked his head to the left, as though he thought about it, and nodded in the affirmative. He shook hands with Celia's free hand and didn't want to let go. He didn't take his eyes off her as he smiled and tripped on his way to the stairs, recovering quickly and looking back at her until he disappeared.

Army smiled. "Looks like Hiran has eyes for you. He's a good man. I'll have him help you move to an apartment nearby. But listen, you can't be a flirtera here. You know that, right?"

"Of course, Armando. You are giving me ..."

She withdrew the ice and placed it on the table, next to her breakfast. She started to cry. "Why you are so kind to me, Armando?"

He looked at her, grinned and placed a hand on her shoulder. "Because you are every flirtera who walks outside my bar day and night, without hope of being anything else. Show me something, Celia. Show them something."

Chapter 14
The Mafia

AT 5 P.M. a clanging alarm clock awakened Army in his bed, where he'd taken a nap after Celia had departed El Carcel. He slipped off the mattress in his underwear and looked at his white pillow. It was smeared with blood from a broken scab during another fitful sleep.

A cold-water shower seemed to help before he dressed and headed for the Hotel Plaza. Along the way he passed a shoeshine boy in tattered clothes on the corner of Animas and Zulueta. The boy flashed a big smile and Army flipped him a large coin.

"Hi Chino, did Hiran give you breakfast this morning?"

"Si. Gracias Armando."

Smiling, he turned the corner and walked up crowded Zulueta, past a mix of poorly dressed Cubans and richly attired tourists. He nodded and smiled at both groups before trotting across the street, dodging honking cars and trucks going both ways. On the other side, tourists were exiting the hotel and casino, in which a mobster had an office.

He thought about how charming Massi could be, as he'd been with Fay on opening night at the Fox Hole. He also knew how dangerous a man Massi was. "Big Joe" had easy access to Mob muscle. What would the former hitman's reaction be when he complained about Tony? He was about to find out.

Sugar Man skirted the lobby on his way to the casino on the right. On a wall outside the entrance were two signs, one in Spanish, another in English: *Pesos and dollars are accepted. Value: 1 to 1.*

Nine round white pillars about 30 feet high supported a second-floor balcony and stood guard around the casino floor, which contained 50 tables. Along the periphery were slot machines. Everything was illuminated by five stained-glass domes 60 feet above and spotlights affixed to the columns. All of the tables were occupied. One of them created a disturbance when a blond American man in his early 30s shouted at a card dealer:

"I am not cheating."

That's when Tony entered the picture. Army was surprised to see him there without Massi. Wearing a natty sports jacket and slacks, the young hotshot grabbed the protester by the back of his shirt collar, dragged him from his chair and pushed him against a pillar.

Army stopped and stiffened as he watched Tony slam the man's head against the stone column, knocking him out. The gambler slid to the green, ceramic-tiled floor while two American women at the table from which the man had been yanked held their mouths in horror.

Tony yelled at them: "This is what happens to cheaters."

He dragged the man along the floor by the back of his suit jacket past the gamblers, through the lobby, and out the front door. The two women followed, protesting.

"Cheaters, huh," he said to no one in particular. "You should know. You're sleeping with one."

Army walked through the casino, turned left and rode an elevator to the second floor. The doors opened and he turned left, past the barber pole and into a hallway that led to a large room in which more card-and-dice tables and slots occupied gamblers. In back of a baccarat table was suite 216, where Babe Ruth stayed during the 1920s. A bronze plate on the door commemorated the Big Bambino's stay. He knocked and a pretty, slim mulata in a black business suit opened the door.

"Hi, I'm Armando. I have an appointment with Mr. Massi."

"Oh yes, please come in and sit down. I am his assistant," she said, pleasantly. She hit a buzzer and within a few seconds the gangster opened the back-office door, poked out his head and waved him in.

A man of average height, Massi didn't look like your ordinary businessman in his white shirt, red tie, and black slacks. He looked like a mobster in a suit, which he was. However, his rough Brooklyn dialect belied his intelligence, which combined the shrewdness of a banker with the quick wits of a gangster. Rimless spectacles sat on a large nose that appeared to have been broken more than once. His lips were beefy, his light-brown hair short and parted on the left. With a firm grip he shook hands with Army and closed the door.

"Sit," he said, pointing to a black leather chair that stood next to another facing his mahogany desk. On the wall behind the desk there were three gold-framed oil-on-canvass paintings: Joe DiMaggio with a baseball bat slung over his left shoulder in his Yankees uniform; teammate Phil Rizzuto scooping a ball at shortstop; and Jake La Motta knocking out another fighter.

Army looked to the wall on his left and saw a large, framed black-and-white photo of Al Capone wearing a dark, three-piece suit with a white handkerchief in the breast pocket and a carnation in a lapel. His left fist was planted on his thigh, and his teeth clenched a fat cigar under a wide-brimmed straw hat with a three-inch black band around it. He looked tough. He talked tough, too. Underneath the photo his words read:

You can get a lot farther with a kind word and a gun than a kind word alone.

Army looked at the photo, read the words, looked at the photo again and at Massi, who had the same tough-guy persona.

"He kinda resembles you, Joe," Army smiled.

In Brooklynese Massi answered: "I take that as a compliment. Al was a pioneer here. In the '20s he stayed at the Sevilla-Biltmore. Took the whole sixth floor. Opened a pool hall in Marianao."

Then the mafioso sat on the front of the desk and turned a framed Capone quote around so that Army could read it.

"This American system of ours, call it Americanism, call it Capitalism, call it what you will, gives each and every one of us a great opportunity if we only seize it with both hands and make the most of it."

The mobster nodded. "He was a great American."

"He seized it with both hands, a kind word and a gun," Army said. "A capitalist with a twist."

They both laughed as the mafioso took a seat in the other leather chair next to him, a sign of friendship.

"How's your father? You know he schooled me on Havana when I came here."

"Fine Joe, thanks. And thanks for coming to my party. My Dad's handling only the Philly operation now, you know, the chocolate production, packaging and sales in North America. He's too old to work here. So, I'm taking care of Cuba, getting the sugar from the plantations to Philadelphia, which is why I'm here."

Massi lit a Montecristo cigar and offered one to him. He accepted.

"Shoot," he said, drawing on the cigar and crossing his legs.

"I went to see my baseball team play Havana last night. It was the first time I'd been to the stadium in a while because, you know, I was spending so much time at the three plantations."

"I know, I know. Nice to have you in Havana, permanent."

"Thanks." Army drew from his cigar. "I mean, it's not that I don't love my team, or that I don't love baseball as much as the Cubans. I played college baseball.

Massi looked surprised. "What position?"

"Pitcher."

The mob boss nodded and looked concerned. "So what's the problem?"

"I found out my best pitcher, El Tigre, threw the game last night. Your guy, Tony, had something to do with it. I'd like it to stop."

Tony's boss took a long drag on his cigar and looked at the ceiling. Silence followed for a few seconds.

"We shoulda cut you in."

"Thanks Joe, but that's not why I'm upset. I grew up in a sports family. I love team sports, the camaraderie, you know, one for all and all for one. To throw a baseball game, to me is like counting cards, to you. You don't tolerate that in your casinos here. To fix any game or to be a part of a fix goes against every instinct in my body."

Massi stood, walked over to the desk, sat, opened the middle drawer, pulled out a ledger book and thumbed through it. He whistled.

"Your father left you with a helluva debt. But I see you been payin' the vig. On time."

"That's right, Joe. I've been paying the interest but we can't pay off the debt because so much of our money here is tied up in running the operation. We're not very liquid at this time. Good thing my bar is doing good. I'm using some of the profits to pay the interest on my Dad's debt. My Mom has banned him from gambling. Plus, he's in therapy."

"Therapy? What's that?"

"You know, he talks to a doctor twice a week about gambling."

"He pays for that?"

"Sure."

"Nice scam. Maybe we can set it up here."

Army smiled. "But what about the baseball team, Joe? I suspended El Tigre for the rest of the season. I don't want my guys taking bribes from your guys."

Just then the assistant buzzed. The mob boss hit the intercom button.

"Tony is here to see you Mr. Massi."

"Send him in."

Army took a long drag on his cigar as Tony swaggered in. He was chewing gum and carrying a 3' x 3' flat package covered by brown paper.

"Hey Boss it's done," he said, presenting the parcel to the mafioso.

Tony looked down and smirked at Army. He shot back a look that would have been lethal if looks could kill.

Massi poked a finger through the paper and tore it all off, revealing an oil-on-canvass painting of a shirtless, young black man wearing red boxing gloves in a classic pugilist's pose. In the lower right corner of the painting were the initials: TS.

"My Kid Chocolate's here, finally. An' it's real good, Tony. I'll hang it next to your DiMaggio and Rizzuto. Thanks."

The portrait was stunningly lifelike. It captured the intensity of the former Cuban boxer's eyes as well as his undisturbed, handsome features.

"Oh, glad you're here for another reason, Tony. This is Army. He owns the Cienfuegos baseball team."

"So?" Tony shrugged.

"So he don't want us fixin' his games no more."

"And?"

"Hold off 'til I talk to Meyer. Got it?"

Tony maintained his focus on Army and shrugged as he spoke. "Got it. By the way, I hada take care of a guy I caught cheatin' at a Blackjack table."

"Did you make an example of 'im?"

Still looking at Army. "Split 'is head open."

"Good. Now get the car. I'm leavin' in ten minutes."

Tony turned toward the door, opened it and walked out.

"Not a bad kid," Massi said. "And a helluva artist. But sometimes he gets in over 'is head."

Standing and snuffing his cigar in an ashtray on the mobster's desk. "He has no idea how far he's in over his head, Joe. Call me when you have an answer."

Chapter 15
Army and Jomar

ARMY STEPPED OUT of the hotel to see Jomar, the baby-faced plainclothes policeman, leaning on the Hudson sedan. The young detective tossed a lit cigarette and approached hastily.

"Sir, you are supposed to call me each morning. I am your driver and I do not want trouble with the lieutenant-colonel."

Shaking hands with the detective. "Leave Grau to me. There will be days when I don't need you, but I understand. You have your orders. So, here's what we'll do. Report to my office at the palace each morning and hang around. If I need you, you'll be right there."

"Sir, you do not understand. I am also your bodyguard. Wherever you go, I go."

Army frowned when he pictured Grau's spy following him everywhere. He looked at his wristwatch.

"Okay. Take me to the palace. I'm late for an appointment. We'll both talk with my staff."

Army opened the front passenger door, but Jomar intervened. "No sir. You are an important person. Please sit in the back."

He sighed and obeyed the order given by his new driver, bodyguard, and whatever else the young man was. So, he lit a Lucky Strike and smoked while the detective drove.

"Where's Grau now?"

"Sir, I am not permitted to disclose the lieutenant-colonel's whereabouts at any time."

Then the chauffeur-bodyguard turned his head toward his passenger, smiled, and for a moment, shed the shackles of formality required of his quasi-military position. "He is having lunch with the president."

"Oh," Army said while the driver parked in front of the palace. In a minute they were in the lobby, where armed soldiers guarded the marble staircase and uniformed police strolled suspiciously. A pleasant-looking, middle-aged woman in a blue business suit emerged from a doorway and greeted them.

"*Señor* Lobo, I am Yolanda, chief of staff. Please follow me."

Army looked at Jomar. "You know her?"

He nodded pleasantly.

Sensing dissatisfaction, Yolanda looked back and added: "I hope you are not disappointed in me as head of your staff."

He simply smiled and followed her through the busy lobby to a large white door that was open. In the middle of the room stood a cedar desk. Behind it, were double vertical windows covered by a white lace curtain.

Yolanda opened a smaller, white door to the right, where male twins about twenty years old sat at a table with three Underwood typewriters and stacks of blank paper. Behind them was a wall-to-wall bookcase filled with volumes of reference, history, geography, and law. *The Havana Post* newspapers were stacked in one corner.

"Gentlemen, this is Walter and Wilmer," the chief of staff said, "law students at the University of Havana. Muchachos, meet Armando Lobo, Minister of Labor, your new boss. You already know Jomar."

The boys rose and shook hands with the men. Wilmer was shorter than Walter and had a lighter complexion. Walter was swarthy, slim and fit. Both wore white shirts and black slacks.

The detective seemed to be as comfortable as a woodpecker in a coconut tree with Yolanda and the twins.

"Muchachos," Army said, "get out your notebooks and pens. I want you to gather statistics. We'll start with the city and province of Havana. What is the population of Havana City and surrounding areas? Its unemployment, underemployment, the number of laborers, skilled and unskilled. Their wages. That also goes for office workers, policemen, firemen, teachers. How many trade schools do we have? Which trades? Cost of living. Rent, food, gasoline."

Walter took notes. Wilmer listened.

"You're going to knock on doors and talk to Habaneros and Habaneras. Hear their thoughts on the economy and other issues. Once we have all of the information we can create a plan and present it to the president.

"The ultimate goal is to get people off the streets and into jobs."

He gestured to his chief of staff. "You will review reports the boys type up and make any necessary changes. Any questions?"

"Yes," came a man's voice from the doorway. "When does this ambitious campaign begin?"

They turned to see the lieutenant-colonel. "Don't you have someone to torture, Grau?" Army said.

"Señor Lobo. I would thoroughly enjoy watching you squirm in my Chamber of Truth. However, right now I need your telephone."

Yolanda led Grau to the cedar desk and shut the door. Army turned to the boys.

"Let's go. We're going to take a survey in central Havana."

The twins and the detective followed their boss out a side door that led to the lobby. They made their way through the police and soldiers, down the palace steps and into the Hudson.

"Detective, drive to Calle Galiano and let them canvas the neighborhood of the Iglesia Monserrate."

"You mean Galiano and Concordia," Jomar said. "If we drive down Concordia one block, there is the San Nicholas neighborhood, where there are many people living all the way down to the Malecón, sir."

"Don't call me *sir*. Okay, San Nicholas."

———— ◆ ————

When they arrived at the barrio the detective parked on the southwest corner of Concordia, near the back door of the white, stucco Catholic church. He and Army smoked cigarettes, leaned on the car, and watched the twins knock, enter, and exit a row of plaster-and-brick row homes built in the 1800s on Calle San Nicholas.

When the boys knocked on the fourth door, which was badly weathered and covered by peeling brown paint, a pot-bellied, bald, middle-aged man staggered out with a baseball bat in his hands. He said nothing to the twins. He didn't have to. He was drunk and in an angry mood. A tall mulatta woman about the same age, with a black eye and a torn, black dress at the shoulder followed him out of the house, pleading with him to stop.

"*Robo, por favor. No,*" the woman said.

Army tossed his smoke and bolted from the car to distract the man from the twins, waving his arms like a rodeo clown at a bull.

"*Amigo, Todo esta bien.* It's okay. *No problema.*"

But the inebriated and hostile fellow wanted to bash someone's head, and it didn't matter whose. So, he wound up the bat and took a home-run swing at Army, who ducked under it. Wind from the barrel rustled his hair.

From out of nowhere Jomar plowed into Robo like a linebacker hitting a running back who'd stalled. The bodyguard's right shoulder drove the man into a brick wall under the house's front window. The bat went flying. The man bounced off the wall and landed on top of the skinny detective.

Army pulled the drunken man off by the collar and said, again. "*Amigo, no problema. Calma.* Relax."

The woman pleaded: "*No, no Robo. Por favor, no mas.*"

But this was one drunk with bad intentions. A crowd gathered around him as he swayed to his feet and stumbled after the detective. Somehow, Robo grabbed Jomar by the shirt and head-butted him. Blood spurted and the detective let out a chilling scream. Enraged, he pulled a pistol and slammed Robo on the head repeatedly, spraying blood as he did.

The woman screamed and with both hands tried to pull the gun from Jomar's hands. But he pushed her away, abruptly holstering it. Neighbors gathered quickly around her, cursing the man with the pistol.

Finally, the drunk fell to the street, backward. But instead of retreating, the detective leaped on top of the felon and punched his bloody face.

Army pulled him off. "Jomar. *No mas.* You'll kill him. *Calma.*"

Disheveled and out of breath, the detective pulled out a badge as angry neighbors closed in. He held the badge high over his blood-splattered face and yelled: *"Policia. Este hombre esta bajo arresto."*

Army tried to calm the agitated crowd while Jomar rolled the drunken man over and handcuffed him behind his back.

"Calma, calma," he said. *"Policia,"* he added as a pool of blood formed around the man's head. He was not moving. The woman was inconsolable.

"My husband is not a bad man," she cried. "He is only drunk."

Just then a squad car arrived with two uniformed policemen. They stepped out with batons at the ready. They seemed to know the detective, with whom they spoke for a few minutes before pulling the sobbing woman from the drunk, who was now moving.

The cops carried the handcuffed and bloody man to the back seat of their 1949 Chevy sedan and threw him in head first. Pressing a white handkerchief onto his forehead, the blood-splattered bodyguard walked over to Army.

"Sir, I must follow these police to the station, where I will file a report. Will you be all right here?"

Patting the detective on the shoulder. "Yes, are you okay?"

"Yes, thank you."

Suddenly a bond was formed between the two, the kind of closeness that arises whenever people join together to repel an attacker. Still, Army was concerned about the way in which his minder lost control of his temper and had become homicidal.

Jomar followed the other police in his car while the twins made their way through the crowd and spoke with their boss.

"Señor," said Wilmer. "The wife of the drunken man wants to talk with us inside her house."

The assemblage of women, men, and teens continued to stand around and talk among themselves as Army and the two law students weaved their way to the woman's front door.

The three entered the woman's home. They walked through a narrow hallway covered by flaking, green paint until they spotted the female, sitting in a creaking rocking chair in front of a table with a lamp that was turned off. The room was dim, illuminated only by the sun peeking through the open door as well as the front window.

The woman greeted them kindly but trembled while pointing to a sofa opposite her.

"Please sit," she said. "My name is Agnelys. I am so sorry for what my man did. He is not a bad man. He is deaf and dumb. He has no work. So, he sits and drinks rum. And when he is drunk he can be violent."

"Agnelys, I'm Armando Lobo, Minister of Labor, and these young men are my assistants, Wilmer and Walter. How can we help you?"

"Find him work. He is good with his hands. A carpenter."

A mahogany table shaped like a heart graced the living room. Four heart-shaped chairs surrounded it.

"He made the furniture," Agnelys said. "He wants to work. His brother, Coco, too. He lives next door. And other men in the barrio. They want work, too. But the city will not hire them. Neither will the Americans."

"Why?"

"They have their own people."

Army turned to the brothers. "Boys, I want you to take names and addresses from this woman. I also want you to check with criminal records at the courthouse. See if any of these men in the neighborhood has a record and if so, the crimes. And…"

He stopped, noticing a 5-by-7-inch, framed black-and-white photo on the lamp table behind the rocking chair. He'd seen the man in the photo before, at the university riot.

In the back of the photo he spotted a Yemaya doll surrounded by short, unlit candles symbolic of Santeria, an Afro-Cuban religion of saints, statues and dolls practiced secretly. He had an eerie feeling.

Army stood and walked to the table, picked up the framed photo and showed it to Agnelys. The picture was of a bald, thin young man with a black beard.

"Who is this?"

"Oh, that is my nephew, Ernesto. We call him Chango. That is his Santeria name.

"Chango? What does he do?"

"He studies law at the university, very intelligent. Very troubled."

Wilmer excused himself, took the picture from his boss, and showed it to Walter.

"I recognize him," Wilmer said. "He is Ernesto, leader of the FEU."

"I saw him involved in a bloody protest at the university," Army said. "The police roughed him up, but he was still defiant."

His aunt pleaded: "He is not a bad boy. He has good intentions."

Army turned to the twins. "The FEU, University Student Federation, is a radical group, isn't it?"

"Yes, revolutionaries, anarchists," Wilmer said. "Ernesto is as radical as it gets. He is in one of our law classes. He has been arrested more than once for inciting a riot. But he is out now. We saw him on campus yesterday."

The aunt interrupted, ominously. "The blood of conquistadors flows through his veins. His mother's side of the family fought against Spain for Cuban independence. He is Chango. He has power over people. You will see."

Army looked at the twins for their reaction. They raised their eyebrows.

Agnelys resumed: "Nice boy. He looks after me. His mother is my step-sister. But she thinks she is too good to come down here."

"What's the muñeca's name?" Army inquired of the doll.

"Yemoja, Mother of Waters, protector of the feminine force."

"Do you mind if I join Yemoja in protecting you?"

"No, I do not," Agnelys said with a weary smile, wiping a tear that ran from her bruised eye. He stooped so that she could see the resoluteness in his face.

"If Robo harms you again when he gets out of jail, call me. If you do not, and I find out he hurt you, I will see to it that he's locked up for a long time."

Army gave Agnelys his card and kissed her damp cheek. He whispered encouraging words into her ear, reached into his pocket and slipped money into her hand.

She nodded a tearful thank you and said. "I will pray for you."

He looked back at the twins. "I'm returning to the Fox Hole. Get to work."

Chapter 16
The Seduction

WHEN ARMY WALKED through the entrance to the Fox Hole the place was electric. The salsa group was playing a little louder than usual. Tyrone Power and Cesar Romero were knocking down shots with US Sailors in whites. Film star Barbara Stanwyck and two other elegantly dressed women sat on stools around small tables, smoking cigarettes, drinking cocktails and nibbling on snacks from small, white porcelain plates.

Army caught a glimpse of Ted Williams to the left of the door through which he'd entered. The baseball star, dressed in a white shirt whose wide collar overlapped the lapels of a light-gray suit jacket, sat on a stool, posing for photos next to a three-foot replica of a bottle of Fox Hole rum.

Williams looked relaxed holding a curled-up racing form in his left hand. He hooked the stool's cross bar with the heel of his left, white shoe while the other one rested flat on the tiled floor. Army was about to walk over to the baseball star when he heard his name, turned and spotted Fay standing at the bar, next to Lora and several young men wearing Boston Red Sox caps. He froze like a rabbit in a fox's gaze.

"Armando," the Corsican called over the crowd noise. "Come here."

With great reluctance he walked over to Lora and shook hands.

"Armando, meet Dom DiMaggio, Yimmy, excuse me, Jimmy Piersall and Sammy White."

Army shook hands with all three Red Sox players, nodded politely to Fay and waved over Hiran, who motioned to Celia to wait on his customers.

"Hiran, drinks for these gentlemen and lady, on me please."

Hiran waved him closer, said he had a guest and pointed to El Carcel. They looked up and saw an attractive woman wearing a cowboy hat and sunglasses sitting at his table.

"I permitted her to wait there, Armando, to prevent a fuss. I hope you are not angry with me."

"Not at all. Did you send up a bottle of our best rum?"

"She asked for it."

Army looked back at Williams. He was busy being photographed. He looked over at the other Red Sox players. They were talking to Fay. He wanted to talk to them, but he didn't want to speak with her.

"Sorry gentlemen, I have an unexpected guest waiting for me. I'll be back in a little while."

He waved to Williams and made his way through the patrons slowly, shaking hands and nodding until he reached the entrance to his private jail. He pulled out a key to open the lock when he felt a hand on his elbow. He turned to see Fay. In the background he noticed Celia watching them.

"Be careful up there," she said. "You might get burned."

He looked into her eyes and shrugged. As he turned back to the gate to slip in the key she stopped him again and ran a finger along the seam of his white shirt pocket.

"Is that blood?" she said. "Are you okay?"

"Yes."

"You're not going to say, 'Some things you don't want to know?'"

"No"

Army turned the key in the lock until it clicked, swung open the gate, pulled it shut once inside, locked it and trotted up the steps without saying another word. In ten seconds he was seated at his private table with the legs that launched a thousand tips. They belonged to Titi. She was sipping from a glass of dark rum. A nearly full bottle of Bacardi Black stood in the center of the round table.

He pointed to her sunglasses and cowboy hat, which now sat on the table, next to the bottle. She wore a blue-and-white western shirt separated from dark-blue denim pants by a brown belt with a silver-star buckle with the inscription, "US Marshall." Brown leather cowboy boots covered her feet.

"Well, yippi yai yo kai aa," Army said as he leaned over and kissed Titi on the cheek. "What's with the cowboy stuff?"

"This is an American bar, no? Why cannot I be dressed like an American?"

"You're speaking English, what a compliment."

"What is this language, Yippi ya ya ya?"

"Oh, it's cowboy talk. Doesn't really mean anything. But I like the sound of your English."

"Only because we are alone, Armando, do I speak English. I feel blue. Only the most handsome man in Havana can make me feel better. But what is this?" she added, pointing to the blood spot on the left breast pocket of his shirt.

"Nothing important."

"It is blood. Over your heart Armando. This has meaning."

He smiled and unbuttoned his white, cotton shirt against which his tanned skin provided an attractive contrast. The open shirt revealed something Cuban men lacked by choice: a hairy chest. His furry pectorals were muscular, accentuating rippled stomach muscles.

He slid the shirt off and his biceps flexed. He tossed the garment onto the couch, reached behind the bar and pulled out a white T-shirt, but Titi stopped him.

"Do you not feel the heat?" Titi said while fanning herself with a colorful silk hand fan. "Please. No pullover."

Titi was titillated. Army was intrigued. He tossed the T-shirt onto the bar, from which he grabbed a cocktail glass. He filled half of it with the Bacardi, added more to Titi's and touched his drink to hers. Rum had a way of filling the hole, the emptiness he still felt despite the insane evening he'd spent at Sailor's Bar. So did the company of a queen.

"Salud," he said as he sat bare-chested opposite her. "Now why would the most desirable woman in Havana be blue? Aren't you Junior's girl?"

"Junior? Armando *mi amor*, these American Mafiosi, they know better how to steal a dollar than to win a woman's heart."

She reached across the table, held his left hand and looked into his blue eyes.

"You are different. I see in your eyes the hurt, the love, the goodness. *Tu eres una persona simpatico.* Your heart is pure. You are a true Cuban caballero."

"You sound like a psychic, Titi."

"What?"

"You know, *psíquico,* someone who senses things that ordinary people cannot."

"Armando, I am Santeria. Maybe that is why I can see into your heart."

Suddenly, the sound of a crash below startled them. They looked down through the ornate ironwork to see a case of beer on the floor and Hiran apologizing to patrons. They also saw Fay make her way to the busy bar, where she found herself face-to-face with Celia.

Army watched with interest as she spoke to Celia loudly over the crowd noise. He listened with rapt attention.

"Hi, I'm Armando's girlfriend. You're new here. Can you please give me the telephone? I have to make a call. Immediately."

Celia stared at her for one or two seconds. "You are Jezebel. I will not help you. Do not bother Armando anymore."

Celia walked away to help another customer and Fay, who'd had too many mojitos, became furious.

"What? How dare you," she screamed above the din of the crowd. "Come back here." Army and Titi heard that.

"She is pretty, but she is not for you Armando" Titi said. "She likes too much to be with the Mafiosi. I know. I see her at Tropicana, at parties. She does not have the heart and soul of a Latina woman. The fire that you require."

Titi rose, carried her chair next to his, sat, held his hand again and picked up her drink.

"*Cin cin,*" she said, touching her glass to his.

"Now you're chirping Italian. Okay, *Cin cin.*"

———— ◆ ————

Two hours passed quickly. The lunch crowd had thinned. The baseball players and their female admirer had gone. The bottle had been drained.

Titi was sitting on Army's lap, running her long fingers through his thick, black hair, thrusting her tongue into his mouth and rubbing his hairy chest. He was in a drunken state of complete and utter surrender.

"Show me your apartment, Armando."

"Can you climb that ladder?" he asked, nodding toward the trap door in the ceiling.

"I climb a mountain for you, *mi amor.*"

He pulled out a key and gave it to her.

"You go first, Titi. I'll be in back of you in case you fall. All you have to do is slip the key into the lock, turn it and push open the door."

"Oh Armando this is exciting. Like we are, how you say, *adolescentes.* We go through a secret door. Ja-ja-ja-ja."

Titi was about halfway up the iron ladder when she stopped and swayed. Army steadied her by placing one hand on her firm, shapely ass while keeping the other hand on the ladder's side rail. He never could have imagined this on the evening of the bar's opening, when she'd presented herself to him in front of an approving audience in which every man in the room wanted to be him.

"Steady, Titi. I hope you don't mind my hand on your *culo.*"

"Oh no, Armando. My *culo* and your *mano,* I think they are in love."

They both laughed and within a minute they collapsed on the couch, holding hands and giggling like high school sweethearts.

"*Mi amor,* you will show me your *dormitorio?*" she said, seductively.

"My bedroom? Of course, it's in back of us. Wait. My hand is talking to me. He doesn't want anything to come between him and your *culo,* like your panties."

"And my bare *culo* wants your hand and his brother to squeeze it. Vamos."

They held onto each other as they swayed to the bedroom door, opened it, snickered, and disappeared behind it.

As Titi lay naked upon his white cotton sheets, he surveyed her body admiringly. Her legs were long and shapely, toned by thousands of hours of salsa, mambo, rumba and cha-cha-cha.

"You are exquisite, Titi."

"Thank you, *mi amor*," she said, smiling and fondling his hair.

Army noted that alabaster best described the color of her skin, from her feet to her shaved vagina to her firm breasts with silver-dollar nipples to her long arms and neck and fantastic face. She moaned as he massaged her clit, then she sat up, pushed him onto his back and mounted him.

After two minutes, four minutes, eight minutes she screamed with multiple orgasms until he hollered too. She was wet. She was hot. She was what he needed. He was what she wanted. Throughout the night they awakened and found each other in the dark, reigniting their passion, punctuated by primal outbursts.

Chapter 17
Killing a Communist

THE FIRST TIME the phone rang was 9 a.m. With his eyes closed Army felt for the table with the telephone and picked up the receiver: "Hello." No answer. He hung up.

The second time the phone rang was 10 a.m. No answer.

"It is your American girlfriend," Titi said in a groggy voice.

"She's not my girlfriend anymore."

"Then pass to me the phone."

Fifteen minutes later the phone rang and Titi answered.

"Armando does not want you anymore. Do not call here again … What? Who?"

She passed the phone to him.

"It is Jostein," she said.

"Jostein? Who? Oh, Hohen Stein, how are you?"

He listened for a few moments and sat up at full attention."

"Okay. I'll be there as soon as possible."

He turned to Titi and hung up the phone.

"I have to go to Santa Cruz. Come with me."

"No, *mi amor*. I must rehearse in two hours. Come to Tropicana tonight to see my show."

He thought for a moment and looked into her eyes. "Titi. If you're still with Junior, we have a problem. He can have your legs broken. Are you still his girlfriend?"

She looked away. "No, I am not his anymore. Please call me a taxi."

A half-hour later the two lovers were kissing goodbye at a cab outside the Fox Hole's main entrance. When he turned back to the building he noticed a man in a blue Guayabera shirt standing on the corner, smoking a cigarette.

"Jomar, how are you?"

The detective walked over and shook hands with his superior, who inspected his bodyguard's forehead. Five stitches had closed a red and swollen wound.

"Robo left his mark, but it'll fade soon enough. How do you feel?"

"I am good. He is in the hospital. He is to be arraigned when he is released. He is looking at a long prison sentence for assault and battery on a police official."

"Hopefully he learns a lesson. As for me, I have to go to Santa Cruz. Trouble at the plantation."

"What kind of trouble?"

"Sabotage."

"My car is around the corner Armando. Vamonos."

Powered by a 145-horsepower engine with a two-barrel carburetor, the Hudson responded to the driver's heavy accelerator foot and the duo arrived at the Santa Cruz railroad crossing thirty minutes ahead of schedule. A large sign read: *Centro Lobo Santa Cruz*.

"Why is this called *Centro?*" Jomar asked.

"Because wherever a sugar mill goes up, a town rises around it. Follow the smoke."

Do you mind if I ask you about the plantations?"

"No, not at all."

"How did your family acquire such land?"

"Actually, my father was poor, an orphan. His parents died when he was a child and a family friend, a chocolate maker, raised him on this Santa Cruz plantation. My father learned everything about the business of planting, growing, harvesting sugar, and converting it into chocolate. He never dreamed that one day he would own the property and two others. Turn right here."

Captivated by the rags-to-riches story, the detective pressed: "So the family friend died and gave the property, the chocolate business to him?"

"No. But you're close. My father's great grandfather, a Spaniard, had disowned my father's father for moving to Cuba instead of Philadelphia, where he started a construction company. So, when great grandfather died he left a lot of money and a fleet of trucks and warehouses in Philadelphia to my father. He was only twenty years old. Turn right again."

"So your father, Lázaro, was lucky."

The Sugar Man shrugged. "Luck is when preparation meets opportunity. With the money he bought the plantation in Santa Cruz and two others. With the knowledge, he built a chocolate business. The warehouses in Philadelphia were turned into chocolate factories. The trucks delivered the product. Turn left, here."

Army sniffed. He could smell the remnants of burning sugar cane stalks the closer they came to the plantation manager's house. Their throats tickled. They coughed.

"I know the business," he continued, "because my father had me work on the plantations from the time I was a child. After the war I took a house in Santa Cruz and worked with Stein, who manages our farms. He taught me a lot. You'll meet him, soon."

The detective turned left onto a dirt road with eleven-foot high sugar cane stalks standing on each side of the path. Thick, black smoke billowed about a quarter mile ahead. Jomar began to sneeze as the wind carried the smoke to them. The ashen air was filled with soot, methane and nitrous oxide. It smelled like burned molasses.

"To burn the sugar cane is normal, no?" the driver said.

"Yes, but the field ahead was set on fire prematurely."

"Why do they burn this?" Jomar said as he rolled up the window. "I mean, under normal circumstances."

"To make it easier to harvest. The inside of the plant doesn't burn. The stem. That's where the sugar is. Fire also kills snakes, clears weeds and makes the stalks easier to cut by hand."

Emerging from the dirty air like a submarine in murky water, the Hudson continued along the unpaved road, past a smoldering field of short blackened stalks, and a sugar mill with three smoke stacks that were not fuming. Army looked at the mill.

"These mills operate 24 hours a day, seven days a week during harvesting season."

The detective smiled. "I see why you are called 'The Sugar Man.'"

Soon they were driving along a cinder road with single A-frame houses made of stone and wood on each side of the street. The nicest home was at the end, on the left. It had an A-frame roof over an entrance of double wooden doors painted red. Windows with red frames and shutters were open.

A black woman in her sixties was sitting and smoking a cigar on a red, creaky rocking chair. She was wearing a gray peasant's dress and a black ribbon tied around the back of her hair. Her forehead was long, her eyes sunken, her nose straight and flared at the nostrils. Her large lips curved downward. It was a sad face. However, when she saw who stepped out of the Hudson, her features lit up like a 200-watt light bulb. She looked radiant. Lovely.

"Mandito," she said, rising from her rocker. She stopped and placed the cigar in an ashtray next to her worn, black shoes on the wooden floor of the front porch.

Sugar Man spread his arms wide as she limped into his caress and kisses.

"How's my Cuban mother?"

"How is my American son?"

Army turned to his driver.

"Jomar this is Nelsa."

"Nelsa, *mucho gusto.*" They shook hands.

Suddenly, a white wolf appeared at their feet. He stood and placed his front paws on his master's thigh. "Obol, how is my handsome Obol?" he said as the alluring animal licked his bowed face. "I miss you so much, boy."

The detective couldn't believe his eyes. "He exists. The white wolf in the picture. In your bar."

"No, that's his grandmother. I grew up with her."

"The Obols go on and on forever," the maid said. "How about some sweet rum and Montecristos?"

"Next time, Mama. I'm sorry, but I have to see Stein right away."

Nelsa's smile disappeared faster than Army's cash in Sailor's bar. "Oh Mandito. We have trouble. Señor Stein is in the barn."

The two men walked around the back of the house, where a large red barn stood. The doors were open and the back of a gray-haired man could be seen standing over a younger man tied to a chair. His eyes were red and swollen. The older man was slapping him.

"Stein," Army yelled. "What are you doing?'

Startled, the plantation manager turned around. A man in his sixties, the German transplant wore a neatly trimmed, white brush mustache that matched his thick, salt-and-pepper colored hair. His beady eyes, peering over an aquiline nose gave him the look of an aging eagle who'd seen a lot. And he had, in Berlin, where he was born, as well as Brazil, where he became a sugar expert before settling in Santa Cruz.

In a German accent, Stein began: "Mandito. This one I found breaking the machinery in the mill. He also set fire to two fields. And he scared the field workers away."

"Any Accomplices?"

"No. He must be punished."

Army pulled Stein aside. Jomar followed.

"What have you found out from him?

"He is a communist."

"Does he work here?"

"On weekends. He said he is a student at the university. He tells the workers they are the owners of the land, not you. That you did not build this. Someone else did. The workers are in their homes. They refuse to come out."

Army thought for a moment.

"Tell your foreman that I'm here. Tell him to round up the laborers. To have them here at the barn as soon as possible."

"What about him?"

"Tell Nelsa to bring two small towels and cracked ice."

"He must be punished."

"Untie him."

"What? He will run."

"Untie him."

Disgruntled, Stein walked back to the saboteur, untied him and stomped off to the house. Sugar Man stood in front of the rebel. His nose was bleeding.

"What's your name?" Army asked, looking down at him.

"Who wants to know?"

"Armando Lobo Armstrong. The owner."

"Armstrong. You are American?"

"Half."

"Well, that half is what we Cubans have a problem with. You take our land. You exploit our workers."

The maid arrived with the towels and a bowl of ice cubes and returned to the house. Army wrapped the cubes in the two towels and presented them to his prisoner.

"For your eyes. They're swollen."

The captive took one towel, shook out the ice and wiped blood from his nose.

Army tossed him the other towel, pulled out a pack of cigarettes and offered him one. He accepted, as did Jomar, who brought over two chairs. The detective lit all three smokes, then let his boss ask the questions.

"What's your name?"

"Pablo de la Torre."

"Where do you live?"

"Near the university."

"Student?"

"Law."

Army picked a piece of tobacco off his tongue while watching Pablo.

"Know someone named Ernesto?"

"I know lots of Ernestos."

"This one is bald with a black beard and is an activist at the university."

Pablo took a drag on his cigarette. "He is one of our leaders."

"Leaders of the FEU?"

"Yes. And the DR."

"What's that?"

Jomar interrupted: "Directorio Revolucionario. A violent group."

"Are you in the DR, too?"

"Yes. We fight against the tyranny of Batista."

"Why are you here in Santa Cruz?"

"To make trouble for you and other foreigners who take our sugar and abuse and exploit the workers."

"How do we abuse them?"

"They die of heat stroke in the fields and factories. And if they live, they do so malnourished, dehydrated, exhausted. The work is dirty, difficult and they do it for what? A few pesos a week? You make all the money."

"Wrong plantation, Pablo. How many of you are sabotaging plantations?"

The saboteur smiled. "You will see."

Just then about thirty workers arrived with Nayade, the foreman. She led them to the barn. They looked at Army and his driver warily. There was an undercurrent of hostile talk. Army heard it and stood next to Pablo in the chair and addressed the laborers.

"*Compañeros,*" he said, pointing to Pablo. "This man says that I have treated you unfairly. That I have cheated you. That I abuse you. That you die in the fields. Is this true?"

The foreman answered. "No Armando. But two months ago, you cut our wages. The muchacho spoke of the injustice of that. The injustices in the country. We work twelve hours a day in the fields and the sugar mill. Seven days a week."

He looked stunned.

"I never authorized such a pay cut."

Suddenly, Pablo leapt to his feet, pointed to Army, and addressed the workers.

"This man is a foreigner with a Cuban name. He is one of many capitalists, imperialists, who own our sugar mills, plantations and mines, filling their pockets with money on the sweat of our brows while we live like dogs."

Jomar pushed Pablo down into his chair. "Shut your mouth, you sabotaging son-of-a-bitch."

Army grabbed Pablo by the shirt, yanked him to his feet and addressed the workers while pointing at him.

"*Compañeros*, I told him he has the wrong plantation. You all know my father, Lázaro Lobo. He was born here, in Santa Cruz. He started out like you many years ago, laboring in the fields. I also worked in these fields as a boy. We know how hard you work. And my father took that into account as he acquired plantations, built sugar mills and a railroad."

He released his grip on Pablo's shirt and turned to the foreman. "Nayade, where do you take your family when they are sick?"

"The clinic."

"How much do you pay at the clinic?"

"It is free."

"Tell Pablo who built it?"

"Your father."

"Tell Pablo who built the school, the recreation center, the grocery store."

She shrugged. "Your father."

Army turned to another worker.

"Carlos, you rent a comfortable home at reasonable rate. Tell Pablo who constructed the houses?

"*Señor* Lobo."

"Sure, there are problems at plantations. There are problems at the mines. Problems with corruption in government. That's part of our history. Since Christopher Columbus. But I'm Minister of Labor now. Things will get better."

"He is a Batista henchman," Pablo countered. "Batista, an illegal president who rules by force and is in bed with the Mafia, the CIA and American big business who plunder our nation."

"This man is a communist," Army said. "He wants a Marxist president who will make everyone equal. Equally poor. While the government takes control of your life. I am a capitalist, like my father, who started out like you. Which means that you, too, can work your way up and make life better for your families. I'm restoring your wages to what they were before they were cut. Will you go back to work?"

Nayade was the first to speak. "Armando, you and your father have treated us fairly over the years. I for one will return."

She turned to the workers. "The rest of you?"

The laborers looked at each other and answered, in unison. "Yes."

"Nayade," Army said. "When the fires are out we have 24 hours to bring the cane to the mill to be cut, shredded and crushed or it will ferment. Let's get to work."

He turned to Jomar.

"Watch Pablo while I find Stein."

He walked to the house and saw Stein sitting on the front steps.

"Hohen, why did you cut their pay without asking me first?"

"Why should I? I work for your father. You pay them more than the other plantation owners and my job is to conserve and show a healthy profit. I have been running this business for the last twenty years and I know what I am doing."

Army bristled.

"You work for me, Stein. My father will tell you that. But even at a higher rate of pay than other 'cane cutters get, we're making a good profit. What did you do with the money you cut from them?"

"I put it back into the company, of course."

"Well, I just restored their wages and they're going back to the fields. But we need to see the damage at the mill. What needs to be fixed?"

Stein shook his head negatively. "The rollers. He jammed the roller machines with tools and without the rollers we cannot produce sugar."

"Show me the machines."

Both hopped into a 1950 Ford pickup truck and the plantation manager drove to the mill, covered by a black cloud of smoke. With their hands over their mouths they hurried inside to find four roller machines jammed with hoes, shovels and fencing bars.

Army looked closer. He discovered that the rollers merely had been dislodged from their adjustable sockets.

"Stein, all we have to do is remove the obstructions and reset the rollers."

Sugar Man pulled out a handkerchief and held it over his nose. Stein found an oil rag and placed it over his. The two men finished the task in less than an hour.

When they returned to the house and exited the truck, they heard a single gunshot. Both ran to the barn.

Lying on the clay floor face up was Pablo. Jomar was standing over him with his pistol. He appeared to be in shock. He turned to the men.

"He tried to take my gun and it fired."

Army knelt beside Pablo. He saw blood flowing from a hole in his left chest. He felt for a pulse in Pablo's neck. It was weak, then it was no more. He looked up.

"He's dead."

Chapter 18
The Torture Chamber

THE RIDE BACK to Havana was quiet. The only sound in the car was night air rushing through open windows. The breeze felt good even though it was steeped in humidity.

Neither man felt like talking. Pablo's body rested in the back seat, wrapped in a white sheet. And the more Army thought about the fatal shooting, the more he wondered. Did Pablo really go for the detective's gun? Or did Jomar lose his temper again, the way he did with Robo? Only this time there were no witnesses and no one at the Fifth Precinct was going to question a detective who shot to death a communist.

Sugar Man lit a cigarette and wondered out loud: "How many more Pablos are out there? How many more times is this going to happen?"

The driver just shrugged.

Then there was Fay. She was very much on his mind. His heart pounded when he'd seen her at the Fox Hole with those baseball players. Still, he became angry at the temerity she'd exhibited. She not only set foot in his place, but also fraternized with ball players. Same old Fay.

As far as Titi went, he really didn't want to get involved with her. There was something wrong, but he couldn't define it. It was a feeling. A bad feeling. He liked the way she mothered him, but she looked too much like his mother. He enjoyed her company, but so did other men in Havana, one of whom was a powerful Mafia boss. She knew his father. But how well did she know him? He cringed at the thought.

"Some things you don't want to know," he muttered to himself.

"Huh?"the detective said.

"Nothing."

"Do you mind coming with me to the police station, Armando? I will need a signed statement from you, an official, in addition to my own report."

Army stared at the dark road ahead for a second or two before answering. "No problem."

Jomar drove straight to the Fifth Precinct on Calle 62 between 7th and 7A in Playa and parked. The duo walked into the blue-and-white building. Ceiling fans stirred the humid, stale air in the lobby. The sergeant, his tie askew and collar open, was seated at a desk on a concrete slab four feet high, which made all visitors look up as they addressed him. He was busy with paperwork, but paused when the young detective addressed him.

"Alex, I have a body in my car, a communist who attacked me and died in the process. Please send someone to remove the corpse and put it on ice pending notification of next of kin. I will be in my office writing up the report."

The detective patted his boss on the back, adding: "This is Armando Lobo Armstrong, Minister of Labor. He will write a statement about the incident."

The desk sergeant nodded and the two men walked to the detective's second-floor office. On the stairwell they smelled urine and heard the sound of a man crying. It seemed to be coming from the basement.

Army held his nose. "Does anyone use the rest room here?" Jomar only smiled while opening the door to his office, a small room without windows but with plenty of filing cabinets. Documents were stacked high upon a desk in the middle. Ceiling fans whirred above to keep the air moving. Still, the room was stuffy.

"Please take a seat,"Jomar said. He grabbed a white pad and pen from his desk. "Just write your recollection of events and sign it. We should not be here a long time."

Army sat on a wooden chair near the door and loosened his collar. While writing he heard the faint screams of a man. He noticed that they were also heard by the detective, who started typing the report on a 1920 Underwood typewriter.

About twenty minutes later he finished his statement, signed it, and handed it to the young investigator. "Where's the men's room?" he asked.

"Down the hall and to the right."

He walked along the hall to a door marked "*Hombres.*" As he was about to push it open he heard a blood-curdling scream that reverberated along the stairwell nearby. Curiosity led him down the steps to the first floor and onward to the basement. From the stairwell he could see men in cell rooms and hear protests.

"Stop!" one prisoner yelled.

"Monster!" another screamed.

"Let us out of here," another hollered while shaking a cell door that sounded like a rattlesnake. Other detainees began shaking the doors of their cells, too, creating a symphony of shuddering steel bars in a dark scene that was playing out before their eyes and ears.

He creeped closer and saw a closed cell room door with ceiling lights in the background. Through the iron bars he spotted a naked man with long hair and a beard strapped to a metal bed frame. At the foot of the frame was a man in a police uniform. He would turn a dial that apparently sent electricity from a car battery through wires attached to the metal structure. The more he turned the dial, the louder the man screamed. And the louder he yelled, the more vociferous the protest by other prisoners. Light bulbs dimmed, cell doors shook and tin cups clanged in a cacophony of condemnation.

"The pain will end when you tell us what we ask," a familiar voice said calmly. "Once again, when will the attack on the palace occur?"

"Go to hell."

Army drew closer. He saw the arms of a man in a white suit pouring water from a metal jug over the nude man on the metal bed.

"Now you will fry and probably die," Grau said. "Turn it up."

The policeman turned the dial to maximum. The man cried out and went into such convulsions that he no longer could scream. His body bounced up and down from the high voltage. His skin turned black and smoldered.

A feeling of overwhelming helplessness overcame Army. In a flash he was transported to the skylight above a hotel room in Berlin, where he'd watched without being able to act as a Nazi SS officer raped and murdered Serena. And like then, his powerlessness turned into rage.

Amid the malodor of burning skin and screams of protest on the cell block, Army flew to the cell room door.

"Stop this execution," he shouted. "Stop this execution, now."

A surprised Grau waved to the uniformed policeman to stop. He turned down the dial and the body stopped bouncing up and down.

Jeers turned into cheers by the other prisoners. The policeman pulled his revolver and trained it on Army; however, Grau waved him off and motioned for him to remove the smoking body, now a corpse.

The officer kept his eyes on Army as he unlocked the gate, unshackled the blackened body and placed it on a gurney.

"Well done," Grau said to the policeman. "Make sure the body is thrown into the street where he lives, er, lived."

Turning to Army, "Welcome *Señor* Lobo."

He was still shaken, but sufficiently calmed to enter the room. He stood next to Grau, who faced him and smiled as though he had the winning hand in a poker game.

"Welcome to the Chamber of Truth, *Señor* Lobo," Then, with a sweeping gesture, as though he were welcoming someone important to his home, he added: "Let me show you around."

Army stood defiantly and watched as the Chief of the Anti-communist Squad stepped to a table with various instruments. The lieutenant-colonel picked each item up and explained what it was.

"These forceps are used to remove fingernails. Sometimes we heat them to increase the pain. This is nine whips in one, a Cat O Nine Tails." He ran the tip of his index finger over the metal barbs on each lash.

"This small screwdriver-like device with a round, metal tip is a branding iron. Next to it, a cattle prod. Look at the two metal prongs that protrude from the stick. And the metal bed on which the terrorist died is a Picana, invented in the 1930s," Grau said with a shrug and a smile. "These are my instruments of truth. This is my Chamber of Truth."

Surveying everything on the table, Army turned and glared into the executioner's eyes. "How much truth did you extract from that man you just tortured to death, Grau?"

Chapter 19

Titi Takes Over

HIRAN AND CELIA were locking the front door of the Fox Hole at 4 a.m. when they turned around to see someone they didn't expect.

"Hiran, I know it's late," Fay said, "but I need to see Army. Can you please let me in?"

"You are too late," Celia said. "He is with Titi. I think he love her."

Just then Titi's limo pulled up. She didn't even wait for the chauffeur to open the rear door for her. The diva was out of the car in her skimpy, jewel-studded dancer's costume, feathered headpiece and all, hot off the stage at the Tropicana. And "hot" was the word, with the temperature in the low 90s.

"I must see Armando," Titi said while waving a handheld fan.

Hiran and Celia looked at Titi. They all looked at Fay.

"Why you are here, American girl?" Titi said. "Armando does not want you." Then, moving closer to her, she added: "And let me tell you something. You do not want to cross a Cuban woman. Maybe you lose your pretty face."

Not one to be confrontational for any reason while sober, the Boston socialite did an about-face and walked away so fast that she nearly fell off her high heels.

"Take me to Armando!" Titi ordered.

Without hesitation Hiran opened the front door and led Titi up the steps to El Carcel where the boss was finishing a drink and swaying on a bar stool. Titi placed her hands on her hips.

"So, Armando, you do not come to my show and you drink without me."

"He wash out that Jezebel again," said Celia.

"Who? What? Hiran, tell William to come here, now."

Hiran ran down the stairs to get the chauffeur and Titi turned to Celia.

"Who is Jezebel?"

"The American girl, Fay."

"Fay? No, fea."

The change Titi made in Fay's name wasn't lost on Celia. "Si, fea, ugly."

Hiran brought back the chauffeur in a flash.

"William, please carry Armando to the car," Titi said. "And someone please open this drapery. This place is for the dead."

Celia drew open the curtain, William threw Army over his shoulder and made his way down the stairs. With every step Army's stomach bounced and rum leaked from his mouth. Titi, Hiran, and Celia followed until William deposited the bar owner in the back seat of the limo. Titi got in with him and the sleek automobile zoomed away.

Hiran locked the front door again and looked at Celia, who smiled.

"What?" he said.

"I do not think we will see Jezebel here again."

———◆———

It was dawn when Army heard a cock crow and felt a mouth on his morning erection. As his penis was about to explode, Titi slipped it inside her and rode him like a jockey. They came together loudly.

Titi collapsed next to him and he looked up from the queen-size bed to see a white canopy supported by reed-style posts painted white. Looking down, he saw pink terrazzo, cool to the feet in a tropical climate. A dresser with a mirror, a chest, and two night stands were all painted white. The lamps, walls, and ceiling were pink.

"Where are we?" he said when he focused fully.

"You are in my jail, mi amor, you are my *prisionaro del amor.*"

He gave her a funny look. "How did I get here?"

"William."

"Oh no, not again."

Sadness overcame her. "You are disappointed?"

"Yes, in myself. I have to stop drinking."

"Well, maybe not today. I have a show at Tropicana. Mediodia."

"12 o'clock noon?"

"Yes, I want you at my private table. I will sing and dance to you, *mi amor.*"

"But I have work to do."

"Your work is people. And you will find the special guests very interesting."

"I don't have a suit here."

Titi smiled. "I have one that will fit you."

After a moment of introspection, he mumbled his mantra: "Some things you don't want to know."

"What do you say, my love?" she said as she walked to the bathroom.

"Nothing."

At 11 a.m. Army was looking at himself in the bedroom mirror. He was wearing a white tuxedo with a pink carnation pinned to a lapel. The tux fit well. The black shoes, too.

Next to the mirror Army noticed a framed head shot of a handsome young boy. He picked it up. The young man was about twelve years old and he was laughing.

"Who's this boy?" he asked, raising his voice so she could hear him from the other room.

"My boy."

"You have a little boy?"

"He is a big boy now," she yelled.

"How old is he?"

"He has twenty years."

"He's cute."

"No more. He makes himself ugly," she said as she reentered the bedroom.

Army put down the picture and looked at Titi looking at him in the mirror.

"The most handsome man in Havana is beautiful in white," she said, softly.

A half hour later Titi looked regal in a simple white dress and heels. Her shoulder-length blond hair was curled at the ends. A string of pink pearls adorned her neck. She had a bottle of Chanel perfume in her hand, sprayed it into the air and walked through it, covering her entire body. The scent was green marine and fruit.

"You smell sweet and look beautiful, Titi."

"Thank you, *mi amor*."

They walked down the stairs leading to the front door, where he spotted another framed photo on a table. He picked it up. It was the same photo he'd seen in Agnelys' house.

"What's this doing here?" he said.

"This is Ernesto. Now my big boy. He shaves his head. Grows a beard. Hates everything, everybody. He cannot love, only hate."

Army stared at Titi. "I saw this photo in a house near Iglesia Monserrate."

Startled, Titi looked at him. "The house of Agnelys? She is my sister. What were you doing there?"

Chapter 20
The Panther of Wagadu

THEY DIDN'T HAVE to travel far to arrive at the Tropicana nightclub and casino. Known around the world for its cabaret, the Trop featured sultry sequin-and-feathered showgirls, exceptional orchestras, singers, and songs in a Latin beat that was the rage of the times. Within five minutes, Titi's chauffeur was driving the couple through the white, front gates and arch along a paved, two-way private road. They continued through a jungle of Royal Palms and lush tropical vegetation on the six-acre estate in the suburb of Mariano.

Titi turned to her lover. "*Mi amor*, you have been to Las Vegas, no? How does this compare?"

"This is wild. We're driving through a jungle. Where's my elephant gun?"

Late-model Oldsmobiles, Henry Js, Hudsons, Nash Ramblers, Chevy's, Fords, Buicks, and Cadillacs were backed up along the right side of the road leading to the club's entrance. So, the chauffeur drove along the left side the wrong way, bypassing the guests' cars until he pulled up to the swanky entranceway parking even with another limousine. It sat under one of several arched, wooden canopies painted white, pink, yellow, powder-blue, or orange. Mamoncillo trees protruded through holes carved for them in some of the canopies, a spectacular sight in which man's creation had embraced nature.

Army observed all of this with delight. And then his jaw tightened. He saw Tony Stabo behind the wheel of the other limousine. The thug saw him, too. He scoffed as he pulled away.

A formally-attired attendant opened the luxurious automobile's rear door and Titi and her man stepped out to applause. They turned and saw a line of men and women in tuxedos and gowns clapping. Army felt a shiver of pride as the Queen of the Tropicana grabbed his hand, blew kisses, sashayed under a white canopy and out to a sunlit tropical garden path that led to the Arcos de Cristal, an immense glass structure that housed the indoor cabaret.

Along the way they passed the Tropicana's icon: The Twirling Ballerina, a white, marble statue of a dancer spinning in the middle of a small, blue reflecting pool. Not far off was a larger blue pool centered by a white fountain called The Dancing Nymphs. Along the rim of the fountain were seven marble figures of naked women holding hands in various stages of dance.

The indoor cabaret was shaped like a cornucopia. It was built with parabolic, concrete arches and glass walls to produce the perfect musical venue for a jungle setting. On a windy day tropical foliage outside could be seen in motion from inside. It was as if the white mariposas, pink orchids, green cypress trees, red Royal Poinciana, and amber Sea Grape trees were clamoring to come inside where the beat of conga and bata drums could be felt. It was a perfect marriage of nature and art.

Individual white, oval-framed black-and-white photos of Celia Cruz, Benny Moré, Nat King Cole, Josephine Baker, Carmen Miranda, Elizabeth Taylor, Debbie Reynolds, Joan Crawford, Liberace, and Marlon Brando were affixed in a horizontal line along the bottom of the stage. They were at eye level for those sitting at tables and resembled a string of cameos.

Titi and Army walked down a red-carpeted runway that divided the room in half. White linen-covered round tables large enough to accommodate ten guests awaited the elegantly dressed clientele who would occupy them.

Titi pointed out a table for two with a single, long-stemmed red rose in a crystal vase below the center of the elevated stage.

"This is our table, *mi vida*. Come. To my dressing room."

He followed her around the right side of the stage, through a doorway leading to a hallway that spilled into a lobby with four white doors. The first one had a large, pink star in the middle. Under it was the name *Titi*. As usual there were special guests waiting to meet the diva.

Titi graciously presented her man to four formally attired gentlemen, who were well acquainted with him. Fowler, who'd attended opening night at the Fox Hole, spoke first.

"Titi, you bring us a fellow plantation owner, the Sugar Man."

"I see that George knows you," Titi said. "So you must know Emilio and Marcelo Ranchero and Michael Tara."

The men all shook hands.

"Please excuse me, gentlemen, while I dress for the show."

Army and his friends nodded with approval and watched her sashay to her dressing room.

"Armando, you've plucked the most beautiful flower on the island," Tara said. "Congratulations."

Seeing a ribald opening, Fowler chimed: "Oh, I wouldn't say plucked, Michael, it's a word that rhymes with plucked."

Sugar Man smiled and the other men roared with laughter. Then the conversation turned serious.

"We heard about the trouble you had with a communist in Santa Cruz," Marcelo said. "We heard that you killed him."

"Is that what's going around?"

"Yes, you did not?"

"No. He was shot when I found him. He died on the spot."

"Well, it is good for everyone to think that Armando Lobo will kill you if you try to dip your hand in his sugar bowl," Emilio said. "It is good for all of us plantation owners. Maybe it will make those sons-of-bitches think twice about creating problems on the farms."

Fowler had an additional concern. "What about these student revolts? Does Batista really have this under control? Every day we read about them protesting this and that. About the police torturing them, killing them."

Army shrugged. "I've seen the torture, that turned into murder, but it didn't yield any information to the police."

"But you are in the cabinet," Marcelo said. "You do not hear anything?"

"We've only had one meeting so far, and discussions about the student problem didn't really happen. However, I saw a riot at the university. The military had to help the police stop it."

Suddenly, the music for the Apertura began. The sugar barons heard the cue, turned, and started walking briskly to the exit.

"Army, let's go," Fowler said. "Our seats. Unless you're gonna sing and dance with Titi."

"I'm on my way," he said, following.

Four lovely Cuban chicas were seated at Fowler's table when the quartet took its seats behind the table with the rose. Army sat and happened to glance across the aisle, where he saw the city's power brokers.

Italian and Italian-American Mafia members who influenced business and politics in Havana - Lora, a Calabrian called Amletta, Florida mob boss Junior A. and Massi - were seated together. With them were Big Bob, his daughter and three other glamorous-looking American women. Tony pulled out a chair and sat next to Fay.

The Apertura by the Tomas Morales Orchestra washed over everyone as Army looked up at the stage to witness a spectacular mise-en-scene. A lush jungle had been reproduced. Palm trees and plants, rubber trees, Genip trees, and shrubs formed a crescent-shaped barrier behind six straw huts. In front of them a tribe of sizzling hot dancers in short, grass skirts, and pasties and Mandingo-like men in gourds danced suggestively to the rhythmic, slap-tone beat of conga drums. The rest of the orchestra had fallen silent, deferring to the beats of the congueros.

A waiter with a bottle of Bollinger Special Cuvee Brut Champagne approached Army, popped the cork and filled his glass. He looked over at Massi, who raised a glass to him. He nodded to acknowledge the gift and sipped from the glass.

A spotlight illuminated a palm tree in which Titi, dressed in a tight-fitting, black panther costume, tail and all, spied on the tribe below still jiggling to the drum beat.

Slowly, sensually, moving to the rhythm she backed down the tree and hid in the shrubs. Sensing danger lurking nearby, a tribesman waved his hands to silence the drums.

He put a hand to his ear. Suddenly, the panther appeared. She clawed her way to the middle of the camp. The congueros struck the congas in a manoteo maneuver in which the palm and fingers produced a sound like drum rolls that increased with each of her movements. The tribespeople cowered as the panther stood and sang to the sounds of trumpets and a piano, The Song of the Panther:

I am the Panther of Wagadu
Here to devour one of you
Which one will it be?
One who pleases me
For I am the Panther of Wagadu.

The lively choreography and drumbeat continued for an hour as the panther picked the frightened tribe members off, one by one. Then, in an unscripted move that startled even the choreographer, Titi sprang forth, leaped off the stage and onto the table occupied by Army, her panther feet straddling the bottle of champagne that bounced up and down. But a half-filled glass of bubbly and the crystal vase flew off the table and crashed onto the ceramic-tile floor.

With the spotlight on her Titi cupped Army's face with a panther claw and sang to the music:

I am the Panther of Wagadu
Here to devour only you
You cannot resist me
You will assist me
For I am the Panther of Wagadu.

The spotlight on her suddenly clicked off. Darkness followed. When the lights flashed on she was gone. The capacity crowd applauded wildly. Guests walked over to Army to shake his hand.

Chapter 21

Falling Out of Favor

ARMY WAS ABLE to slip away from his table in an effort to join Titi back stage only to be grabbed by Massi.

"Was that planned?

"No. I was as surprised as everybody else."

The mobster laughed and introduced his friends. "You know Amletta, owner of the Banco Atlantico. And Junior. His father ain't Cuban, like yours, but he's been doin' business here for years. You know Big Bob."

He wasn't thrilled to see the big one; however, he shook hands with all of the men. He took special note of Junior, who had the disarming look of a college professor with his round, wire-rimmed eyeglasses and a gray bow tie clipped onto the white collar of a tuxedo shirt. The Mafioso's hand felt like a dead fish.

Sugar Man pulled Massi aside. "Joe, I never heard from you about my baseball team. What gives?"

"Sorry. Can't help you. Meyer said when it comes to casino gamblin' the house always comes out on top anyway. So, no funny business. But when it comes to sports' bettin' anything goes."

He stared at the bad news bearer in stunned silence.

"Another thing. Junior's upset that you're messin' with Titi. They had a, ah, fallin' out, and she's been givin' him the brush off. Now he knows why. This is just a friendly warnin'. The guy has a lota resources, if you know what I mean."

Army thought about how Titi had looked away when he'd asked her if she was still Junior's girl. He knew that he should have asked. He sensed trouble on the horizon, excused himself and started to walk to the stage entrance when someone else stopped him. It was Fay. She looked radiant.

"Can I speak with you for a sec?" she asked.

"Sure," said Army, always the gentleman.

She picked black lint off his lapel while speaking. It had attached itself from Titi's costume and he sensed that Fay would've liked nothing better than to detach anything Titi from him.

With sad eyes she began: "I'm sorry I hurt you. I've had a lot of time to think about what I did. I'm filled with remorse."

He looked into her eyes. She looked down.

"How can I ever trust you?"

She looked into his eyes. "Please. Give me a chance to prove myself."

He nodded at the table where the mafiosi were sitting. "Face it. You always had a soft spot for Italian bad boys. Tony's waiting for you."

Chapter 22

Trouble at the Bar

It was summer in Havana. The sun baked creatures bold enough to move under its brilliance without cover. And if man or beast found a shady spot in the city and there was no breeze, suffocating humidity made every pore pour perspiration.

Havana was one hot tamale.

The plantations and mines were peaceful. Student protesters had scattered. It was a time of the year when Cubans and tourists fled to the beaches. Those left behind did the best they could.

It was also a Thursday, Army's 36th birthday. He had no special plans. But Hiran and Celia had conspired secretly to have a birthday cake and a few guests at the Fox Hole for lunch.

Minister of Public Works Muja sent his regrets. But Titi, Don Lora, Alain the baseball manager, Fowler, and Jomar had RSVP'd.

Army was sitting in his usual spot at the end of the bar, near the back of the room, chewing ice from a tall glass of Coca-Cola. The top two buttons of his white Guayabera shirt weren't fastened. Titi, who sat on a stool to his right, slipped her right hand inside his shirt and rubbed his hairy chest while kissing him on the neck.

Spinning fans above kept them from overheating. Behind the bar the windows were pushed open with the hope that a breeze would chase air inside. But that didn't stop American tourists, gamblers, entertainers, and athletes from packing the place and filling it with cigarette and cigar smoke. They adapted by removing their ties.

Threw their suit jackets over the backs of chairs. The pretty people perspired, puffed, prattled and poured from Fox Hole bottles of rum and Hatuey beer. They nibbled on cheese and chorizo on white porcelain plates. The place was already a party.

As Titi spoke with Celia, who leaned over the noisy bar to hear her, Army happened to glance at the entrance where the salsa band was playing. He saw someone who made his skin crawl. It was the troublemaker from the university, the young man with the bald head and black beard. The one described by his own mother, whose back was to him, as ugly and hateful. It was Ernesto.

Army noticed that the rebel had two long-haired, bearded friends with him. Other Cubans called them "Barbudos," the bearded ones, unwashed and unshaven revolutionaries, terrorists, anarchists. The ones on whom Grau had been inflicting lots of pain and death.

He signaled for Hiran, who finished pouring a shot for a patron before walking over to him. Army nodded in the direction of the three threats to civility and spoke into the bartender's ear.

"See those guys over there? Keep a close eye on them and tell me if there's a problem."

"I will wait on them personally, Armando."

Ernesto and his peers were wearing light-brown short-sleeved shirts and dark-brown pants, a political uniform worn by Cuban communists. Ernesto's shirt was the only one that wasn't tucked under a belt.

The three Barbudos, sweating and fanning themselves with their hands, were polite in edging their way to the busy bar. Their odor was overwhelming to some of the customers, who moved away voluntarily. Ernesto smiled at them and signaled for Celia. However, Hiran stepped in front of her. Army watched.

"*Puedo ayudarte?*" Hiran said.

"Why do you speak Spanish, brother?" Ernesto said in a baritone voice. "Is this not an American bar?"

"Sorry. May I help you?"

"I want the chica to wait on us. I never had a chica barmaid."

"She is busy. I will help you."

"No, brother. I want the chica to wait on us. She is much prettier than you."

The rebel turned to his friends on each side of him and laughed. They all laughed. But the bar was busy. Other patrons were pestering bartenders for drinks. Still, he stood his ground.

"Please, tell me what you want to drink. I have other customers."

"Okay, Okay. Three doubles. Not the Lobo brand. That is piss. Bacardi."

Hiran set up four shot glasses and filled them. He raised the first one in front of his lips.

"Salud," he said. "This round is on me."

The others nodded their appreciation. "Salud, brother," Ernesto said.

Hiran filled their glasses again and collected the money before signaling another bartender to take over. He walked back to Army, who was still chewing ice and listening to Titi talk with Celia about the Tropicana. Titi was unaware that Ernesto was in the room as the bartender poured the rest of a Coke bottle into Army's glass, leaned over the bar and spoke.

"The bald one will make trouble, Armando. Do you want me to put him and the others out?"

"No. Not now. Let's see what they're up to. But pay close attention to them. I don't want anyone to get hurt."

Army felt a tap on his shoulder and turned to see Lora, Fowler, and Alain smiling.

"Happy birthday, Armando," they said in unison.

Celia placed a chocolate birthday cake with thirty-six candles aflame on the end of the bar and Hiran signaled the band, which broke out into "*Cumpleaños Feliz.*"

"I hope that's Lobo chocolate," Army said as guests sang along with the band and he blew out the candles. Hiran waited for applause to fade before making an announcement to the patrons.

"Attention everyone. Attention, please. In honor of Armando's birthday, a round of drinks is on the house."

The crowd roared its approval and the band played an upbeat salsa song. Birthday boy looked around and smiled at patrons who danced in place.

Lora, his lips loosened by several rum and cokes, leaned over and whispered into Sugar Man's ear.

"Armando, tomorrow night I will have fresh bundles of heroin and cocaine as well as a new assortment of chicas from Colombia. You are most welcome to join me and the girls for an evening of bliss. It will be my birthday present to you."

Army looked up at Lora and smiled. "Thank you, Don Lora."

Chapter 23

The Beautiful Stranger

INTO THIS FESTIVE atmosphere Ernesto spotted an innocent dreamer enter from outside. She was lithe and taut at 5-feet, 7-inches. Her thick, black shoulder-length hair shined like silk. She had soft brown eyes with long lids and lashes, a short, straight nose that showed character and full lips devoid of artificial color. Her skin, covered with perspiration, was olive in complexion. It glistened.

She was a vision from heaven in a worn, blue dress with a thigh pocket that looked newer than the rest of the old garment. Wondrous and wandering into another world, she walked in worn, flat shoes and paused to admire American women of fair skin and hair, expensive jewelry and the latest in summer couture. Conversely, when she stopped by their tables to admire them, the Hollywood set cut short their conversations and smoking to assimilate the outsider, the personification of a beautiful, sad song.

"Isn't she just stunning," the rebel heard a slim blonde say. She was seated with three other women who could have won beauty contests in the US.

"And clearly so poor," said another blonde at the table, holding up a lit cigarette.

"Honey, she would look good in a burlap bag," said a tough brunette.

That was obvious to Ernesto, a dark cloud that hovered over the sunshine crowd. He watched as the beautiful stranger looked up at the fans and around at the attractive American women and moneyed men who competed for their attention. And as she passed him at the bar, he reached out and grabbed her damp arm, heated by the summer sun. If it was hot outside, the mercury level had just shot up to the top of the thermostat. Aroused, Ernesto spoke to this starry-eyed country girl whom he was about to devour. Or so he thought.

"Are you lost, sister?" Ernesto said, earnestly.

She smiled. "No. I am looking for someone."

"Who?"

She pulled from her pocket a faded, black-and-white photo of a slim man elegantly dressed in a suit and tie. He had his arm around the shoulder of a dark-haired woman in a white dress.

"This is you on the right?" Ernesto asked, pointing to the woman.

"No. My mother."

"Sister, you and your mother look like sisters." He sneered and added: "The man you seek is a Mafioso. He enslaves women at the Hotel Sevilla Biltmore."

"Please," she said. "The man. Is he here?"

Ernesto pointed to the back of the crowded room.

"The capitalist bloodsuckers are at the end of the bar," he said, his hand pointing and returning to her arm. "Stay here with your own kind. Let me tell you what they have done to us. And what we will do to them."

She shook her head no, thanked him politely, took the photograph from his hand, and continued walking along the crowded bar.

Ernesto stood on the bar's brass foot rail and craned his neck over the other patrons to watch her. That's when he spotted his mother at the end of the bar. Titi stood there with her back to the crowd, running her fingers through Army's hair.

"*Puta,*" Ernesto said. "*Puta grande.*"

He sat down, picked up a double shot, downed it and wiped his mouth with the sleeve of his shirt. "Barman, another double."

Ernesto waited while Titi kissed everyone goodbye and exited through the back door. Then he slowly made his way near the capitalists.

"Such a shame she cannot stay," Lora said.

"The show must go on," Army said, reclaiming his seat at the bar and chewing ice from an empty coke glass.

Behind him the beautiful stranger finally had arrived after catching the attention of patrons and bartenders, including Celia. Army didn't see her. He was surrounded by Lora, Fowler and Alain, who faced the open window behind the bar.

Ernesto noted that Lora wasn't wearing a suit on such a hot day when the girl tapped on his shoulder. He turned around, tipsy. He blanched at the sight of her. It was as though he'd seen a ghost. He actually stuttered as he spoke.

Ernesto heard him stammer: "You, you are, who are you? ..."

"Bonita Di Riva. You know my mother, no?

"Oh my God," Lora said. He beckoned her to sit with him at an empty reserved table near the bar. She joined him.

"My God," Lora said. "You look so much like Dolores. What is your name again?"

"Bonita. Bonita Di Riva."

Ernesto took it all in.

Bonita sat there, observing Lora as he collected himself. She pulled the photo from her pocket and presented it to him.

"Where did you get this?" he said.

"The brothel of Doña Marina. She told me that you fell in love with my mother and took her away years ago. I have been looking for her. She abandoned me as a baby in Santa Clara. Is she still with you?"

The poor girl looked worried. Ernesto watched a somber Lora reach across the table, grab her hands in his and look into her eyes. "Your mother is gone," he said. "Killed in an automobile accident. A year ago. I loved her very much."

The rebel scoffed.

Bonita bowed her head and closed her eyes as if in prayer for about five seconds. She opened them and looked at his hands on hers.

"Did she ever speak of me?" she said, withdrawing her hands from his.

"Yes. She felt tremendous guilt about leaving you with your father. Running off with her lover to Havana."

"Her lover?" she said with sad eyes.

"A young man she knew in Santa Clara," Lora said, softly. "She told me that not long after your birth the affair began and they ran away to the capital. But he deserted her a few years later, after your father died.

"She found herself without money, family, or friends. In the streets. She ended up at Doña Marina's bordello, the safest place for a beautiful young woman with no place to go."

The interloper scoffed again.

"That is where I met her. It was love at first sight. She moved in with me. We were married."

Lora reached back for his wallet, opened it and pulled out a dog-eared, black-and- white photo of him and Dolores on their wedding day.

Bonita looked at the photo and smiled. "You both look so happy."

Her smile faded into a frown. "Why didn't she look for me while she was with you?"

"I do not know the answer. However, we had a child. That may have filled the void in her life."

Startled, she asked: "Girl or boy?"

"Girl. She died with her in the auto accident. She was two years old."

Again Bonita lowered her head and remained silent. A tear trickled from the corner of her eye as she rose silently and shook hands with Lora. Abruptly turning to her right, she bumped into Army, who'd risen from his bar stool. He nearly knocked her over.

He reached out to steady the stranger. They looked into each other's eyes as though they'd known one another for a thousand years. He wiped away her tear gently with a thumb, just as he'd done to the beautiful stranger in his dreams.

"Pardon me," she said, embarrassed, forlorn, and stunned by the handsome stranger.

And then she turned and ran for the entrance, bouncing off bar patrons as he froze in place, remembering her face, the same one he'd seen in those fitful dreams the night he thought his life might end in Sailor's bar.

"Where did she go?" Lora said.

"Who is she?" Army said.

He walked by Ernesto and the bar crowd as quickly as he could, past the salsa band and out the entrance, where the hot air felt like an oven door had opened in his face. He looked up and down sun-soaked Calle Zulueta. All he saw were a few tourists, beggars, and police walking by in the bright afternoon sun.

Lora joined him in the heat. "Where is she?" he asked.

Army shrugged. "You know her?"

"No. Her mother. And she is a handmade woman like her mother."

Chapter 24
A Troublesome Revelation

ARMY RETURNED TO the bar to hear a deep, loud voice yell over the music. "No, I want the chica to wait on us."

It was Ernesto, drunk and unruly. Army approached him and the two other Barbudos when he noticed a protuberance under the ringleader's shirt. Hiran was trying to calm down the rebel, but he didn't want to hear it. He continued to act belligerently. So, Army interceded, tapping the bald-and-bearded one on the back.

"Excuse me, what's the problem?"

Ernesto turned around, looked up at him and grinned. "Hello brother. Good to meet you. After all these years. Do you know who I am?"

"Yes, I do."

"Oh, do you? Really?"

"What do you want, Ernesto?"

"So. You know my name. But you do not really know who I am, brother."

"Don't call me brother. You're trouble. That's who you are."

The rebel looked at the two Barbudos standing next to him and smirked. They appeared to be waiting for a signal from him to get physical. But Ernesto turned his attention to Army.

"Yes, I am trouble and I am troubled that you do not know who I really am. You see, I know who you are."

"You've had too much to drink and I want you and your friends to leave," Army said as he stepped closer to Ernesto to neutralize any aggressive move he might make.

Seeing this, Hiran and three other male bartenders hopped over the bar and surrounded the bearded ones. The music fell silent, as did most of the patrons.

"Another thing. We don't allow firearms in here."

Ernesto looked down at the bump under his shirt and up at Army. "So, brother. Tell me what I have concealed under my shirt and I will tell you what has been concealed from you."

"A pistol."

"That is good," Ernesto said without lifting his shirt. "A .32 caliber Belgian Browning. I carry it for protection from those who are angered by my views. But I am angry, too. Wouldn't you be angry if you found out you are the bastard son of a whore and a capitalist swine who would not give you his name?"

He paused for a reaction. He got none. Then, he added the punch line.

"That same swine gave *you* his name. He also gave you the plantations he stole from the people who sweat and die in the fields."

Army's mind started spinning as he processed what Ernesto said. He looked at the miscreant in another way now, studying his eyes, nose, mouth and imagined him with a head of hair. In a flash he saw glimpses of his father, Titi, and even himself.

He stood stiffly as the unsteady undesirable, two inches shorter, reached out with both arms, held him by the shoulders and kissed him on both cheeks. "My big brother," Ernesto said, looking up into Army's intense eyes. "Happy birthday."

Then the malcontent stumbled and giggled toward the door with his two friends following. Two seconds later they were gone. The band played. The customers resumed talking, and the bartenders, except for Hiran, returned to their duties.

"Armando, he lies. He hates you because you are special and he is nothing."

He didn't respond. His anger smoldered. He thought about his years of denial. The wall that he'd built around his father to protect his mother. It crumbled in an instant. She'd been wronged and he hadn't been able to protect her. Suddenly, he turned and charged out the front door, where he ran into Jomar.

"Armando."

"Not now."

"But I came to wish you a happy birthday."

Army ran around the corner to his car and peeled out of his parking space, passing a stunned birthday guest. Twenty minutes later he arrived at the Tropicana. He raced into the Arcos De Cristal and saw the choreographer giving instructions to the dancers on the indoor stage, but Titi was absent.

"Where's Titi?" he said to a stage hand.

"In her dressing room."

He walked briskly through the stage entrance, down the hall, into the lobby and to the door with her name on it. He barged in to see Titi sitting with her back to him, naked from the waist up, looking into the mirror and applying eyeliner. Her instinctive reaction was to cover her breasts with her arms. She spun around to face him.

"Armando, what are you doing?"

"*Descarada*! Have you no shame?" he screamed as she stood and continued to cover her exposed parts. "Did you think I'd never find out about you and my father? That Ernesto is my brother?"

Her reflexive reaction was defiance. "You knew. You had to know. How could you not know!"

He let out an agonizing sound that came from somewhere deep inside, as though he were being exorcised: "N N N No I didn't. I couldn't. I wouldn't allow myself believe that."

Hearing his own words, Army stopped and cupped his mouth, trembling.

Reacting to his pain Titi stopped hugging herself and squeezed him tightly to her bosom. "Oh Armando, *mi vida*," she cried. "I am so sorry. I could not help myself. You are so beautiful. So much like Popi, who I loved so much. But he did not love me in the same way. So, I went with other men. I prayed to Oshun, Goddess of Love. And she sent you to me. So perfect."

He shoved her. Titi was crying now, her hands covering her face, smearing her freshly-applied makeup. He was starting to feel sorry for her, but he allowed rage to overcome civility.

"Perfect is right," he said. "The white tuxedo and shoes fit me so perfectly. Now I know why. And when I think about it. Wearing my father's tux and shoes, I wanna puke."

Suddenly, Tony Stabo and another man in a suit appeared at the open door. They were carrying baseball bats. Someone else was angling for revenge this night.

Army spun around to protect her as the men charged. He backed Titi into a corner of the room as Tony swung the bat at the mirror, shattering it into a hundred pieces. Shards of glass flew into the air as he clubbed the makeup table and chair into broken bits of wood and metal that sprayed the room. The other man banged holes in the walls and smashed lamps.

When the demolition ended, Tony walked to an alabaster statue of a six-foot nude female dancer with long lean legs and took aim. He swung the bat through the legs and they disappeared into a cloud of dust. Out of breath, he turned and pointed the bat at the frightened couple.

"Junior says that's what'll happen to your legs if yous two stay together."

The two men looked at each other, laughed, and walked out. Titi, still behind Army, sank to the floor in tears.

He turned around to see royalty in ruins, the Queen of the Tropicana cowering in a corner like a cretin outside a cheap cabaret near the capitol building. He turned toward the door, crunching broken glass and plaster under his shoes as he walked out.

Chapter 25
A Picture of Poverty

ARMY INCARCERATED HIMSELF in his private jail suspended above a dwindling Fox Hole crowd. He'd been sitting at the small bar, collar open, sipping from a bottle of rum that purposely was not the family brand. He looked at himself in the mirror. He wanted to be alone with his thoughts about his father, Titi, Ernesto, Massi, Tony, Fay, and everyone else in his life. He stood and drew the drapes shut.

Sugar Man needed to talk to someone, but who? He couldn't worry his mother. And he didn't want to trouble his younger sisters, Victoria and Julia. So, he spoke to a legend, a bottle of Maximo Legendario Elixir, a sweet dark rum. When sipped from a snifter, fumes traveled from the palate to the nostrils and exited like fire, turning whoever consumed it into a human dragon.

"*Señor* Legendario, I have a problem maybe only you can solve," he said to the bottle.

But before he could breathe fire, a familiar male voice shouted over the noise below: "Can I come up?"

Army pressed a buzzer under the bar, the iron door unlocked and before long the man in the disguise was sitting next to him and Legendario. He had a box of cigars tucked under an arm.

"You look like shit," the spy said as he sat down at the bar.

"I feel like shit. Ever meet my friend, Maximo Legendario?"

He unscrewed the metal cap on the bottle, filled half a snifter and slid it to the CIA guy, who took a sip and nodded approval.

"Sweet fire," he said, toasting Army. "Happy birthday amigo. I couldn't let the day get away without giving you a present."

He flipped open the box and presented Montecristos to the birthday boy. Soon they were puffing furiously until the ceiling fan chased a cloud of smoke.

"Thanks, Cutter."

"What's wrong?"

Army looked straight ahead at his friend in the mirror behind the bar. "Today I found out that I have a brother who's a crazy communist and his mother is the woman who's been seducing me: Titi."

Cutter puffed and listened intently while his former colleague sipped from the snifter. "I lost my socialite girlfriend to a mafia goon and I've been working to pay off the gambling debts of the 'Charmer from Santa Cruz' while he pretends to be a good husband and father."

"That's a lot to chew on," Cutter said as he chewed on his cigar and sipped rum. "Does your mother know?"

"I doubt it. I'm trying to protect her from this."

"I'm guessing Ernesto is your crazy commie brother."

"You're not guessing. Why didn't you tell me?"

"What's that you say? Some things you don't want to know? You're in denial. You've been in denial. About a lot of things. I thought I'd let you find this out on your own. But don't worry. Grau'll snuff him out eventually. Titi's a different story. A rose with thorns. Thorns with poisoned tips."

Cutter puffed on his cigar and toasted him. "To friendship."

Army agreed. "Friendship that goes back to our high school athlete days," He sipped more rum. "Only you would understand my rant."

He blew a smoke ring and thought for a moment. "I don't know anymore. I don't care. Power. Glory. Debts. Deceit. I came to Havana from the plantation to forget the war, not to fight communists. I became a minister for power and glory and the benefits that go with it. But things keep popping up. Sometimes I ask myself why I'm not dancing with the devil in Sin City."

Cutter swung his arm around his friend's shoulder. "You can't escape your true nature, amigo. Decency and fair play, since we were kids."

Army sipped more sweet rum and let it roll around on his palate so that fiery fumes could exit his nostrils. The spy did likewise while his friend sucked on the cigar and blew smoke rings toward the ceiling fan.

Suddenly Celia appeared, hands on hips, seen in the mirror by both men.

"So, you do it again, Armando. I see you drink Coca-Cola today and I think maybe you stop rum. But now you are with Legendario."

He couldn't help it. He let out a huge laugh. He spun around to face her.

"Sit down," he said. "I'm not drunk. Sweet rum's like candy. Isn't that right Mr. Cutter?"

The CIA guy nodded in the affirmative, swiveled on the bar stool and shook hands with Celia. He motioned for her to sit with them.

"Thank you, sir. But I have work to do. And sweet rum is still rum. Make you loco."

"I'm your boss. Sit down. Besides, you didn't come up here to lecture me again. Or did you?"

"What is lecture?"

"You know, tell me what to do."

"No, Armando. I cannot tell you what to do. But I must to ask you to do something for me. A priest come here yesterday. He ask for clothes for the orphanage on San Lazaro. Tomorrow I go there. You have something to give?"

"I don't know. I'll look. Are you off tomorrow?"

"Yes."

"Where's the orphanage? The address."

Celia pulled a thin wallet from underneath her apron and opened it. She read from a piece of paper.

"San Lazaro and Marques Gonzalez. Next to the hospital."

"Stop by around 3 o'clock."

"Thank you."

Celia looked at him. "You looking for that pretty girl with the bad dress?"

"No," he said, swiveling back to the bar, blowing more smoke rings and looking at his only female bartender in the mirror. She studied his reflection in the glass for a moment, then walked to the stairs.

"I am sorry for you," she said under her breath, but he heard her.

"And I'm happy for you," he said. "You make me proud."

The phone on the bar rang. He didn't answer. It stopped and Hiran yelled. "Armando. Your father is on the phone."

"Tell him I'm out."

Hearing the gate below close, Army looked at Cutter polishing off his glass of rum.

"So here I am, paying off his gambling debts. For what? What am I doing here?"

"You'll figure it out," his drinking buddy said as he rose. "Happy birthday."

"Wait. I have something for you," Army said. "Lora invited me to another heroin and cocaine party. He said he'll have fresh bundles tomorrow night."

The spy smiled. "Thanks, amigo." He slipped the cigar into his mouth again and shook hands. Army watched him turn and walk away when his eyes drifted to the floor where Celia had stood. He spotted what looked like a yellowed piece of cardboard and picked it up. There was writing on it that read: *La Familia Tramiño.*

When he turned it over he saw a photo of poverty: A father, a mother, and four small children shabbily dressed outside a ramshackle cottage with weeds around it. One of the angelic faces was older now, but still recognizable. It was Celia. He stared at the picture and Cutter's words echoed in his ears: "You'll figure it out." His eyes welled.

He snuffed the cigar in an ash tray, slipped the photo into his shirt pocket, walked around the bar to a shelf where there were books, and grabbed a copy of Ernest Hemingway's *To Have and Have Not.* He retreated to the couch and read until he drifted to sleep.

As night turned into morning the treachery of the previous day sent his mind spinning into a maelstrom of dreams that flooded his senses. He twitched like a sleeping hound after a day of fox hunting.

In the dreams he saw smoke rings morph into the usual people and places from the past. They ended with the beautiful stranger shedding a tear and his thumbing it away.

"Are you real? He shouted. "Are you real? Are you real?"

Suddenly his left shoulder shook violently.

Hiram's voice cried out: "Armando! Armando! *Despertarte!* Wake up!" Army looked around; he was sweating profusely. "Are you all right?" Hiran said.

Sitting upright, he held his head in his hands. "Yes, yes. I had a bad dream, that's all. A bad dream."

"Jomar, Walter and Wilmer are downstairs. They said they work for you at the palace.

"What time is it?"

"Ten o'clock."

He followed Hiran down the steps to a table on which there were four cups of espresso and sweet cakes in a bread basket. Jomar and the twins were indulging when he sat down and exchanged greetings. It was two hours before opening.

"Armando, we compiled the information you wanted and typed it," Walter said. "Yolanda reviewed it. Here it is."

Wilmer gave Army a report four inches thick. "It says, basically that in this city of 850,000 people unemployment is about 20 percent overall and 50 percent among blacks and mulattos."

"Is that why Robo and his friends on the block aren't working?" Army said as he grabbed a cake.

"Possibly, but we also checked their criminal records. They all have one, for minor things like drunk and disorderly, resisting arrest, you know."

"So that wouldn't prevent them from being hired?"

"It should not," Wilmer said. "They all should be eligible for unskilled work in construction."

Army sipped from a cup of coffee. "The next cabinet meeting is in two days. I'll present these statistics to the president.

"Jomar, pick me up tomorrow morning at 11:30. We have some things to do."

Chapter 26

Field of Honor

THE NEXT MORNING at 11:45 Jomar pulled the Hudson in front of the Fox Hole. He was about to explain his tardiness when Army waved him off.

"Today we have two stops: the baseball stadium and an orphanage. I want to be at the stadium before the game starts, so let's go."

Hiran poked his head out the doorway and yelled: "Armando, your father is on the phone."

"Tell him I'm out."

About a half-hour later the Hudson arrived at the blue-and-white stadium's main gate. Security guards allowed the detective to park along a driveway with the cars of other VIPs. The duo alighted and ambled through a tunnel that led to the field, where the Wolves were taking batting practice. The stadium was filling with fans.

Army waved the manager and the players to the infield. He stood on the pitcher's mound surrounded by a curious pack of Wolves. He surveyed their faces as if it were the last time he'd see them.

"Gentlemen, I'm thinking about selling the team."

The players grumbled. They looked bewildered.

"Why, Armando?" the third-baseman said.

"Because I asked a Mafia boss to stop sending his man to bribe my players and he said 'no.'"

"It is El Tigre. It is his fault," the player said.

"It's not all El Tigre's fault. Those who are taking money know who they are," Army said. "I used to play baseball. I was a pitcher. I loved competition. Loved to test myself against another man, another team. To see if I was better than he was, my team was better than the other team. To throw a game is sickening to me. This team has already sold one game that I know about. And you will take bribes again because the money is good."

He looked at the faces surrounding him. "You don't make much money playing baseball. That's why you all have jobs. So, you have to ask yourselves a question. Why do I play?"

He scanned the players again and saw Jose, a seasoned pitcher, shaking his head side-to-side.

"Jose, why do you play?"

"I love baseball. Baseball is the son I never had."

Another player scoffed: "If I played baseball for the pay, I would starve."

Other players laughed in agreement before he added: "But I love the game. So does my family."

"Would you do anything to dishonor your family?"

"Of course not," the player said.

Army nodded. "When someone gives you an envelope to lose a game, you dishonor your family. You dishonor the field where you bare your heart, soul and body with every swing of the bat, every stolen base, every catch, every pitch, every collision with a catcher. You dishonor yourselves. You dishonor your children."

As he was speaking from his vantage point on the mound, Army saw the stands filling up. He also spotted Tony sitting next to the dugout, a perfect spot from which to make eye contact with players. Then he saw Fay and her father making their way over to him. He made use of the moment.

"Gentlemen, I just noticed that the Mafia's lapdog, Tony Stabo, sits next to our dugout. Some of you may know him. He's the one who brings envelopes filled with cash. And the man who wants to buy the team is about to take a seat. He is an American who could care less about Cuban baseball. Or about you."

Without warning he stepped off the mound, pushed through his players and marched towards the grandstands. The Wolves watched.

When Tony returned his attention to the field he saw Army standing in front of him. A cyclone fence about three-feet high separated them.

"Get out!" Army shouted.

"Fuck you!" Tony said without hesitation.

It only took a second or two. Army didn't even think about it. He reached over the top rail with his left hand, grabbed a fistful of the goon's white, cotton shirt near the throat, used the fence for hip stability and let out a "Kiyai" as he initiated a shoulder throw, flinging the 200-pounder over the rail and onto the hard dirt. Tony rolled a few extra feet before standing and doing what earned him his nickname. Tony "The Blade" pulled a switch-blade knife and ran full speed at Army, whose back faced a frightened Fay and her excited dad. Fast hands followed.

As the point of the blade came within inches of Army's face, his left hand pushed the knife hand upward. Simultaneously he reached out with his right and grabbed the mobster's shirt in the same spot. With these hand placements he was able to use Tony's momentum against him in what the Japanese Jiu Jitsu Masters call a Seoinage or shoulder throw.

Thrusting his right handful of Tony high and steering the human missile with his left, Army sent the mobster flying into the vacant third row. His face slammed into one of the metal arms of an empty seat and split open his forehead as well as the bridge of his nose. The knife sailed. Blood sprayed. Tony collapsed like a rag doll and landed between the wooden floor planks and the seats.

Fans nearby in the stands and players still surrounding the pitcher's mound let out a collective sound when they saw the collision.

"Ouuuuuuu."

Army heard Fay scream. Her father stepped over two rows to pull up Tony by both arms and drop him into the seat that had rearranged his face. He marveled at Big Bob's compassion. The big man removed a white handkerchief from the back pocket of his worn black suit and pressed it on Tony's bloody wounds.

"What the hell was that about?" Big Bob said as the crowd noise escalated.

Army climbed over the fence and seats to confront the thug, who looked dazed while his friend held a hanky to his face. Then he leaned forward, coming within inches of a battered face.

"Don't even think about coming back."

"Fuck you!" Tony intoned through a broken, bloody nose. Army responded with a bored expression. Turning toward the dugout, he was startled to see players from both teams standing near the fence and pumping fists into the air, recreating what he'd just done with the slightest of effort. He also saw his manager standing next to the detective.

"Alain, we need a trainer and an ambulance, and tell security never to let this guy back."

Army stepped over empty seats in rows two and one before he looked down at Fay. She held both hands to her face in horror while her father cleaned up Tony.

Noticing his gaze, she dropped her hands and gave a look of helplessness, which she reserved for extreme situations.

On the field players shook their heads in approval and patted him on the back. Most didn't know who Tony was. They just enjoyed how the team owner had handled himself.

Jomar joined Army in the tunnel and placed his right hand on his shoulder while they walked toward the light.

"Where did you learn that, Armando?"

"Europe."

"How did you remain so calm?"

"I was afraid."

"Afraid? To me you showed no fear."

Turning to his admirer. "Fear is like fire. If you control it, you can make it work for you. Fear makes you more alert, like a fireman who senses when to run out of a burning building."

Jomar thought about it for a moment as Army stopped to light a Lucky Strike. He had to use both hands. His match hand was shaking.

"Armando, you just sent a Mafioso to the hospital. They will want revenge."

"I know," he said, taking a drag.

"What will you do?"

He shrugged. "I don't know."

Chapter 27
Clandestine Artists

IT WAS 3:10 p.m. when Army and Jomar walked into the Fox Hole looking for Celia. Instead, they saw that tables had been cleared for two dancers. The band was playing *Camarera del Amor*, a salsa song about a customer who falls in love with a waitress. A handsome Cubano in his 20s was twirling a slim, sexy American in a blue dress while the two men deftly skirted them on their way to the crowded bar.

The humidity was low. The ceiling fans were on high. Hollywood was happening. The beautiful people and their sycophants sucked up the space at the bar and around the tables, drinking mostly cocktails and smoking cigarettes.

The couple finished dancing and the onlookers erupted in applause. Waiters pushed back tables and chairs to their original placements. The band switched to tenor Benny Moré's *Como Fue*, a love song.

Army looked around the crowd and spotted Ernesto and his two bearded friends sitting at a table in a corner. He elbowed his bodyguard and pointed to the rebels.

Ernesto looked away, avoiding their stares. Army and the detective saw something else. Three Cuban men in white shirts and ties enjoying beers at a table near the Barbudos.

With the three troublemakers behaving, Jomar excused himself, walked to the men and sat with them. Army spotted Celia and waived her to the front of the bar.

"I have a lot of clothing for you," he said over the noise of the crowd. "It's in the Hudson. We'll drive you to the orphanage."

Surprised and delighted by the offer, Celia shouted back: "Oh, thank you Armando. I have four bags under the bar. I will get them."

While surveying the customers in their colorful couture, Army saw Jomar waving him to the table at which he was seated. He made his way through thirsty patrons lined up three deep at the bar and others seated on stools until he reached the quartet.

"Armando, I present Jorge, Jose, and Julio, detectives with me at the Fifth Precinct. "Gentlemen, this is our Minister of Labor."

They all shook hands. "Is the Fifth Precinct busy these days?" Army asked as he sat.

"Judging by the screams coming from the basement I'd say yes," said Jorge, a middle-aged man with overbite. He was joined by his colleagues in laughter.

"Who are the offenders?"

"Mostly students from the university," Jorge said. "And I see that one of their leaders is here with his friends."

Army turned back and glowered at his step-brother and his fellow Barbudos. He turned back to the policemen. "I've been wondering how he got out of jail after he started a riot at the University. Isn't that a serious offense?"

"Which riot?" Jomar said. The other detectives chuckled. "His mother has clout. But if we catch him in an act of violence against a policeman no one will save him from my uncle."

Celia made her way through the elbow-to-elbow drinkers and smokers without dropping one of the four brown bags of clothing she hugged.

Sugar Man looked at the detectives. "Gentlemen, I'm sorry but we have to go now."

Jomar excused himself and rose first, taking two of the bags from Celia and wended his way through the patrons. Celia followed him out the door while the boss shook hands with two patrons who stopped him on his way out. When he resumed his exit he bumped into Ernesto near the door. An artist's pad fell to the floor. Army picked it up quickly and saw a detailed drawing of the three detectives. The rebel tried to grab it but his step-brother held onto it and asked:

"Who's the artist?"

"We all are," Ernesto said angrily. "Now give it back."

Army ripped off the page with the drawing and returned the pad to the enraged Barbudo leader, who yelled: "What's mine is mine and what's yours is mine, brother."

Army smiled: "Spoken like a true communist," *brother.* "Then, with a poker face he added. "No spying in my place, *brother.* That's the second time you crossed the line. Three strikes and you're out."

The rebel sneered. "Just like baseball, my American brother. To you Americans everything is a game."

"You have to learn how to relax, Ernesto. It must be stressful being a full-time, commie-pain-in-the-ass."

The illegitimate one snarled: "Hijo de puta!"

"Me? Son-of-a-bitch?" He turned, walked to the detectives' table and gave them the drawing. "Compliments of the Barbudos."

Chapter 28

Bonita

Jomar pulled in front of a three-story building that covered an entire city block. Crosses and spires stood like sentries atop the sprawling complex that housed a convent, high school, orphanage, and clinic.

School had let out and chatty children with red-and-white uniforms flooded the sidewalk, looking for their parents. Watching over them like a mother hen was a middle-aged American nun, and like a bird she looked as if she could fly with a coronet of white wings that shaded her hand-stitched black robe from the Havana sun.

Asserting her authority as Protector of the Gate, she crossed over and spoke to Army curtly through the open car window on the passenger's side.

"Can't park in front of the entrance, move it back, and watch out for the children."

He nodded and turned to the detective, who acknowledged the order. But first he and his bartender exited the auto.

"Hello, Sister," Celia said enthusiastically. "A priest come to the bar last week and ask me for clothes for the orphanage."

"The bar?" said the nun derisively. "That would be Father Luís. He solicited clothing at a bar? I think I know why, but go ahead."

Undaunted by the dour one, Celia continued with verve. "We bring clothes for the orphanage. Where do we put them?"

"We call it the House of Charity. We are the Sisters of Charity. And I am Mother Superior Maria José."

Annoyed by the imperious nun, Army interrupted.

"Look, Mother, all we want to do is donate clothes. Where do we put the bags?"

Maria José pursed her lips, studied her challenger for a moment and issued an order. "Follow me."

The three strangers removed some of the twelve big bags of clothes from the car's back seat and trunk and followed the Holy Terror through a large portal, past the front desk and through a doorway leading to an open-air courtyard illuminated by the sun. The two men placed their bags on a stone bench and returned to the car for more while Celia waited with the nun.

When Army came back with more clothing, he stopped when he heard the nun say: "I'll have one of our teachers take it from here, Oh, here she is now."

At that moment the Fox Hole's elusive visitor entered the courtyard, her silken hair aglow in the sunlight. She was wearing the same shabby dress.

"Bonita. These kind people are donating much-needed clothing. Take care of this, please. I have a meeting to attend."

Mother Superior turned and shook hands with Celia, whose mouth was agape. As Maria José headed for an exit she turned back and issued one last statement with a righteous smirk and then disappeared.

"Father Luís met them in a bar. He's at it again."

"Oh really, the teacher said to the bartender, who shook hands with her. "What bar?"

"The Fox Hole. You were there last week. Remember?"

Startled, she stammered. "Yes...Yes, you were there?

"I am a bartender there."

"Oh. I did not see you. But I remember the people. They looked like movie stars."

"They are. All of the time. From Hollywood they come to Armando's bar."

"Armando?"

"The one you bump into. Do you remember? Before you leave the bar."

Blushing, she hesitated for a moment. "Yes, the handsome man with the blue eyes. I have not forgotten him."

Transfixed by the scene, Army walked up to her. His heart was pounding.

"And I haven't forgotten you."

The girl with the bad dress turned to see him. Startled and embarrassed, she reddened again as she pressed her hands together as if to pray and placed them over her lips.

"The last time I saw you, you were upset. You ran out. Why?"

She was about to answer when her eyes widened and her mouth dropped. "You. You. What are you doing here?"

He turned around to see Jomar, who looked sheepish. "I bring clothes."

"You two know each other?"

Bonita grabbed a bag of clothing from Army and threw it at the detective. "This man killed my fiancé. He murdered my Pablo. Beast. Get out! Get out!"

"Pablo? Pablo de la Torre? I can explain," Army said.

She looked at him in a different way now, as though something clicked. "He killed my Pablo on the Lobo plantation. You are Armando Lobo?"

"Yes."

"Get out! All of you. Get out!"

Overcome, he attempted to embrace her, but she shoved him and ran to the door from which she'd entered the courtyard. The silence that followed was broken only by the sound of flowing water from the Tranquil Fountain, an ornamental structure about five-feet high.

Army and Celia looked at Jomar, He shrugged.

"She claimed his body the next day. I was at the precinct. She asked me what happened. I told her. She said she did not believe me."

"I will speak with her Armando," Celia said.

"No," he said, disappointed and distraught. "Let's go."

Chapter 29
The Day After

SITTING BETWEEN BLANCO Rico and Grau in another cabinet meeting, Army once again felt as though he was in a snake pit. Back and forth the dangerous duo went with their reports to the president about student activists, labor union activists and the way the government was handling them. They also spoke about the military's role, a subject about which Batista showed great interest.

Then Grau mentioned the Fox Hole.

"My informant tells me that the leader of the FEU, a founding member of the militant *Revolucionario Estudantil Directorio*, has been seen on more than one occasion in an establishment owned by one of our own ministers."

Grau looked at the faces of the cabinet members along the table until he got to the Minister of Labor, who figured that Jomar was the "informant."

"So we are asking ourselves what he would be doing there? Why would he be in an American bar with other subversives? We found out. He and his fellow Barbudos are surreptitiously drawing pictures of our detectives. Putting their wellbeing in danger."

Many of the ministers shook their heads as if to say: "Ah ha!" Grau paused to allow it all to sink in. Then he added the punch line.

"What would he be discussing with his brother, the owner? I am speaking about Armando Lobo and Ernesto Randal."

A chaotic din suddenly filled the air as the other ministers expressed surprise and disdain at the news. Batista looked disturbed.

"Is this true, Armando?" the president said.

Army stood. "Yes, Mr. President, Ernesto is my brother. Through an illegitimate birth caused by an unfaithful husband and father, the student radical leader shares my blood. But that's all we have in common. He's angry. He's capable of violence. He incites rebellion. And he's a communist."

Army turned and looked with contempt at Grau.

"So I must ask you, Grau, guardian of the government, why is this reprobate still on the street?"

Most of the other ministers looked at Grau now and nodded in agreement. Most, but not all.

"Why do you allow him to come to your bar, Armando?" Blanco Rico said.

"That's enough," Batista said. "Grau and Armando need to settle this on their own time. What I want from you now, Armando, is your report on the labor situation."

Looking down at Blanco Rico for a moment instead of the report Army began:

"Mr. President, unemployment is about twenty percent overall, but fifty percent among blacks and mulattos. With all due respect, you are of mixed race, you know what it's like to cut 'cane in the fields, so together we have to solve this problem.

"An entire block of mulatto and black men was out of work when my bodyguard, Jomar, and I visited a central Havana neighborhood. At least one man was a skilled worker. There were probably more."

Grau interrupted. "Which neighborhood?"

"San Nicholas."

"Criminals. The state does not hire felons."

Army looked directly at Batista. "Misdemeanors, Mr. President. The state does hire small-time offenders and all of the men in that area have minor offenses on their records. Except for one. And he's incarcerated."

Batista nodded. "Go on."

"Skilled workers are making a livable wage, but police, firemen, and teachers are all underpaid, as are office workers. At the end of the month they are fortunate to have a few pesos left over after paying for rent, food, and transportation. That's why so many play the lottery."

Batista smiled. Army paused, realizing that the lottery was nothing to be taken seriously by anyone in the room. It was rigged in their favor. So, he continued.

"The best-paid workers are dealers, croupiers, pit bosses, and floor managers in the casinos. But they are employed by the Italians from New York. They bring many of the workers from Las Vegas and Florida.

"The worst paid are the plantation workers. That goes for Havana province, which sets the tone for all of the other provinces. My plantations are the exception because I take care of my workers and they respond by out-producing their peers on other farms."

Batista nodded at the Minister of Public Works, seated opposite the Labor Minister.

"Muja, why don't you sit down with Armando. The Public Works' projects we are planning will require lots of strong shoulders to build roads, tunnels, and bridges. After all, we do not want any obstacles standing in the way of American tourists who desire to spend money in the Las Vegas of the tropics."

Chuckles followed and all of the ministers voiced their agreement with the president on that one. Some even applauded.

"Why don't we open a school for dealers here?" Army said. "Use our own people to man the tables."

Batista smiled: "Meyer is doing that as we speak. But not with Cubans. That will take time. Now what is this I hear about you killing a communist?"

Army hesitated for a moment to compose himself. He was digesting news about the dealers' school and his being a killer.

"I heard the same story about the communist. But I wasn't the one who shot him. The young man went for my bodyguard's gun and it discharged, killing him. As a member of the Sugar Stabilization Institute, gentlemen, my worry is that there may be other saboteurs like him out there. They want to turn the workers against the plantation owners."

Batista laughed. "Do not worry, Sugar Man, We will protect the 'cane at all costs. We do not want half the world to be deprived of Cuban sweetness. Grau, are you on this?"

"The killing?"

"Yes."

"The case is closed. Self-defense. The detective - my nephew I am proud to say - killed a radical law student who engaged in sabotage at the Lobo plantation."

"Good. I have ordered the commander at Camp Columbia to dispatch soldiers to protect the crops in the region."

Batista rose and the ministers did likewise. He looked at his wristwatch.

"Now, if you will excuse me gentlemen, I must go directly to my canasta game. I am late. *Buena suerte, caballeros.* Enjoy the rest of your summer."

Before the dictator left the room, the head of the Secret Police handed him a heavy attaché case. Blanco Rico usually brought the leather bag to the president's office on Monday mornings. Its contents: Skim from the Havana casinos, a cool $300,000 in cash, the weekly price the Mob paid El Mulato Lindo for casino gambling in the capital.

Army and others who did business in Cuba, such as building contractors, mining operators, car dealers, and plantation owners had to pay twenty percent of their gross income to the dictator. The Minister of Labor was no different. Furthermore, some of his bar profits were used to pay the vig on his father's gambling note. His earnings from sugar cane production were not only plowed back into a growing business but also used to support the clinics on three plantations.

So, with a pleasant wave of the hand Batista, a former United Fruit Company 'cane cutter, left the room for an afternoon of card playing.

As soon as the president exited, the ministers commenced an impromptu debate about their two peers. Army chose to take the high ground by remaining silent. However, Muja spoke out.

"I sympathize with Armando, his problems with the rebel brother and at the plantation. Obviously, Armando the capitalist has no influence over Ernesto the communist. I have been dealing with these Marxists for years. They have this romantic notion of taking from the rich and giving to the poor. Like Robin Hood. Maybe that worked in England. It will not work here. If the workers take the sugar cane plantations, then what? They can plant and they can harvest, then what?"

"I'll tell you what," Army said. "The workers take the land for themselves. Then the state takes the land from the workers. So, the workers are back where they started, only worse. Because now they're working for the government, not for themselves. And the government tells them what to do, not the other way around, as we do in America."

Muja nodded in agreement and looked around the room. The other minsters concurred. They talked among themselves as Muja handed Army the public works report.

"Now, when it comes to jobs, Armando, please read my report on the public works we have planned. And by the way, more jobs are coming because the Italians from New York are preparing to build at least three hotel casinos. Hotels that will create more jobs and business in Havana. Let the communists complain about that."

"You're a champ against communism, Muja," Army said. "I know that you were the one who took control of the labor federation from the communists in 1947."

"Thank you, Armando. I could not have done it without your father's help."

The two ministers reached across the table, shook hands and left the room while the others talked among themselves.

———•◆•———

It was 2:15 p.m. when Army and his driver parked in front of the Fox Hole's main entrance. From outside they could hear the quartet blasting a mambo tune called: *Cuentame Te Que Paso.*

Jomar opened the door to the Fox Hole and motioned for Army to pass. As soon as he did, a dancer fell into his arms. Startled, he looked around the room to see that tables and chairs had been cleared for two costumed, Cuban dancers to perform in front of the band, which was in full swing. The trumpeter was blowing a loud riff to a refrain, backed by a piano, guitar, and conga drums. The Hollywood set and its followers were gathered along the periphery of the makeshift dance floor, watching, listening, tapping feet, and nodding to the mambo beat.

"*Pao pao*," the chica playing the piano sang, "*pao pao*" in a one-two-three-four beat.

Army gently pushed the dancer forward and attempted to sidestep her; however, she embraced him in a dance position and moved with him, rhythmically. Again, he sidestepped. Again, she danced with him. Seeing this, her partner bowed and spread his arms as if to say: "the floor is yours, Armando."

And the crowd - many of the onlookers knew him – cheered. So, the son of the Charmer from Santa Cruz did what his daddy would have done. He smiled and let the beat carry his feet. He took the chica's right hand with his left, placed his right on her side and pulled her past him in a "dile que no [tell him no]" move. He twirled her twice, her short skirt spinning like a saucer, and spun himself. Caught up in the intoxicating salsa rhythm, his feet snapped quick-quick, slow, quick-quick slow. "*Cuen-Ta-Me Te Que Pa-so, Cuen-Ta-Me Te Que Pa-so*," the singer sang with the piano taking the lead, followed by the guitar, conga drums, and trumpet. Around the floor they traveled quick-quick, slow, quick-quick, slow. He led her past him again, switched places with her, and did a move in which they spun each other with combined arms above, whirling like eggbeaters. They finished with his holding up the small of her back in the palm of his hand after she swooned backward, her long black hair touching the floor.

"Sabor!" yelled a Cuban gentleman in a beige summer suit, applauding. "Sabor!"

The onlookers erupted in applause. And then they joined in the refrain even though most did not know that Sabor, literally "flavor," in this case meant "feeling." The audience felt it. "Sabor!" the people shouted. "Sabor!"

Army and his dance partner took bows, after which he had a difficult time walking through the multitude. Well-wishers offered congratulatory handshakes and shouted compliments like: "so suave" and "simply smashing."

It took a while, but the suave one and Jomar finally made their way to the other end of the bar, where the boss usually sat. However, a half-dozen American naval officers dressed in white uniforms, drinking shots and beers had overtaken the spot. Army was okay with that, but Hiran wasn't there and he wondered why.

"Celia," he shouted. "Where is Hiran?"

"Out back to throw trash," she yelled.

Army stood in back of a man-made storm generated by firewater and foul language and signaled a bartender for a drink.

While waiting he heard a scream, faintly at first, followed by another and another. Louder and louder. It was coming from the back entrance. It was Celia.

He raced through the door that led to an alley. There lay Hiran on his back next to the trash, his face bloodied. A baseball bat and a business card sat on his chest.

Chapter 30
Celia and Fay

JOMAR SPED DOWN Zulueta while Celia pressed a handkerchief to Hiran's forehead to stop blood flowing from a wound above his nose. He remained unconscious with his head on her lap in the back seat of the Hudson.

"Don't worry, he'll be okay," consoled Army from the front seat while the detective leaned on the horn, passing other cars turning onto the Malecón.

When they arrived at the Hospital Concepcion de la Inmaculada emergency room, the men carried the injured bartender inside. Nurses directed them to a gurney.

"Look, he is awake," Celia said, hugging him. "How do you feel, baby?"

"My head. What happened?"

"Let the doctor examine you, amor. Do not talk."

A nurse with gauze soaked in antiseptic cleaned blood seeping from a cut on his forehead and an elderly man in a white lab coat palpated the nasal area.

"I am Doctor Gomez. Your nasal bones feel as though they are fractured. Your skull could be fractured, too."

The physician dabbed a fresh gauze pad on the bloody cuts on Hiran's forehead and bridge of his nose: "I will stitch you now, send you for X-rays and keep you under observation. You may have a concussion."

Celia turned to Army. "I will stay with him."

He nodded his approval, kissed Celia on the cheek, and walked out of the room with Jomar before opening his wallet and pulling out the card found on Hiran. It read: Joe Massi, Plaza Hotel and Casino.

"Son-of-a-bitch. This is my payback for Tony. I'm so sorry for Hiran. It should have been me."

———◆———

The next morning Army drove to the hospital, where he bumped into Massi and Fay waiting next to the elevators. She looked down and the mobster looked straight ahead without acknowledging him. The doors opened and all three entered in silence.

He could feel her eyes upon him as he stood in front of her and the Mob boss during what seemed like an interminable ride. The doors finally opened and the trio stepped out. He turned to the mafioso.

"Joe, can I have word with you?"

Massi nodded to Tony's lover to go on without him. Army was defiant.

"I'm visiting my bar manager. He was beaten with a baseball bat. Your card was found on him."

The mobster simply stared at him without a response. He continued: "I know this is about Tony. But he had it coming. Fucking Fay. Fucking with my team in front of me. He's a hood without a code."

Massi nodded. "I can understand your beef about Tony and your ex. But I told you the decision about baseball. Now I don't have no driver, no muscle because he's in this hospital."

"And I don't have a barman, a manager."

The mobster pointed an index finger at Army's face. "You did the same as Tony did, but with Titi. You were warned about that. Now I'm warnin' you again. You're the one who should be in the hospital. Respect for your father is the only thing keepin' your legs under you."

With that admonition Massi turned and walked down the hall. A minute later Army was in Hiran's room. There, the bar manager sat in a padded chair next to his bed. He had two black eyes. Celia was at his side.

Shaking hands. "Hiran, you're up, how do you feel?"

"Oh, I have headaches, Armando. They say I have a fractured skull. They are trying to find the right medicine. Do you know who did this to me?"

"It was the Mafia. I hurt one of their soldiers and they hurt you. I'm sorry."

Celia interrupted: "Do not worry, honey. I will protect you."

Army smiled, but his bar manager looked worried. "The doctor will not release me until my headaches go away."

"Don't worry. Take your time. Don't rush back to work."

After an hour at his bedside the visitors left. They were walking outside the hospital when Celia stopped suddenly.

"Armando. You know who is in the building next door? The convent. Please allow me to speak to her. She has feelings for you. And you for her. I have eyes. I can see."

He shot her a look of hopelessness. "I'll wait in the car," he said.

Army sat with the Chevy convertible's top down, watching palm trees sway in a tropical breeze on a cloudy day. He thought about Fay and how good she looked. He noticed something else. The hole in his soul seemed to be closing. And then he was startled to hear her voice.

"Hi."

Army looked up and saw his former lover walking by with Massi. When he acknowledged her she stopped. The mobster kept going.

"How's Hiran?"

"Headaches. They're keeping him for a while. How's your boyfriend?"

Before she could answer, Massi started blowing his car's horn for her to join him. Army saw that she was undecided.

"We'll take you home," he said.

"All right."

Fay waved the Mob boss off and slid into the passenger's seat next to him.

"I was saying, how's your boyfriend?"

"Tony? He's not my boyfriend. I have no boyfriend. How's your girlfriend?"

"What girlfriend?"

"The barmaid. The one I just saw you with."

"She's not my girlfriend."

Suddenly, he looked up to see his female bartender looking down at the new passenger.

"It's okay, Celia. This is Fay. Fay this is Celia."

His former girlfriend opened the door, stepped out, smiled, nodded and pushed the seat forward so the Fox Hole's only female bartender could sit in the back. That didn't sit well with Celia. So, before he started the car she began a monologue that prevented any dialogue between her boss and his former girlfriend throughout most of the fifteen-minute drive to her house in Miramar.

"Armando, she say you return at 9 o'clock tonight. She look so beautiful. She wear a lovely black dress. With her nice skin color the dress is, how you say, *maravillosa*. I think she is more beautiful than Titi, in a different way of course. More Latina. And you need a Latina woman. They have the passion. Your blood is Latino."

Fay frowned. He shrugged while driving along the Malacón toward Miramar.

"And she teach, Armando. Very smart. She teach English. To the little ones. Another thing. She apologize to me. She say she is, how you say in English, grieve?"

"Grief," he said, turning toward her. Simultaneously, he pulled from his pocket the family photo she had accidentally dropped on the floor of El Carcel and handed it to her. She looked at it with surprise and pressed it to her heart as she continued her monologue.

They were in the tunnel now. It funneled loud cars, trucks and buses to Miramar, so Celia turned up her volume.

"Si, grief over her dead fiancé. So sad. But she is without a man, Armando. I tell her I am so sorry for her. I tell her how nice you are. How you are generous and kind. How you care about poor people. How you take me off the street and teach me bartender. How you help me with my family."

Which made her pause and look at the photo. Tears started streaming down both cheeks. Army looked back with concern. Fay looked at him with sadness. But Celia continued while sobbing: "Maybe she can teach me, too. My English not so good. But she speak English like an American. Like you. She is so smart. And wonderful. Like you."

The light at the end of the tunnel was approaching and Celia wiped her tears with her fingers as she continued her long speech. She leaned forward.

"And she live in the convent. Is that not good?"

When Army's car emerged from the tunnel onto Fifth Avenue, Celia leaned forward a little more so that the front-seat passenger could hear every word, amplified.

"And she do not drink and smoke and sleep with men. I think she is, how you say in English, virgin, Armando. A virgin waiting for you."

Fay placed her hand over her mouth to keep from laughing out loud. Army snickered: "Celia. You are such a story teller," he said as he turned right onto 30th St. "Such a gossip."

"What is gossip?" Celia said with a frown.

"You know, *chismoso*."

He pulled in front of the house.

"Would you like to come in?" Fay asked. "My father enjoys talking to you."

He gave her a sarcastic look. "No thanks."

"Well, good luck with your date tonight. Sounds enchanting."

She leaned over and kissed him on the cheek, stepped out, and pushed the seat forward for her tormentor to alight and move to the front seat.

Looking into Celia's eyes. "You are delightful. Please continue to watch over him. He needs a guardian angel like you."

Fay extended her hand. After those kind words there was nothing to do but shake. Thus, a truce was effectuated between the former *flirtera* and the society girl.

———— ◆ ————

When Army and Celia arrived at the Fox Hole it was lunchtime. The place was noisy and packed as usual. He looked for El Angel.

El Angel de la Muerte, the Angel of Death, was his nom de guerre in the professional wrestling ring. A little man with large hands, El Angel had mastered the sleeper hold, which would render opponents lifeless.

Army watched him open six beer bottles swiftly. He signaled the bruiser to meet him at the front of the noisy bar

"Angel, it looks like Hiran will be out for awhile. I'd like you to manage the bar until he returns. Okay, amigo?"

"Si, Armando. Until he returns."

Chapter 31
Second Chance

A T 8:55 P.M. Army pulled up to the convent. He parked just short of the main entrance and grabbed a bouquet of red roses from the passenger's seat. He walked swiftly through the eternally open portal to the main desk and spoke with an elderly nun wearing one of those winged coronas.

"Hello Sister. I'm here to see Bonita, eh, Bonita…"

"Di Riva," the nun added.

"Thanks. She's expecting me."

However, before the nun could pick up the telephone, the school teacher opened a door behind the sister and summoned him. She was wearing a plain black dress with no accoutrements and no lipstick or makeup. She didn't need any.

"This way, please."

Army followed her through the doorway into the open-air courtyard. In the center was the Tranquil Fountain, from which water shot upward and sprayed outward in a perfect circle. At the base of the fount was a shallow pool surrounded by lush, tropical plants and colorful stones. It was in this serene setting that he presented his peace offering.

Bonita accepted the flowers with a smile and a bow and motioned for him to sit on a nearby stone bench with her. She cradled the bouquet as if it were her child.

"About the other night," she said.

"You don't have to explain."

"I must. You see, I'm still in mourning over Pablo. He was my best friend and my first and only love. I have heard different stories about how he died. So, I do not really know what happened. However, there is one thing that you can do to help me."

"What?"

"I would like to see the spot where he was killed. The very place where his heart stopped beating. It would rest my soul."

"I understand," he said, nodding. "He died in a building on my plantation. I know that you're angry about that."

"My first reaction is to hate you. But I'm a Christian, raised by God's servants. Not only do we preach love, we demonstrate it each day in our nurturing of students, patients and the penniless. Here in Cuba we have the rich and the poor, none in between."

"I know. I'm trying to help..."

Bonita interrupted: "By giving us some clothes? That's like dispensing band aids to earthquake victims."

Army looked at her questioningly. She saw the hurt in his expression and immediately tried to comfort him. She placed her hand on his.

"I'm sorry. I was too harsh. But we work with the impoverished children of Cuba every day. There are many of those little ones. It's so sad. If Jesus were here, he would have worked for the redistribution of wealth."

Recognizing this statement as a dig at capitalism, he cleared his throat but said nothing in response. She continued. "I'm a communist. I believe in common ownership of the means of production and a classless society, not one in which the rich subjugate the poor on plantations and in factories."

He frowned. "Pablo taught you that?"

"He showed me that I was a communist, like him."

Army swallowed hard and nodded at what she said as though he expected it. "Okay, can I take you to the plantation?"

"Yes, please. Is Sunday suitable? After 10 o'clock Mass at the cathedral in Old Havana?"

"Yes."

"I have to prepare for tomorrow's English class now. Thank you for the roses."

"My pleasure."

He didn't attempt to give her the customary kiss on the cheek this time. Instead, he squeezed her warm, soft hand. He felt her energy and his passion. But she wouldn't look into his eyes as he said goodbye.

———◆———

Sunday Mass at the cathedral was an event. Built between 1748 and 1777, the principal church of the diocese was mammoth and ornamented in the Baroque style of the times. It attracted waves of Cubans from all walks of life and in all manner of dress - mendicant to millionaire - and they rolled into and out of the massive doorway every hour between 9 a.m. and noon on Sundays.

The plaza in front of the cathedral was packed with churchgoers when Army arrived at 11 a.m. Bells were clanging and the crowd was abuzz with church talk as he meandered through groups of parishioners waiting to enter. When he arrived at the bottom of the front steps he watched people pour slowly out of the building and into the September sun until he fixed his gaze on a young woman in a black dress.

"Bonita," he yelled.

She could have been mistaken for a young, tanned Ava Gardner, who'd spent her honeymoon with Sinatra at the Hotel Nacional. But there was no mistake. It was Bonita, placing a hand over her eyes to shield the sun's glare as she scanned the crowd. He waved. She waved back and soon they were walking down a side street to Calle Obispo. They turned left onto Obispo and entered the Plaza de Armas, past the American Embassy and the Hotel Santa Isabella. When they came to the famous Ceba tree, symbolic of Cuba's first settlement in 1519, she stopped and turned to him.

"The first Mass on the island was celebrated under the tree in that spot. Legend says that if you walk around the tree three times and make a wish, it will be granted."

Army watched while she walked up to the tree, elevated on a mound of fresh soil, and walked around it. He wanted to ask what she wished, but didn't. He led her to a taxi parked next to the ship pilot's building.

"Train station," he said to the cabbie as he opened the rear door.

"So how was church?" he said when they sat.

"I was surprised to see Father Luís saying Mass. Usually he's at our church, but I hear they were a priest short today."

"What brings you here? I mean, your church is right there, next to the convent."

"Oh, I go to Mass every morning there. This is a nice change. Do you go to Mass?"

Army started to squirm as the taxi accelerated. "I used to be a good Catholic, you know, Mass every Sunday. Then the war came. It changed me. Now I attend Mass on Christmas and Easter. To keep from being excommunicated. So, what did the priest talk about today?"

"Corruption. About how people enslave themselves to material things."

Army shook his head in agreement. "The whole world is corrupt. The war taught me that."

"But it doesn't have to be that way."

"The way Mother Maria Jose spoke about Father Luís, I got the idea that he's corrupted by the bottle."

"Yes, Father Luís does have a weakness for alcohol. But he is a good man. A good man with a flaw. None of us are perfect, although we should strive to be so, the way Father Luís does. He is trying to conquer his demons."

Nodding, Army added: "Aren't we all."

"What are your demons, Armando?"

He laughed. "Too many to list. Let's chalk 'em up to corruption. To the corrupt world in which we live."

"But we can change the world, Armando, no?"

"I'm a pragmatist. I try to succeed within the framework of the world I'm in. Especially here in Havana. If you only knew."

He glanced out the window as the taxi sped along Avenida Del Puerto, past Calle Cuba and Sailor's Bar.

"Oh I know," she said. "Pablo used to tell me things. Things about Batista, the Mafia, and the secret police. Things about the American capitalists. Are you an American capitalist, Armando?

He looked at her and smiled. He didn't know if she was joking or serious. He liked the way she said "American Capitalist." So, he gave her a direct answer. "Yes. I am an American Capitalist. Thanks to my father, born poor here in Santa Cruz."

The taxi pulled up to the station, where Cubans dressed in their Sunday best listened to the baritone voice over a loudspeaker announcing trains and tracks. Army paid the driver and instinctively took his guest by the hand so they wouldn't be separated by passengers jostling their way to Tracks A, B, C ,and D.

Not used to being led by the hand of a man other than Pablo, Bonita allowed it as he tightened his grip on their way to the trains. She felt his energy.

"Santa Cruz Track A," the voice on the speaker resonated. Within fifteen minutes they were on the train and she took in the sights as they sped past the beaches of Santa Maria on the left.

Army observed her and smiled: "So why do you live at the convent?"

"That is the only home I know. I was an orphan, a baby when the Sisters of Charity took me in."

"The Don, Lora said something about your mother. She knew him?"

"She loved him. But she did not love me enough to raise me." Then, she pulled out the old photo from her purse and showed it to him.

"She looks like you. You carry this around with you all the time, don't you?"

The convent girl shrugged. "A child needs a mother. My mother was Mother Superior."

"Mother Maria Jose? Oh, I'm so sorry," he said.

"No. Don't be sorry for me. She provided the discipline I needed. Her assistant, Sister Celeste, nurtured me. She was kind to me until her death last year. I thank God for her every morning."

She bowed her head.

"When I was growing, Mother Maria Jose used to tell me that my beauty was the work of the devil. This affected me deeply. I did not have the courage to harm myself, so I prayed that the Lord would take me. God forgive me."

Army reached over, squeezed her hand and looked into her soft brown eyes.

"What a nasty thing to say to a young girl. Your beauty is the work of the creator. Be thankful."

"I'm all right now," the former orphan said. "Mother Maria Jose has made me into a teacher and I love my work. She has also rearranged my schedule so that I can earn my undergraduate teaching degree at the University."

"I'm impressed," Army said. "You'll be one of a handful of female teachers with a university degree in Cuba, the way Celia is one of a few chicas who tend bar in Havana."

"You hired her as a bartender?"

"On-the-job training. In my bar."

"That's commendable. Maybe it's time for the Church to have a woman defend her in a courtroom, too. I would like to study law."

He nodded in approval as the train stopped to pick up passengers in Boca de Juraco, a tiny coastal town in which cars, buses, and boats refueled. Bonita studied him for a moment, smiling.

"Have you been married, Armando?"

"No."

"Why?"

He squirmed. "I haven't found the right one."

She laughed. "Where were you born?"

"Philadelphia. In a state called Pennsylvania in the United States."

"Your mother is not Cuban?"

"Oh no. She was born in Ireland. Her family moved to Philadelphia when she was a baby."

"She must be light in color. You have her eyes, no?"

"Yes."

"They are beautiful. You are a beautiful man."

"Don't tell Mother Maria Jose."

They both chuckled. About thirty minutes later they arrived at the station in Santa Cruz, not far from the Centro Lobo plantation. Hohen Stein was waiting for them, leaning against a 1948 Chevy sedan when they stepped off the train.

"Hello Stein, this is Bonita." The elderly man tipped his straw hat to her. "Bonita, Hohen Stein is my plantation manager."

She nodded and smiled as Stein turned to Army.

"This is the car I would like you to drive back to Havana. It must have a tune-up."

"How's everything else?"

Stein frowned. "Dangerous."

Chapter 32

At the Plantation

S TEIN PULLED IN front of the plantation house. Obol was on the front porch and he began to bark, drawing the maid to the screen door.

Army kissed and hugged Nelsa and made the proper introduction, in Spanish.

"Mama, Le presento Bonita."

"Que bella. Bonita is a perfect name for you muchacha. Please sit while I bring some cold lemonade."

Stein walked to the barn while the visitors petted Obol, who had an eye on the beautiful guest.

Army excused himself. "Pardon me for a moment. I have to speak with Stein."

The plantation manager was sharpening a machete when Army arrived. "Mandito, what a beauty. Where did you find her?"

"She was the fiancée of late Pablo de la Torre."

"Who?"

"The guy who died here. Where you're standing."

"The communist? What does she want?"

"To see the spot where he died."

"Why?"

He shrugged. "It's a personal thing. Any more trouble?"

"I hear that more saboteurs are in the area," Stein said as he ran a finger along the side of the sharpened blade.

"What about the army?"

"I have not seen it."

Army nodded. "Why don't you come up to the house for some lemonade so I can walk her here. Okay?"

Stein finished his work and walked with Sugar Man to the porch, where his Cuban mother and the bereaved beauty appeared to be in deep conversation. They stopped and put down their drinks when Stein approached first.

"Mandito will take you to the barn now Miss, if you want."

"Thank you. Please give me a moment."

Bonita walked to the car, opened the back door and picked up a purse she'd left on the seat. She opened it and pulled out a 1x2-inch head shot of Pablo and her mugging for the camera. She kissed it and slipped it into her pocket. She held the purse as she walked back to the porch. Army escorted her to the barn.

"It was here," he said, pointing to the dry clay floor, where four depressions had been made by the chair on which Pablo had sat near the entrance. "Jomar said Pablo went for his gun and it went off. We heard the shot and came running. He died instantly."

"What was his crime?"

"He sabotaged the refinery. He also set fire to a field of 'cane prematurely and tried to turn the workers against us."

Bonita shook her head sadly to acknowledge Pablo's transgressions. She kneeled and used her fingers to dig a small hole where the chair had stood.

"Can I help?"

"No, I can do this."

The bereaved one removed the photo from her pocket, kissed it again, placed it tenderly in the hole and filled it. She removed a short, round candle from her purse, placed it on top of the freshly-filled photo grave and lit it. She blessed herself and prayed silently.

He bowed out, not wanting to distract her. He walked to the house and found Stein sitting on a rocker, sipping from a glass of lemonade. The manager handed him one.

"Thanks. You know, the president has assured us that the army is protecting the plantations. But I'm not so sure. Look at what one man was able to do here."

Stein shook his head in agreement. "My vigilance is unshakable. Sometimes I do not sleep at night."

Army patted him on the knee. "While I'm here I'd like to take a look at the books. Do you mind?"

"Of course not. Go in. The door to my office is open."

He spent more than an hour going over ledgers, receipts, bills, and pay stubs. Everything seemed to be in order. When he finished, he walked to the front porch where the women were still conversing quietly.

"Are you all right Bonita?"

"Yes."

"Where's Stein, Mama?"

"In the barn again."

Army sat and relaxed on a rocking chair next to his guest. All three rocked and talked as Obol moved from Bonita to his master.

"I tell her stories about you, Mandito. When you are a boy. Now you are in trouble."

Army smiled and looked at his guest. She seemed comfortable. He listened to them talk, and before long his eyes closed and he drifted to an unaccustomed peaceful sleep. When he awakened alone on the porch, darkness had fallen and the aroma of roasted pork stimulated his nostrils. He opened the screen door and saw the table set.

"We were just going to call you," the guest said. "Nelsa has prepared your favorite meal."

All four dug into the fresh salad, pork, rice and beans. Fried plantains and boniato chips were an extra treat. Fresh coffee from the Sierra Maestra Mountains and flan followed. Dinner was delicious and devoured quickly.

Army looked at Bonita admiringly as she engaged in conversations with the others. She seemed to have thoroughly enjoyed the food and the company. Occasionally he'd catch her glances at him. But she would look away quickly before he could acknowledge her with a smile.

When they all gathered on the front porch to say goodbye, Bonita turned to her new confidant: "I came here with a hurting heart. I leave here with the hope of healing and moving on."

"We are always here for you, dear," Nelsa said, hugging her.

It was 10:00 p.m. when the couple hopped into the Chevy. A few minutes later they arrived at the railroad crossing that traversed the entrance to Central Lobo.

Black-and-white checkered barriers descended, lights flashed, and the frenetic sound of bells rang while they waited. Soon, the black-and-silver Southern 63 freight locomotive began pulling its load. The steam engine hissed, snorted, and blew white smoke like a Brahman bull in winter. Then came a deafening whistle. The coal cars that followed weren't carrying black rocks. They were overflowing with white and brown gold, refined and unrefined sugar headed to port in Havana Harbor. Army counted aloud as they screeched along slowly.

"One ... two ... three ... four ... five ... six.

"Seven? ... eight? ... nine? ... ten? ... eleven? ... twelve?" Bonita observed his look of bewilderment.

"Anything wrong?"

He turned to her. "The last six cars. They aren't ours. Somebody's hitching a ride on my train. At my expense."

He pounded the steering wheel. "I've got to get to the bottom of this."

Sugar Man sat there in thought as the flashing barriers rose. Who could be glomming onto his sugar train?

He stepped on the accelerator and except for the Chevy's headlamps, the road ahead was pitch black. He sped along the costal route where only the stars, lamps in a few scattered houses, and lights from a cruise ship in the distance pierced the darkness. In this setting the Chevy felt cozy, safe. The music on the radio summed up how the driver felt. Dick Haymes was singing *It Might As Well Be Spring*.

Bonita interrupted.

"Thank you for taking me to the plantation, Armando. I feel as though I communicated with Pablo. I could feel his presence. If this had not been such a sad occasion, it would have been joyful. Nelsa was so warm and kind. She told me a lot about your father and you. The free clinic, education, and housing for the workers. This is so amazing to me. That your father and you would be so good to the workers."

"You mean we capitalists aren't so bad?"

"I think you are the exception. Pablo did not speak about that possibility."

"There are others, Bonita. Lots of others."

Chapter 33
Communism Vs. Capitalism

IT DIDN'T TAKE long for spring to turn into winter.

Bonita bowed her head in thought and turned to Army. "Pablo was passionate about his beliefs. Even fanatical. But he had good reason. From the time of Machado, and then Batista, and political gangsters, and now Batista again. Our country suffers, bleeds."

"Bonita, corruption's been part of our history since the US kicked Spain out of Cuba in 1898. Political violence, too. I don't like it. But it's our way. It's a cultural thing."

The school teacher shook her head in disagreement.

"The House of Charity is full, Armando. Outside Havana there are few doctors, hardly any schools, and little medicine."

"I'm working to fix that. I'm working on a plan. I don't know if you know this, but I'm the new Minister of Labor."

She looked surprised. "You are in Batista's cabinet? What about the secret police? The torture. Kidnappings. Murder. I know. Pablo told me."

Mention of Pablo's name set him off. He raised his voice. "Pablo wanted the violent overthrow of the government. Destruction of the economic engine of this country."

She pursed her lips and looked down for a moment, gathering her thoughts. She spoke softly.

"You know that worried me. He had a violent side. Never with me. With the system."

She looked down. He apologized. "I'm sorry. I know you're hurting."

Passing through a small, sleepy town he tried to hold her hand but she resisted. When they arrived at the convent, he walked her inside, held her by the shoulders and looked into her eyes.

"I don't want this to come between us. Let's talk about other things next time."

She shook her head negatively. "Armando. I'm not ready for this. Please understand."

He turned and left.

Chapter 34

More Bad News

THE MORNING SUN seeped through the shutters and shone on Army's eyelids, forcing them open. He shaded them with a hand when the phone by his bed rang.

"Armando?"

"Yes?"

"I am Livan, Livan Orlando, your third-base coach."

"Is there a problem?"

"Alain the manager is in the convent hospital. Two men last night attacked him."

"What the hell? Is he all right? What happened?"

"He has broken legs."

Army sighed. "Okay Livan. I'll meet you there in an hour."

When he walked into the hospital room the manager was on his back in bed. Two hard casts surrounded his legs from the ankles to just below the knees. The coach was sitting in a chair next to the bed. He rose and shook hands with the boss.

"Alain, how are you feeling?"

"Bad."

"Who did this?"

The manager signaled to the coach, who presented Massi's business card. On the back it read: "Now we're even."

Army stared at the card for a moment, thinking. He looked at Alain.

"Where were you attacked?"

"In the tunnel leading away from the stadium. After practice."

"What did your attackers look like?"

"They wore hoods."

Army patted him on the shoulder. "Okay. Anything you need, just call. Meanwhile, who do you want to replace you for now?"

"Livan can do it. He is qualified and the players respect him."

The owner patted him on the back. "Okay. The job is yours until Alain heals."

Army walked down the hall to visit Hiran. Celia was sitting with him, holding his hand. His eyes were now black and blue.

"How are you feeling today, Hiran?"

"Headaches, Armando, headaches. They are still testing."

Celia looked up and smiled. "How was your day with the girl?"

He thought for a moment. "So-so."

"Why?"

"Long story. Please be in work by eleven o'clock to get ready for a big day. A cruise ship is coming in from New York."

Chapter 35

Sugar Thieves and Aching Hearts

ARMY PULLED THE Chevy in front of the Central Train Station in Old Havana. He parked across the street on Calle Belgica, where he could see the white building with twin bell towers that rose above the Banyan trees and black iron gates that guarded the entrance.

"Can I see yesterday's train log?" he asked a clerk in the office.

"Who are you, sir?"

"Armando Lobo, owner of the Southern 63 freight train that pulled in last night."

The clerk pulled the log book, thumbed the pages until he reached "L" and closed it. "Sorry. It is not here. Let me try today's book."

The man reached under a metal counter and pulled up another log book and fanned the pages to "L."

"Here it is. It shows six cars of sugar."

"What about the other six?"

"Other six?

"The six that I saw last night in Centro Lobo, attached to the first six."

"We have no indication of that here, sir."

"Where's the train now?"

"In Regla."

"When's the next ferry to Regla?"

"It sails in fifteen minutes from the dock near the Iglesia San Paula."

Army bolted to his car and sped away. When he pulled into the parking lot at the harbor, the cruise ship was docking and travelers were disembarking. He boarded the ferry that crossed Havana Bay and held his nose. Garbage floated around the vessel. About ten minutes later the boat docked amid more garbage. Passengers held their noses as they filed off the boat and scattered throughout Regla, a town across Havana Bay.

Army walked briskly for six blocks, turned right and trotted alongside railroad tracks littered with trash and children playing perilously close to the rails. He passed a baseball game on the left, where the scoreboard showed the home team Refleros leading the Carribes, 3-1. Five minutes later he was inside the Regla train station's office, thumbing through the logbook. The Southern 63 had pulled in at 2 a.m.

The book showed six cars of sugar. The train was on Track 6. He walked to Track 6 and saw twelve cars hooked to the locomotive. All were empty.

"Where's the sugar?" he yelled to a worker on the tracks.

"On its way to the ships," the young man answered.

By the time Army walked to the dock, the SS Pennsylvania was loaded and ready to sail. He entered the Harbor Office, identified himself and asked to see the ship's manifest. It showed that six cars of sugar from the Southern 63 had been loaded and were Philadelphia bound.

"Was there another ship loaded here today?" he asked a clerk.

"The SS Maine. It sailed an hour ago."

"Can I please see a copy of the Maine's manifest?"

"Can I see your identification, sir?" the clerk said.

"Army pulled out the owner's card from the Southern 63. The clerk looked in the logbook, then pulled the official document giving comprehensive details of the ship and its cargo.

"Here it is. Six cars of sugar from the Southern 63 bound for Boston."

"Boston! That son-of-a-bitch."

Fifteen minutes later Sugar Man was on the ferry. When it docked in Old Havana, he saw his reflection in the garbage-filled water. He felt like the refuse surrounding his image. Within the last twenty-four hours he'd lost his bar manager, his baseball manager, and had transported six carloads of sugar for free. Big Bob was involved. Maybe Stein, too. He knew that he should speak with his father, but he didn't want to. He thought about confiding in Bonita, but mentally she was still in Pablo Land.

Money for the mob loan was due. He toyed with the idea of not paying, even though he knew the consequences. Maybe a sit down with Legendario was in order.

Army disembarked with about thirty others and walked to his car. He drove straight to the convent. School was letting out and Mother Maria Jose was lording over the students and parents when he pulled up to the entrance.

"Are you here to see Miss Di Riva?" the nun asked through the open passenger's window.

"Yes, Mother."

"Well, she is not here."

"Where is she?"

"At the University. It is Tuesday."

He frowned. "Can I wait?"

"Where would you do that?"

"In the courtyard."

"If you wish."

———— ◆ ————

Army backed up the car and parked. A few minutes later he was sitting on the stone bench in the open courtyard as students and faculty members sauntered by. When they had gone, he could hear the sound of flowing water from the Tranquil Fountain. He looked up and saw a large crucifix on one wall and a statue of the Blessed Virgin Mary nearby. Standing in front of a third wall was a life-size figure of Michael the Archangel.

He walked to the statue and became lost in it. Upon closer inspection, he noticed that the archangel's facial features were cherubic. However, he wore a vest of silver armor, the color that matched the large wings rising from his shoulder blades. His left hand held a silver shield with the inscription: *Quis Ut Deus*. His right hand was raised at eye level and held a spear whose tip rested on the right eye of a serpent with a grotesque head that looked almost human. It rested near his foot.

His careful examination was interrupted by a soft voice calling his name.

"Armando?"

He turned to see Bonita standing there with books pressed to her bosom. What a sight for an aching heart.

She noticed his distress. "What's wrong?"

"Oh nothing. Mind if we sit?"

"Not at all."

They sat on the stone bench. She faced him, held his hands and looked into his troubled blue eyes. He looked down.

"What is it?"

"Bad day. Just wanted to see you."

He disengaged his hands from hers and rose with a distressed look.

"Maybe this is a bad idea, my coming here. I mean, you're still in mourning. I have no right to come to you for comfort."

She looked up at him. "Come," she beckoned, extending her hands. "Sit down next to me. We'll talk."

Army clasped her hands and sat silently, admiring her shining hair, inviting eyes and luscious lips.

"Armando."

He didn't answer. He bowed his head. She moved closer. She released his hands, embraced him warmly and soon her lips caressed his face until they found his mouth. Passion that had been a fond memory to both suddenly erupted, hearts pounded, bodily fluids bubbled. The kiss was long and heated. And duly noted by Mother Superior.

"Miss Di Riva!" Maria Jose huffed. "Mother of God. Comport yourself!"

Chapter 36

The Wolf and the Foxes

ARMY WAS SOUNDLY asleep when his ear picked up a sound: *Wuu-wuu. Wu-wu. Wu-wu.* Again and again he heard the faint sound of a train whistle. The sounds formed images as his eyes darted left and right under closed eyelids.

He saw the train's engineer, Big Bob, smiling and pulling on a cord that released the whistle: *Wuu-wuu, wuu-wuu.*

"I'm gonna ride this sugar train straight to Boston," the big guy said with a chuckle. "Ain't that right, Stein?"

"No, you cannot do that," said the plantation manager. "The train cannot go there."

Suddenly, both vanished; however, the sound was still there when Sugar Man opened his eyes: *Wuu-wuu, wuu-wuu.*

He slipped out of bed in his boxer shorts and followed the sound to the window with the open plantation shutters. He looked down on Calle Animas to see a young boy blowing into a train whistle on a balmy Havana morning. He shook his head, closed the shutters and looked at the clock on a nightstand. It was 9 a.m. Cutter's starting time at the barber shop. He needed a favor. It was time for another trim.

"*Hola* Armando," the shoeshine boy said with a smile as Army walked by. He looked down and reached into his pocket for a coin. There was none. So, he pulled a pen from his pocket.

"*Chino, dame tu mano*" he said and the boy presented his hand.

Army wrote on the palm: "Angel, one dollar." He signed it with his initials. "Angel will make you breakfast when he arrives at 11:00." He patted the muchacho on the head. "Hiran is not working now."

"Si, Armando. Gracias."

He resumed his walk, dodging a group of Italian tourists on his way to the Plaza Hotel, where he took the steps up to the second-floor barbershop.

"What brings you here so early, amigo?" said Cutter, sitting on a barber chair with a copy of *The Havana Post.*

"I need a wiretap."

The barber rose so his friend could sit and spun him to face the mirror. He threw a barber's apron around his neck, picked up a pair of scissors and began to trim the back of his head.

"Who?"

"My plantation manager."

"Why?"

"My sugar train just got a lot sweeter."

"Whatdaya mean?"

"It's complicated."

"When do you need it?"

"Before next Wednesday,"

"Where do you want the tap?"

"The manager's house in Central Lobo, Santa Cruz. He has an office there."

Cutter stopped cutting, chuckled, and looked at Army in the mirror.

"Funny you mentioned a wiretap. We've been listening to your buddy, Joe Massi. You've been a bad boy."

"Why?"

"Tony Stabo."

He shrugged: "I snapped."

Cutter paused. "It's really getting to you now, amigo. Game fixin' is the last straw. Isn't it."

Cutter started trimming again.

"When Tony and those guys messed with the baseball team, my baby, something snapped, Cutter. Consequences no longer mattered."

The barber stopped and spun him around so that they were face-to-face.

"You reached your limit, amigo. There's only so much corruption a decent man can put up with. I sank into the same slump after the war. Couldn't work for a long time. Until I found my way back to the agency."

Army shot him a knowing look.

"Speaking of the agency," the spy said, "thanks for the cocaine-and-heroin tip. We seized a half-ton on a military transport headed for Parris Island."

"I owed you one. Who'd you bust?"

"Cubans. Lora's guys were nowhere around."

Army was silent for a moment. "Massi retaliated against my bar manager for what I did to Tony and I feel bad about that. But I'm suspicious about what happened to my baseball manager."

"Your baseball manager?"

"Long story. Oh, I need something else. A doctored freight train's manifest."

———— ◆ ————

When the Southern 63 arrived in Regla the following Tuesday at midnight, Army was there counting cars. There were twelve. Dressed in black, he waited until the engineer left the cabin to check the cars. Stealthily he made his way into the locomotive. The paperwork was hanging on a clipboard next to the windshield. Army replaced it with forged documents and slipped into the night.

The next afternoon the phone rang inside his apartment. It was Cutter.

"Hey. Wanna hear some interesting conversation?"

"Surprise me."

"Stein received a call this morning. Here it is on tape."

> *Stein, what happened? Six carloads never made it to the Main.*
>
> *Well, I am asking the same question. Everything was in order when the train left Central Lobo.*
>
> *My cars were attached?*

Of course.

Then what happened? What coulda happened? How did all that sugar end up on the Pennsylvania? If you're screwin' me …

I am not screwing you.

You lost six carloads of my sugar. What's worse is that it went into Lobo's boat. I expect results.

And I am taking a big risk.

Oh yeah? Did ya forget about that gamblin' note I hold?

All right. I will look into it.

Cutter cut in. "Who's the other guy?"

"Big Bob Flanery."

"He doesn't have a train to haul his sugar?"

"He did until the used engine in his locomotive blew up last week. He's waiting for another one. Cheap bastard. He should have bought a new one from the start."

"So why doesn't he just pay you to haul his sugar?"

"Pride. He keeps telling me he wants to buy me out."

"So he's prideful and cheap. How's he gonna buy you out?"

Army laughed. "He still has his recess money. Maybe he'll spend it. But now I have to replace a man who's worked for us for twenty years. This is the second underhanded thing Stein has done. That I know about. I just can't trust him anymore."

"Did you know he was a gambler?"

"Sure. But not a gambler with a problem. He's the kind of man who prides himself on self-control."

"So much for willpower."

"The worst part is that I have to tell my father. I haven't talked to him since the Titi thing. And I don't plan to."

Chapter 37
The Phone Call

THE GOOD SON didn't have to call his father. His sister called him after he hung up the phone with Cutter.

"Army, it's Victoria."

"Victoria? Hey, how are you, sis?"

"It's Popi. He's not doing well."

"What happened?"

"Too much to explain. He's in the University of Pennsylvania Hospital. He wants to see you."

He paused. "How bad is it?"

"It's not good."

"Okay. I'll be there as soon as I can."

After he hung up, his first thought was about Bonita and the radicals at the University. He wouldn't be able to protect her if she needed him. That realization made his stomach churn. Then there was Big Bob and Stein. He bristled when he thought about their conspiracy against him. He'd planned to deal with them that day.

Three hours later, Army was aboard the legendary Cubana Airlines Lockheed Constellation winging toward Miami. The flight carried revelers from the Tropicana Cabaret via the Hotel Nacional. Most were spent after a weekend of non-stop debauchery and he was all right with that. He had a lot to think about while they slept. He'd been avoiding his father's calls out of anger and he felt guilty.

Victoria and Julia met him at Philadelphia International Airport. The sisters filled him in as they walked to the car. Lazaro Lobo had pancreatic cancer.

"We're driving straight to the hospital," Victoria said.

When they arrived at the patriarch's private room, their mother, Grace, was there holding his hand. She and her son hugged until he turned to see his father and hardly recognized him. The Charmer from Santa Cruz, a robust, powerful, handsome man who'd once dazzled women on dance floors from here to Havana, was a shell of himself.

Lazaro looked up at his son and smiled. Army had intended to give him a perfunctory kiss on the cheek; however, when his lips touched his father's face a torrent of hot tears erupted. He embraced the man who'd taught him so much in a foreign land during his formative years. He couldn't pull away.

"Son, my son," Lobo the elder said in a weak voice.

Army could hear his mother and sisters weeping. He composed himself and stepped back, wiping his damp cheeks with a handkerchief. His father spoke, but he had to lean over him to hear what he was saying.

"Everything all right at the plantations?"

Army cleared his throat. "Yes, Popi. All's well."

"In the city, too?"

"No problem."

"Good. I am proud of you, son. I knew you could handle it. My regret is that I put that big debt on you. Are you square with the Italians?"

"*Tutto bene.*"

"You must be spending a lot of time with them. Listen to what they say and watch what they do. Never trust them."

A nurse entered with two pills and a glass of water. "I'm sorry but visiting hours ended fifteen minutes ago," she said.

Army hugged his father, who whispered in his ear.

"I love you, son."

Not expecting to hear that, he fought back more tears.

"Thank you, Dad. I love you too. See you tomorrow."

Chapter 38
Protector of All Women

AT THE LOBO mansion in Bryn Mawr the aroma of percolating Maxwell House coffee filled the kitchen while Grace, the girls and Army sat around the table. Grace started pouring when Girard, Julia's husband, walked in with their two young children, who raced to the living room to join Victoria's two kids.

"I just received a message that we're expecting a double load of sugar tomorrow," Girard said as Grace slid him a cup of coffee. "Things must be really good on the plantations."

Sugar Man smiled. "How're things going here? How much cash is available?"

"We're up twenty percent in Pennsylvania and ten percent over the rest of the country," Girard said while mixing milk with his coffee. "But most of our money's tied up in new machinery and trucks. Plus, there's that new plant we're building in South Philadelphia. We don't have much cash available here. What about Havana?"

"We're not liquid there either," Army said, sipping from his cup. "We're still paying off the locomotive and the mortgage on the electric plants."

"Why are you talking about cash, son? Still paying off your father's gambling debt?"

He flinched. Girard looked surprised. Grace smiled. "My husband has been indebted to the Mafia for quite a while, Girard."

The son-in-law raised his eyebrows and looked at everyone in the room. "How much money are we talking about?"

"A substantial amount, we'll talk about it later," Army said, turning his attention to his mother and changing the subject. Girard looked at Julia, who shrugged.

"How're you holding up, mother?"

"Oh, you know, I'm spending more time at the hospital and less time with the field hockey team. But we're still undefeated."

"How many years have you been coaching field hockey, Mom?" Girard said.

"Oh, too many to remember."

"How many championships?"

"Who knows?"

"We know," Julia said, toasting her mother with her coffee cup. "Twenty-nine. She's won twenty-nine titles in the twenty-nine years she's been coaching at Bryn Mawr College."

"That's right," Victoria said. "Didn't you ever check the dates on the trophies in the trophy case, Girard?"

"There were too many and the light's dim in the basement. But I saw Army's."

"I didn't play field hockey," he said with a straight face.

"If you'd been a girl you would have," Grace said. "You always had the athletic ability and field awareness, but you weren't a vociferous player."

Girard turned to his brother-in-law. "I heard you trained in Jiujitsu? Where did you learn it?"

"Istanbul. But let's talk about the girls and mother. They're the ones who won championships. I only have an MVP trophy."

"But you have character," Grace said, holding her steaming cup near her lips. "That's what competition builds. Have you been doing any charitable work in Havana? I pray for those poor people and you every day."

He shrugged. "I delivered clothing to a convent."

"Which one?" Grace said.

"*Concepcion de Inmaculda.*"

"Immaculate Conception. The Blessed Mother. Was that statue there?"

"Michael the Archangel? Yes."

Grace returned her cup of coffee to a saucer, smiled and surveyed everyone at the table as if she had something important to say. She was animated by the memory.

"My young man was seven. I asked him what name he'd chosen for his confirmation. He said, Michael. I asked why. I mean, there are no Michaels in the family. Either side. Then he told me about Sister Catherine."

Girard and the ladies looked at Grace with intense interest. Victoria and Julia knew the story, but always enjoyed hearing their mother repeat it.

"In Mother of Devine Grace church, Army had seen a statue of an angel with a long spear and a serpent at his feet. When he asked the nun who the angel was and what he was doing, she replied that he was Saint Michael the Archangel, the serpent was the devil, and Michael was protecting the Blessed Mother."

Grace leaned over and mussed his hair, the way she did when he was a boy. "Well, that's all he had to hear. Next day, my little man was Armando *Michael* Lobo Armstrong, protector of the Virgin Mary. Protector of all women."

Pushing back his hair he interrupted. "Popi had something to do with it. He used to tell me that I was the man of the house while he was away. I had to protect you and the girls."

"That's true, but mainly it's your nature, son. You are our Archangel."

He unconsciously reached under his shirt for the bent gold medal of St. Michael the Archangel and rubbed it between his index finger and thumb. He stared at the white tablecloth and his thoughts raced, including the obituary of his brother's death in the Battle of the Bulge. Images of the two men he killed during the war flashed, too.

"Still wearing the St. Michael medal I gave you?" Grace said. She turned to Girard. "The medal is bent. The girls know how it happened. Do you?"

"No, Grace. Please enlighten me."

Army pulled out the medal and looked at it. "It stopped a bullet from a German Luger. Point-blank range. It should have gone through." He looked up at Girard. "I'm living on borrowed time."

Grace got up and hugged him for a long moment. His sisters did, too. Grace began to weep, initiating a torrent of tears from all three women.

"I miss my brother," he said after they took their seats.

"We all do," his mother said, drying her tears with a hanky.

There was a pause of introspection. Girard puffed on a cigarette and observed. Victoria broke the silence.

"Army, what about Fay? You haven't mentioned her."

"It's over."

"What happened? You've been seeing her for quite a while."

"Another man."

"I knew it," Julia said.

"She was always stuck on herself," Victoria said.

Grace grimaced. "A trollop. Is there someone special in your life now?"

Army rubbed the medal again.

"Not sure."

"Not sure?" Julia said. "How's that?"

"It's complicated."

Chapter 39
The Patriarch

THE NEXT DAY was much better for the patriarch. He was watching the *I Love Lucy Show* when Army walked into the hospital room.

"Popi. You're sitting up."

Lazaro smiled. "Desi Arnaz is from Santiago de Cuba. Did you know that?"

"Yes. He was in the Fox Hole a few months ago."

The old man signaled the nurse to lower the volume on the TV. She did so and exited.

"How is the club doing?" he said as Army kissed him and pulled up a chair.

"Packed every day. Your voice is stronger. Your color is back. You look good. How do you feel?"

"Good today. Yesterday bad. Tomorrow, who knows?"

Then the elder Lobo lowered his voice. "Tell me the truth. Pull no punches. How are things over there?"

"I'd like to pay off the debt, Popi. I don't like these Mob guys having their hands around our throats."

"I know. I wish I could make them go away. What about the plantations? Does Stein have everything running smooth?"

"Stein said he works for you, not me. Plus, he looks like he's about to jump ship."

The old man frowned. "Jump ship?"

"He's getting too close to Big Bob."

Lazaro shook his head in disgust.

Army spoke about his interactions with Massi, Batista and Grau, and what happened to Alain and Hiran after he put Tony Stabo in the hospital.

"Massi took away your number one like you took away his," Lazaro said. "I can understand that. But not your baseball manager. He would not do that. Bad for business. I have been dealing with these Mafia guys for years. I know how they think. The baseball team is a contender, attracts bettors. Whoever had the manager beat up wanted you to think it was the mob. Someone like the guy who called me twice to buy the team."

Army shook his head in agreement. "I'm not surprised. Big Bob says he wants to buy the entire operation."

"I know. Stein is another story. He has been with us for a long time."

"He's gotta go, Popi. Can't be trusted. He's a gambler with debts, too."

The old man nodded. "I know all about gambling debts. Thank God I'm out of that world now. If you feel like you must replace him, George Fowler would know where to find another plantation manager. He has plantations in Colombia."

Then the patriarch nodded. "But Stein is part of the family, son. With me a long time. Get him help for his gambling, like you did for me. What is Batista like in your meetings?"

"He listens and seems to want to help."

"And Grau?"

"An animal. I don't like him and he doesn't like me."

"Be careful. He has power. He can hurt you. Stay out of his way. He is not important to us. What about this communist you killed in Centro Lobo? Are there more of them out there?"

Army looked astonished to hear that question from his father. "You too?"

"What?"

"Think I killed the commie. It was my bodyguard, supplied by Batista. But yes, I am concerned about sabotage. However, the president has the garrison at Camp Columbia on alert about trouble on the plantations."

"Are you making the vig payments directly to Massi?"

"Yes. But still, I'd like to pay this thing off."

The old man shrugged. "You have to think ahead. The big one is close enough with the Italians to buy the note from them. Then he will squeeze us out.

"But he's a cheapskate. Besides, what leverage does he have? He's not Italian. He doesn't even like Italians. And I'd bet that they'd put him in a pine box if they had a reason for it."

The old man sighed. "Forget cheapskate. He has big money. He also has Irish muscle in Boston. He could bring it to force us to sell. We do too much good for our plantation workers and their children to let the big goof or anybody else get their hands on the business."

Army smirked. "The Irish Mob, in Havana? That's like Eskimos in Arizona. Seriously, a war would break out with the New York Mob. It's more likely that he'll hire communists to sabotage us. If we can't produce and we can't pay the vig or the principle, we lose everything to the note holder. Then the big boob could buy it and force us out."

Lazaro didn't miss a beat. "That's where the muscle comes in, whether it's Irish or Italian."

A coughing spasm had Lazaro reaching for a pitcher, which his son grabbed quickly and filled a glass with water. The old man sipped and the coughing stopped. He took a deep breath.

"I was an orphan. Had it not been for the kindness of a landowner and a stroke of good fortune, we'd all be laboring on a sugar cane plantation. It's good that we remember where we came from. Good that we give back."

Army gripped his father's hand and squeezed it. He felt his emotions rise and his eyes well, but he fought it. His voice cracked.

"That's right, Popi. But we don't have that much more to give." He let go and composed himself.

"How was your relationship with Massi before the fight?"

"Good."

"What about Junior?"

Army paused.

"What about Junior?"

"Not good."

"Why?"

He swallowed and waited a beat.

"Titi."

"Titi? What does she have to do with this?"

Army looked his father in the eyes. Suppressed anger rose.

"Junior sent his bodyguard, who brought Tony along to smash up her dressing room with baseball bats. I was there with her. When it was over, Tony said: 'Junior says that's what'll happen to your legs if yous two can't keep your pants on.'"

His father didn't blink. This boosted his anger a notch and his voice rose.

"Before that happened, the leader of the FEU came into my bar. He said he was the bastard son of a whore and a capitalist swine who gave me the plantations. His name was Ernesto."

The old man showed no remorse. A long, deep breath parted his lips.

"I knew that you would find out, son. Sorry you had to learn this the way you did. One thing led to another and …

"Did you love her? Did you love Titi?"

Lazaro thought for a moment. He didn't want to answer. But his son pressed him.

"Dad, did you love her? Did you love Titi?"

The elder Lobo looked down at the tube in his right wrist rather than answer.

Army turned his head and stormed out of the room, nearly knocking over his mother and sisters, who were entering. The ladies looked at each other, perplexed, then at the elder Lobo sitting up.

———•◆•———

That evening the family gathered at the house for a pheasant dinner in the dining room, where a large gold-framed painting of Liam in a US Army dress uniform hung.

Army was quiet. He blew cigarette smoke rings while his sisters, their husbands and children, aunts, uncles, and cousins all sat around a massive table eating and chatting about school, sports, business, politics, and chocolate. All were happy that the Charmer from Santa

Cruz seemed to be coming around. He'd been watching TV and that was a good sign.

Army excused himself and retreated to the den. He sat at his father's desk, clicked on a small lamp, picked up the telephone, and tried the convent in Havana, no answer. He called the bar. Celia answered. It was 10:00 p.m. and the background noise was loud. He had to shout.

"Celia, it's Army. How is everything?"

"Someone looking for you today."

"Who?"

"Big Bop."

"Anyone else?"

"No."

The line went dead.

He hung up the receiver and fell back into his father's leather chair. His heart ached for Bonita. He worried about her. Where was she? What was she doing? Was she with the rebel in the family?"

He sat there in the dim light of his father's desk, thinking, until he could no longer ignore the hubbub in the dining room. He clicked off the light and stood when the phone rang. He picked up the receiver in the dark.

A man's voice said: "Hello, is this the Lobo residence?"

"Yes, this is Armando Lobo."

"This is Doctor David Fischer from the University of Pennsylvania Hospital. I'm sorry Mr. Lobo. Your father passed a half hour ago. He died peacefully in his sleep."

Stunned, Army hung up and sat motionless for about five minutes before walking into the room full of cheer. But one look at his face brought about a hush.

"He's gone," Army said with a shrug.

Grace put down her fork and bowed her head. Victoria and Julia looked at each other and embraced. The children became quiet. All of her children rushed to Grace and hugged her.

Chapter 40
The Funeral

ON THE FRONT page of *The Philadelphia Spotlight* the next day below the fold of the eight-column broadsheet, there was a 5x3 black-and-white photo of the patriarch in his prime. He was movie-star handsome, a sort-of George Raft look-alike with black hair slicked back over dark eyes, a straight nose and lips that women loved to kiss.

Army looked at the photo and thought about his father's infidelity. But the overriding emotion was grief. He missed Popi.

The passing of the head of the family kept Sugar Man in Philadelphia much longer than he'd anticipated. Bonita was foremost on his mind.

There was also the vig. The due date for the interest payment already had passed. A late payment would double it. But the remaining vig died with his father. At least that's what Army thought.

He also ruminated about a cabinet meeting taking place without him that day. Would Grau undermine him even more? If so, would it affect his plans to put people to work? Was Ernesto creating more problems for him?

He called the convent every fifteen minutes from the Bryn Mawr house. No answer. Finally, someone picked up the phone.

"Hello, this is Armando Lobo calling from the United States. Can I speak with Bonita Di Riva please?

"She is not here," the voice on the other end replied, curtly."

"Well Mother, will you please tell her to call me, collect? My phone number is …"

"She cannot use the telephone for personal business. Thank you for calling." The line went dead and he sizzled. He smashed the phone into the cradle. When he cooled off he called the Fox Hole. It was 11:00 a.m. and El Angel answered.

"Angel, this is Army, how is everything?"

"Good Armando. I saw the newspaper. Sorry to hear about your father."

"Thank you. Where is Celia?"

"One minute."

Celia took the phone. She was out of breath. "Armando. I just come to work. Where are you?"

"Still in Philadelphia. I won't be back for a while."

"I am so sorry to hear about your Popi."

"Thanks. Do me a favor. Find Bonita and tell her to call me collect from the Fox Hole. You have my number."

"Are you okay?"

"Yes, thanks. But please tell her to call me."

———— ◆ ————

Army was in his father's study the following night when he received a collect call. "Hello, Armando," Bonita shouted. The background noise was loud. "Celia allowed me use the phone behind the bar. I'm sorry to hear about your father. How are you?"

"Okay now. It's so good to hear your voice. I'll be tied up here for a while. What have you been doing?"

"I just came from my class at the university. The students are demonstrating every day. I listen to their complaints. I agree with them."

"Fine. Just don't get involved. It's dangerous. You can get arrested, or worse."

"What did you say?"

"I'll be home in a week. I miss you."

"I miss you too."

The line went dead.

Chapter 41
Ernesto and Bonita

WHEN BONITA HUNG up the phone she noticed a familiar face squeezing through an opening at the noisy bar.

"Señorita. You are working here?' Ernesto said loudly.

She looked at him warily and shook her head negatively.

Celia intervened, shouting: "What do you want, Barbudo?"

The rebel looked at her, stroked his beard and answered. "A Hatuey."

Celia reached down into a metal tub filled with ice and beer and slammed a bottle of Hatuey on the bar directly in front of the rebel. She opened it so that it sprayed him in the face, collected his fifty cents and waited on another customer.

Meanwhile, Bonita made her way around the bar and headed through the crowd when she found herself face-to-face with the miscreant. He was wiping away the suds on his beard with a handkerchief.

"Please," he said. "I have seen you at the University. Can I speak with you?"

"About what?"

"Pablo."

He took her breath away. She was more shocked at hearing Pablo's name than the source from which it came. And more curious about what was to be said than who was saying it.

"Pablo?

"Yes. He was a good soldier for the cause. Can we talk?"

She followed Ernesto to his usual unoccupied table in a corner of the room near the main entrance. They sat facing each other, the rebel with his back to the crowd, and Bonita with her back to the wall. He knew that he had her full attention and he milked it.

"Pablo always spoke about his girlfriend and how he planned to get married. I did not know it was you until I saw you at the University. So, I made an inquiry."

"Inquiry? Who did you speak with?"

"Manzanillo."

Her eyes widened. "Yes, his friend. Oh my. He was to be our best man."

The reprobate reached across the table and placed his hand on hers. At that moment Celia appeared, placed a hand on a hip and confronted the bearded one.

"What do you think you are doing, Barbudo?"

Ernesto looked up at his antagonist and answered calmly: "Having a discussion with a friend, sister."

"I am not your sister and she is not your friend."

Bonita withdrew her hand. "It's all right, Celia. He knew my Pablo."

"Pablo? *Aye, mi madre.*" Celia walked away.

He continued. "Funny how Pablo never mentioned you by name. Manzanillo put the name with the face." And then the reprobate shook his head sadly: "I was so distraught to learn that my brother killed Pablo, my good friend."

"Your brother? Jomar?"

"No. Armando."

"Armando is your brother?"

"You did not know? *Que carajo.* His father impregnated my whore mother, Titi Randal. I was the result, a bastard without his capitalist father's name. I am a son of a bitch. And Armando is worse. He slept with my mother."

"What?" Her mouth was agape while Ernesto bit his bottom lip in anger. "Capitalists and whores invade my life!" he exclaimed."

The Barbudo clenched the cocktail glass into which he'd poured his beer so tightly that it exploded, sending shards and suds in all directions. Bonita jerked backward and wiped her face and chest with her hands. Celia returned with a short towel and a wet rag. She handed the towel to Bonita and used the rag to push the suds and broken glass onto Ernesto's lap before storming off into the crowd.

He stood in anger, his hand bleeding. "*Muchacha*," he shouted at Celia. "Are you stupid or crazy?" Onlookers at tables nearby frowned at the scene and followed Celia to the bar with their eyes.

On his way to the men's room the student leader crossed paths with Grau, who'd just entered the Fox Hole. They stared at each other momentarily.

The convent communist stood behind the chair, wiping herself with the towel when the communist hunter made his way to a table where three men sat nearby. They saluted him upon arrival.

Taking her seat, she overheard a conversation between the well-dressed man, and the others. "That communist son-of-a-bitch," the well-dressed man said. "He will be mine. It is only a matter of time. Who is the girl, Jorge?"

"She is the fiancé of the communist. You know, the one killed on the Lobo plantation."

Bonita looked directly at the inquisitor, who turned around to look at her. She did not know that he was the Chief of the Anti-Communist Squad.

"Interesting," he said, looking at her up and down.

She handed the towel to the still-fuming rebel when he returned. He wrapped it around his wounded hand and sat with wet, khaki pants. Without turning around, he lifted a thumb and pointed it backward.

"See those men behind me?" he said. "Animals. Batista's dogs."

But she was still thinking about what Ernesto had said about Armando sleeping with his mother. Was Ernesto telling the truth?

She stared at him. His explosive temper reminded her of Pablo. And like Pablo, the rebel was dogmatic, intellectual, and unshaven. She'd heard Ernesto's fiery speeches, which had frightened and fascinated her. She decided to set him straight.

"Armando did not kill Pablo.".

"What?"

"Armando. He did not kill Pablo."

"You are so naive."

"And you are telling a false story. Armando took me to the scene. I spoke with someone who was there. It was not Armando."

Ernesto looked surprised. "Armando took you to the plantation?"

"Yes."

"You are seeing him? That capitalist swine, pretty boy? My mother's fucker?"

"He is a good man. You should try to know him."

The rebel's anger seethed. "And he should try to know me. Better yet, you should know me. And what Pablo fought for. What I fight for. What we fight for. What you should fight for in Pablo's name."

She didn't back off. "I agree with the cause, but not the violence. Pablo's passion to change things scared me. You scare me."

"But you loved him, no?"

She stared at him. "Yes."

Ernesto pulled a piece of paper from his shirt pocket, wrote something with his injured right hand and gave it to her.

"We are having a meeting tomorrow night at the University. Please come and hear what we have to say." He nodded at the table where Grau and the detectives sat and added: "Now I must leave before the hounds devour me."

Chapter 42
The Reception

THE VIEWING AT the Cathedral of Saints Peter and Paul in Center City Philadelphia was well attended. Local dignitaries as well as State Department representatives and even the Mayor of Havana were present. The Havana Mob appeared in the form of flowers. Batista, too. The stragglers were Big Bob and Fay, who'd arrived together on a late flight from Miami.

The patriarch had the kind of sendoff reserved for a head of state. It was well deserved. Lazaro Lobo Figueredo might not have had scruples when it came to his marriage vows, but he had a social conscience, like Grace. Coupled with their hard work and charitable endeavors, they gave capitalism a good name on both sides of the Atlantic at a time when communism was gaining ground in Europe.

———◆———

The luncheon that followed the burial was held in the ballroom of the Bellevue-Stratford Hotel. Army sat at the center of the dais. Grace and his sisters were to his right. On his left was the Most Reverend John Joseph Sheen, C.S.C., archbishop of Philadelphia. He was a large and loquacious man, but he had a serene quality that drew people to him.

He spoke Spanish fluently because of his schooling by the Franciscans in Havana in the 1920s. As Delegate to the Military

Vicar during the war, he had appointed the chaplains in Europe, including the one who'd ministered to Army after the deaths of his brother and Serena. He knew the family well.

Rising and giving guests the traditional mealtime blessing, the archbishop sat and spoke with the new head of the family while they waited for the servers.

"So Armando, how are you doing spiritually?"

"Spiritually? I don't know. I guess I haven't thought about it, Archbishop."

"Are you over the young lady you lost and your brother?"

He shook his head in dismay. "I still have nightmares."

The Archbishop nodded in sympathy. "Once you can look inward, you'll find answers. It must be difficult to get your bearings amid all of the corruption in Cuba. Capitalism has its drawbacks."

He gave the prelate a look.

"I'm not talking about you, Armando. You and your family have been very generous and fair. When capitalism is propelled by greed it's destructive. And those blinded by greed will be devoured by it."

"There are many other generous capitalists, Archbishop. Too bad Katherine Drexel isn't here. She has given away a fortune to help American Indians. Her father, an investment banker, was a philanthropist before she was. Here in Philadelphia."

The Archbishop shook his head in agreement.

Army pulled a pack of Lucky Strikes from his coat pocket and offered one to the priest, who declined. "Capitalism has its flaws, Archbishop. But what about communism? It subjugates its workers to the party bosses, who reap the fruits of their labor."

The Archbishop looked at him with disappointment. "I do not espouse communism, Armando."

"Maybe not communism, Archbishop, but you have to admit that the Church practices socialism, the cousin of communism. And I understand that. Your mission is to help the poor."

He lit a cigarette and blew a cloud of smoke into the air. "I can live with capitalism, even if it is corrupt."

The Archbishop shook his head as though he understood. "So you've succumbed to corruption?"

Army exhaled smoke from his nostrils: "Some things you don't want to know, Archbishop."

Out of the corner of his eye he noticed Fay and her father entering the room. The big man waved to the Lobos and accompanied his daughter across the floor to a round table with a white table cloth, where there were two empty seats among twelve.

They sat and ate with the rest of the guests and when they were nearly finished Army walked over to them. Big Bob had forked the last chunk of steak into his mouth when he looked up at him.

Still chewing, he said: "Your father was a great man and I'm sorry for him leavin' us so soon."

He nodded in the affirmative.

"Meantime, I just wanna remind ya that I'm ready to make a fair offer for the whole shebang, the plantations, the refineries, the railroad, the team. Whatdaya say?"

Army scoffed. "If you have all this money, why are you mooching off me?"

"Mooching? Whatdaya mean?" the big man said as he wiped his mouth with a linen napkin.

"My sugar train. You've been hitchin' a ride."

Big Bob thought for a moment. "I'll have to talk with my plantation manager."

"Not a bad idea. You don't know who you can trust these days. And oh, Massi said he's upset about what happened to my baseball manager."

He made up the last part, and his adversary looked worried. But he came right back at his rival, standing and looking down at him. "I will have it all, one way or another. I promise."

Before a retort could be given another voice interrupted. "Sorry I'm late, I had some business in New York and took the first train out."

Army turned to see Fowler, his plantation-owner peer. They shook hands and stepped away from the table.

"George, good to see you. Thanks for coming."

"Thanks, I'm so sorry I never got to tell your father how much I admired him."

"Thank you, George. My father mentioned you before he died. He said you might know a good plantation manager for us."

"What happened to Stein?"

"I have to replace him."

"Sorry." He thought for a moment and added: "I was in Colombia last week. There's a guy who managed plantations for me, until his wife and children were killed in a freak accident at the mill. He hasn't worked since. I'll talk to him."

"Thanks George."

"Have you had any more problems with sabotage?"

"No. You?"

"My farm in Cienfuegos. Torched the mill. Bastards. We caught 'em and turned 'em over to Grau's squad."

"Did I hear Grau's name?" a middle-aged man interrupted.

The two turned to see the Mayor of Havana, short and stout Aldo Agremonte. "First let me give you my condolences, Armando. Batista sends his, as well. He has also sent more soldiers to secure the plantations on the outskirts of the capital. The situation with the communists is worsening."

Chapter 43

Fay Almost Has Her Way

WHEN AGREMONTE AND Fowler drifted away, Fay stepped in, kissed Army on the cheek and hugged him.

"Everyone loved your father. He was so charming. He was always nice to me. I'm so sorry."

"Thanks."

"Join me for a drink?" she said.

He shrugged: "Okay."

They walked to the overcrowded bar, where well-wishers shook hands with him and offered consolatory words. She ordered two Bacardis and Coke and as time ticked by they drank more and more. Suddenly, Victoria and Julia appeared. They waved to their brother and his friend, who waved back.

"We're getting ready to return to the house," Victoria said.

Julia interjected: "Are you coming, Army?"

Obviously, the guest wasn't invited.

Feeling her angst and his sisters' displeasure, he smiled: "I'll catch you back at the house."

Julia raised an eyebrow, looked at Victoria and they walked away.

Fay waited until they were out of sight. "So how was your date?" she said.

"What date?"

"At the convent last week. You forgot?"

"The date? No. I didn't forget."

Pushing up her breasts she repeated: "So how was it?"

"Fine. What do you want me to say?"

"Nothing, really. It's just that a convent is an unusual place for a date."

"Maybe she's unusual"

The former Boston beauty queen adjusted Army's tie and ordered two more cocktails. They drank until the bar closed, and steadied each other while walking to the lobby

Without warning, Fay pulled Army into an open elevator. She pressed a button, the doors closed and they were on their way. He knew that she and her father had rooms upstairs. Any thought he had about resisting had been suppressed by alcohol.

But it was his curiosity more than rum that made him go along for the ride. She was the embodiment of pleasure and pain. Had anything changed?

"I'm going to freshen up, make yourself comfortable," she said after they entered her room, illuminated by street lights and neon signs shining through a picture window.

Army sauntered to the queen-size bed and sat on the edge facing the bathroom. He saw a light under the door, leaned to the right and gently laid his head upon a fluffy pillow. Within a minute he was asleep. He dreamed about Bonita, felt her warm breath on his neck and relaxed in her caress until morning, when he awakened with Fay's arms wrapped around him.

Gently he disentangled himself from her embrace, turned and looked at her in repose. He admired her naked body for a moment, turned and tip-toed out the door.

Chapter 44
Cutter's Call

ON FRIDAY MORNING Army trotted down the stairs to have breakfast and saw his mother on the telephone. She handed it to him.

"It's a friend."

"Sorry I couldn't show my face, either one, at the funeral," the caller said. "Did you get the flowers?"

"Yes. Thanks Mr.Cutter. How are things over there?

"I have a copy of 'The Havana Post.' Somebody you know made the news. The headline reads: *'Three Wounded as Police Break Up Student Rally.'* Listen to this." He read:

Shooting erupted at midday yesterday at 23rd and L Sts. as police tried to dissolve an incipient student demonstration. The students had strung a length of black cloth across L St. and put up posters. Undergraduate student Bonita Di Riva, 25, was arrested at San Lazaro and Infanta as she was pinning black crepe on the lapels of passersby. A group of students stoned a police car. Police fired into the air. Students erected garbage-can barricades. They also set off a series of powerful rockets that sounded like machine guns and alarmed the neighborhood. Ernesto Randal, 20, president of the Federation of University Students, was arrested while lighting a bonfire on the grand stairways of the university. Firemen were pelted with stones. Police fired 200 shots into the air. Three young men were held at the disposal of Urgency Court. At the Ninth Police Station 25 more students were under arrest and awaiting court action.

"Looks like little brother's in trouble, again, Cutter said. "Maybe this time Grau'll get ahold of him."

Army exploded. "Son-of-a-bitch!"

"What?"

"I warned her about Ernesto."

"Who?"

"The girl. The hell with Ernesto. Get over to the Ninth Precinct. You've gotta get Bonita Di Riva out. Quick. Don't let Grau get his hands on her. Do whatever you have to. I'll be there tomorrow."

Cutter hadn't heard that kind of urgency in his buddy's voice since Istanbul. He asked no more questions as he hung up and went to work.

———— ◆ ————

It was Friday afternoon when the chauffeur arrived at the mansion to drive the Lobos to the law offices of Kelly, Penn, and Pepper. In the limo Army kept thinking about Bonita, the rebel, and the communist hunter. He pursed his lips. He was seething with anger. Mainly at Ernesto.

Suddenly, he felt his mother's gentle hand on his clenched fist.

"What's wrong, son?"

Feeling her tender touch, hearing her soft voice momentarily reclaimed him from the world of dark thoughts. He turned and looked into her blue eyes, partially obscured by the black, netted veil surrounding her pillbox hat. He sighed and placed his hand on hers.

"Business, Mother. Just business."

On the fifteenth floor of the Land Title Building in Center City the reading of the will went on with no surprises, until the end.

"…and finally," the attorney read, "I leave my former accountant's house in Santa Cruz to the Randal family of Marianao."

That was it. No explanation. Just the Randal family of Marianao.

Grace and the girls looked at each other, then at Army.

"Who are the Randals? Son?"

He felt his mouth going dry. The only sign that he was unnerved by the inquiry was that he pulled a pack of Lucky Strikes from his shirt pocket and spilled four cigarettes onto the carpeted floor. He gathered them up quickly before anyone else could help. He looked up red faced and smiled. He knew that his answer had to be vague if he were going to protect his mother and sisters from his father's infidelity.

"A family in Marianao."

"But who are they?" Victoria said. "Why would Popi leave them a house?"

He shrugged. "I guess he had a good reason."

"What kind of a house is it?" Victoria said.

"Stone and wood. It's like a little fortress when the shutters are latched."

"Do you know them?" Julia said.

"Yes."

"Well, what do you think, son?"

He pulled on his shirt collar. "I think we should move on, mother."

Grace looked at the girls, who shrugged.

Army turned to Victoria's husband: "Girard, I'm putting you in charge of the entire operation here, with the proviso that all major business decisions be cleared with me, first. These things are defined in the documents already drawn up by Mr. Kelly."

Kelly handed legal papers to Grace, who signed the first set of documents in which her dead husband's business was transferred to her. In turn, she signed over the company to her son, who delegated authority to Girard. Army kissed his mother and shook hands with Girard and Kelly. With that, all legal matters were closed.

Chapter 45
Flying Blind

THE FLIGHT FROM Philadelphia to Miami was uneventful. But the Cubana connector to Havana was delayed. Army paced the floor at Miami Airport and looked at his wristwatch. It was already 6:00 p.m. and three calls to Cutter had gone unanswered. He had no idea what he was flying into when he got back, but he wanted to get there as soon as possible. Then the public address system echoed:

"Cubana Air Flight 3231 will board in thirty minutes at Gate Five."

When he arrived at the gate he found himself standing among men only. That's when he realized that this was no ordinary flight. He was on the Tropicana Special. The party plane that would be met by a bus that transported male passengers to the Tropicana Club Casino and Cabaret, where they would see a production with the finest-looking showgirls this side of Las Vegas, drink, and gamble the night away. Also available were cocaine, heroin, marijuana, and beautiful young Cuban women offered by taxi drivers who loitered at the entrance.

Army stepped onto the tarmac, where he saw Cubana's Lockheed Constellation Airliner. The propeller-driven, four-engine airplane looked like a giant seagull. Inside, the first eight seats had been removed and replaced with a stage and curtain.

About ten minutes after takeoff the drapery opened and a quartet of costumed musicians started playing a salsa song while a sexy singer and her male counterpart began gyrating.

Within minutes the chica danced down the aisle, plopped herself onto a passenger's lap and pulled him out of his seat. Thus, a conga line was born. The gentlemen were being prepped for a weekend of overindulgence in sensual pleasures.

Army had a window seat and was beyond the grasp of the lovely young dancer. He was too upset to enjoy the mid-air party, anyway. He noticed a copy of a newspaper smashed into the back of the seat in front of him. He pulled it out and saw that it was The Havana Post's Thursday edition.

He scanned the headlines: *National Association of Sugar Mill Owners Visit Minister of Agriculture; World Sugar Labor Meeting Opens Here; Batista's Doctors Declare Him Cured of Chicken Pox; Pittsburgh Pirates beat Havana, 3-2.*

He searched for more news about the students' clash with the police. He found none.

When he deplaned, he picked up his luggage with the partiers, walked through the airport and out the entrance to hail a cab. But he didn't need one.

"Over here," yelled Cutter.

The spy was wearing his brown wig-and-mustache disguise and waving from the driver's seat of a 1950 Ford sedan. He slipped on a pair of black-framed sunglasses when his passenger tossed his suitcase into the back seat and hopped into the front.

"How'd you know I was on this flight?"

"The only other one was cancelled."

"What's the situation?"

Cutter shrugged. "I couldn't get her out. Grau said ..."

Army exclaimed: "Grau? Is she at the Fifth Precinct??

"No, the Ninth."

"So what's Grau got to do with this?"

"She must have mentioned your name to the police at the Ninth. They held her for the Chief of the Anti-Communist Squad. Who is this chica, anyway?"

"I thought you knew everything. Even before it happens."

Cutter smirked. When they arrived at the Ninth, he waited in the car while Army raced inside and up to the desk sergeant. He flashed his credentials.

"Good evening. I am Minister of Labor Armando Lobo, here for a prisoner named Bonita Di Riva."

They sergeant looked up her name in a ledger and delivered the bad news. "She has been transferred to the Fifth Police Station."

Chapter 46
Bonita's Ordeal

IT WAS 9:45 p.m. when Cutter parked in front of the Fifth Precinct. He waited in the car again while Army rushed in.

He ran up to the long, elevated mahogany desk that stood in front of the back wall, overlooking the entrance to the building. He looked up at the sergeant, a thin man who appeared to be in his early twenties.

"Good evening, I'm Minister of Labor Armando Lobo." He showed his credentials. "I'm here for a prisoner."

"Who is it, sir?"

"Bonita Di Riva."

The sergeant's eyebrows raised as if he knew the name.

"Oh. I am sorry, sir. Only Lieutenant Colonel Grau can release her and he will not return until Monday morning."

Army glared. "Call him, now."

"At his home?"

"Immediately!"

Afraid to challenge an official, the sergeant picked up a telephone receiver and dialed.

"Sir, this is Arturo, desk sergeant at the … Yes, thank you. I am sorry to disturb you at home but … Yes, thank you. The Minister of Labor is here for the prisoner you instructed us to hold. What shall I do?"

The sergeant handed the telephone to him.

"Hello, Grau, this is Armando Lobo. Thanks for taking my call on a Friday night. At home."

"Si, Señor Lobo. Normally, I do not take calls when I am relaxing with my wife and children; however, this case has my ear. Give me a second to move the phone to a quieter room …

Army looked up at the dim lighting, sniffed the stale air and wrinkled his nose in disgust. He soaked up the depressing atmosphere with a sigh.

Grau returned to the phone. "Okay, the young lady said she knows you. I remembered her from your bar, where she was with your miscreant brother, last week. She is the fiancé of the communist killed on your property. Should I be concerned?"

"No. She is not a communist like her deceased boyfriend. And she's not violent. She's just a student who has fallen in with the wrong group."

Grau scoffed. "The wrong group? Ernesto is the worst. Only his mother saves him from me. But that will not go on forever."

"I'd like to bail her out."

The line went silent for a moment. "Humm. And why should I help a cabinet member who challenges me at our meetings?"

"Because it's the right thing to do."

Silence followed for several seconds until he spoke again. "On one condition, otherwise I will find a way to hold her indefinitely."

"What?"

"That she refrain from anti-government activities. If she is arrested again, I will show no mercy to her because I know who she associates with."

"I'll tell her what you said. You've been reasonable. Thank you."

"One more thing. How is she in bed?"

Army gritted his teeth. "I wouldn't know."

He passed the phone to the sergeant and soon a policeman led him to a window where he paid $100 bail. The officer led him to the basement stairs. As they descended, the odor of urine intensified.

The cell nearest to Grau's torture chamber held one person: the female protester from the convent. The three dungeons next to hers held women. The ones across housed men, who continually tried to engage them in conversation, especially Bonita. However, after more than forty-eight hours of the insanity of incarceration in the Fifth Precinct basement, where each female used the cell room toilet in full view of the men and vice versa, the teacher was silent.

"Honey, I want to see you pee again," a prisoner in a lockup across from her said when the Minister and the police officer arrived in the basement.

"Shut up, pervert," another inmate said. "Take your clothes off, sweetheart."

Army observed Bonita sitting quietly on a bench when the policeman slipped a large key into a brass lock. She was wearing the same worn dress she had on during her first visit to the Fox Hole. He choked up at the sight.

"Armando!" she exclaimed as the gate swung open. She ran to his embrace.

"Armando!" the pervert yelled.

"Armando!" the pervert's critic yelled.

Unable to talk, Army embraced her tightly.

Before long all of the men were yelling Armando's name repeatedly during the long embrace. The policeman urged them out of the cell and up the stairs to freedom.

They were out of the precinct and into the auto in a flash. The couple sat in the back seat and the car sped away from the police station. Bonita placed her head on his shoulder and held his hands in silence until Cutter turned right onto Fifth Avenue.

"Wanna talk about it?" Army said.

"Just hold me."

"Cutter, the Fox Hole."

Cutter sped through the tunnel that connected Fifth Ave. to the Malecón and within five minutes they were passing the convent. Bonita raised her head, looked, and said nothing. Ten minutes later they pulled in front of the Fox Hole and parked in back of his Chevy on Animas. Luggage in hand, he guided her up the outside stairs to the sliding doors, opened them with a key, and locked them after they were inside.

"How about a drink," he said.

"I need a shower," she replied.

Army led her to his bedroom. He showed her the shower, towels and a white robe that had been left there by Fay. He retreated to the living room, made himself a Bacardi and Coke and relaxed. Bonita appeared thirty minutes later in the robe, her black hair wet, wild, and gleaming.

"Cuba Libre?" he said.

"Yes, please."

He prepared the cocktail and gave it to her with a look of displeasure.

"What's wrong?" she said.

He sipped his drink and sat, facing her at the kitchen counter.

"What's wrong? I warned you about Ernesto. What's wrong? You didn't listen. What's wrong? You were arrested. Even worse, you were arrested with the worst agitator in Cuba. The bad seed of my father."

She placed her drink on the counter and defied him. "I wanted to help the cause. I had no idea that violence would take place. You know that I oppose brutishness."

"Ernesto is a brute. Violence is his cause. And now you're associated with it."

"The cause is just," she shot back. "Even if he is not."

Army raised his voice. "Let me tell you who is not just. Grau. He released you to me with a warning. No more demonstrations. He is the Chief of the Anti-Communist squad. He tortures communists. Leaves their dead bodies in the street. He is vicious."

Alarmed but not bowed by his bluster, Bonita remained stoic. He studied her and saw a picture of intransigence, a strong will counterbalanced by his own. He sat closer to her while she sipped the cocktail. She got up, walked to the couch and sat with arms folded in front of her. He followed and sat next to her.

Looking straight ahead she said: "Is it true that you slept with Ernesto's mother?"

She turned to see his reaction. He didn't hesitate. "Yes. Before I meet you. I didn't know the devastating story about her, Ernesto, and my father until the very day I saw you. The happiest day of my life."

He moved closer to her, placed one of her soft hands in his and stroked it. Her head fell onto his shoulder. Her body went limp. And soon she fell asleep.

Gently, he laid her down on the couch and placed a pillow under her head before stepping back and admiring her. She was irresistible. He scooped her into his arms, walked through the open bedroom door and gently placed her on his bed. He turned out the ceiling light, stripped down to his boxer shorts and laid next to her, stroking her hair as the fan above chased warm and humid air. He saw her eyes open.

"You don't know how much I missed you," he said.

She reached up with both hands and pulled his head down to hers. She kissed his lips once, twice, and then engaged them fully. Their tongues danced to the beat of their hearts. Her robe came undone, laying bare her firm, round breasts, petite nipples and shaved vulva. He was harder than a steel hammer. He wanted to bury it between her luscious thighs.

But as he prepared to mount her she stiff-armed him.

"No!" she said.

"What?" he said, breathless and confused.

She looked him in the eyes in an apologetic way. "I am a virgin."

"What? What about Pablo? You said you were engaged."

"Yes, engaged, not married. We never consummated our union. I would not, until I was married. And I will not, until I am married. I made a pact with God. My mother was pregnant with me by my father before they married. Then, she ran off with a former lover shortly after I was born and abandoned me in an orphanage. How do I know that you will not abandon me?"

Crestfallen, Army tried to understand. Was she telling the truth? Was she another Fay? Or worse? By now, his hammer had turned into a soft rubber toy.

"Did you love Pablo?"

"Yes.

"Do you love me?"

"I'm afraid. My feelings are so strong for you. What about you? Do you love me?"

"I loved you before I even met you."

"What do you mean?"

"I saw you. In my dreams."

She drew him to her bosom like a suckling baby and that's the way they slept until morning.

At sunrise, he slipped out of bed without disturbing her. He tip-toed into the kitchen and brewed a pot of coffee. He followed the aroma back to the bedroom. She opened her eyes, saw him, and smiled.

"Smells good," she said, stretching.

"Tastes good, too, come on."

Army was seated at the counter and reading Muja's report when she walked in. He hopped off his stool and grabbed the coffee pot, pulled out a stool for her, poured the coffee into two cups, and pushed a plate of sweet buns to her as she sat.

"How was your sleep?

"Restful," she said in a mournful way.

He hugged her tenderly.

"What are you reading?" she asked.

"This guy, Muja, Minister of Public Works, wrote a long report about the construction projects planned throughout the city, including three new hotels that are scheduled to go up. That means jobs, jobs, and more jobs."

"That's nice," Bonita said, sipping from the mug.

"I told Batista I wanted more of the inner-city people hired and he seemed to be okay with that. I want more people working. Better wages. Better schools."

In a quiet voice, almost a whisper, she countered.

"That's fine, but what about the corruption? The profits go to the dictator and his friends. Do you really think that he will increase wages, or hire those without connections?"

Army smiled. "He has to. The labor force is here. He'll need lots of labor, and I'm the Minister of Labor."

He toasted her with his cup and lowered his voice. "Are you all right to talk about what happened while I was gone?"

"No, I am not. Not yet."

"How long will you let this fester?"

"I don't want to talk about it now. How is your family in Philadelphia? How did everything go?"

He studied her and didn't respond.

Chapter 47
Army Warns Bonita

Bonita scanned the apartment from her perch on the kitchen stool. "Beautiful. I have never been in an apartment like this. The rug, the furniture, the art, the phonograph. What is that photo over there? Near the record player?"

Army stepped to a table on which the phonograph sat and picked up a gold-framed, 8 x 11-inch, black-and-white photo of the Lobo family thirty years earlier. He handed it to her.

"I think I can pick you out. You are the second boy on the sofa. Who is the first one?"

"My brother, Liam. He was killed in the war."

"I am so sorry. Who are the girls?"

"That's Victoria next to me and Julia next to her. We're all two years apart."

"And all so good looking. Your father and mother, too. I like the way they are standing in back of the couch guarding the nest, so to speak."

"My mother was the guardian more than my father, who was away most of the time. So, he assigned me to protect them all."

She looked at him. "Is that why you are so protective of me?"

He smiled. She grabbed his hand, nuzzled it and kissed it and looked up at him. "Did you inform Ernesto of your father's death?"

Army withdrew his hand. He bristled at the question. "Ernesto? Why would you bring up Ernesto?"

She paused. "He is your brother, no? At least that is what he told me."

"When?"

"The day I called you from your bar."

She became annoyed and stood, hands on hips. "Why did you not tell me he is your brother? Why did I have to learn this from him?"

Army looked away. He felt like he'd just been punched in the stomach, the same feeling he had when Ernesto revealed who he was. He spoke softly, barely audibly.

"I'm sorry. I'm still in disbelief. I'm having such a hard time accepting that I share the same father with such a grotesque figure."

Feeling his pain Bonita began to caress him.

"That my father might have loved him. That you might love him."

"What?" she said, pulling back. "How could you even think that? He is evil."

Army's eyes met hers. The volume in his voice turned up a notch.

"What happened in the bar?"

She stomped her foot on the floor like a petulant little girl. "I will not tell you. Not the way you are talking to me."

He pulled back and looked at her in a different way. Her fiery Latin temper aroused him. His heart began to pound. He reached out with both hands, pulled her to him roughly and planted a passionate kiss on her lips. She melted. For a moment. Then pulled away, turned and stomped to the living room, where she sat on the couch, arms folded, pouting.

At first he looked at her with concern, then with yearning desire. No woman had done that to him. He wanted her to love him, unconditionally. He walked slowly to the living room and sat near her.

"You must learn to trust me if I am to trust you," she said, staring ahead and still pouting.

"Trust?" he said. He moved closer to her. Stroked her silken hair. He looked into her alluring eyes. His lips close to hers. "I love you so much it hurts."

Her lips swallowed his. He scooped her into his arms, carried her to the bedroom and loved her to the limit imposed by her. They laid there naked afterward, engaging in small talk when Army brought up his rebel brother again.

"What happened that night in the bar?" he said.

She stared at the whirling ceiling fan. "Ernesto stopped me on my way out."

"What did he say?"

"He spoke about you. And he invited me to an FEU meeting at the University."

"And you said?"

"Yes. At the meeting he invited me to the demonstration."

He shook his head as though he'd expected that answer. "Well, guess who spotted you and him in my bar? Grau."

She faced him. "The man in the white suit." She looked frightened. "We were just talking."

"What about the riot at the University? You were pinning something on people's lapels. He was setting a fire. Shots were fired."

"How do you know this?"

"Your names were in the newspaper."

Stunned, she said: "It started out peacefully."

"It ended with you in jail." Army lowered his voice to a whisper. "And let me tell you something. You don't want to cross Grau. You should know. He placed you in a cell next to his torture chamber."

She stopped and recalled her incarceration in horror. "I heard the screams. It was terrifying."

"And don't forget about the smell of urine and creepy prisoners on the cell block. Don't ever forget it." He hugged her tightly. He whispered into her ear.

"Grau gave me a message for you before I bailed you out. Your next stop is the chamber if you're arrested at another demonstration. Don't demonstrate. And stay away from Ernesto. Please. For me."

His admonition was interrupted by the telephone. It rang three times before he picked up the receiver.

"Armando, this is George Fowler."

"George, are you back?"

"I'm back with good news. The Colombian I spoke about. He wants out of the country, but not the business. His name is Pastrami,

Jorge Pastrami. He's coming here tomorrow for the World Sugar Labor Meeting."

"Good. Can you set up a meeting?"

"No problem."

<h1 style="text-align:center">Chapter 48</h1>

<h1 style="text-align:center">A Good Bet</h1>

A T THE Fox Hole Army stuffed the weekend's cash earnings into a brown-leather satchel, zippered the top and buckled two leather straps stitched to the sides. He slung the bag over a shoulder in preparation for his weekly visit to the bank.

But first he walked to Massi's office to give him the final vig. The secretary said he was at the Oriental Racetrack.

He walked out of the Hotel Plaza and spotted the detective inside the Hudson smoking a cigarette. He wasn't surprised.

"Oriental Racetrack," he said. "Stop at the bank first."

Jomar made a right and cruised along the Prado. A tropical breeze blew through the open windows and it felt refreshing.

"Anything new while I was away?"

"No, Armando. Just the usual. Oh, there was something. The man who manages your farm. I was with a friend last week at the Sans Souci. We saw him win $10,000."

"Ten thousand? What was he playing?"

"Blackjack. Then he lost it all in one bet. Crazy guy."

Army nodded. "He's a crazy guy all right."

When they reached the Malecón, the breeze along the ocean boulevard was strong, cutting the mugginess in the air. But before they could enjoy it the engine stopped. Jomar coasted to a curb.

The detective popped the hood and steam hissed from the radiator. He looked underneath the car and saw fluid leaking.

212

"Armando, the radiator is broken."

"Okay. I'll walk back to my place and call a tow truck. Stay with the car."

Twenty minutes later Army pulled up to the Hudson in his convertible. "The tow truck is on its way. I'm going to the track."

"But I should be with you."

"Don't worry, I'll be okay."

He drove along the ocean boulevard, passing people young and old standing, sitting or fishing along the seawall, as they did day and night in a city where unemployment was high.

Rounding a curve in the highway near the convent, he spotted a beautiful girl sitting on the seawall. She was holding an umbrella in one hand and an open book in the other. The wind was blowing through her hair, lifting it off the collar of her white blouse.

He pulled over, blew the horn and she jumped.

"Hey honey, want a ride?" he hollered.

Bonita ran to the car. "Armando. You scared me."

"Why aren't you teaching?"

"A pipe burst in the classrooms. They are flooded."

"Get in. We're going to the racetrack."

"But I should remain close to the convent. In case Mother Superior needs me."

"Get in."

Captivated by his carefree command, the duty-bound schoolteacher tucked the book under her arm, secured the umbrella and hopped into the front seat. They both laughed as he sped away, their hair blowing in the wind like two teenage truants.

"What are you reading?"

"A new novel by Hemingway called *The Old Man and the Sea*."

"Great writer."

When they arrived at the Oriental Park Racetrack and Casino's parking lot in Marianao it was filled with American cars, Harley-Davidson motorcycles, and small trucks and buses. Army parked in a VIP space near the grandstand and stepped out of the car. She didn't budge.

"Are you coming?" he said.

"I don't know if I am dressed for this."

"You look fine. Come on."

She stepped out of the Chevy and joined him alongside the grandstands. When they entered the first row, they saw a sea of fancy hats in different colors worn by women in dresses designed to impress. Bonita stopped in her tracks.

"Armando, I'm not dressed for this."

"I forgot. This is like Kentucky Derby Day in the States. But we're here now. Please. We'll run up top where we won't be seen."

Before she could protest, he grabbed her by the hand and ran in front of the first row, past an animated assemblage of gamblers, thoroughbred racing enthusiasts, dilettantes and bon vivants eager to be part of a big event: The Oriental Stakes.

They raced up the steps to the clubhouse, but along the way he spotted Massi sitting near the top of the stands, even with the finish line. Next to him was a large man. Army stopped, nodded to the men and introduced Bonita, who looked embarrassed. Massi shook hands with her.

"Hi doll. Ain't you pretty," he said.

"Yeah, pretty," the big man agreed.

Bonita waited with her arms folded in the aisle while Army slipped onto an aisle seat next to Massi. He noticed that No. 7, Billy Boy, was circled in the last race on the program. Suddenly, he heard a voice that sounded familiar.

"Hey, how are ya?" said a man looking up from a seat below the mob boss. It's me, Sal, Sallie, remember?"

"Yes, I see you finally made it to the track."

"You know Sal?" the mobster said.

"Met him at the University. We got a good education."

As Army shook hands with the New Yorker he noticed that No. 7 was circled in the last race on his program, too. He turned to Massi and handed him an envelope.

"This is the last payment, Joe," he said.

The Mafioso counted the money.

"You're light."

"Light?"

"You missed the deadline. The vig doubled."

"My father died. I was in Philly for the funeral."

"Yeah, sorry about that. Did you get the flowers?"

"Yes, thanks."

The Mob boss didn't budge from his earlier statement. "Well, you have until the end of the week."

"For what?"

"The vig doubled. You were late."

Army became angry. And loud. "The vig's over. The debt's done. He's dead."

He didn't realize that he was shouting. Bonita leaned down and tried to pull him out of his seat. "Let's go Armando."

"That ain't the way we see it," Massi said, calmly. "The note was made in the name of the Lobo Corporation and signed by it's CEO, Lázaro Lobo, your father. You been payin' the vig, right? When you pay off the debt, the vig's done, the debt's done."

Army could contain himself no longer. He leaned forward, looked into the gangster's eyes and raised his voice in making a declaration for all within earshot to hear.

"My father's dead. The vig is over. The debt is over!"

Alarmed, the large man rose and attempted to grab him by the throat. However, he saw it coming, grabbed the man's wrist with his right hand and bent back his thick fingers with his left until the big one screamed.

Bonita blanched. "Armando!" she exclaimed.

Massi, seated in the middle of the altercation, looked up and issued a command.

"Stop it! Botha yous."

Army released his grip, the big man cradled his right hand with his left and sat like a child who'd just been spanked.

When the two calmed down, the Mafioso pointed to the big man. "This is Trabo. He'll be collectin' from you 'til Tony gets back. Pay off the debt and this is over."

Without uttering another word, Army rose, turned toward a sheepish Bonita and motioned for her to walk with him into the clubhouse.

"What happened?" she said.

"Follow me." He was still seething.

She trailed him to a wire rack where there were racing forms. He picked up two and gave her one.

"What just happened down there?"

Army looked at her. "Some things you don't want to know."

Bonita followed him outside, to empty seats at the top of the grandstand, from which she looked toward the racetrack. She remained silent for a while, watching the horses enter the gates. When the last jockey and horse trotted into the final gate she turned to her tutor.

"Oh, the horses are so beautiful. What magnificent creatures they are."

He smiled. "They're Pure breeds, originally from English mares and Arab stallions. We're going to bet on number seven, okay? We're lucky to be here for the last race."

"Is that what he said?"

"What?"

"Number seven?"

"No."

She opened her booklet to the final race.

"Armando, number seven, Billy Boy, is 15-to-1. That's bad, no? His chances of winning are not good."

"No, they're not. That's why we're betting on number seven, the chestnut colt. Here's $10. When you get to the window tell the clerk you're betting $10 on number seven to win in the last race."

"I'm nervous. Ten dollars is a lot of money. I could give this to the orphanage."

"Just do what I said, please."

The House of Charity teacher did as she was told and stared at the betting slip while Army gently moved her out of the way to place his bet. Then he did something reckless, something his father would have done. He'd never made it to the bank, so he unstrapped the leather bag, unzipped it and dumped the entire week's earnings onto the clerk's counter.

"Count it. Number seven, Billy Boy, to win, last race." The clerk's eye bulged. He counted the money for about five minutes, making others in line grumble. Finally, he gave the big bettor a slip.

The couple stood at the top of the grandstand seats and watched, fanning themselves with their programs under a sunny sky.

"Look, Billy Boy, he's behind gate nine, Armando."

"It's poor position, too much clutter in a twenty-horse field running a mile-and-a-quarter race."

"He's in a bad spot and he is 15-to-1. Why are we betting on him? Why not bet on this one, Rocket? He's favored, no?"

"Yes. Just hold tight."

The gun sounded. Rocket blasted out of the first gate. He beat the others to the rail. Billy Boy was last. In between, the rest of the field raced in a pack behind Rocket, who set a torrid pace in 90-degree heat, galloping the first quarter-mile in 22.30 seconds.

At the half-mile marker Rocket held a four-length lead, clocked in 45.40. The rest of the field followed in pairs along the rail. Billy Boy moved up steadily on the outside. On the last turn the jockey angled Billy Boy in front of the second-place horse. Rocket was the only obstacle between the chestnut colt and the finish line.

In the final furlong Billy Boy was running next to the rail, two-and-a-half lengths behind Rocket and closing on him fast.

The lovers were screaming hysterically now. They were joined by other spectators shouting for Billy Boy, Rocket, and other horses, a Tower of Babel amplified a thousand times.

Rocket was running out of fuel. His nose fell even with Billy Boy's on the outside. Rocket faded. Billy Boy surged. A half-length. A full length. A length-and-a-half when he blew past the finish line for the victory.

Billy Boy brought down the house. The ecstatic couple threw their programs into the air and hugged tightly. They jumped up and down in a circle for so long they almost fell off the top step. Others were doing a victory dance, too. Billy Boy paid $32.60 and the school teacher won more than two year's wages. Meanwhile, Army bagged a small fortune as the clerk pushed endless stacks of $20 bills to him with apologies. A happy, expectant Massi watched from the next window.

"Sorry about the twenties señor," the clerk said. "We have given you all of the $100 bills we have."

"*No problema,*" the big winner said as he shoveled the stacks into his leather bag and looked over at the leering mob leader.

But instead of handing over the doubled vig to the grinning Mafioso, Army winked. Massi stood there with a fast-fading smile.

Army turned to Bonita.

"Let's go."

"Must we?"

<hr>

During the drive down 41st Street Bonita was aglow. She held up the cash for him to see.

"I have never been so excited in my life, Armando. Look at this money! I can do so much good with this. Oh, what a day. I wanted to stay at the race track."

"The first thing to learn about betting is to quit while you're ahead. My father never learned that lesson, and I'm still paying for it."

"Those men. They are the Mafia? The ones you must pay?"

"I'd rather not talk about it."

"Are you in danger? I'm worried."

He shrugged and swung left onto 10th Street past the Clinica Ciro Garcia. A few blocks later he turned right onto Fifth Ave. and headed toward the Malecón.

"Please take me back to the convent," she said. "I must prepare a test for my students."

Bonita leaned over and kissed Army on the lips. He nearly crashed into another car as he entered the tunnel. Ten minutes later he pulled in front of the convent's entrance. She picked up her book on the front seat and gave him a peck on the cheek.

"Thank you for a beautiful afternoon, she said." He smiled.

As the teacher alighted from the car, she bumped into Father Luís, a wiry and bald little man who looked older than his fifty years. He wore a black cassock with a large gold crucifix dangling from a gold necklace. He seemed to be preoccupied.

"Oh, Father," Bonita said. "Are you okay?"

"Yes, thanks, but I am on my way to Iglesia Monserrate," he said in an Irish accent." Do you think your friend can give me a ride?"

Overhearing him, Army waved the priest to the car. "Hop in, Father. I know the church."

Chapter 49

Drinking Buddies

ARMY SPED ALONG the ocean boulevard and the little priest sized him up.

"You are Armando Lobo. Mother Maria José told me about you."

Army smirked, "I heard what she said about you, too."

"Touché," the clergyman said. "You do not look like Satan."

Army laughed. "And you don't look like a hopeless drunkard."

"I am not, really. But I do enjoy a glass of rum, occasionally. It assuages the stress of the job the Lord has given me. Mother and the rest of the nuns do not understand."

"There's nothing like a bottle of rum and a Montecristo to slow down the world, Father. Would you like a cigar?"

"Of course, my son,"

Army pulled two cigars, a Windmaster lighter, and a cutter from the glove compartment and gave them to the priest. He snipped the ends, lit them both, and gave one to the generous businessman.

"I do not remember seeing you at services," Father Luís said, puffing away.

"That's because I've never been inside," Army said while relighting his cigar.

"Then why don't you come in with me? I want to show you something. I have a surprise in my desk drawer."

At the direction of the little man of God, Army parked in front of the church on the corner of Galiano and Concordia. He grabbed the leather bag, slung it over his shoulder and walked into the church.

Inside he saw men, women, and children in and around the pews waiting for something. Some 100 adults sat there, many with blank looks on their faces, while their children played in the aisles. All of their clothing seemed to be hand-me-downs and most hadn't been washed for a while. It was a malodorous crowd.

"What are they waiting for, Father?" Army whispered as they bumped into children playing along a side aisle.

"Food. We feed them once a day. But supplies are dwindling. Money is tight. The Church in Rome can send only so much cash and the government here doesn't really help."

Army felt a tug on his sleeve. It was the boy who shined shoes outside the Fox Hole. He wore a big smile that put a shine on his soiled white T-shirt, torn trousers, and worn sandals. He greeted his benefactor.

"Armando."

"Hi Chino," Army said, shaking the sticky hand of his little admirer.

"I want you to meet my mother and father," the boy said, turning to a couple sitting in the pew to his left. "Mama, this is Señor Armando, from the Fox Hole."

A gaunt woman of about thirty-five and her husband of the same age looked up from their seats and smiled vacantly revealing rotting teeth. The bar owner tried wiping his sticky hand on a handkerchief before shaking hands with both. He pulled out pesos equivalent to ten dollars and handed them to the mother, who thanked him with a smile.

"You have a nice boy," he said, not knowing what else to say before turning to the muchacho.

"How has El Angel been treating you, Chino?"

The boy grinned. "Good, sometimes he even gives me lunch."

Army nodded happily. "You know, our dishwasher is leaving next month, Chino. It pays $3 a week. Are you interested?"

"Wow! Yes. When do I start?"

"Talk to El Angel."

Father Luís interrupted: "Come, come Armando." He pulled his new friend by the arm to get him past the people and through a doorway in back of the altar. Up a set of wooden stairs, they trotted, puffing on their cigars until they arrived at a door with the clergyman's name on a bronze plate—*Padre Luís, Pastor Luís.*

Once inside, the little priest flipped on a light and headed straight for a cluttered desk at the back of the room. He sat, opened a bottom drawer, pulled out a fresh bottle of rum with no label, and issued an order.

"Shut the door, Armando. Put down your bag and have a seat in front of my desk."

He complied, sitting on a simple wooden chair, sucking on his cigar, and thinking about how similar the situation was when he'd sat with Massi. The two chairs that faced the priest's desk weren't leather. And the paintings on the walls weren't of famous Italian-American athletes. But he was interacting with a much more powerful force than a mob boss and he knew it.

The petite padre eyed him. "You just shook hands with a dirty little boy and his mendicant mother and father in a church filled with paupers." Luis stretched both arms to place two empty water glasses next to a foot-high ceramic statue of a white dove with its wings spread on the front of the desk. "Now what does that tell me about a man who wears hand-made Italian shoes and expensive clothes?" he added, filling the glasses with a clear, white liquid.

Army looked at the statue of the dove and had a brief flashback to his evening in Celia's room. "Maybe I care," he said. "But I'm drinking with a priest who has a bottle of rum hidden in his desk in the same church. What does that tell me about him?"

"It tells you that being loving to his flock can be overwhelming at times and in the end, he is just a man, like you."

Army smiled and touched glasses with him. A loud knock on the door startled them.

"Who is it?" Father Luís said.

"Sister Mary. We are having a difficult time lighting these ovens again. The people are hungry."

"Call Fernando. He can do it."

Sipping from his glass and drawing on the cigar, the little man of the Lord opened a middle drawer and pulled out a baseball with signatures on it. His eyes lit up.

"This is my prized possession."

Catching a possible transgression, the priest looked heavenward and apologized. "God forgive me for coveting a material thing." He looked at his new acquaintance again and added, enthusiastically: "I have many of the New York Yankees' autographs on it going back to the 1930s, including Babe Ruth and Joe DiMaggio. I also have many of the old Boston Red Sox and players from other teams. But there is one player in particular that I am missing—Ted Williams. I heard he visits your bar. Do you think you can get his signature on here? Then, maybe I can sell this and pay for a new kitchen."

He gave the ball to his new drinking buddy, who twirled it and whistled. "Babe Ruth, Lou Gehrig, Joe DiMaggio, Lefty Grove, Mel Ott, Carl Hubbell, Jimmie Foxx, you got all these guys to sign this?"

"Yes. What do you think?"

He exhaled a smoke ring from his cigar. "I think you have a new kitchen without Ted Williams. But give me the ball before I leave and I'll have him sign it for you the next time he visits."

"Thank you, thank you," the priest said enthusiastically.

The two baseball fans touched glasses and didn't stop talking about their favorite sport until their final toast. By then the bottle was empty and they were lit like the cigars they'd smoked.

Throwing his head back and staring up at the cracked and discolored ceiling, Army blew smoke rings into the air. "You know, Father, I feel at peace here. At the convent, too."

Then he sat up and snuffed the cigar stub into an ashtray on the desk. Father Luís did likewise and nodded approvingly. Sugar Man bowed his head in thought and stared at the rotting, hardwood floor. "I have a secret, Father. Never told anyone this. Not even my best friend." He paused and looked up at the pie-eyed priest. "I wanted to become a priest. When I was in prep school."

Sobered momentarily by this personal revelation, Father Luís took on the somber visage of a pastor in a confessional. "I see God in you, Armando. The way you care about the less fortunate among us. Your compassion and love for them. So, what happened to your priestly ambitions? Your calling?"

He bowed his head, a tortured soul if ever there was one. "The war. I did things. Unforgivable things."

"Unforgivable things? Only the Lord can decide that. Do you want to talk about it?"

Army looked up: "Some things you don't want to know, Father."

"Me or you?"

"Huh?"

"Some things I don't want to know or you don't want to know, Armando? You cannot live your life in denial and have a real relationship with those around you and Christ."

Without turning around, the priest pointed a wobbly index finger at the back wall, where there hung a crucifix. "He died nailed to a cross. Hung there for hours in agony. Until his lungs collapsed and he suffocated." His voice rose and he pointed upward, as if he were giving a homily. "So that God the Father would forgive us our sins. There is no denying that. Everything is forgivable as long as you have a truly contrite heart." His voice lowered, he withdrew the finger. "And, of course, you confess, in a confessional."

Army rose slowly without commenting. He caught himself listing and leaned against the desk.

"Wow! What kind of rum was that, Father? Who made it?"

"Let us say only that some talented people attend services here."

Army laughed as the short priest rose and teetered with him to the door, where they shook hands and hugged.

"Please come around more often, Armando. I think we can become good friends."

"I do, too, Father."

"Wait," the little man of God said. "I forgot to give you the baseball."

The priest staggered back to his desk and picked up the ball when he noticed that Army's attaché case was on the floor nearby. He picked that up too and carried it to his guest.

"Here is the baseball, Armando. And here is your bag. It is quite heavy."

Army looked at the ball, twirled it and put it into his pants pocket. He grabbed the handles of the bag, stumbled back to the desk and opened it. With both hands he scooped up stacks of money and dropped them over documents, prayer books, newspapers, and a bible on the desk.

With eyes widened the priest looked at the pile of greenbacks and whistled. "Good Lord! How much is there, Armando?"

Silently he closed the bag, which provided him with balance as he swayed to the door. He glanced back at the crucifix on the wall and the dove on the desk. Then he turned to the priest and winked.

"Much more than the cost of a new kitchen, Father." He grabbed the priest's right hand and slapped the baseball into it. "On second thought, why don't you keep this until Ted returns."

Chapter 50
Bonita's Balloon Bursts

ONITA FELT AS though she was dancing on a cloud after the win at the track. She pressed the Hemingway novel to her bosom and waltzed into the courtyard. She spun in circles several times near the Tranquil Fountain.

"Oh what a day, the happiest day of my life," she said aloud as she tossed the book onto the stone bench and almost fell off when she sat. Drunk with delight, she laughed at herself and pulled the cash from her pocket. She stared at it.

"We can do so much good with this. I cannot wait to tell Mother."

"Mother is here," Maria Jose said from the main entrance to the courtyard.

Pushing the cash back into her pocket, an excited Bonita said to the nun: "Mother, what would you say if I told you that we have enough money to repair the pipes?"

"Well, I would say it was a blessed day."

"And what would you say if I said that we can also fill our pantry with enough food to last the rest of the year?"

"I would say that the Lord has heard our prayers. But what is it, Bonita? I have never seen you so excited."

The House of Charity dweller pulled the cash from her pocket and showed it to the nun. "Mother, look. We can pay for the pipes and give the rest to the House of Charity."

"Where on Earth did you get that money?"

"I won it."

"You *won* it? Where?"

"At the racetrack."

"The racetrack? You mean that pit of capital vices? A place where the seven cardinal sins thrive? No, we cannot accept that money. I am disappointed in you, Miss. We raised you to be virtuous."

Crushed by the remark, Bonita stamped her foot on the stone floor.

"But I am."

"You are keeping company with a man who wallows in corruption at many levels.

"How do you expect to live a virtuous life under those circumstances? Material pleasures are fleeting. Social justice is what you should be striving for. That is virtuous."

Maria Jose looked at her wristwatch.

"Time for Mass with Father Luís in the chapel. Join me?"

"No," she said, stamping her foot again

"Fine then. You can remain here and pout all you want. I will pray for you."

Bonita stood there feeling empty and alone. She shoved the money back into her pocket and muttered: "I know what to do with this."

Maria Jose shook her head with displeasure and began to walk away when Luís' voice echoed in the courtyard.

"Glory be to God. Glory be to God in the Highest. Glory, glory, glory."

He joined the teacher and Mother Superior and exclaimed, "What a great day for the parishioners of *Iglesia Nuestra Señora de Monserrate* and its environs."

"Father, have you been drinking again?" asked Maria Jose. "How on Earth will you say Mass in that condition?"

The tipsy little clergyman ignored her and looked directly at Bonita.

"As a matter of fact, I have been drinking. And I was doing so with our new benefactor, Armando Lobo."

"Armando?" Bonita said with a smile.

"That capitalist?" Mother Superior said with a scowl.

"He made a donation that will impact my church for years to come."

Mother Maria Jose became angry. "Father Luís, what a disgraceful example of a religious person you are to this young, impressionable lady and your flock. Accepting money from that … that … capitalist, who rubs elbows with a dictator, gamblers, torturers, and thieves. That is unconscionable. God knows what he did to acquire that currency, and now it is in your hands."

Again, Father Luís ignored her. He spoke directly to Bonita. "Now, that was not very charitable by the leading Sister of Charity, was it?" he said while wagging an index finger at Maria Jose without looking at her. He turned to the nun, adding: "And as far as thieves go, let me remind the good Mother Superior of the penitent thief on the cross who said: '…Lord, remember me when Thou comest into Thy kingdom. And Jesus said unto him, Verily I say unto thee, Today, shalt thou be with Me in Paradise.'"

The imperious nun refused to capitulate. "Father, you do not appear to be appropriate to say Mass. Ugggh!" She threw her hands up as if to surrender and walked away in a huff.

But not before the priest added: "Appropriate at this time is a verse from Matthew 6:1-4: 'Beware of practicing your righteousness before other people in order to be seen by them, for then you will have no reward from your Father who is in heaven…'"

The priest bowed to Bonita, extended the palm of his right hand and said: "Coming to Mass, my dear?"

She grasped his hand, curtseyed, and replied with a big grin: "Yes Father."

Chapter 51
"Batista Get Out"

THE UNIVERSITY OF Havana was quieter than usual on this windy, cool evening. No anti-Batista signs. No groups of students huddled together. No police. Perhaps it was the weather.

Bonita looked around as she walked up the Grand Staircases previously set ablaze, but saw only a few students there sitting, standing, or scurrying to and from the main building. She arrived at class on time, took a test and walked out of the classroom with other students when she felt a sudden chill in the air.

"Bonita," Ernesto said. "I was hoping to find you here. What happened? Did Grau harm you?"

Sensing insincerity, she looked askance at him and remained silent while walking and pressing her books close to her chest. "There will be no more demonstrations for me. I abhor violence and I found myself surrounded by it."

The rebel pulled her by the elbow to a stop. "Sometimes things get out of hand. Surely you are not going to let that incident prevent you from fighting for the cause."

"I'll fight in my own way," she said angrily.

"Please tell me what happened," he said in a calm, caring voice. "Did Grau or his men hurt you?"

She paused, reflected, and spoke in an accusatory tone. "No. It was more psychological. He put me in a cell next to the torture chamber. I heard the screams. I endured the insults of the male prisoners. It was a horrifying experience."

Ernesto was overly empathetic. "You poor thing. He had me in that cell, too. It was horrible. The next stop is usually the chamber. But I have managed to stay out."

"How?"

"My whore mother. She knows important people."

"You shouldn't continue talking about your mother like that."

"What? Calling my mother a whore? I would rather say it first before anyone says it behind my back."

"No one is going to call her that behind your back."

He smiled at her with pity. "You are so naive in the ways of the world. That is your charm."

"Well I have something to tell you. Grau said that if I'm arrested again at a demonstration, he will take me to the chamber."

"He told you that?"

"No, Armando did."

Ernesto scoffed. "Lies. He lies."

"Why do you hate him? What has he done to you?"

"He exists."

"He bailed me out. He spoke with Grau directly to free me."

"So you are scared to demonstrate?"

"Of course."

He looked at her for a second or two and changed his tone. "Look, we are having a meeting in the auditorium. Come and listen."

"No."

"It is only a meeting, not a demonstration. In the Great Hall. Come with me. Please. You will be safe. Think of the cause, which is greater than ourselves."

She thought for a moment. "If you are lying to me …"

"I am not. It is a rally for a demonstration. Not a demonstration. Demonstrations take place in the streets. This is a rally only."

When the couple walked through the double doors of the Great Hall the seats that descended from the back to the front of the stage were filled with students and teachers. A huge banner hung on a valance over the stage. It read: "Batista Get Out!"

Ernesto found a seat in the front row for Bonita and trotted up the stairs leading to the stage. He stood at the podium, looked at the audience, scratched his bald head, and stroked his beard like a professor about to lecture. He spoke into a microphone.

"Good evening comrades. Most of you know me. For those who do not, I am Ernesto Randal, citizen, law student, President of the *Federacion Estudiantil Universitaria*, founding member of the *Revolucionario* Estudantil *Directorio*, proud son of Cuba and follower of Jose Marti, hero of the republic. I have been arrested, incarcerated, beaten, and threatened with torture because I, like you, cannot remain silent in the face of an illegal government that promotes corruption.

The assembled crowd roared, "Batista Get Out!"

"Corruption in the form of graft, extortion, and the Forrajeo System in which every business must pay a 'tax' to the local police precinct to operate.

He lifted his hands upward to encourage the audience to join the refrain.

"Batista Get Out!"

"A levy on every beer truck, milk truck, cigar stand.

"Batista Get Out!"

"A 'tax' on lotteries that give so many poor people hope.

"Batista Get Out!

"Prostitution and drug trafficking that plague our society while politicians pocket payoffs and look the other way.

"Batista Get Out!

"Police who arrest and torture and kill us and throw our bodies into the streets.

"Batista get out!"

"An illegitimate president who ignores Marti's doctrine.

"Batista Get Out!"

"The doctrine that calls for the respect of human dignity, liberty, integrity, democracy, equality.

"Batista Get Out!"

He looked over the audience and lowered his voice for effect.

"The doctrine that states, 'When politics has as its object merely changing its form in a country, without changing the conditions of injustice in which the inhabitants suffer, when politics has as its object, under the name of liberty, of replacing those in power with even hungrier authorities, the duty of the honest man will never be to stand aside and permit unchained corruption.'

"Batista Get Out!"

"The doctrine that says, 'Every man of justice and honor fights for liberty whenever he may see it offended, because that is to fight for his integrity as a man, and the one who sees liberty offended and does not fight for it, or helps those who offend it, is not a whole man.'

"Batista Get Out!"

He looked directly at Bonita and raised his voice.

"The doctrine that decries one-crop economics, in which a foreign power, the United States, uses ownership of our sugar plantations to dominate us politically.

"Batista Get Out!"

Surveying the audience, he added, softly, "I would like to end with this thought about another great fighter against the oppression of the masses.

"Marti wrote: 'Karl Marx was not only a titanic mover of the anger of European workers, but a profound seer in the reasons for human misery, and in the destinies of men. He was a man eaten with the desire to do good.'

"We too are eaten with the desire to do good. By sending this message to the Dictator:

"Batista Get Out!"

The audience rose as one. The applause was deafening.

The sensational speaker left the stage and was immediately surrounded by jubilant supporters. Bonita, like them, was still aroused by the electricity he'd generated in the auditorium. But she remained in front of her seat until things settled down. Eventually, the popular speaker took her by the hand before another lecturer claimed the stage.

"How about a cup of coffee?" he said.

Enchanted by his speech and wary of his intentions, Bonita hesitated for a few seconds. "Okay."

Ernesto walked with her through the campus until they arrived at the School of Agronomy. They skipped down the stairs to the basement, where a muscular student with an FEU armband guarded a door. When he saw the rebel leader he nodded in the affirmative and permitted entry. It was a cafeteria and they were alone, but there was a repetitive noise coming from a side door. She acknowledged it. He ignored it.

"What's that noise?"

"It comes from comrades. How did you like my speech?"

"It was exciting. You speak the truth. You arouse people."

They sat at a table and he placed his hands on hers and smiled, suggestively.

"Did I arouse you?"

She pulled away her hands. He smiled, rose, poured coffee from a canister into two, small cups and set them on the table. He lit a cigarette, sat with his legs crossed and studied her for a moment.

"The ignorant man has not yet begun to be a man, so I have started a literacy campaign to educate people. Forty percent of Cubans cannot read and write. We meet in a classroom in the Spanish Department on Thursday evenings. Would you be willing to help?"

"I could come after my class."

"Do you have any books to donate? We do not have money to buy them."

Bonita pulled out a wad of cash from her pocket. Ernesto's eyes bulged.

"Chica, where did you get that?"

"Just take it. For books, paper, pens, and pencils. Not for guns."

He smiled. "Of course, not for guns."

Three students with FEU armbands entered, opened the side door and disappeared downstairs. With the door open the repetitive noise was louder now.

"Bang-bang-bang-bang."

"What is that?"

"Come with me."

Ernesto led her through the door and down the steps, where a shooting gallery came into view. Young men and women were firing mostly M1 carbine semi-automatic rifles and American Colt M1 911 .45 caliber semi-automatic pistols. They all had as their target a caricature of the president's head. They aimed for his eyes.

"Batista Get Out, no?" the rebel rouser shouted to no one in particular as the noise overwhelmed any possibility of conversation. Turning to Bonita, he yelled,

"Would you like to fire a gun?"

Upset by the scene, she shook her head no and folded her arms.

When an attractive young woman presented a pistol to Bonita, she turned, and ran up the stairs. The student leader pursued her.

"What is wrong?" he said when they reached the cafeteria.

"This is wrong. Violence begets violence."

"Non-violence begets violence, on us."

"You are a skilled orator. Use your voice and your mind to bring about change."

He grabbed her by the shoulders.

"I am not asking you to be violent. But we need your help. Will you help me to spread Marti's message? Assist in educating the people?"

"I will do so, but not with a gun."

Ernesto kissed her lips roughly. She pushed him away, hard.

"Beast," Bonita yelled. "I will help the cause, not you." She ran for the exit. He followed her with his eyes and smiled.

Chapter 52
Trust a Gambler?

FROM HIS PERCH in El Carcel, Army saw Fowler enter the crowded Fox Hole with the Colombian. It was noon when he greeted and sat with them at the round table.

Meanwhile, two flirteras sat at the bar, playing cards and drinking rum while the men exchanged pleasantries.

Sugar Man lit a cigarette and nodded. "Gentlemen, thanks for coming."

"Armando, this is Jorge Pastrami," Fowler said.

They shook hands. "Jorge, the ladies are Gloria and Daisy."

The girls flirted with the Colombian, a plain-looking, middle-aged man of average height and weight, nothing like the cultured Fowler.

"Are you going to be all right here? We're a long way from Cali."

"That is why I am here. I cannot bear to be in the same places where I lost my family. This will be good for me. To dig my hands into the soil again."

Army shook his head sadly. "I heard what happened." He took a drag on the cigarette and appeared to be in deep thought. Maybe the ladies can help you forget."

Squirming in his seat, the Colombian focused his eyes on the floor.

"Would you like one? Or both?"

"No, thank you. I have not had a woman since my Marta died a year-and-a-half ago. I prefer to be alone."

"Would you at least like to play cards with them?"

He looked up. "Oh no, señor. I do not gamble."

"How about some cocaine, a glass of rum?"

Pastrami looked at Fowler, who was amused.

"What kind of a man do you bring me to, Señor Fowler? I do not gamble, sleep with strange women, use drugs, or drink rum."

The plantation owners looked at each other and laughed. They patted Jorge on the back.

"Relax, amigo," Fowler said. "It was a test and you passed."

El Angel brought Cuban sandwiches and beers for everyone. Jorge requested a Coca-Cola. The three men chatted about the sugar industry until Army was satisfied about the Colombian's ability to take over from Stein.

"When can you start, Jorge?"

"In three weeks."

"Good."

———— ◆ ————

On Saturday morning Army picked up Bonita at the convent. They drove to the train station. He held her hand and his heart thumped. She glowed.

"Why aren't we driving?" she said.

"It's good to take the train as often as possible. To see if there are any problems."

"Problems?"

"My father used to say, when you value something, pay close attention to it or you'll lose it."

"Why are we going to Matanzas?"

He ushered her to a window seat and sat next to her. "To fire my plantation manager."

"What did he do?"

"He lied. Cheated. Betrayed me."

Two hours later, the train stopped in Santa Cruz for more passengers. It continued along the coast, past Playa Jibacoa, Arroyo Bermejo, and then inland towards the plantations of Matanzas. The line ended in the barrio Versalles on Calle 55. They disembarked with light luggage and waited. Army looked at his wristwatch.

"Stein should have been here a half-hour ago. Let's hail a taxi."

At Parque Libertad they found a cab. The driver took the Carretera Yumuri route, which ran next to the Rio Yumuri, a scenic drive next to a wide river. The trip lasted ten minutes until the road split and the driver veered right. When they arrived, Army paid the taxi driver and knocked on the door of the manager's house.

"Strange. He's not here, either."

"Maybe he is on his way to the train station."

"Not him. He's precise. Something's wrong."

Army unlocked the door, put their bags inside and locked up. He led her around the back of the house, where the plantation began.

"Stein," he yelled three times.

When there was no answer he took Bonita by the hand. They walked between neat rows of sugar cane plants about hip high. He stooped to the ground and dug the earth with his fingers. She squatted next to him.

"The soil on this island is rich," he said. "See how dark and moist it is? Together with the sun, temperature, and rainfall the conditions are perfect for growing sugar cane..."

She interrupted. "And coffee, tobacco, mangos, everything. Were these stalks just planted?"

"No. They started as stems. Now they're in the tillering phase. In a few months they'll be in the Grand Growth Stage, where they'll be taller than we are. The final stage is the Ripening Stage."

"God bless this land and its fruit," Bonita said, bowing her head and blessing herself.

Army led her to a shed on the other side of the house.

"The Chevy's still here, but his Ford is gone. Come on. We're going to look for Stein. I have a hunch about where he is."

The old Chevy was difficult to start. Persistence paid off and soon they were on their way, but not before he stopped at the house again for two beach towels. The trip was short. The Flanery Plantation was a few minutes away.

The Chevy pulled up to the main plantation house, where Stein was sitting on a rocking chair on the porch, alone. When he saw

Army alight, he stood and placed a hand on his head, as if he had a headache.

"Mandito. I completely forgot you were coming today. I am sorry."

Army walked to the porch while Bonita waited in the car.

"What are you doing here, Stein?"

Big Bob answered from inside the house: "He's workin' for me now," he said, opening a squeaky screen door and stepping out.

Stein stood with a painful expression. "Mandito. I wanted to tell you. Your father's death. It was the end for me. I do not think I can work for you."

"Because you've been working for him," he said, pointing to the big man.

"Whatdaya gonna to do now?" Bob chuckled. "You have three plantations and no plantation manager. And soon we'll have another harvest. Where ya gonna find a manager now? You're chocolate without sugar. Rum without molasses."

Fay walked out of the house at that moment.

"I thought I heard your voice, Army."

She kissed him on the cheek and pretended she didn't hear the conversation. "What a pleasant surprise," she added. And then, out of the corner of her eye she spotted Bonita in the car.

"Is that your friend? Why don't you invite her to the house?"

Before he could respond, she walked to the car.

Army turned to his former plantation manager. "Stein, I came here to fire you. For running his sugar on my train. For cutting wages without my consent and for being untrustworthy. Who can trust a compulsive gambler?"

Turning to Big Bob. "Can you?"

The large one looked down at his challenger and sighed. "As I recall, your father was a compulsive gambler and your business is still doin' good. But let's talk about you. You still don't have nobody to run the show."

"Come on, Bob. We've been coming to Cuba long enough to know that you always need a Plan B. And my Plan B is better than yours."

Army walked to the car and slipped behind the steering wheel while the two women chatted through the front passenger's window. Slowly, he pulled away.

Chapter 53

Army, Bonita and Fay

ONCE THEY WERE out of the plantation Army drove along the Yumuri River until it led them to Matanzas Bay, a popular estuary for locals. They parked in a secluded area, slipped on their bathing suits, grabbed the towels from the trunk, and walked to the beach.

The afternoon was sunny and warm. Cubans were relaxing on towels taken from their bathrooms and placed on the hot sand. They also played in the water as the couple walked hand-in-hand until they found a spot away from the crowd. They placed their beach towels next to each other neatly and sat.

Bonita rested her head on his lap and he applied sunscreen carefully to her face. She looked up at him.

"Fay used to be your woman."

"She told you?"

"Yes."

"You spoke to her for three minutes and she told you that?"

"Women don't hold back that kind of information very long. Did you love her?"

He stopped and looked into her eyes. "I thought I fell in love with her near the end, which I didn't know was coming until …"

"Until what?"

"She betrayed me. I lost trust in her."

"That's the second time I've heard you say someone betrayed you. Are you unforgiving?"

"No. Protective. Protective of me. I forgive others. I just don't want to be around them."

"How did she betray you?"

"You might say she was in bed with the Mafia."

"Are you not in bed with the Mafia?"

"Not by choice. She had a choice."

He rubbed sunscreen on her chest and arms and she sat up.

"Armando, look into my eyes."

He did so and cupped her face in his hand. A smile creased his lips.

"What do you see?" she said.

"The love of my life."

Bonita smiled broadly and kissed his lips tenderly. "When I look into yours, what do I see?

He shrugged. "A lovesick fool?"

"I see a wounded soul. Which needs nurturing."

They kissed. She opened her eyes, glanced down beach and saw someone unexpected in the distance.

"Look, there's Fay. We should invite her."

He turned, saw his ex and turned back.

"She's all alone Armando."

"Give her time. She makes friends fast."

"Here she comes."

Fay had left her towel and belongings and approached the couple apologetically. "I'm surprised and embarrassed. I didn't know you were going to be at this beach. I left my L'Oreal at the house. Do you have any sunscreen?."

"We have Coppertone," Bonita said. "Is that okay?"

"That is lovely. Thanks.

Fay kneeled on the sand, poured some onto her hand and applied it to her face and arms.

"Why don't you sit with us? You are all alone over there."

Army gave her a look. Fay caught it.

"Oh, I don't want to impose on you lovebirds."

"No, really, bring your things over here," he said, sarcastically.

"Are you sure?"

"We are," Bonita said.

The interloper stood and walked back to her towel to retrieve her things.

"Armando, that was very nice of you." He rolled his eyes. She laughed.

About ten minutes later the third wheel returned with her belongings, sat and complimented her former boyfriend's girlfriend.

"Your hair is so beautiful. I wish I had thick, black hair like yours. And look at your breasts. Mine are puppies compared to yours."

"I wish I had your beautiful skin," Bonita said. And for the next two hours the two women talked about girl things while he feigned disinterest. All three swam together and even ate dinner at a nearby restaurant. By the time they finished dining it was too late to catch the train back to Havana, so the couple said goodbye to the guest and returned to the Lobo plantation house.

At midnight they went to bed, where passion once again almost overcame the convent dweller. Almost.

"I'm sorry. But I will remain a virgin until I am married," the determined Catholic girl said, breathlessly.

Army propped himself up with both hands behind his back and looked into her eyes. "Then let's get married."

"What?"

She sat up.

"I can't."

"Whatdaya mean, you can't?"

"We have not known each other long enough."

"How long do we have to know each other?"

"More than three months."

"You're scared."

"I want to be sure."

He stroked her hair. "When we met, I felt like a thunderbolt hit me."

"I felt it, too."

They kissed, heatedly.

"Armando, I know our culture and how men here cannot exist without sex. So, if you want to sleep with another woman, I understand." And then she looked intently into his eyes.

"But not with Fay."

"I thought you liked her. You just spent an afternoon with her."

"I wanted to know her. On the outside she is very pleasant. But inside I am not so sure. She's hiding something. I saw how she looked at you, too. I didn't like it."

"You're jealous. Jealous of Fay. I'm happy to hear you say that. I was beginning to think …"

Bonita kissed him passionately and once again they became overheated, for naught.

Chapter 54
Swimming Upstream

A TAXI TOOK THEM to the train station the next morning. On the ride to Havana Bonita turned serious.

"Remember when you said that you are in bed with the mafia, but not by choice? I heard a speech. The speaker said that when someone sees liberty offended and does not fight for it, or helps those who offend it, he is not a whole man."

Caught off guard by her sudden philosophical outburst, Army looked at her, perplexed.

"What else did you hear?"

"That the duty of the honest man will never be to stand aside and permit unchained corruption."

"So I'm not a whole man, an honest man? Where did you get this?"

"It's from Jose Marti."

"So when were you talking with him? And I know he's dead."

The convent communist put her hands together as if in prayer and became excited. "I was at a rally. Oh, Armando, it was so inspiring. You have no idea."

"And who was quoting Marti? The family communist?"

"Yes. He is a brilliant orator."

Army raised his voice, disregarding the other passengers.

"Oh really? I guess he told everyone how great Karl Marx was, too."

"Yes, he did."

He shook his head in frustration. "Communists like Marx and Ernesto the Orator want one thing: To take from the rich and give to the poor."

"What's wrong with that?"

He looked at her with incredulity. "What's wrong is that in the process they dismantle the economic engines built by poor people who became rich. And when they level the field and make everyone 'equal,' everyone will be poor. The only ones to gain will be the party bosses, which is what Ernesto will become. They'll live well while everyone else is poor because the government will decide how much of their earnings they can keep."

The House of Charity teacher squirmed in her seat. "You cannot deny that the United States has used ownership of our plantations to dominate us, politically."

He nodded and smiled: "I'm trying to change things on the inside. Give me a chance."

"What if you can't?"

He had no answer. He'd thought about that, but no one had ever confronted him about that possibility. He was swimming upstream with iron boots, and he knew it. The frustration was enormous. Perhaps that's why he bit his bottom lip, stared straight ahead, and didn't speak the rest of the trip.

———◆———

A taxi delivered them to the convent, where capitalism and communism kissed goodnight.

"See you tomorrow evening? he said.

"I'm teaching a class of illiterates."

"Where?"

"At the University."

He frowned. He suspected that his step-brother was behind it.

"Why don't you stop in? It's between 8:00 and 10:00 p.m. Classroom 77 in the main building. Bring some people who cannot read and write."

He looked at her. "Maybe I will."

Chapter 55
Unpleasant Surprises

WHEN ARMY WALKED down to the Fox Hole bar for breakfast early the next morning, El Angel handed him a letter from Titi.

My Dear Armando:

I have received notice from an American attorney that your father willed to me and Ernesto the accountant's house in Santa Cruz. My shock is limitless. I did not know he died. Was he sick? Was it an accident? I am so sorry for you and your family. I do not know Santa Cruz. If you would show me the property I would appreciate it. Ernesto, of course, wants no part of it.

Sincerely, Nefertiti Randal.

Army threw the letter into the trash and walked to the end of the bar. He sat down and started drinking a cup of espresso prepared for him by the new bar manager. He was nibbling on a sweet bun when out of the corner of his eye he noticed a large, menacing-looking man in a dark suit at the entrance. He turned and recognized him as the same one who'd tried to choke him at the race track.

He bristled. "Why is the front door open, Angel?"

"Sorry boss."

"Hey. I'm here for the vig." the big man said.

Army glowered at him from the bar stool. "Trabo, right?"

"Yeah. The vig, you're late."

"And you're early. We're not open. And I'm not paying a double vig. In fact, I'm not paying, period."

He watched Trabo walk slowly toward him and sit five stools away.

"Gimmie a shot, Bacardi Superior," the giant said to El Angel.

"We are not open."

Trabo reached across the bar with his right hand and grabbed a fistful of the little bartender's shirt collar, pulling him over the bar.

"I said gimme a shot of Bacardi Superior, midget."

Army gave the okay. "Give it to him Angel."

Trabo grinned at his rival as he released the bartender, who gathered himself before pouring Bacardi Superior into a shot glass and sliding it to the intruder. He swilled the shot and slammed the solid little glass atop the bar.

"Another," he said to Angel, who looked at his employer for approval. Army nodded as he sipped more coffee while facing Trabo. The large one downed the second shot and appeared to be placing the solid little glass on the bar. But suddenly, like a pitcher throwing a baseball, he wound up and threw the glass at the bar owner's head. Reflexively, he raised his coffee-cup forearm in time to deflect the missile, which skipped off the bone in his right arm, sending a nauseating pain throughout his body. Steaming coffee that splashed on his neck exacerbated the pain as he hopped off the seat.

Trabo followed up by rising from his heavy wooden stool, lifting it with his right hand and throwing it at his foe, who couldn't get out of the way. Felled by the impact the seat made on his head, Army looked up from the floor. He was dazed and bloody from a wound over his left eye. Helplessly, he watched El Angel jump onto the bar and leap onto Trabo's back and attempt to apply a sleeper hold around the big man's neck.

However, Trabo shook him off like a flea on a rhino. As the bartender tumbled to the ceramic-tile floor, his head struck the brass rail at the bottom of the bar. He was out, cold.

Meanwhile, the mob's enforcer was on the move. He grabbed his stunned victim by the throat with his left hand and lifted him off the floor, choking him. Army tried to break the hold but he couldn't.

So, he jammed two fingers into the big man's eyes. Reflexively, the attacker released the grip to cover his eyes and his prey fell to the floor. He attempted to stand but tripped over the stool.

Blinking, Trabo grabbed the back of Army's shirt with his left hand, spun him around and with a straight right hand landed a heavy blow to the cut over the left eyebrow. Blood gushed from the wound as he fell again, dazed by the blow. The giant ripped a leg off the broken wooden stool and raised it high above Army's head. But when he began to swing it down to bludgeon him, a shot rang out.

The behemoth stopped in mid-strike and turned to face the direction from which the bullet traveled. He dropped the wooden leg, looked at blood pumping through a hole in his left chest and collapsed like a mammoth felled by an elephant gun. He landed with a thud that shook the floor.

Army looked toward the front door and saw Jomar standing there with a smoking revolver.

"Armando, are you all right?"

He staggered to his feet, pressing a handkerchief over the cut to his forehead. "Good shot," he said. He met his bodyguard at the bar where El Angel laid face down. Together they turned him over.

"Angel!" they yelled, shaking the bartender.

Jomar grabbed a pitcher of water on the bar and dumped it on the bartender's head. The little man opened his eyes and looked around.

"*Que paso?*" El Angel said as he stood a little wobbly and rubbed the back of his head. "What happened?"

"The big guy attacked us," Army said, holding a handkerchief over his wound. "I think he's dead."

The three men walked to Trabo's body. Jomar crouched over him and felt a wrist for a pulse. A pool of blood under the brute's left arm was growing larger.

"No pulse," the detective said.

At that moment Celia entered the Fox Hole, surveyed the scene and placed her hands atop her head. "*Dios mio. Que paso?*"

Caught off guard, Army removed the handkerchief from the wound, exposing a bloody gash over his left eye. Celia cried out and ran to him, sobbing.

"Armando, oh Armando," she said, hugging him tightly. He pressed the handkerchief to the wound again with one hand and patted her back with the other.

"I'm okay. Please, get me a towel."

Celia raced to the bar and returned with a white, wet towel. He pressed it on the wound. "You must go to the hospital," she cried.

"No, not now. We have to deal with this first," he said, pointing to the dead body.

"I will call the precinct," Jomar said. "They will send someone from the coroner's office. I cannot leave the scene until they arrive; however, you and Angel should go for treatment."

The bartender rubbed the back of his head. "I am good. You go to the hospital, Armando."

Army said nothing. He walked to the entrance, locked the door and took a seat at a table nearby. El Angel joined him. The detective walked behind the bar, set the phone on it, and dialed the police station.

Still upset by the scene, Celia blurted: "I will bring you some ice, Armando." She darted behind the bar as Jomar hung up the phone and made his way back to the two men.

"Officials from the Coroner's Office will be here shortly," he said.

"Bring a bottle of rum too, please, Celia" Army shouted. She nodded, but first she picked up the telephone receiver and made a call. For the next hour, she sat next to the man who'd changed her life, pressing ice in a towel to the wound while he and the bartender sipped rum.

Meanwhile, the detective frisked Trabo's dead body, pulling his wallet from his back pocket, keys from his pants' pockets, and personal papers from inside his suit jacket.

A knock on the door brought Celia to her feet. Before Army could say anything, she opened the door, through which Bonita and a man in a white lab coat and medical bag entered.

She rushed to Army, hugged him tightly and looked at his forehead. "What happened, mi amor?"

"It's all right," he said, forgetting that the bloody gash over the left eye was exposed when Celia ran for the door.

"Oh no," Bonita said, looking at the wound. She started to cry. "I brought the doctor."

"How did you …"

"Celia called me."

"All right," the physician said, "Push some tables together and get me a good flashlight."

With Army lying on his back on four tables Celia found a flashlight behind the bar and held it over the cut while the doctor cleaned and stitched the laceration and applied an adhesive bandage.

"You are lucky," he said. "The wound is not that deep and you did a good job of stopping the bleeding. I will remove the stitches in a week."

"Please take a look at my bartender, Doc. He was knocked out."

"Then I suggest that he come with me to the hospital for a thorough examination," the doctor said.

El Angel shook his head "no," but he was overruled by everyone else.

Army walked the doctor and El Angel to the door when a detective and two men from the coroner's office appeared and introduced themselves. They asked for Jomar, who showed them his badge and described what had occurred. About twenty minutes later Celia locked the front door after the men had removed Trabo's body on a stretcher.

"We're closed today, Celia. Please put a sign on the door," Army said as he lit a Lucky Strike and sat on a stool at the end of the bar. Jomar joined him.

"We have a big problem, Jomar. The man you killed. He was an enforcer for the Mafia. So, you know what's coming."

Overhearing him, Bonita cried out: "Armando, I can hide you in the convent."

He smiled. "You can't hide from these people."

Jomar interrupted. "Armando, all I know is that my job is to protect you. He looked like he was going to kill you. There is only one thing to do."

"What?"

"Call my uncle. He is the one who assigned me to protect you on orders from the president."

———— ◆ ————

Two days after the mafioso died, a meeting took place in a back room of the capitol building, where political deals were crafted. Present were Blanco Rico, Lansky, Massi, Army with a black eye and a white bandage over his left eyebrow, and Jomar.

Blanco Rico began.

"Gentlemen, as Chief of the Secret Police and a member of the Batista cabinet, I have been ordered here to solve a serious problem. I stress the words TO SOLVE because the president does not want this to escalate to a point where it will interfere with our relationships.

"So let us go to the basics. The detective, acting as Minister of Labor Armando Lobo's bodyguard, shot and killed Trabo Torres, who was assaulting Señor Lobo at the time. Trabo had been sent by Señor Massi to collect money owed. Something went wrong."

"Yeah, Trabo ended up dead and we never got the vig," the mafioso said.

"You mean double vig," Army said. He looked at Blanco Rico. "The vig doubled because I was in Philadelphia attending my father's funeral and tending to his business affairs. So I was late with the vig. The final vig, because he died."

Massi interrupted. "I explained the situation to him at the racetrack. He don't want to believe it." He shrugged: "The thing is, this is at the point where we don't have to explain nothin'. We can just ..."

Lansky raised his hand to stop him from continuing with a threat. Dapper in a tan-colored suit, blue shirt, white tie and brown fedora he interjected: "We've been friends with your father for a long time. We don't want regrets on both sides."

Army looked at Lansky and responded, heatedly.

"I feel as though you all disrespected my father, me and my family. You say you were friends with him. You worked with my father. You even sent flowers when he passed. And then when I was late with the last payment while at his funeral, I got slammed with a double payment."

Lansky interrupted: "And then you said the debt was settled by his death, right?"

"Yes, the debt died with him."

"No, it didn't," added Lansky, the Mob's accountant, negotiator and strategist. "He signed a note as chairman of the Lobo Corporation. The obligation belongs to the company until it's paid off. And now you are the company."

"I'm disputing your claim," Army said. "My attorneys are looking into it."

Massi laughed. "Your attorneys? We don't care about no attorneys. You owe us. Period."

"How much is the debt?" Blanco Rico said.

Lansky pulled the note from his shirt pocket and waved it. "Six-hundred thousand. And we have a man in a pine box. A man who protected Charlie "Lucky" Luciano when he was here in 1946 and 1947."

Massi nodded: "Charley Lucky. Capo de Tutti Capi, Boss of Bosses."

Blanco Rico continued: "Well, Armando did not kill Trabo. And Jomar was just doing his job in protecting him. So here is my recommendation, gentlemen. Señor Lobo will pay for Trabo's funeral and give the family $1,000. Señors Lansky and Massi will forego the late vig payment. And Señor Lobo will resume vig payments next month unless he pays off the debt in its entirety.

"Any questions? Objections?"

Army looked up and blew smoke rings from a cigarette. His presidentially appointed bodyguard watched him. The Mob members observed Blanco Rico as his eyes scanned the room.

"All right? Are we done here, gentlemen?"

Blanco Rico rose and shook hands with Lansky and Massi, Jomar, and Army. In turn, the aggrieved parties reluctantly shook hands to seal the deal.

Chapter 56
Setting Things Straight

Jomar drove Army to the palace the next morning for a meeting in the Minister of Public Works' office. He brought the file the minister had given him.

"What happened to your eye?" Muja said.

His peer smiled: "I ran into a bar stool."

Muja grinned. "Please be more careful. Cuba needs its Minister of Labor."

"Which reminds me, I never thanked you for recommending me for the job, Muja."

The Minister nodded. "I know you care about the people, Armando. That is why I brought up your name to the president. Your father was the same way. Good man."

Army smiled. "I went through the report and I find it very interesting. How many of these projects are currently in progress?"

"About 10 percent. The little jobs like building a post office, planting trees, cleaning streets, installing parking meters."

"I can get workers to do any or all of that. Where shall I direct them?"

Muja removed his eyeglasses and looked at him. "Armando, now is not the time. We have the men we need. Wait for six months, when ground is broken for the big projects."

"But these men need work, now. You and I talked about this before. You said they could do the small jobs."

The Minister shrugged. "I am just a planner. I do not assign workers."

"I'm the Minister of Labor, so I'll go ahead and assign workers."

Muja put on his glasses and issued a warning. "Be careful. You do not want to anger the wrong people."

"If I wait for the wrong people to make things right, I'll be old and they'll be dead."

"Or vice versa."

Their meeting lasted an hour, after which the young cabinet member shook hands with his peer. "Thank you, Muja. Maybe you and I can make a difference."

The Labor Minister walked to his office down the hall. His unscheduled visit surprised the twins, who were playing cards. They looked up at him like students caught cheating on a test.

"Aren't you two supposed to be writing an addendum to the report you wrote a few weeks ago?"

"Sorry Armando," Wilmer said. "We were taking a break. What happened to your eye?"

"Long story. Wilmer, I want you and Walter to go back to the San Nicholas neighborhood, knock on doors and see who wants to work first thing tomorrow morning. Tell them to be outside their houses at 6:00 a.m. tomorrow. Where's Jomar?"

The boys shrugged.

Army looked for his bodyguard. He found him outside the palace, smoking a cigarette and talking to an attractive chica.

"Jomar, we need a truck," Army shouted from the entrance, where uniformed policemen watched everyone coming in and out of the building.

The detective tossed the tobacco, kissed the chica on the cheek, and walked over to his boss.

"A truck?"

"Big enough to carry a work crew."

"Then we must go to the yard in Marianao. Vamanos."

Army hopped into the back seat of the Hudson. The driver accelerated, turned right onto the Prado, and left onto the Malecón, where the ocean spray once again crashed over the seawall.

"Angry ocean," Army said.

"It will calm down in a few hours, when the clouds lift and the sun returns," Jomar said, turning left on Paseo. "The sea air feels so refreshing."

Five blocks later, at the corner of Paseo and Linea, he stopped for a red light.

"See this here?" Army said, nodding toward the corner.

"The construction site?"

"Yes. A new post office is going up here and we're going to supply the labor."

The detective nodded and turned onto Linea. Within twenty minutes they were entering the Department of Public Works' lot where municipal cars and trucks were parked. Army walked into the office and requisitioned a pickup truck. He gave a pink slip of paper and keys to the detective.

"Jomar, follow me in that red truck. I'll drive the Hudson to the corner of Galiano and Concordia. We'll park next to the church."

About twenty-five minutes later, the mission was accomplished. Jomar got out of the truck and met Army, who said: "Tomorrow morning we're going to transport workers to a job site. Meet me here at 6:00 a.m."

———— ◆ ————

The next morning the detective greeted his boss outside the church, where Wilmer and Walter were waiting with pens and paper.

When they stepped into Calle San Nicholas and looked down the undulating, narrow street, they saw men young and old; black, white, and mulatto standing in front of their doorways.

"Good job in getting them out, boys. Take down their names and addresses so they'll be paid. Tell them to get into the truck. It'll be at the end of the street.

While Jomar and the brothers did his bidding, Army decided to call on Agnelys. He knocked on the door and was surprised to see who answered.

"What are you doing here, brother?" Ernesto said.

Pokerfaced. "Where's Agnelys?"

The rebel stared at the black circle under his brother's eye and the bandage over it. "What happened to your pretty face? Lose a fight with a communist?"

"Where's Agnelys?"

"Here I am," said a friendly voice behind the door.

"It's me, Armando. Just checking to see how you are."

Agnelys slipped in front of Ernesto. "What happened to your eye?"

He ignored it. "Are you okay?"

"Yes," she said, looking up at her nephew and smiling. "My Ernesto sees to that. Excuse me. I have something on the stove."

Army caught a whiff of chicken soup in the air while the reprobate resumed the conversation. "What are you doing in this neighborhood, brother?"

"Being helpful."

"Really? Trying to impress someone?"

"Who would that be?"

"You know. What you might not know is that she is a communist."

"No. You're the communist. She's an impressionable girl with a good heart. And if you care about her, you'll stay away from her. She's been on Grau's radar screen since she was arrested at your last demonstration."

"That is the price of freedom from capitalist oppression, brother. She could end up in his torture chamber."

Army raised an eyebrow. "You don't care what happens to her, do you?"

"I want to see you suffer."

Army leaned in as he spoke. "If anything happens to her, you'll wish Grau got to you first."

The reprobate laughed in his face and slammed the door shut.

Fuming, Army walked to his car. He drove to the end of Calle San Nicholas, where a truck full of men waited. He motioned for Jomar to follow him in the truck. Within fifteen minutes they were in front of the construction site on the corner of Paseo and Linea. The Labor Minister summoned the manager. He flashed his credentials.

"I have thirty men who will work on this site."

"But sir, we are using a new method. We are pouring concrete. Laying the foundation. It is skilled work."

"You need men to mix and move the cement, correct?"

"Yes sir."

"And after it hardens, who builds on top of the concrete?"

"Brick layers and laborers."

"Well, you have thirty laborers. Show them what to do."

"But the Construction Company belongs to …"

Army waved to the men. "Over here, boys. This gentleman is the boss."

The workers jumped out of the back of the truck. The site manager threw up his hands in surrender and led them to a tool shed. He knew there would be consequences.

Chapter 57

Flirteras and Chango

A RMY WAS SEATED in his office at the Presidential Palace doing paperwork when he stopped and telephoned the Fox Hole. "Hola?"

"Bonita's teaching people how to read and write tonight at the University, Celia. Do you have friends who want to learn?"

"I know only flirteras."

"I know. Let's go to Sailor's Bar and see what they have to say."

"Armando, I am working here."

"Not tonight. El Angel is back. He and the other bartenders will have to pick up the slack."

"Can we just take the girls off the street?"

"I'm sure they'd much rather come with the Minister of Labor than the Chief of Police."

"But what can I do?"

"You're a success story. They'll follow you anywhere."

The line went silent for a few seconds before she responded: "Yes, Armando. I will do it."

————— ◆ —————

The classroom was filled with people of all ages and genders when Army poked his head in and winked at the teacher. She smiled at him while writing her name on the blackboard. He motioned to six flirteras to take the empty seats in the back of the room.

A sight to behold to the rest of the class, the street walkers sauntered in one-by-one in standard flirtera issue: plunging necklines around which cheap jewelry and perfume were evident; painted lips, narrow hips, miniskirts, and stiletto heels.

Army grabbed Celia's hand. "Here's the money. But don't give it to them until the class ends. I have to go to the Fox Hole and finish my paperwork. I'll see you there afterward."

The bartender, who'd exhibited better taste in flirtera wear when she'd met her future employer in Sailor's Bar, was the last to take her seat. She was in her work uniform.

The male students' reaction to the troupe was predictable—smiles and laughter. The females were a little more dignified. They giggled for the most part. But the men and women seemed thrilled to be part of their first reading-and-writing class.

———◆———

Army sat at the round table in El Carcel. He pulled official documents from a briefcase, read, and signed them. The hours passed quickly until he heard the brass lock below click and footsteps scurry up the metal stairs. Celia appeared at the table, out of breath.

He looked up. "How'd it go?"

"Good, Armando, until the Barbudo come at the end. He make a speech about how Bonita give him money for books and things. Then he talk about Batista and Carlo somebody."

Army dropped his pen on the table. "She gave him money? What else did he say?"

Celia became fidgety, playing with the strap on her red handbag. "I do not know. I go to the bathroom. But when I pass the classroom I hear him speak. He talk about a big demonstration next week."

"Where was Bonita?"

"With him."

"When is the demonstration? What day?"

"He did not say."

Army stood, stepped to the bar, and grabbed a bottle of Fox Hole rum.

"Who else was with him?"

"Barbudos, like him."

"How many?"

"I see four or five when I pass. Bonita wave to me."

"Jesus Christ," he said.

"I know, Armando. Ernesto is evil. Maybe he have her under a spell."

He lit a cigarette. "A spell?"

"Santeria."

Army scoffed. "I don't believe that stuff." He took a drag and sipped some rum. "Ernesto's aunt is into Santeria. She has dolls, you know, muñecas."

"Which muñecas?"

He shrugged. "I don't know what they're called. Why?"

"I know that Oshun is Goddess of Love. Chango's lover. Her hair is blond."

He took another sip. "Chango is Ernesto's Santeria name. I remember a blond doll."

Celia became more animated, and worried.

"Chango is God of fire, thunder, lightning. His strong words draw women to him like slaves to their masters."

Chapter 58
Bad Intentions

THE MAN IN the dark was visible only by the light of the cigar he was smoking when Ernesto entered and closed the screeching iron door to Mausoleum 107. The burial chamber contained twelve tombs, six on each side. An odor of must and tobacco filled the air.

"I was told to come here," the rebel leader said to the obscure figure, who was seated at a table in the back. "But all I know is that you are willing to give money to my cause."

"I don't care about your cause, sonny. I need somethin' done an' I need ya ta do it."

Ernesto approached the man cautiously, hoping to see who he was, but he couldn't because he wore a black hat with a wide brim and sunglasses. Still, he could tell that he was a large man.

"What do you want done and how much will you pay?"

"There's a sugar-cane plantation in Matanzas. Another one in Cienfuegos. They belong to Lobo. I want ya ta torch 'em. Destroy 'em."

"Lobo? So, he has an enemy. The enemy of my enemy is my friend. How much will you pay, friend?"

"Two-thousand dollars. I'll give you $1,000 now and $1,000 after."

"Why me? You do not care about my cause. So why me?"

"Because Lobo's our enemy and money's your friend."

The Barbudo cocked his head to the side, thinking. "Why do we meet in a house of the dead?"

"Look around, sonny. Dead people don't talk."

"Who are you?"

"Nona ya damned business. You wanna do this or not?"

Ernesto hesitated, angling for a better deal. "This is a dangerous operation. Soldiers guard the 'cane. Five-thousand dollars."

"Three."

"Four."

"Thirty-five hundred."

"No."

The rebel leader turned to walk away when the man caved.

"Okay, four thousand. Two thousand now."

Ernesto walked back to the man, who handed him an envelope. He opened it and tried to count the money but it was too dark. So, he just slipped the envelope into a pocket.

"Whenaya gonna do it?"

"Midnight. Friday. When the soldiers are drunk. When do you pay me the rest?"

"Midnight the next night. Right here."

The Barbudo started to walk away when the man added: "One more thing. There are two plantations in Matanzas. Side-by-side. Stay away from Flanery."

Ernesto departed the same way in which he'd arrived at the mausoleum, along a narrow blacktop that separated a city of raised coffins encased in white cement, marble or stone, depending upon the century in which they were constructed. Under a crescent moon he crept, looking side-to-side into the darkness that surrounded him as he made his way to the main road, where a younger Barbudo was waiting on a silent Harley-Davidson motorcycle. It was so dark that the driver didn't see him when he hopped onto the back of the bike.

"*Aye mi madre,*. You scared me. This place I do not like."

They were at the intersection of Calle G and Avenida Cristoból Colon in Christopher Columbus Cemetery, a 140-acre necropolis on a rectangular grid with numbered and lettered streets.

"Vamos," Ernesto said. The engine roared and lights clicked on. They blasted off on Colón, which ran straight from the central chapel through the neo-Romanesque northern archway to Calle Zapata.

About thirty minutes later, they roared into the Plaza de Armas in Old Havana and parked in front of a small cafe near the neoclassic El Templete, the Little Temple, and the celebrated ceiba tree.

"Hurry up," Ernesto said as he hopped off the back of the cycle and walked briskly through the eatery's entrance. He looked past tourists occupying most of the tables and made eye contact with a clean-cut waiter standing in the rear. The server nodded and motioned for him to sit at an empty table in the back.

"What will you have, sir?"

The rebel leader whispered: "Guns, lots of guns," and pulled the envelope from his shirt pocket to flash the cash. The waiter whistled. He spoke softly: "Where did you get that?"

"Never mind. Call your capitalist contact tomorrow morning. Arrange a meeting for tomorrow night." He laughed. "Capitalists will sell you the guns you shoot them with." He leaned in closer: "Also, come to the University at 8 p.m. Friday and bring five Barbudos."

"But I work Friday night."

"Not this Friday night. We have to earn this money before we are paid the rest. Bring gasoline and torches."

The server thought for a moment and shook his head affirmatively. He raised his voice when an elderly man passed by on his way to the men's room.

"All right, I will bring a couple espressos."

The young cyclist joined them and pointed to the bulging envelope sticking out of Ernesto's breast pocket. He whistled. "That looks like a lot of money. Have you ever thought about how it would be if you were rich? Lived in a fine house like one of those plantation owners?"

The devout communist grew angry and loud.

"I would not live in a plantation owner's home if he gave it to me."

The young man recoiled.

Ernesto leaned in to him and spoke softly. "I know that you are young and new to the cause. Think before you speak. Think about why you have joined the fight against the capitalists, the government, the police, the system."

"I apologize, sir. You are correct to chastise me."

Ernesto patted him on the hand. "That is better."

Chapter 59
The Anonymous Note

AT 9:30 THE next evening – dismissal time for night school students - a police van pulled in front of the Grand Staircases of the University of Havana. Riding shotgun, the Chief of the Anti-Communist Squad watched with delight as officers dragged two men with broken feet to the bottom step and removed their handcuffs. The policemen returned to the van and led three others to the base of the stairs. They sat and the cops uncuffed them, exposing bloody fingers without nails. They seemed to be in shock.

With his arms folded on the open window, Grau said, smugly: "Say hello to your classmates, gentlemen. Tell them how you informed on them."

Students skipping down the stairs heard his comments. They stopped to look at the five tortured hombres deposited by the police. Their faces showed the horror they felt.

About twenty minutes later, Grau thanked the van driver for taking him to his five-bedroom house in Vedado, where two Doberman Pinschers greeted him in the front yard.

When he walked into the dining room, he saw Beverly seated at one end of a French antique dining room set with seven empty chairs. The drapes were drawn. She was alone, sipping a glass of red wine and finishing a plate of lamb and rice in a room dimly illuminated by a chandelier. The remnants of a roasted shoulder of lamb and a large bowl of rice sat in the middle of the table, where the maid was gathering five plates from which children had left their half-eaten dinners. He leaned over, gave his esposa a peck on the cheek and handed her a small box of chocolates. He surveyed the room.

"This place looks like a mausoleum. And is that my plate at the other end of the block, I mean table, dear?"

"You know this is lamb night and for the third straight week you are an hour late," Beverly said, ignoring his attempt at humor. "So we are no longer waiting for you."

Grau walked to the other end of the table, picked up the empty plate and set it down next to her. "I am sorry, dear." Looking down at her he raised his voice: "But I have been busy protecting the country from the vermin who threaten the existence of this government and thereby you, me, and our five children."

Unruffled, Mrs. Grau wiped her lips with a white napkin, stood and faced her agitated husband. She spoke softly: "Well then, as long as you are pleasing Batista, I suppose that I and the children should be happy. So tonight, you will eat alone, as we do every night. You will sleep alone as well."

She started to walk away when she stopped, slipped a hand inside her pocket and pulled out a white envelope with his name on it. She handed it to him.

"This came with the mail." She left the room.

Grau looked at the envelope curiously. "No postage. No return address." He turned it over. "Nothing on the back."

He tore open the envelope and pulled out a 5x4-inch folded note. It read: *Ernesto Randal will be at Mausoleum No. 107, Cemeterió Cristobal Colón, at midnight, Saturday, after his return from Matanzas and Cienfuegos.*

It was signed, *A Friend.*

The Chief of the Anti-communist Squad sat there, thinking.

Chapter 60
Total Destruction

ON SATURDAY MORNING Army and his driver picked up the Colombian at the airport and drove him to the plantations at Cienfüegos, Matanzas and Santa Cruz. It was a long day and the new plantation manager was happy to settle into Stein's former residence and eat a hot meal prepared by Nelsa.

"The sugar crops at Cienfuegos and Matanzas are young. The fields here are burned, why?" Pastrami said while the maid cleared the dinner table.

"Sabotage," Sugar Man said. "But we were able to save the sugar. You can start planting again this week."

The Colombian was alarmed. "Sabotage? Is that why I saw so many soldiers on the roads and in the fields?"

Army shrugged. "Yes, student radicals. People who hate capitalism and Batista. They'll do anything to destroy the engine that drives the car."

They walked outside to the porch and sat on rockers. "I caught a saboteur here," Jomar said, sipping from a glass of clear rum.

"What did he do?"

"Set fire to the field, jammed the machines, but he paid a price."

"What price?"

"His life."

Jomar smiled. Pastrami flinched. Army frowned. The Colombian pressed.

"How did he die?"

"He went for my gun. It went off. Boom. Dead."

Pastrami squirmed in his chair. "Can I expect trouble here?"

"Hardly," the detective said. "You are protected by the Cuban army."

Army interjected: "Which means that we'll sleep well here tonight, Jomar, I want to go over the books and discuss a few things with my new manager in the morning."

Pastrami stepped into the house and the telephone rang. Two minutes later he ran out. He was hyperventilating.

"Armando, the army called. A captain in Matanzas."

"What happened?"

"The plantations in Matanzas and Cienfuegos. They are destroyed."

Sugar Man looked stunned. "Destroyed? How?"

"Fire. Someone set the fields on fire and because the crops are young they are gone. Oh my God. You are ruined."

Army said nothing. Stricken, he leaned against a porch post while the Colombian ran back into the house.

Jomar marveled. "The army. It could not stop them. What now?"

Army pounded a fist into his hand. "I thought the army could protect us."

"I can make a few calls. To see if they caught anyone."

The plantation owner remained silent for a few minutes. He cringed at the thought that his world and that of his workers was collapsing around him. Obol poked him at the knee with the bone before he answered. "Okay."

But Nelsa opened the screen door and stepped onto the front porch. She was upset. "Mandito. Señor Pastrami is very frightened. He does not feel safe here."

The sugar baron became annoyed. "Where is he?"

"On the telephone. He speaks with Colombia."

"Colombia?

Army turned to Jomar.

"Maybe he's ..."

Pastrami pushed open the screen door, agitated: "Armando, you told me it was safe. Where was the army? What if someone comes here and burns the house while we sleep?"

Army stopped the rant, cold. "You want to go back to Colombia? Because if you do, we'll drive you to the airport right now."

The Colombian stopped abruptly. Army turned to Jomar. "Forget about calling anyone. Let's go to Matanzas and talk to the captain."

The sugar baron turned to the Colombian. "Are you with us?"

His head bowed in thought, the manager looked up. "Yes, yes I am with you."

The threesome piled into the Hudson and zoomed off into the evening.

———— • ————

Army looked at the accountant's house in Matanzas. It was covered by thick, black smoke. A captain and two other officers were on the front porch. They held handkerchiefs over their mouths. The detective chased the fumes with his left hand and shook hands with the captain. They conversed while the Colombian used a flashlight to survey the property.

"It is as I expected," Pastrami said, coughing, covering his mouth and shining a light on the blackened earth. Everything must be uprooted and replaced."

"How long will it take? Army said, covering his mouth.

"With the proper number of field workers, a month. But there is Cienfuegos, too. Then we have to wait until the ripening stage. It could be a year before you see sugar."

Jomar interrupted. "Armando, the officer said the fire was set in two locations, assisted by the wind."

"Did they catch anybody?"

"No. But the captain said he spoke with my uncle, who told him he received an anonymous tip about Ernesto. Communists have been seen in this area and in Cienfuegos."

———— • ————

The next morning on their way back to Havana, Army thought about the ramifications of his soon-to-be sugar shortage. So many people would be affected adversely. Good people. People who'd been working for his family for years. He sighed. His driver heard him.

"Armando. Your Wolves are playing Havana today."

Devastated by the day's events, he nodded.

"Maybe it would be good for you to go to the game. I mean. To take your mind off things."

Army stared straight ahead. "We have to take Pastrami to Santa Cruz."

"Okay, but really Armando. Big game. Make you forget about your troubles for a while. You should go."

He turned to the detective. "You wanna go?"

Jomar shook his head sadly. "I cannot. I have something important to do. But I can drive you to the ballpark."

Army thought for a moment. "Can we stop at the convent first?"

The detective nodded, and less than two hours after they dropped off Pastrami they were cruising along Avenida del Puerto past tugboats, tankers, a US Navy ship, Plaza de Armas on the left and Castle Morro on the right. And then the convent.

Who knew what he would find there?

Chapter 61

Lucifer and the Archangel

ARMY SAT ON the stone bench, enjoying the peacefulness washing over him in the open courtyard. Spotting the statue of St. Michael the Archangel, he walked to it and moved deeper along the wall to the back, where murals had been painted on walls in a secluded, dark corner made dingier by a black cloud hovering over the quadrangle.

As he squinted to see who'd signed the paintings, he heard Mother Maria Jose.

"So how long have you been head of the Student Federation?"

"Six months, Mother," a familiar baritone voice replied. Army stiffened.

"I heard your speech in the auditorium the other day and I agree with you, Ernesto."

Army grimaced when he heard his step-brother's name. He wanted to rush out and grab him by the throat. Instead, he listened and watched from behind a large rubber plant.

"You were in the audience, Mother?"

"Yes. I had just finished giving a classroom lecture on corruption and salvation in current day Cuba when I passed by the auditorium. I was drawn in by your words. I enjoyed the way you quoted Marti, particularly how he projected domination of Cuba by the US based upon ownership of our plantations. The United Fruit Company and other American-owned businesses here pay the workers poorly. Just look around here, at the orphanage. So many parents have given up their children for adoption because they can barely feed themselves."

He nodded and pursed his lips. He wasn't surprised to hear what she said. And then he heard the sweetest voice in the world.

"Ernesto, what are you doing here?" Bonita said, coming into view.

Army saw the disappointment on Mother Maria Jose's face at the intrusion. "Well, it was nice speaking with you and good luck," the nun said. "I'll run along now."

The rebel leader took her left hand and kissed her on the cheek.

"What is that odor on your clothes?" she said. "You look tired. What's wrong?"

"Nothing. I was up all night. I just wanted to sit down and talk with you."

He led Bonita to the stone bench, where they sat. He held her hands and looked into her eyes. He spoke with urgency. His stepbrother watched intently.

"Come with me tonight. Someone is donating $2,000 to our cause. I want you to collect it. I want you to be our treasurer."

Sensing something amiss as he moved closer, the teacher pulled her hands from his. "Why should I? You still haven't purchased books, paper and pens with the money I gave you."

The rebel dismissed her concern. "Come with me."

"I'm waiting for Armando."

"Armando? The Sugar Man? Ha-ha-ha."

Army stepped out of the shadows. Bonita and the reprobate looked up in shock. She ran to his arms; Ernesto sprinted out the door. It was as if Lucifer had been surprised by Michael the Archangel.

"That bastard," Army said, "are you okay?"

But before she could answer Army ran out of the courtyard, past the elderly nun at the front desk and onto the street in front of the convent. He yelled to the detective sitting in the Hudson. "Did you see Ernesto run by here?"

"No, I saw no one." he said, stepping out of the auto and joining his boss on foot around the back of the building.

"Call your uncle. Tell him Ernesto is in the area."

Bonita was sitting at the Tranquil Fountain when Army returned to the courtyard. He was agitated. "He got away. He must have had help."

She was looking at her hands, smudged with a dark substance. He looked at them too.

"What is this?" she said.

He smelled the soot on her hands. "Methane and nitrous oxide."

"How do you know?"

"My plantation in Matanzas was burned to the ground last night. Destroyed. Cienfuegos, too. Methane and nitrous oxide were in the air."

Her jaw dropped. "What are you going to do now? I mean. The workers."

"If I didn't have to deal with the debt, I could keep them on the payroll. I could even keep the clinic open."

"Oh my God, the clinic. I forgot about that. How will you keep things going?"

Army shrugged. "Profits from the Fox Hole, I hope."

Bonita wrapped her arms around him. Lost in the comfort of her embrace, he looked into her eyes, sighed and said: "Jomar suggested a baseball game, to take my mind off this. What do you think?"

"There are dark clouds above. But who cares. Let's go."

Chapter 62

Avoiding the Chamber

S ATURDAY NIGHT AT 11:15, a Harley with two riders parked across from the northern archway to the cemetery under a half moon. Ernesto and a young Barbudo dismounted and walked across silent Calle Zapata, under the archway and trotted straight down Avenida Cristoból Colón. At the central chapel, they turned right and ran along Calle G for about a quarter-mile past tombs and mausolea grand and less noteworthy. On Calle 6 they turned left along a narrow path separating more above-ground sepulchers until they were in a direct line with mausoleum No. 107.

They hid behind a large tombstone and watched the house of the dead. Ernesto looked at his wristwatch. "We are thirty minutes early," he whispered. "We will wait and see who goes in or comes out."

They waited for an hour, thirty minutes past the deadline. No one had gone in or out of the burial chamber. The rebel leader looked at his teenage accomplice.

"Are you afraid to go in there?"

The biker swallowed hard. "This place makes me nervous. But I will go in to prove myself to you."

Ernesto smirked. "Relax. Here, take my hat. You are my size and build. And your beard is full."

"What do I say if he is in there?"

"You say: 'The job is done. The envelope.' There should be $2,000 in it. Here is a flashlight. Count the money before you leave."

The young man with a big heart put on the hat, took a deep breath, and stood . Ernesto watched him walk along the narrow path directly to the mausoleum with the iron gate. He pulled open the screeching door and walked inside.

Suddenly the Barbudo-in-charge saw two men in suits emerge from behind the vault and stand guard at the iron door. His heart pounded. He knew he could not warn the teenager without risk. So, he waited silently.

And then he heard Grau yell from inside: "Ernesto Randal, you are under arrest for arson, conspiracy, reckless endangerment and acts of terror."

The two men grabbed the Barbudo when he ran out. They handcuffed him. Grau took the flashlight, shined it on the teen and yelled in Spanish. "*Que carajo*! It is not him. Where is he?"

"Who?" the young man said.

"You know who."

"I do not know what you are talking about."

Grau became enraged. "I will get it out of you before the night is through."

The chief, his two men and their prisoner disappeared into the darkness and the rebel leader sat there with a pounding heart. He'd engineered his own reprieve, but for how long?

Chapter 63
The Power of Chango

ARMY WAS HAVING his morning coffee and burnt toast at the end of the bar when a surprise visitor appeared.

"Army."

He looked toward the entrance: "Meyer?"

Lansky was alone. That was surprising because he knew that the Mafia's most valuable asset, Batista's Casino Czar, usually walked with his bodyguard/chauffeur.

Army dropped everything, walked to the important visitor, shook his hand and turned to El Angel. "Bring us some coffee."

Lansky waived him off. "My driver's waitin'" he said in a gravelly voice. "Can't stay. Can we talk private?"

"Sure." They sat at a table in the corner, the rebels' spot.

"Last week the Minister of Labor took a work gang to a construction site. He replaced my workers with his. You are the Minister of Labor. Correct?"

"Yes, I am. I didn't know that you were constructing the building. I just wanted to give some Cubans in a poor neighborhood a ..." Lansky cut him off.

"It took me a week to straighten this out. I had to go to the top. Your guys are gonna have to find another job. And you owe me $500.00 for the problems you created at the construction site. You have until tomorrow."

Army blinked. "Meyer, I've lost three plantations to sabotage. Sugar production is non-existent. Cut me some slack."

"Sorry, kid. Nothin' I can do. I walk a tightrope every day here. I gotta keep everybody happy. When they're not happy, I gotta find a way to make 'em smile. You know what I mean?"

He didn't answer.

"Well, you're creatin' a lotta bad will for yourself here. The vig. The problem with the construction site. Shape up, kid. Take some advice: You need balance. Balance in your personal life and in business."

The Mafia's financial genius stood and looked around. "Nice place."

Then, he turned and walked out without further word.

Army sat there like a sad clown.

"More trouble?" El Angel said.

Army stared at the floor. "More trouble."

Celia rushed in. "Armando, I have news about Ernesto and Santeria." He looked up. "He dress in a costume. Dance to drums. Sing and put people in a trance. Especially women. He become Chango."

"So he's a song-and-dance man."

"What?"

"Never mind. He's a wanted man. Police are looking for him. Where does he do his little dance?"

"He keep it secret until day of the dance. Then, Santeria people go to watch him and bring Chango gifts like frogs and chicken legs and things."

Army winced. "Find out where the next dinner dance is and we'll surprise him."

———◆———

The first-floor hallway in the School of Education was deserted. Bonita was walking with other students out of a classroom when she heard her name.

She turned to see an old friend. "Manzanillo!" she exclaimed. She ran to him and they hugged. "I heard that you left the University."

"I did, for personal reasons. But how are you? Are you still in mourning over Pablo?"

A sad look crossed her face. "I will never be over Pablo, but I am in love."

He was surprised. "In love? Already?"

"I did not plan this. It just happened out of the blue. He is a special man."

"Do I know him?"

"His name is Armando Lobo."

Manzanillo raised his eyebrows. "The plantation owner? The capitalist?"

She laughed. "Yes, the capitalist. Are you still with Juliet and the other communists?"

He looked at his wristwatch. "I am. Juliet and I are meeting in five minutes. There is a Santeria ceremony in the basement. In a classroom. Would you like to come?"

"I am not a believer in Santeria. But I would love to see Juliet. How long is the ceremony?"

"An hour or so. Come on. *Vamanos.*"

She followed Manzanillo to the basement, where they joined other students filing into the room. Juliet, a bleached blond with a natural tan, waived to them from a seat in an empty front row below a small stage. Bonita sat on one side of her and Manzanillo on the other.

"It is so good to see you," Juliet said as she stood and hugged her. "I did not know you were interested in Santeria."

"I'm not. I wanted to say hello to you."

They sat and were about to begin conversing when the sound of drums overtook the room, which filled to capacity quickly with about forty adults.

A black woman dressed in a long white dress and two black males in white shirts, slacks and shoes started doing Orisha chants. A bata drum player sitting in a folding chair accompanied them. The drum - made of caoba wood - was wide mouthed on one end with a small opening on the other. It rested on the lap of a drummer, also dressed in white. He tapped the wide part rhythmically with each hand as Chango danced onto the stage.

Caught off guard, Bonita said to Juliet, rhetorically: "Is that Ernesto?"

"Yes. Do you know him?"

Fascinated by the chants, drum beats, and dance, she didn't answer. It all had a hypnotic effect, somewhat like that of a snake charmer who mesmerizes a Cobra by playing the same tune over and over on a pungi. So, when Juliet and Manzanillo left their seats abruptly after being summoned by a security guard, the suggestible schoolteacher didn't notice the strangers who'd replaced them.

Soon she became the Cobra, captivated by Chango, who looked down and saw her. He danced to the repetitive beat directly in front of her. His performance went on for an hour, during which he took note of her susceptibility to his power. To boost her state of suggestibility near the end, he produced a pinwheel of red and silver, the colors matching his blouse, on which there was an embroidered silver star surrounded by a circle. He crouched and held the pinwheel in front of the easily swayed convent girl.

Round and round twirled the wheel, bop-bop-bop … bop-bop-bop sounded the drums repeatedly and before long Bonita followed the spin up the steps to the stage, where she danced in a trance to the beat. Chango whispered into her ear as she stared at the spinning wheel in his hand.

"Ernesto is Pablo … Ernesto is Pablo … Ernesto is Pablo."

The audience followed the action with rapt attention. Gradually, the chant and drumbeat faded, Chango stood still and the pinwheel stopped turning. Chango led Bonita back to her seat to end the ceremony. The spectators showed their respect by remaining silent.

When the audience left the room, Bonita remained in the chair, still spellbound. A few Barbudos loitered around the stage, but exited when their leader, back in his khaki outfit, nodded for them to leave.

He sat next to her.

"Are you all right?" he said.

"Yes, but I feel confused."

"In what way?"

"I can't explain it."

"Tomorrow we are planning a protest, but no violence."

Bonita looked at him dreamily. She put her hand on his.

"I have been waiting to hear you say that for a long time, Pablo."

The reprobate leaned over and kissed her on the lips. There was no resistance. He kissed her again and thrust his tongue into her mouth. She began to breathe heavily.

Chapter 64
Bewildered Bonita

Army was waiting for his sweetheart in his Chevy parked in the dark near the entrance to the convent, when a 1939 Ford sedan pulled in front of his car. A spotlight above the portal enabled him to see four people in the automobile. The male driver and a woman in front turned to a couple in the back seat of the car with open windows.

"Are you sure you are all right, Bonita?" the driver said. "You look bewildered."

Army heard every word and wondered who the driver was. His heart pounded as he listened, watched and smelled his lover's perfume in the air with the intensity of a wolf in waiting.

"I'll be all right," she said. "Pablo will walk me to the door."

"Pablo?" Juliet said.

"Pablo?" Manzanillo said.

"Pablo?" Army said.

The back door of the car swung open. Army pounded his fist on the dashboard when he saw Ernesto step out first, followed by Bonita. She clasped his hand and Army sprang from his Chevy.

"Oh no you don't, Pablo or Chango or whoever you are today." He shoved Ernesto and Bonita fell, striking her head on the pavement. Immediately he knelt by her side and lifted her, gently.

"Are you okay honey?"

She placed a hand on her forehead. "Where am I?"

Out of the car by now, Manzanillo and Juliet knelt next to her and rubbed her hands. "You are at the convent," Manzanillo said. "We drove you. Remember?"

"No," Bonita said standing with the help of Juliet. "The last thing I recall is the Santeria ceremony."

"Where is Ernesto?" Juliet said. They all turned to see him disappear into the darkness.

"We saw him kissing her in the empty classroom," Manzanillo said. "After the Santeria ceremony. He said they were lovers. But earlier she told me she was in love with you, Armando. She seemed confused so we insisted on driving her back to the convent."

"Santeria ceremony?"

Bonita interrupted. "At the University. In the basement. I think I saw Ernesto."

The two men looked at each other. "She *thinks* she saw Ernesto?" they said simultaneously.

Juliet responded: "Ernesto, er, Chango has been known to draw people into a powerful trance. Sometimes entire audiences."

Army felt Bonita's forehead. "You'd better stay at my place tonight."

"No, I'm all right. Please. Just walk me to the door."

He accompanied her inside the convent and remained at her side through the courtyard, looking for the Svengali until they came to a locked door. She opened it with a key, kissed him goodnight, and closed it behind her.

The couple was gone when Army returned to his car, still looking right and left for his shapeshifter half-brother. Within a minute or two he was driving along the Malecón, searching for him. He spoke aloud.

"We'll meet again, you bastard. And you will feel the pain."

Chapter 65

More Than Rum

THE FOX HOLE's early-evening patrons were loud. Army stood and watched them from his ornate jail. American sailors were shouting and gulping shots. A gaggle of gamblers gathered around Errol Flynn, showing a card trick at a table. Aspiring Hollywood starlets smoked and drank within earshot of Tyrone Power and Cesar Romero, who seemed to enjoy sharing ribald jokes with the navy boys.

Army turned to the small bar, where he retreated with a bottle of his own brand rum. He sat, sipped, lit a cigar and blew smoke rings toward the ceiling. He heard a click at the gate below and footsteps over the din of the crowd.

"Celia allowed me to come up," Jomar said. "I hope you do not mind."

"Grab a seat," Army said, pulling a stool next to his. "Grab a glass. Let's make it a party. You, me, and Fox Hole."

The detective did so and toasted the man who'd been in his charge for some time. So, when Army offered him a cigar he accepted and made a feeble attempt to blow smoke rings like his host. They both laughed.

Jomar placed the cigar in an ashtray. "Armando, I have known you for a good while now and I have come to admire you. Respect you."

Army was flattered by the sudden compliment. "Well thanks. You know, when Grau assigned you to me, I figured you were his spy. I felt I had to watch my back. But that feeling faded over time. I respect you too."

"You have always treated me as a friend, Armando. And that is why I am here. My uncle did want me to spy on you, but my heart was not in it. Actually, I do not respect him. The only information I gave him was about Ernesto visiting the Fox Hole with his Barbudos. But he received that from other detectives as well. He even saw it."

Army patted him on the back. "Don't worry about it."

"This morning my uncle told me something that might be of interest to you. He said Ernesto was supposed to go to a mausoleum to collect money for setting plantations on fire. But it was not Ernesto who went to collect the money. The muchacho who did so ended up in his Chamber of Truth."

Stunned, Army snuffed his cigar in the ashtray. A lightbulb went off in his head. "He called it a 'donation.'"

"What?"

"Ernesto. In the courtyard at the convent. He asked Bonita to go with him to collect a 'donation.' That could have been her. Son-of-a-bitch."

The detective nodded in agreement and sipped some rum. "Detectives interviewed Ernesto at the Fifth Precinct about the arson, but he had an alibi confirmed by his mother and an important Mafioso. Furthermore, there was no evidence to link him to the crime. They had to release him.

"Who was the Mafioso?"

"Junior."

Army nodded. "I'm not surprised."

"I am sorry, Armando," Jomar said, standing. "I must go now. My father needs my help with a project he is working on tonight. Thank you for the rum and the cigar."

They shook hands and the nephew of the Chief of the Anti-Communist Squad skipped down the stairs. Passing him on the way up was Cutter in his disguise. The two acknowledged each other, although they'd never met.

El Angel interrupted from below. "Armando, please pick up the telephone.

Army did so and was surprised to hear who was on the other end of the receiver.

"It's Big Bob. Courtesy call. Just want ya ta know I hold your gamblin' note now. An' I expect ya ta keep up the vig payments, unless ya can't, in which case I'll take over your operations here."

"Over my dead body."

"That can be arranged."

Sugar Man slammed down the receiver.

"What?" Cutter said.

Army poured him a glass of rum. "The big bastard. He says he bought my father's note."

Cutter sipped. "The plantations are ash."

"That's right. Can't produce for a year."

"How's he plan to enforce collections? The Irish Mob?"

"That's what I said to Popi."

He stared at Cutter. Something clicked. "Big Bob was the 'donor.'"

"What?"

"He paid Ernesto to destroy my plantations. Then he set him up for Grau. The way Ernesto tried to set up Bonita. But it didn't work, both times.

The spy became animated. He swilled his drink. "So why don't you go on offense? He has a plantation."

Chapter 66
"Ernesto Is Pablo"

ERNESTO WAS SITTING at the teacher's desk in classroom 77 when the teacher arrived with books under her arms. He was playing Orisha chants on a phonograph. The lights were dim.

She became angry when she saw him. "Why are *you* here?"

Unruffled, he responded softly: "Please, close the door. I am preparing for the rally. You remember. The rally."

Those last two words sidetracked her. "Oh," she said, recalling the words from the Chango episode. "The rally."

Bonita shut the door and sat at a small desk facing him, like a student waiting for a professor's instructions.

"Hear the chant, Bonita? It is for good fortune. That we may have a good rally without violence or arrests. Remember the wand?"

The son of Santeria held the spinning red-and-silver pinwheel in front of her and spoke softly while the hypnotic music played in the background. The wheel turned. Her eyelids became heavy. When he thought she was more suggestible he spoke softly.

"Ernesto is Pablo… Ernesto is Pablo… Ernesto is Pablo."

The more he repeated, the deeper she sank under his spell. And then he told her the plan, softly.

"You are fighting for the cause. A cause that is just. Against an evil dictator. You will say this to the crowd. In front of the Fifth Precinct. 'We are here to protest Fulgencio Batista, an evil dictator, and his hatchet man, Lieutenant Colonel Emilio Grau.' In the name of Pablo de la Torre, we condemn the brutality of the Anti-communist Squad.

"But first. After class you will ask your students to follow you to four buses at the bottom of the staircases. The buses will drive you and me to the Fifth Precinct."

The Santeria scoundrel waited a few seconds, stopped the music and rose to turn on the lights. Students began filing into the classroom. Bonita blinked. She looked around and he and the phonograph were gone.

The classroom hour went by quickly before she made an announcement:

"Buses are waiting to take us to a rally in front of the Fifth Precinct. A rally to protest Batista and Grau. Those who are interested can follow me."

Most of the pupils followed her to the first of four buses. Ernesto appeared and Bonita took his hand. Together they stood up front in the bus and led the students singing La Bayamesa, the Cuban National Anthem.

The demonstrators stepped out of the buses and gathered at the entrance to the most feared police building in Cuba. A policeman in a guard tower picked up a telephone. Within minutes a half-dozen officers tried to break through the blockade in order to penetrate the siege by about 200 dissenters. They failed.

In a flash, the maniacal Marxist produced a soap box and placed her on top of it with a bullhorn. She raised the amplifier to her lips.

"We are here to protest Fulgencio Batista, an evil dictator, and his hatchet man, Lieutenant Colonel Emilio Grau," she began. "In the name of Pablo de la Torre, we condemn the brutality of the Anti-communist Squad."

The hoodwinked school teacher repeated the statement over and over as about 30 policemen swinging nightsticks encircled the demonstrators, who were packed into a tight formation. The group fought back as one, with fists and placards as well as clubs they wrestled from the officers. The battle was at close quarters There were cries by young men and women. There was blood, lots of blood, including Ernesto's as officers swinging billy clubs made inroads into a forest of fury.

A cop clubbed Ernesto and he stabbed the officer in the gut. Bonita saw the attack and snapped.

"Stop," she cried. "Stop the violence. Stop! Stop!"

She was hysterical when police pulled her off the soapbox, dragged her through the skirmish and into the lobby of the station house. She looked around for her Svengali, but he was nowhere in sight. Two policemen had her by the arms when Grau appeared with his detectives, Jorge, Jose, and Julio.

"So, you challenge me at my front door," Grau growled. "Where is Ernesto?"

"Ernesto is Pablo."

"Pablo, huh," he said as he reared back with his right hand and slapped her face with such force that it turned her head thirty degrees and knocked her unconscious.

"Drag her to the chamber."

Chapter 67
Fit to Be Tied

SCREAMS AND CRIES could still be heard from outside as Grau followed the prisoner. Her captors hauled her through the odor of stairway urine to the basement, where the detainees were shouting and jumping around in an excited state like frightened zoo animals. When they saw Bonita pulled into the chamber they yelled, almost in unison.

"Nooooo. Noooooo. Nooooo."

But the Chief of the Anti-communist Squad was undaunted by the disturbance. Once they were all in the torture chamber he gave the order. "Strip her, tie her to the iron bed and hose her down."

The three detectives looked at each other and at the chief and then complied as the young woman, now conscious, cried for mercy.

"No, please do not do this. No, please," she pleaded as the policemen ripped off her blouse and skirt, bra and panties.

Hearing her pleas, the inmates became more agitated, rattling the iron bars, stomping their feet and screaming: "Nooooo, Nooooo. Nooooo."

The ruckus was so deafening that three uniformed policemen raced to the scene with their guns drawn. By now, Bonita was naked and tied to the metal bed, pleading for her life.

The exquisiteness of her body wasn't lost on all of the men in the room as well as the cops outside looking in. In fact, they all became so aroused by what they were witnessing that Grau became uncomfortable. He didn't want this to turn into a gang rape.

"Untie her!" he shouted.

"What?" said Jorge, who tied her.

"Untie her!"

The detective untied the alluring prisoner and Grau threw her a blanket to wrap around herself. He ordered everyone out of the cell and handed her the clothing that had been stripped from her. They all watched as she dressed in tattered clothes amid the tumult outside. The Chief's heart pounded with excitement. Other hearts were pounding, too, from outside the bars.

Grau looked at the crowd of cops in front of the cell room door and spotted one of his detectives. "Jose, take her to the room upstairs, next to my office."

The room to which the detective escorted Bonita was like a cell, a foul-smelling chamber, although the door was wooden, not iron. Inside there was one rectangular window high up on the back wall and it had iron bars, through which the fading sounds of a rally gone awry could barely be heard. There were four bunk beds, two on each side, and three young women in bras and panties standing around when the detective pushed her to the dirty floor, turned and slammed the door shut on his way out.

"Muchacha, what did they do to you?" a blonde said as she and her fellow prisoners helped Bonita to her feet. Too shaken to speak, the newcomer wept as they led her to a bottom bunk and sat her.

"Bring her some water," the blonde said.

Bonita drank from a plastic cup, after which multiple hands stroked her hair and rubbed her arms.

"There, there," the blonde said, sidling next to her on the bed. "Tell us what happened."

"They stripped me in the chamber. They tied me to the metal bed, naked. Then Grau ordered them to put me here."

"Did they rape you?"

"No. Thank God."

The blonde gave a knowing look. "Grau wants you for himself. That is why you are here, with us."

"You mean..."

"Yes. Soon you will be in his bed. Next door."

Then the blonde did something that heretofore had been unimaginable to the virgin from Convento Inmaculada. She kissed Bonita on the lips, thrust her tongue inside her mouth and grabbed a breast. Bonita recoiled like a frightened cat, ran to the back of the room and curled into a ball on the dirty tiled floor. A cockroach and a spider fled for their lives.

The blonde shrugged and looked at her friends. "Poor baby," she said. "She has nowhere to go."

Chapter 68
Grau Has His Prize

THE TOWHEAD ROSE, removed her panties and bra and started to walk toward the newcomer when suddenly the door sprang open. Grau stood there, surveyed the room and summoned Bonita with his index finger.

"Come with me young lady."

Afraid to go and scared to stay, slowly she rose and warily she walked. She decided to take her chances with the man who'd freed her from a bed of iron. So, she willingly accompanied the chief to the office next door, where he took a seat on a black leather sofa across from his desk. He grabbed a bottle of sweet Legendario Elixir rum and filled two snifters halfway.

"Sorry, I would rather not," she said.

"My, my. What a short memory. I am the one who saved you from gang rape. Would you like to return to the chamber?"

His captive thought for a moment, accepted the drink and sipped it. Within an hour they'd consumed half the bottle and she was drunk. The captor took her by the hand and led her like a child through another door.

Once they were inside the room he flipped on a switch, revealing a large bed with a nightstand on which there stood a clear glass pitcher of water. The wooden floor was dirty. Cockroaches and spiders scattered. She turned to him.

"Please. I am a virgin," she slurred.

"A virgin? Really! You have been with the lowlife Lobo, Ernesto. You have been with the highlife Lobo, Armando, and you are a virgin? I do not believe it. I will have to see for myself."

Grau sat at the foot of the bed and watched her.

"No, please," she said, unsteady on her feet.

"How many years do you have?"

"Twenty five."

"Unbelievable. Remove your clothes."

"No, please."

"Take them off or I will. And I will not be gentle."

The prisoner slowly pulled off her torn blouse and slipped out of her ripped skirt. Grau ogled her. She was in her bra and panties, trying to maintain her balance.

"The rest. Take off the rest."

Inelegantly she removed her bra and panties. He started to breathe heavily as she stood naked in front of him. He leaned over and kissed each voluptuous breast while his hands enveloped her buttocks. She quivered. He rose, scooped her into his arms and laid her on the bed. She watched as he slipped out of his leather loafers, unbuttoned his white shirt and threw it onto a chair. A spider ran as one of the cuffs smacked it on the floor.

She looked away as she heard him unbuckle his belt, unzip his slacks and pull them off. Next were his undershorts and sox.

"Hail Mary, full of grace …" Bonita began.

Grau kneeled on the floor, spread her legs and buried his face in her vulva. As he explored it with his tongue he panted until the urge to penetrate her overcame the pleasure of tasting her. He rose with his penis at attention.

"… and blessed is the fruit of thy womb, Jesus …"

She continued to pray as he pulled her toward him, preparing to rob her of her virginity. Then, with unexpected suddenness he screamed in anguish.

He looked down. On his right foot was a scorpion. Its furry stinger was imbedded in the flesh near the big toe. He attempted to shake the eight-legged arthropod from his foot in vain. He trembled and fell to the floor, shaking. He was going into shock.

Startled by the sudden turn of events, Bonita sat up and watched her would-be rapist quivering on the floor, as helpless as she'd been. Unsteadily, she gathered her clothes, dressed and looked around the room. She saw a door near the nightstand. But something made her look back at her impotent attacker. He was trying to speak. She looked at the door, then at Grau on the floor. He was sweating and shaking profusely.

"Oh God. What do I do?"

As nervous as she was and as much as she wanted to run, the daughter of the House of Charity staggered to her fallen attacker, kneeled and put her ear to his lips.

"Medicine," he whispered. "Drawer," he pointed.

She swayed to the nightstand and opened the drawer. Inside were dildos, handcuffs and a vial with one white tablet. She pulled off the top, slid the tablet into her hand, stumbled to the dying man and dropped the pill onto his tongue. As she was about to leave he grabbed her ankle.

"Water," he mumbled.

A knock on the door froze her on the spot.

"Sir, Jorge here. Sorry to disturb you. But you have an important call."

Shaking in her shoes, the prisoner staggered to the nightstand and grabbed the pitcher. The knocking grew louder.

"Sir, the Chief of Secret Police is on the phone."

Her heart pounding, the detainee stumbled to her fallen attacker and poured the water into his mouth. She placed the empty pitcher on the floor, wobbled to the door next to the nightstand and pulled a rusty bolt to the right. It resisted.

The knocking grew louder. "Sir, sir," shouted the detective, pounding on the door."

Bonita struggled with the bolt. She jiggled it until it slid open. Through the door she staggered down a dark, narrow staircase two flights to another door. She heard the door upstairs burst open and a man scream. Her trembling fingers fumbled with a small nodule on the doorknob. Suddenly, the door opened and she was outside in a dark and barren field.

Celia and El Angel were sweeping the Fox Hole floor when they heard a knock on the front door.

"Go away," Celia yelled. "We are closed."

But after another knock El Angel opened the door. He expected to see a vagrant. Instead, he saw a young woman slumped on the pavement in front of the entrance. Upon closer inspection he realized who it was. Celia joined him.

"Bonita!" she cried.

Celia and El Angel lifted her by the arms, carried her into the bar and sat her at a table.

"Water, Celia, a glass of water," El Angel said, holding her in place.

Celia ran for the sink behind the bar. Quickly she returned and lifted the glass to her injured friend's bruised and swollen lips. She poured gently.

"Celia turned to El Angel: "Get Armando."

The bartender ran to El Carcel's gate, unlocked it and raced up the stairs. He saw the boss passed out on the couch. An empty bottle of rum was on the floor next to him.

"Armando, wake up, wake up," El Angel said while shaking him."

"Wha, What? What's going on?"

"Bonita."

Army staggered down the stairs to the table where Bonita sat in torn clothes, smelling of rum and staring into space. One look at her sobered him. He dropped to a knee and hugged her for a long moment. She was mute. He pulled back and spoke softly. Her eyes were bloodshot; her face swollen.

"Honey, what happened?"

"Rally. Fifth Precinct," she slurred.

"Ernesto?"

She didn't answer.

He turned to the other two. The look on his face would have scared a murderer.

"Angel, help me bring her upstairs. Let's take the steps outside. Celia come with us. Stay with her until we get back."

Chapter 69
Search for a Scoundrel

WHEN BONITA WAS safely seated with Celia on the sofa inside his apartment, Army darted to the bedroom and slipped on fresh pants, shoes and a black T-shirt. He opened the bottom drawer of a dresser and pushed aside neatly-stacked socks and shirts to reach a metal box. He opened it with a key and pulled out a fully-loaded 9 mm Luger, the one that almost killed him. He also grabbed a garrote and a folding knife issued by the O.S.S. He opened and closed both ends. One had a four-inch spike; the other a four-inch razor. Pleased at the ease with which the knife still worked, he slipped it and the garrote into his right pants pocket. He pushed the pistol into his waistband, sprinted to the living room, and waved to El Angel to follow him. Out the sliding doors and down the stairs they ran to his car.

Within five minutes Army pulled in front of Agnelys' house. Before he got out he pulled out the pistol and handed it to El Angel.

"Wait here, Angel. If you see anyone follow me into the house, take 'em down."

Army pounded on the front door. It was 4:35 a.m. It took a while for Agnelys to answer. When she did, he pushed past her and walked quickly into the house.

"I apologize for this, Agnelys, Where's Ernesto?"

"Why are you here at such a time?" she said, following him into the living room.

"When did you last see him?"

"I do not remember."

Satisfied, he left her in a quandary. "Sorry I disturbed you, dear," he said on his way out.

Army then did something he thought he'd never do again. He drove to Titi's house. It was 5:15 a.m. when he and El Angel arrived. Titi was just getting home. She was with Junior at the front door, which she'd just opened with a key. Hearing footsteps she turned cried out:

"Armando, what are you …"

He burst through the threshold and up the stairs, checking each bedroom. Junior, Titi, and El Angel stood together on the first floor when Army hurried down the stairs and checked the other rooms.

"Where's Ernesto?" he said, ignoring the Mob boss.

"I have not seen him. Why?"

Army looked at Junior with contempt. "Hi, Junior." Then, turning to El Angel: "Let's go."

Titi followed them out the door. "What about the house in Santa Cruz?"

The hot-pursuit duo hopped into the Chevy, where the bartender returned the pistol to him. They sped away and arrived at the Fox Hole in record time. When Army walked into his apartment he saw Celia sitting on the sofa alone, watching a movie on television.

"Where is she?"

"She took a shower and went to sleep in your bed."

"Did she say what happened?"

"No."

He tiptoed into the room and watched Bonita toss and turn. He laid next to her. Startled, she started to pummel him until she realized who he was and where she was. She broke down, crying.

"It's okay," he whispered. "It's me. I'm here for you. No one will ever harm you again. I'll protect you. Forever."

With that assurance, Bonita Di Riva fell asleep in the secure arms of Armando Michael Lobo Armstrong.

Chapter 70

Mad Enough to Kill

Armed with the weapons of his former trade the next morning, Army wiped his mouth with a linen napkin after finishing breakfast with Bonita in his apartment. "Are you going to be all right here?" he said. "Celia and Angel are downstairs if you need them."

She looked worried. "Where are you going?"

"To the plantations. I'll be back tonight. Maybe you should call Mother Maria Jose and tell her you're here."

She bowed her head. "What she thinks no longer concerns me."

He hugged her for a long moment and kissed her lips. She clung to him as he broke her embrace.

"You're safe here, honey. Don't worry. I'll be back as soon as I can."

With that assurance, Army slipped through the trap door to El Carcel and down the stairs to the Fox Hole. He saw Jomar smoking a cigarette and sitting alone at a table.

"Have you eaten breakfast?"

"Yes, the detective replied. "Where are we going?"

"Santa Cruz."

Something fell from under his Guayabera shirt and the detective picked it up.

"What is this for?" Jomar said, holding a 12-inch length of piano wire with small, wooden handles.

"Some things you don't want to know," Army said, taking it from him. "But this time I'll tell. I'm gonna kill Ernesto."

Jomar raised his eyebrows and drew on the cigarette. "Kill Ernesto?"

Army didn't flinch.

"Then why use wire?"

"Because this is personal."

"Then let me help you find him. He stabbed a policeman last night in front of the Fifth Precinct. The officer died. Bonita was there, too. Speaking out against my uncle."

"What happened to her?"

"I was not there. However, other detectives told me that my uncle had her taken to the chamber."

Army bristled. "And then?"

Jomar became uneasy, almost reluctant to say more. He stumbled over the next word. "He, he, he had a change of heart and transferred her upstairs."

"Upstairs?"

"Armando, I do not know what happened from there. But she escaped somehow." He dropped the lit cigarette on the floor and ground it with a foot. Without looking up he waited to hear his boss's reaction.

"I'm going to hold Grau accountable once I find out. Right now, Bonita isn't talking about it. But I know that bastard Ernesto intentionally put her in harm's way."

———◆———

It was noontime when the Hudson pulled in front of the former accountant's house that Army's father had given Titi and Ernesto. The place was abandoned but the exterior appeared to be well maintained. The sun overheated everything on and near it—the slate roof of the A-frame house, the red shutters, grass, and palm trees out front.

Pistols drawn, the two men split up. Army walked to the front of the house and the detective to the rear.

Army looked through a window in the front door to see a house that was comfortably furnished. He turned the knob and was surprised to see that the door opened. It squeaked. He moved slowly and noticed that the dining room had a broken window pane big enough for someone to climb through.

He walked to the kitchen and opened the back door for his bodyguard. Without speaking they split up again. The plantation owner tiptoed up the stairs and the detective descended to the basement. Army noticed that someone had slept in the first bedroom. The other two were tidy.

"Armando," Jomar yelled. "Come down here. Quick."

He ran to the basement to join the detective, who used his fingers to pry the lid off a crate. It contained 20 Springfield T 25 rifles. There were two more containers filled with Thompson submachine guns. Another packing case was marked: "Explosives." Another noted: "Ammunition, Frankford Arsenal." All the crates were stamped "USA."

Jomar ran up the stairs to make a call, but before he reached the phone soldiers were at the door. The plantation owner heard them and raced to the scene.

"Sorry for the intrusion gentlemen," an officer said. "There was more sabotage last night. At the Flanery plantation in Matanzas."

Sugar Man was startled. "What happened?"

"Arson in the field, the electrical plant and the processing plant. The main house burns as we speak."

Army looked at Jomar. "He's ruined."

"Who."

"Big Bob."

Turning to the officer. "Anyone hurt?"

"The plantation manager. He was burned to death while fighting the plantation fire."

Army shook his head in sympathy for Stein and sat down heavily on a wooden chair. He looked up. "Sir, you'll find weapons and explosives in the basement. I think we're all looking for the same man."

Chapter 71
The Wrath of Big Bob

Big Bob stood in the middle of his dying plantation. A long, wet black towel covered his head. Protruding was his bulbous, red and craggy drinker's nose. He was shrouded in dark smoke billowing from a field and two burning factories. He watched helplessly as flames flickered through the windows of the main house and the roof collapsed in a fireball.

Teary-eyed from the chemicals in the air, choking on the poison that entered his lungs, he conjured a witch's brew of evil thoughts, ready to act out a violent play reminiscent of a Shakespearean tragedy. All he needed was a pointy hat.

Suddenly, rain fell from a passing cloud. Thunder and lightning followed in what appeared to be a moment that only could have been crafted by the Bard of Avon: "Fair is foul and foul is fair. Hover through the fog and filthy air."

The big man was visualizing an assassination, not of Macbeth's King Duncan, but of Cuba's Minister of Labor and his brother. He wanted the Sugar Man and the rebel leader dead. He thought about how Ernesto had double-crossed him by ruining his property and how likely it was that Army had put him up to it.

With this misconception in mind the big man walked to a small house formerly occupied by his plantation manager. On the front porch he spotted a note in black ink on a 3x5 piece of white cardboard pinned to the back of a rocking chair. He picked it up and read it: *R.I.P. Young Barbudo.* A photo of the teenager Grau arrested at the cemetery and tortured to death was under it.

Too devastated to even try to discern the meaning, he tossed it on the chair and entered the house. He picked up a telephone and dialed the operator for Boston.

"Shawn? Big Bob. I have a job for you and Mickey. Here in Havana."

Chapter 72

Gettin' Hitched

Copies of Ernesto's picture had been posted all over Cuba under the Spanish and English headings: SE BUSCA MUERTO O VIVO and WANTED DEAD OR ALIVE respectively. Grau had ordered them. He didn't pursue Bonita. And Army decided not to go after him, for now. The cop killer was No. 1 on both of their lists.

A week passed. Ernesto was nowhere in sight and Bonita had recovered sufficiently enough from her ordeal to speak about how she had ended up with him at the Fifth Precinct. A meeting with Juliet, Manzanillo, and Celia in El Carcel helped her piece together the evening of Santeria, the torture chamber and near rape.

Army listened to the story and looked at Bonita. "I want you to stay here instead of the convent. Celia and Angel are here. And even Hiran. He's returned to work part-time. You'll be safe."

"But I must go back to the convent school to teach. And what about my own studies at the University?"

He was firm. "No. No University until that bastard is captured or killed."

While the search for the bad brother continued, his sensitivity to her needs had drawn them closer to each other. She watched him butter her toast at the breakfast table one morning and smiled.

"Armando, Celia once told me that you could have any woman you want here in Havana. I believe her. Yet, you have sacrificed to be with me."

Tenderly he cupped her face with his right hand. With his thumb he gently rubbed the healed cheek that had been bruised. She stared at the discolored skin around his left eye.

"Armando, I know about your desire to work within a corrupt system for the benefit of the people. Are you succeeding?"

He shook his head sadly. "I'm not. I've been kidding myself. I can't change anybody here. The corruption is systemic. I can only continue to help the people who work for me. It'll be difficult."

She looked at him lovingly as he poured her coffee. Her eyes welled. She grabbed his free hand and kissed it.

"You have a big heart," she said. "You have my heart. I'm ready."

"Ready? For what?" he said, stroking her hair.

"I'm ready to marry you. If you still want me."

"If I still want you?" He lifted her, chair and all and kissed her lips as she squirmed, fearful that she was going to fall, but confident that he wouldn't allow it.

———— ◆ ————

The next evening, with Bonita standing by his side at the Fox Hole, Army made the announcement at his corner of the bar.

"Drinks are on the house," he yelled to a plethora of patrons. "We're gettin' hitched."

A roar surged from the drinkers. They held up their glasses to salute the couple. The musicians played *Besame Mucho*. Caught off guard, Celia looked at Hiran in disbelief. They joined El Angel, Hiran and the rest of the staff in pouring themselves a shot of rum and saluting the couple before serving the crowd at the bar. It was a happy time. And it went on for hours.

At closing time Army sat at the bar with his future bride and waved goodbye to the last customer exiting the front door when he spotted the spy entering in his usual disguise.

Cutter walked to the couple and shook hands with Army. He looked at Bonita's bloodshot eyes and the empty cocktail glass in her hand.

"I see you've had a few," he said, smiling.

She frowned.

"It's okay, honey, you remember Mr. Cutter. He drove us home from the Fifth Precinct."

"I didn't mean to upset you," Cutter said, shaking hands with her.

A little tipsy, she smiled: "I don't really drink much. But tonight, is special." She grabbed Army's hand and kissed it. "We're engaged to be married."

With a surprised look Cutter congratulated them. "I'm happy for both of you."

With that, the bride-to-be excused herself and said goodnight to all.

"Do you mind if I talk with Mr. Cutter for a while, honey? I'll help you up the stairs first."

"It's okay. Stay. I'll take the outside stairs."

"Hiran, go with her please," the bar owner said, pouring rum into a cocktail glass for Cutter.

Hiran left with Bonita and Celia. Army turned to Cutter. "Wish me luck." They touched glasses and sipped rum.

"You're gonna need it."

"You think I can't handle marriage?"

"Oh, I'm sure you can. But I don't know if you can handle what I'm about to tell you."

What?.

"Tony Stabo's back."

Army shrugged, "So what?"

"He wants to get even. There's more. Our agents at the airport reported that Shawn Fitzpatrick and Mickey O'Shaughnessy, two Boston hitmen, cleared customs here eight hours ago. The address they wrote on their visas was 3029 Third Ave. in Miramar. In other words, the home of the daughter of one Big Bob, who picked them up."

The groom-to-be put down his drink on the bar and stared at it for a moment.

"Son-of-a-bitch. He was right."

"Who?"

"My father. The Irish Mob. They're here in Havana. To hit me."

"I can't give you protection. Double up on your bodyguards."

Chapter 73

Revenge

Mother Superior was sitting on the stone bench near the Tranquil Fountain, reading a prayer book when her protege entered, smiling. A newspaper was folded under one of her arms. With her palms crossed against her chest she exclaimed: "Mother, I'm getting married."

Maria Jose looked up with resignation. She put down the book, rose and embraced the beautiful young lady she'd helped to nurture for more than two decades.

"I hope you are doing the right thing, my dear. I pray for you every day."

Bonita pulled *The Havana Post* from under her arm and opened it to page two for Mother Superior. Over a 3x5 head shot of Army, the headline read: *Minister to Marry*. The story followed. However, she closed the page before Maria Jose could read it.

Suddenly, a sober Father Luís entered, greeted Maria Jose and hugged the happy bride-to-be. "I just heard you deliver the happy news, dear. Let me see that paper. Before she could dissuade him, he opened it and read the story aloud.

"Minister of Labor Armando Lobo Armstrong usually is planning more jobs for the unemployed," Father Luís read. *"However, last night in the Fox Hole Bar & Restaurant, which he owns in Old Havana, he announced plans for his wedding.*

"Lobo, 36, said he and Bonita Di Riva, 25, are planning to marry sometime next summer. Which proves that affairs of the heart and politics make strange bedfellows. Lobo, son of the late Charmer from Santa Cruz, Lazaro Lobo, is a wealthy capitalist whose home is in Philadelphia, Pennsylvania in the United States. Di Riva, an orphan reared in the Convent Inmaculada Concepcion, is a radical student supporter. She was labeled a communist after she was arrested with Federación Estudiantil Universitaria President Ernesto Randal during a student demonstration at the University of Havana last month."

Mother Maria Jose gasped. "Bonita, you never told me this."

Unfazed, Father Luís continued to read while Bonita blanched: *"The FEU is listed as a radical student organization by the Havana Police Dept. Randal, 20, is wanted for the murder of a police officer during a protest outside the Fifth Precinct last week."*

Mother Superior shifted one of her hands to cover her mouth.

"The student leader was one of about 200 demonstrators who blocked the entrance to the police station while Di Riva was speaking against the government. As police attempted to disburse the mob, Randal stabbed an officer in the stomach, according to witnesses. The policeman was rushed to Hospital Calixto Garcia, where he died the next day.

"Good gracious," Mother Maria Jose said.

"Randal has been charged with murder. He is a fugitive. No charges have been filed against Di Riva.

"Mother of God," the nun cried.

"The capitalist and the communist plan to ride the Friday night train to Matanzas, where they will host an engagement party at the Town Hall the next evening."

"God help you," Mother Superior said, looking up at Bonita.

Chapter 74

Ernesto the Outlaw

ONE PERSON FOR sure would not be attending the engagement party: Ernesto.

Now a rebel platoon leader, the miscreant and a dozen other armed Barbudos dressed in dark green fatigues were sitting along the banks of the Santa Cruz River near a railroad bridge. They were studying a map when three female rebels joined them.

"Look at this," a short chubby one said, handing Ernesto a copy of *The Havana Post*.

He puffed on a cigar and studied his step-brother's photo. He read the article next to it, looked up and asked: "Where did you get this, Carmen?"

"Outside the church. In your Aunt Agnelys' neighborhood."

He glanced at Army's photo and looked up at Carmen. "Where is the nearest telephone?"

"There is a house in the woods about five kilometers from here."

"Vamanos."

The rebels picked up their rifles and knapsacks and made their way over an open field about 100 yards long. They entered a forest of tropical trees and thick foliage, streams, and brush, and continued to a clearing in which a log cabin stood.

While the others remained hidden, Ernesto walked 30 yards across an open field and knocked on the front door repeatedly. No one answered so he stepped to a window along a side of the building. He pulled open the shutters and slipped a knife under the window turning the blade upward, raising the frame about an inch. He slipped his fingers under the opening and lifted the window, climbed through and disappeared inside the house.

After going through each room, he returned to the living room where he found a telephone and dialed a number. Titi answered.

"Mother?"

"Ernesto? Where are you? The whole country is looking for you."

"I need money."

"And why should I give you money? Why should I help you?"

"Because I am your child, Mother. Have you forgotten? I am the one who grew up as a bastard, without love, without a father, or a real mother. I do not even have my father's name."

"Well, you have his house, or one of his houses, but you rejected it."

Ernesto paused, thinking about the accountant's house in which he and his fellow rebels had broken into and stored explosives and arms.

"Mother. Still, I need your help. Please help me. Please."

"You are a monster."

"I am your son. Please help me, Mother. Please. I need money. They want to kill me."

The phone line went silent for a few seconds. "How much?"

"Whatever you can spare. Take the Friday night train to Santa Cruz. Then go to the house Lobo left us."

"I have no address."

"Just tell any taxi driver to take you to the accountant's house on the Lobo Plantation. And please do not tell anyone about this."

As he hung up, Carmen fell to the floor under the open window. She'd landed with a thud.

"What are you doing here?" the Barbudo leader said.

"I have a call to make, too," she said somewhat defiantly.

"Then you can meet us. At the bridge."

———— ♦ ————

Within an hour the rebels had fanned out along a bank of the Santa Cruz River. They looked up at a railroad bridge over which the train to Santa Cruz and Matanzas traveled regularly.

They opened their knapsacks, revealing dynamite sticks, blasting caps and rubber-coated wires, which they retrieved gently from each bag.

Ernesto pulled a wooden dynamite plunger blasting box from his sack and placed it on the grass. He looked up and made a sketch of the bridge on a white pad, circling key structural points.

"We will work in teams of two he said to his men and women. "In the seven spots I have noted. Teresa and Luísa will cover our flank while we are rigging the dynamite. Carmen will help when she returns."

It was dark when the last rebel hopped onto the river bank from the bridge's criss-cross supporting structure, which now presented a spider's web of black, interconnecting wires that fed into one cable at the base of the bridge. The cable traveled to the wooden ignition box's pump handle, which stood high, next to Ernesto's knee.

"Is Carmen here?" he said.

No answer.

"When the locomotive is halfway across the bridge I will detonate. Until then, we wait."

Chapter 75

Death Train

Aloud car horn sounded outside Army's apartment, bringing him and Bonita to the iron stairs with their luggage.

Jomar stood outside the Hudson waiting for them. He loaded their bags into the trunk and introduced them to a tall man who emerged from the front seat.

"This is detective Alejandro," he said. "He is here to assist in your security."

Bonita looked at Army. "Security?"

"Yes, honey. Just a precaution. I'm in Batista's cabinet and the newspaper gave away our itinerary."

While Alejandro drove to the train station Jomar divulged the security plan.

"Armando, when we arrive I will wait in the car with you and the señorita while Alejandro checks the platform for suspicious characters. The train has only two cars and a locomotive. You will sit in the car hooked to the locomotive. I will stand in front of the door to the locomotive, watching your back. Alejandro will stand at the other end, facing you and me."

The tall detective pulled in front of the train station and quickly disappeared through the main gates. About fifteen minutes later, he reappeared and gave the okay signal.

The couple boarded the first car and sat in the middle, facing the rear as instructed. In seats facing them were Hiran and Celia.

To the right of Hiran, across the aisle sat Titi, whom Army was surprised to see. He nodded to her and she smiled at him. Seated next to her at the window was Agnelys, two sisters estranged for years and brought together by their concern for a boy gone bad. The Sugar Man nodded to acknowledge Agnelys as Titi turned to her and whispered something.

———— ◆ ————

"All aboard," yelled a conductor outside, leaning with one hand from a handle on the first car, from which he spotted a large man and two smaller ones wearing suits and fedoras racing to the second car. Big Bob, out of breath after their sprint, boarded with Shawn and Mickey. They found a side seat at the rear of the half-filled car. The train's whistle sounded three times, a bell clanged, steam puffed from the locomotive and the chug-chug-chug and screeching silvery-grey metal wheels echoed at the platform. The iron horse slowly left the gate.

The big man pulled a photo of Army from his shirt pocket. He showed it to the hitmen. "This is your mark, lads. Shoot him in the head. But wait 'til we're about to stop in Santa Cruz. There'll be a lotta confusion when we get to the station. I have a car waitin' there for us."

Big Bob dipped back into his pocket and pulled out a handwritten note in black ink on a small sheet of paper bearing the Hotel Plaza logo. He unfolded and read it to himself as the train rocked back-and-forth and the two Irishmen lit cigarettes. He seemed amused by its contents.

This is a promissory note in the amount of $600,000 to be paid to the owner/operator of the Hotel Plaza Casino. It was signed: *Lazaro Lobo, C.E.O. Lobo Chocolate Company, Philadelphia, PA., January 1, 1951.*

An addendum in blue ink and a different handwriting indicated: *This note for $600,000 has been legally transferred to Robert F. Flanery known as Big Bob.* It was signed by Joe Massi and Keith Ballentine, attorney at law, and dated October 1, 1953.

The big man tapped the note against his Timex wristwatch and mused: "Looks like I'm the new Wolf in town."

The cars had been rocking along for a while when Jomar looked at his watch. It was 9:00 p.m. The conductor yelled: "Santa Cruz, next stop." He looked at the other end of the car. Alejandro was gone. Concerned, Jomar started walking the length of the car. Along the way he passed the happy couple. He overheard her distress.

"Mi amor, I must have dropped an earring."

Army ducked under the seat in front of him, but the detective didn't stop walking until he made his way to the end of the car. There, he observed a man in a sports coat leaning against a window in the last seat near the sliding door. A tilted fedora with a wide brim concealed most of his face. He appeared to be sleeping.

The policeman looked at him while he grabbed a handle and slid the door to his right. As he stepped through the doorway he looked left and right to see the two grinning Irishmen standing between the two swaying cars. Before he could pull his pistol, Shawn grabbed the bodyguard's belt and pulled him toward him while Mickey slammed the door shut. Shawn disarmed him and Mickey secured him in a full Nelson.

"Now you can join your amigo," Mickey said, spinning the detective 180 degrees while pushing his neck downward. Jomar heard the clackity-clack of metal wheels and watched wooden planks and iron rails race by. He struggled to break free. He couldn't. So, he placed his right foot on a large bolt protruding from the back of the other car and pushed back. However, Mickey was strong enough to twist Jomar to the right, release the hold around his neck and use his chest to bump him off the train.

The detective flew head first toward the tracks but managed to grab onto a loose chain that dangled from the second car. The train rocked. The wheels clacked. And Jomar bounced off the second car, perilously close to the wheels and track. The two Irishmen used all of their strength to lift the chain off a hook and watch him tumble to the side of the track.

The foreboding sound of a wolf howling caught the attention of the hitmen.

Hear that?" Mickey said. "Yeah, weird."

Army didn't notice the dangerous duo sit in empty seats behind him. He'd been searching for the elusive piece of jewelry.

The groom-to-be suddenly sat up holding a silver earring with a red stone. "Is this it?" he said.

"You found it," a surprised and exultant Bonita said, hugging him tightly. He laughed and relaxed in her embrace, closing his eyes while the car rocked back and forth, lulling him and her into a state of sweet serenity.

When he opened his eyes he noticed the man with the tilted fedora rise and walk toward them. He had his right hand in his pocket and when he stopped in front of the happy couple he pushed back his hat to reveal Tony Stabo. However, he stared at someone in back of his target.

"How's ya sista, Dago?" Shawn said with a grin.

Tony flipped open a six-inch blade. "I'm gonna slice you Micks up."

Out of the corner of his eye Army saw a handgun emerge along the left side of his seat. It was aimed at Tony.

Army pushed the pistol up. A bullet discharged, shattering the window next to Agnelys. She screamed. Shawn stood. Tony and Shawn struggled with the knife and gun.

Armando Michael Lobo Armstrong sprang into action, shielding Bonita and Celia. Another bullet discharged and he fell to the floor.

———◆———

Meanwhile, on the ground the rebel leader and his cohorts watched the train reach the crossing. Suddenly, a faint voice could be heard from afar as Ernesto gripped the handle of the ignition box.

"Ernesto no!"

He turned to see Carmen in the open field 50 yards away. She was running toward him. He looked up at the train entering the bridge. He looked back at Carmen, now closer with soldiers in hot pursuit. She was waving at him now and shouting.

"No Ernesto. No!"

Perplexed, he turned back to the bridge. The locomotive and two cars were closing in on the center of the bridge. He turned toward her. The soldiers started firing. His fellow rebels returned fire. Bullets whizzed back and forth between the two groups. Still, he kept both hands on the ignition box handle.

He looked up. The train was nearly halfway across the bridge. He looked at the rebel girl. She was within a few yards. The gunfire continued. She was in the soldiers' line of fire.

"No Ernesto, no," she shouted. "Your mother and aunt are on the train."

"My aunt?" In horror he looked up again. The locomotive roared to the midpoint of the bridge. He looked back at Carmen. A bullet exited between her eyes. She fell dead.

Ernesto screamed in anguish. He pushed the handle down with all of his strength. The wooden span lit up like fireworks in New York Harbor on the 4th of July. Large planks flew in all directions. Iron rails splayed. Train lights extinguished. Tons of iron on wheels hurtled toward the river.

"Death to capitalists and whores," he shouted, his words echoing in the canyon.

———◆———

Army heard other passengers scream hysterically. They tumbled down the aisle with him. Shawn and Tony had flipped first, slamming into the closed, iron door. Their bodies cushioned Army when he followed. Mickey skidded into him.

Titi, Celia and Bonita respectively smashed into them next. A pileup of bodies shifted and turned like batter in a blender as the car twisted and flipped.

"Armando," Titi shouted.

"Armando," Celia cried.

"Armando," Bonita bellowed.

He felt a soft hand slip between bodies and clasp his. He squeezed it tightly when he heard the car uncouple from the locomotive in midair. He felt the car twist like a corkscrew as it sped to the river a thousand feet below.

The locomotive impacted the water first, sending a huge spray upward. Combined with steam from the engine, the collision looked like a geyser.

Careening into the water next was Army's car. It landed next to the locomotive with a kaboom! Water seeped in slowly through the closed doors but not the shot-out window, which faced the sky.

The car in which Big Bob was a passenger tumbled until it landed on top of the locomotive with a loud whump, flinging one passenger outside through an open window.

In the quiet that followed, Army heard a bird cooing. Dazed in the darkness, he opened his eyes to see a light surrounding a white dove spreading its wings on the broken window's sill.

Still holding the hand, he squeezed it and heard a woman moan. He attempted to see who she was, but couldn't in the dark, twisted pileup of humanity. He looked up at the dove, blinked and it was gone. His eyes closed. His hand went limp.

———◆———

A full moon illuminated the river, in which the body of a large man floated face down near the locomotive. A small piece of white paper fluttered nearby as though it were a bird attempting to catch up with its mate. However, a gust of wind pushed it toward the river bank, where soldiers had gathered.

Chapter 76
The Awakening

Liam Lobo looked as though he'd stepped out of the framed painting in the family's Bryn Mawr home. Dashing in his US Army dress uniform, he sat opposite his brother at a white table in a brightly-lit room. A white dove sat on his shoulder.

"Liam, is that you?" Army said, shielding his eyes from the glare of the intense light. "I mean …"

Liam smiled at him. He was dressed in a white tuxedo like the one their father used to wear.

"Mother asked me to speak to you," Liam said, smiling. "Seems you've been away."

Army studied him for a moment. "How is she?"

"Worried. You know how she gets when you don't call for a while. What are you waiting for?"

He sat silently for a few seconds staring at Liam and the dove until a figure in a wedding dress appeared at his side. A veil covered her face. Without looking at her he made the introduction:

"This is my bride." Turning to her, he added: "Honey, this is my brother, Liam. You know. The one killed in the war."

Liam smiled and addressed his little brother. "You need to follow the dove," he said.

"Where?"

Liam pointed and Army turned around to see a black pinhole in the distance. "There, that spot."

"Why?" he said, turning back to Liam. "How?"

But suddenly the dove launched, flapping its wings furiously with Army pulled in its wake. Soon the black dot in the distance expanded to the size of a railway tunnel with him and the dove in it. He looked back at Liam sitting in the brilliance of some supernatural light. The bride had disappeared, but the urge to return was overwhelming. He tried to resist the force of the bird but couldn't. Still, he was able to look back again at where the lovely veiled lady had been. He tried to call her name. But no words emerged, only tears.

———•◆•———

"Look, mother, tears," Julia said. "He's awakening. He's trying to speak."

Army turned his head side to side. His lips struggled to form his first word in two weeks. It came out loudly: "B O N I T A!"

Moist blue eyes opened in a white bed to see his sister dabbing them with a tissue and his mother watching him with hope.

"Come, come quickly," said Julia, waiving to someone sitting in a chair.

He saw a female figure hobble on a crutch to him. She was a sorry sight with a black eye and Plaster of Paris casts on a leg and arm.

"Armando!" she cried. "Oh Armando, Armando, Armando" she repeated, weeping, kissing and stroking his face. We didn't know if you would ever wake up."

He wiped her tears with the fingers of his left hand, consoling her and looking at his mother and sister. He felt a large, white bandage surrounding the top of his head and tubes embedded in his veins.

Grace hugged and kissed him and cried. "Thank God. Oh, thank God. My prayers have been answered."

Bonita questioned him softly. "Do you remember what happened on the train, amor?"

"No," he said, rolling his eyes, thinking. "The last thing I recall was looking for your earring."

He disengaged his right hand from his mother's to stroke Bonita's hair when sudden pain gave him pause. He looked at his shoulder and saw a round, discolored depression the size of a quarter.

315

"I was shot. I was shot, wasn't I?" He became emotional. "What happened to Hiran and Celia? And the others?"

"Calma, calma mi amor, shhhh, shhhh," his wounded lover said. She paused and bit her bottom lip. She gripped his hand. Her eyes welled. Shaking, she continued. "Hiran is gone, mi amor. Titi and her sister, too. By the grace of God, I was brought back to life by a doctor who happened to be at the scene. Celia is being cared for here in Santa Cruz Hospital. So is a man from Ireland."

His eyes filled, but Bonita wiped away the tears with a tissue as he absorbed the bad news.

"The river. How did the train fall into the river?"

"All I know is that Ernesto blew up the bridge when the train was passing over it. I overheard police talking about it."

Army clenched his jaw. He spoke through gritted teeth. "Did they catch him?"

"No."

"So he's still out there."

"Who's Ernesto?" Grace said.

Julia chimed in sorrowfully: "Why would he do such a dastardly thing?"

Bonita looked at them. She answered with firmness.

"He is a rebel. A violent communist rebel." Turning to Army, stroking his face gently, she added: "Mi amor, the train is lost. The plantations are gone. The sugar business is finished. And one more thing, the Fox Hole, it was burned to the ground. You have lost everything."

With his mouth agape, he thought about the flattened Lobo fortune, balled his fists and spoke with resolve: "If I have to do it myself, I'll rebuild. Brick by brick. Stalk by stalk."

And then he relaxed his hands and looked into her sad eyes. "Besides, I haven't lost everything. I still have you."

ABOUT THE AUTHOR

William M. iezzi, a retired sports writer for The Philadelphia Inquirer, first visited Cuba in the summer of 1997. His first question to a Cuban walking past Havana's Hotel Riviera was: "Who is your best baseball player?" The gentleman, Diego, answered: "Orlando 'El Duque' Hernandez." He added that the pitcher had been banned from the game for trying to escape and his whereabouts were unknown.

A few days later Diego returned to the hotel and said he found Duque at a psychiatric hospital. Diego and iezzi spoke with Duque through a chain-link fence on the hospital grounds, where the former star hurler for the Industriales – the Yankees of Cuba – had been ordered to play softball catch with mental patients. Humiliating.

That was the catalyst for an abundance of stories about Cuba written by iezzi for national magazines and newspapers, including the Pulitzer-Prize winning Inquirer, over a period of 21 years.

In 2018 his first novel, *Armando's Havana Loves*, came to fruition. The midcentury romantic suspense story embodies knowledge gained over two decades of interviews and research on the communist island.

iezzi is a member of the Philadelphia Sports Writers' Association and the Pen and Pencil Club, America's oldest daily operating press club. He is also a General + PRO member of Romance Writers of America.

Currently, you can find him at www.facebook.com/HavanaBananaBill, where he updates us about occurrences in Cuba, past, present, and future.

What did you think about
Armando's Havana Loves?

Please take a moment to write a review and post it on the *Armando's Havana Loves'* sales page at Amazon.com or the retailer who sold you the novel.

Please tell others about *Armando's Havana Loves* and share something about it on social media. Upload the cover image to Instagram, sit back and read www.facebook.com/havanabananabill for more stories about Cuba and when we'll see *Armando's Havana Loves II.*

And don't forget to go to YouTube and play Havana Sugar Man.

ACKNOWLEDGEMENTS

What a ride. The journey that carried me to this midcentury romantic suspense story actually started 21 years ago during my first trip to Havana, Cuba.

Wilmer Morales and a series of other interpreters helped me interview Cubans about whom I wrote stories for newspapers and magazines in the states. One interviewee was Jorge Miguel Jorge Fernández, Frank Sinatra's valet in the 1940s and '50s. FBI records substantiated some of his claims.

But it was interpreter/translator Nayade Tramiño Gilroy who stuck with me. I found the then thirty-two-year-old teacher in 2010. She was giving English lessons to Cubans in a Havana City church.

With Nayade's help I interviewed Eusebio Leal Spengler, historiador of Havana City. He introduced us to the two-volume *Book of Cuba*, the complete history of the island. Nayade and I also interviewed Estela Rivas, historiadora of the Hotel Nacional, Ciro Bianchi Ross, columnist for Juventud Rebelde as well as a TV and radio host, and Ernesto Iznaga Coldwell, manager of storied Sloppy Joe's Bar.

Septuagenarian Jesus Escandel told us he'd been a rebel conspiring at Sloppy Joe's with others who plotted against the Batista regime in the 1950s. Nayade accompanied me to the Biblioteca Nacional De Cuba José Martí to research the decade, which included the history of the world-famous cabaret Tropicana, where many hearts were broken.

All of that was the springboard for diving into a novel about Havana in its glory years, when the Mob, American big business and a dictator were in cahoots under the watchful eye of the CIA.

Special thanks to my Beta readers: Author Jerri Williams, Beverly Kessler Rosa, Antoinette Stabilito, and Professor Rosemary Rys. Her Public Relations students gave this work a boost.

My gratitude also extends to members of the Philadelphia Romance Writers Limited Affiliate Chapter, especially author Susan Scott Shelley, who guided me through the publishing process.